THE
NIGHT
SINGER

Johanna Mo was born in Kalmar, Sweden, and now lives with her family in Stockholm. She has spent the last twenty years working as a literary critic, translator, and freelance editor. *The Night Singer* is her English-language debut.

THE
NIGHT
SINGER

Johanna Mo

Translation by Alice Menzies

HEADLINE

Published by arrangement with Ahlander Agency

First published in Sweden as *Nattsångaren* in 2020 by
Romanus & Selling, Bonnier Sweden

First published in Great Britain in 2021 by
HEADLINE PUBLISHING GROUP

First published in paperback in Great Britain in 2022 by
HEADLINE PUBLISHING GROUP

1

Cataloguing in Publication Data is available from the British Library

ISBN 978 1 4722 8116 6

Typeset in Garamond by Avon DataSet Ltd, Alcester, Warwickshire

Printed and bound in Great Britain by Clays Ltd, Elcograf S.p.A.

Headline's policy is to use papers that are natural, renewable and recyclable
products and made from wood grown in well-managed forests and other
controlled sources. The logging and manufacturing processes are expected
to conform to the environmental regulations of the country of origin.

HEADLINE PUBLISHING GROUP
An Hachette UK Company
Carmelite House
50 Victoria Embankment
London EC4Y 0DZ

www.headline.co.uk
www.hachette.co.uk

For Mika

The Last Day

Four more steps, then he turns around again. Doesn't trust
the silence behind him. All he can hear is the chirping of the
grasshoppers. No engines, no birds. He misses the night singer.
Its high, fast song keeping the darkness at bay.

A shadow by the edge of the road makes him jump, and
pain radiates out from his broken rib.

It's just a bush.

The darkness is full of shapes dancing around him – faster,
closer – making it difficult to breathe. Could his broken rib
have damaged his lung?

Finally, he sees the light. A tiny dot that slowly grows to a
square. His head is pounding, nausea washing over him,
twitching in the light, but he tries to fix his eyes on it. That is
where he needs to go.

His legs give way and he drops to his knees, breaking his fall
with his hands. The sharp taste of bile fills his mouth. It feels
like someone has rammed a fist into his chest and started
rummaging around inside.

Staying right there on the ground feels incredibly tempting,
but he is so close now.

He crawls back onto his feet and staggers forward. Hears something crunch behind him. Footsteps? No, it can't be – it must be an animal.

He pauses, noticing movement in the light. His eyes take in what he is seeing, but it's like they don't want to pass it on.

Why?

The question tears at him, at the ground beneath him. Everything is about to crumble.

Wednesday 15 May

Chapter One

Hanna Duncker followed the gravel path down to the wrought-iron gate, which creaked in protest as she pushed it open. The list of things that needed repairing was getting longer and longer. She had moved into the little white house with the blue corner panels just over a month earlier and, like Kleva, the small hamlet it stood on the outskirts of, it was tiny – under fifty square metres in total. Hanna had grown up on the other side of the island, in eastern Öland, but moving back there had never been an option. If she did, she would forever be nothing but Lars Duncker's daughter.

Lars had finally drunk himself to death last autumn, and it was while Hanna was clearing out her childhood home, alone, that she had realised what she wanted. Driving over the bridge for the first time in years had woken a powerful sense of longing in her, a longing for everything she had been missing in Stockholm. Öland was where she belonged.

Buying a house that needed so much work wasn't something she had really thought through, but it had been the best place available within her budget. Once she had made the decision to come back to the island, she hadn't been patient enough to let the process drag on. Within the space of just three weeks, she had sold her apartment on the outskirts of Stockholm, bought the house and found herself a new job.

Only then had she called her brother, Kristoffer, in London. He had reacted more or less exactly as she had expected him to.

There's something seriously wrong with you, he'd hissed.

They hadn't spoken since. Yes, she had spat out a few harsh words herself. There was just so much pent-up anger between them. Over the fact that he hadn't come to the funeral, or that he had left it to her to draw up an inventory and empty the house they had both grown up in. There was only a year between them, and for a while they had almost been like twins.

From the very first morning in the new house, Hanna had developed a ritual: she walked the seven hundred metres down to the beach. After fifty or so metres, she passed Ingrid's grey stone house, which had to be at least twice the size of her own.

That morning, she saw Ingrid on the swinging seat in the garden, eyes closed. Silver hair and wrinkled skin, a blanket draped over her legs. The resemblance to Hanna's grandmother was striking. Granny spent her days doing much the same now that the haze of forgetfulness had enveloped her.

Hanna tried to sneak past without the old woman noticing her – she wasn't in the mood to talk to anyone right now, not even Ingrid – but Ingrid's eyes snapped open and the resemblance was gone. Her eyes were dark brown, not greenish-blue like Granny's, and there was a pronounced alertness in them. She had probably come outside specifically to wait for Hanna. The views were better on the other side of the house, where the poker-straight fields stretched out into the distance. On this side, the landscape was flat and rough, and would likely be developed before long. But Ingrid was more interested in her neighbours than the countryside.

The blanket dropped to the ground as she got up and took a few steps forward.

'Hello,' she said. 'Big day today.'

Hanna nodded. It was her first day as an investigator with the Kalmar Police. She would be investigating serious crimes across Kalmar County, which also covered the east of Småland and the whole of Öland. Her new boss, Ove Hultmark, had decided to ease her in as gently as possible by having her start on a Wednesday.

Why had he hired her, considering their history? Hanna still couldn't make sense of it, and that made her uneasy: was there something going on that she didn't understand?

'Just don't cause a fuss, and you'll be fine,' Ingrid told her.

In Ingrid's eyes, causing a fuss was about the worst thing a person could do.

A few days after Hanna moved in, Ingrid had knocked on her door with a box of freshly baked biscuits. Hanna had tried to keep their conversation in the doorway, but Ingrid had invited herself in, asking for a cup of tea to drink with the biscuits. Black tea, nothing too floral or funny. When she saw the mess inside, she snorted: *So, this is what you didn't want me to see?* Ingrid's bluntness had brought Hanna's walls crashing down. Her grandmother had been exactly the same, and Hanna knew she probably wouldn't have survived without her.

Within the space of just a few minutes, Ingrid had told Hanna all about her life. Hanna knew that her surname was Mattsson and that, after years of longing, she had finally given birth to a son when she was thirty-six years old. That he now ran the farm she had inherited from her father. That she had

7

three grandchildren, and that the two eldest were at university, in Linköping and Umeå. That the youngest was a much later addition, an eleven-year-old with Down's syndrome. That Ingrid had a troublesome hip. By contrast, Hanna had revealed her own surname only at Ingrid's direct request.

Does that make you Lars's daughter? Ingrid had asked.

Hanna had nodded, and the topic had never come up again. For a moment, however, Ingrid's brown eyes had been full of compassion. Perhaps Hanna should follow Kristoffer's example and change her name. He was a Baxter now, like his wife. But Hanna didn't want to do that; she hadn't done anything wrong.

'What are you doing today?' Hanna asked now.

'It's Wednesday,' said Ingrid. 'I always take the bus to Mörbylånga and have a bit of a flutter on the V65.' Seeing Hanna's blank face, she added: 'Harness racing.'

Hanna excused herself, telling Ingrid she had an appointment she had to keep, and continued down the path towards Kleva strandväg. To date, there were only two houses on the little strip of land by the road down to the water. A family with young children lived in one of them, but the other seemed to be empty. Perhaps its owners used it as a summer house. Ingrid had spent much of her second visit to Hanna's house going through the various inhabitants of Kleva – there were no more than thirty of them in total – but she hadn't said much about the people living on the coastal road. In fact, she had spent most of the time talking about Jörgen, the Stockholmer who had moved to the island with his wife a few years earlier, and liked to complain about everything from the horse dung on the road to the people who let their houses fall into disrepair.

What a bloody moaner, Ingrid had said. *I'm not going to replace things that work perfectly well just because some grumpy mainlander tells me to.* Despite the years Hanna had spent living in the capital, Ingrid still thought of her as an islander. And according to Ingrid, she was a welcome arrival. She was a police officer, after all.

For Hanna, the road down to the beach characterised Öland: a straight gravel track flanked by grain fields. Small, straggling forage maize crops, and some other plant she didn't recognise. The weeds in the ditches were so high that the low stone walls were almost entirely obscured from view. A few hundred metres ahead, the trees were like a promise of something better. Beyond them, the Kalmar Strait.

The trees slowly drew closer, and the tang of fertiliser gave way to pine and seaweed. Hanna tipped back her head and let the wind caress her face. She had missed this. In Stockholm, she had lived her life in a cramped five-storey building surrounded by people she knew nothing about. On Öland, she felt like she could breathe.

After another few metres, the strait appeared like a streak of blue between the trees, growing with every step she took. The gravel track opened out onto a small car park, and Hanna cut through it, turning south and ignoring the beach. It wasn't quite bathing season yet, and it was still early in the morning, but she didn't want to risk bumping into anyone. She saw an elderly man and his Labrador walking towards her, and nodded in greeting.

Maybe she should get a dog. Yes, she would be at work all day, but she suspected Ingrid would be more than happy to look after it. For an eighty-one-year-old, she was still incredibly active; the problem with her hip was barely noticeable.

But no. Hanna didn't even like dogs. Besides, her loneliness felt less tangible here on the island, despite the fact that she hadn't really spoken to anyone but Ingrid. There was no one in Stockholm she would stay in touch with. Definitely not Fabian.

Hanna followed the path a little further before pausing to look out at the Kalmar Strait. She breathed in the scent of seaweed and salt air. The wind had bent the trees inward, and there was an upturned rowing boat on the ground beside her, the white paint scraped off along its hull. She actually preferred the view from the other side of the island: the sea blending with the horizon, seemingly never-ending. From where she was standing now, she could make out the mainland on the other side. Ingrid wasn't alone in thinking that most of the island's problems stemmed from the mainland, and she also wasn't alone in using 'mainlander' as an insult. Hanna had bristled when she'd first noticed it in the newspaper after returning to Öland. On page four, there had been two articles about crimes that had been committed, and both went to lengths to point out that the perpetrator was a mainlander.

A sudden sense of longing took hold of her, an echo of what she had felt as she drove over the bridge last autumn. The desire for a life that wouldn't slowly suffocate her.

She was twelve the last time she was genuinely happy.

Her fingers dug beneath the sleeve of her jacket and sweater. She didn't need to see the tattoo to feel its presence, her pulse like a fluttering bird's heart beneath the black ink. Touching it always seemed to calm her down.

If Hanna was going to make it to the police station on time, she knew she would have to head back, but she couldn't quite bring herself to move. The plan was to meet Ove Hultmark and then join in the morning meeting. It was the first part that made her most nervous. She had been nineteen when she'd last sat opposite the man, as he questioned her about her father. About what he claimed her father had done.

There's something seriously wrong with you.

Kristoffer's words came back to her, gnawing and niggling away. The suspicion that he might be right after all. That what he had said before hanging up was true:

You've got no idea what you're dredging up. You're going to ruin everything.

11

Chapter Two

'Breakfast!' Rebecka Forslund shouted, knocking on the door beneath the picture of a unicorn Molly had drawn for her big brother.

The painkillers had numbed her headache to a dull throb, but the nausea was going nowhere. Rebecka had barely slept a wink last night; the alcohol leaving her system had only worsened her anxiety. She had tried to lie still at first, to avoid disturbing Petri, but at some point in the small hours, she had crawled out of bed and taken a hot shower before returning. When his alarm went off that morning, she had pretended to be asleep, and though she was awake, it had been a struggle to get up when her own alarm started ringing. Joel hated having to rush in the mornings, and he wouldn't appreciate being woken up with just half an hour to get ready for the bus. His classes didn't start until nine on Wednesdays.

Rebecka didn't wait for an answer before opening his door. The boy could sleep through anything. A few nights earlier, Gerd's garage had burnt down, and the fire engine had arrived with sirens wailing. Joel was probably the only person in the whole of Gårdby who hadn't woken up.

Fortunately the fire hadn't spread.

His room smelled faintly of sweat and hormones and the awful incense sticks he insisted on burning. Rebecka moved over to the window, raised the blind and opened it, breathing in the cool, crisp air. Having a teenager was nothing like she had imagined it would be. Joel could be moody sometimes, but he kept it all inside, spending hours hunched over his sketchpad or staring at the computer. He almost always did as he was told, and she rarely had to nag him about clothes on the floor or doing his homework, yet the worry was always there: that he would end up a homebody. That he wouldn't be able to manage life out in the real world. The darkness in him frightened her.

Rebecka turned around, and it took her a moment to process what she was seeing: Joel's bed was empty. His black duvet was heaped in the middle of the mattress, though that was nothing new. She didn't want to impose rules on the kids that she herself didn't keep, and since she had heard that bed mites preferred neatly made beds, she only bothered when they were expecting company.

Her mind raced back to the night before. They had gone over to Gabriel and Ulrika's for a barbecue. As a rule they stayed home on weeknights, but it was Gabriel's fortieth birthday and Ulrika had bought him an expensive grill, inviting them over to try it.

Memories of Gabriel paralysed her for a moment, but she quickly brushed them to one side. Thinking about him was too painful right now. Joel had brought Molly home and put her to bed around nine o'clock. When Rebecka and Petri got back a few hours later, she had looked in on both of them. It wasn't just the outline of Joel's thin body she had seen in bed: she specifically remembered seeing his dark, messy hair. But now his bed was empty. What did that mean? Joel didn't usually sneak out at night, and particularly not when he had school the next day.

Rebecka headed down to the kitchen as her anxiety levels continued to rise. Molly sensed it and looked up from her cereal.

'Do you want me to go and wake him up?' she asked.

Rebecka occasionally sent Molly upstairs to drag Joel out of bed. However stubborn and withdrawn he might be in the mornings, his little sister almost always managed to get through to him. There were nine years and a messy relationship between them. Rebecka sometimes wished she had met Petri sooner, so that he could have fathered both her children.

She should call him now, she realised. Petri had left for Kastlösa an hour earlier. A young couple had hired him to renovate the kitchen in their summer house before they came to the island in early June. Rebecka doubted Joel had snuck out without her noticing it – not after four o'clock, in any case – but she couldn't be sure, and Petri might have given him a ride. He did that sometimes, whenever Joel missed the bus or needed to get to school earlier. Mörbylånga was on his way, after all. She tried to find her phone, convinced she had left it on the kitchen worktop.

'Mummy?' asked Molly.

'Joel has left already,' Rebecka told her. 'He's going on a school trip today. I forgot.'

The lie came out so easily.

'I want to go on a trip too!'

Molly looked up at her, waiting for a reply, but all Rebecka could do was nod. Where the hell was her goddamn phone? She rummaged through a pile of old newspapers, moving a box of cereal so abruptly that it tipped over. Another wave of nausea rose up in her, and she raised a hand to her mouth, took a few quick sips from the glass of water she had filled to wash down the painkillers. Eventually she found her phone on top of the microwave, where she always left it.

Rebecka went out onto the porch to call Petri. She didn't want Molly to hear her. He answered after three rings.

'Did you give Joel a lift this morning?' she asked.

'No, his classes start later today.'

'Did you see him?'

'No, why?'

'His bed was empty when I went up to wake him.'

Saying it aloud gave fuel to her fears, and Rebecka let out a sob.

'I'm sure he just got a ride with someone else,' said Petri. 'Or took an earlier bus.'

He was trying to reassure her, but his words had the opposite effect. There was no logical explanation for Joel's empty bed. He didn't have any group work to prepare, no homework he had forgotten, and those were the only reasons he ever went to school before he absolutely had to.

'Have you tried ringing him?'

'Of course I have,' Rebecka snapped, hanging up.

What the hell was wrong with her? Calling Joel had never even crossed her mind. She scrolled down to his number, but his phone was switched off. Maybe that was why she hadn't immediately tried to reach him, because she had known it would be. That excuse felt better than blaming her hung-over, sleep-deprived, emotional wreck of a head, in any case.

Fifteen years of parental guilt came crashing down on her, making her sway. No matter how hard she tried, she was never enough. But rather than wallow in that, she called Joel's friend Nadine.

'When did you last speak to Joel?' she asked, without even saying hello.

'Yesterday, why?'

'Do you know what he's doing today?'

There was a brief silence that Rebecka interpreted as hesitation.

'Going to school, I guess,' said Nadine.

Rebecka didn't have the energy to argue. The teenager's hesitation could be down to so many things. Nadine had moved from Gårdby to Kalmar, on the mainland, three years earlier, but she was still the person Joel spent most time with. Rebecka sometimes wondered if they were a couple, but she had learned not to ask. In truth, she hoped they weren't. Joel had never said anything, but Rebecka knew that Nadine had tried to kill herself at least once, that it was one of the reasons she had moved.

'If you talk to him, would you ask him to call me?'

'Sure.'

Molly came out onto the porch wearing her pink unicorn backpack. She probably needed a jacket – it wasn't quite warm enough to go without yet – but Rebecka decided not to fetch one. She didn't bother asking if Molly had brushed her teeth either. Apparently that was something children typically lied about anyway. Instead, she took her daughter's hand, and they started walking towards Gårdby School. It was no more than eight hundred metres away, but Rebecka didn't trust Molly on the road; the girl was far too easily distracted. She also didn't trust the people racing by in their cars. Too many of them ignored the speed limit.

Molly giggled.

'What's so funny?'

'Are you really going to walk to school in those?'

Rebecka looked down at her feet and realised she was wearing Petri's wooden clogs, which were at least seven sizes too big for her.

'Whoops,' she smiled.

But her smile quickly faded as she remembered the question going round and round in her mind: where was Joel?

They passed the burnt-out garage. The back wall was all that was left of it, the rest a pile of warped black beams and planks, sticking up like arms waving for help. The smell of smoke was still so sharp that it made her nose sting. There had been a storm that night, but many people were convinced the fire was deliberate. Fires were a touchy subject in the area. For a couple of years in the late 1950s, a pyromaniac had terrorised eastern Öland, and the police had never managed to catch the culprit. Then, in March 2003, Ester Jensen had died when her house was set alight with her inside. Between 2005 and 2012, a further six people had died in fires in the north of the island. The last of those, in a garage, had been started in an attempt to cover up a double murder.

Molly didn't even look up as they passed the garage. Instead, she spent the whole walk to school talking about what games she was going to play during break. Something about kings and knights. Molly's bike had got a puncture over the weekend, but she hadn't pestered anyone to fix it. Rebecka murmured often enough to get away with not really listening.

After a quick hug, Molly ran off into the yellow school building Rebecka herself had attended thirty years earlier. There had been fewer children back then, but plenty was still the same. Rebecka paused for a moment, at a loss for what to do next.

'Hello.'

She turned towards the voice. It belonged to Ulrika, who was dropping off Elias. He would be nine that autumn, and wasn't particularly keen on having his mother chaperone him. Ulrika forced him into a hug before letting him go.

'Thanks for last night,' said Rebecka.

'It was nice, wasn't it.'

Though she had drunk her fair share the previous evening, Ulrika looked considerably fresher than Rebecka felt. She had showered, and was wearing a light face of make-up; there was just a slight hint of shadow beneath her eyes that her concealer had failed to cover. Ulrika was hopeless when it came to planning, and had invited them over across the hedge the same day, whispering that it was a birthday surprise for Gabriel. In addition to Elias, they also had a daughter, Linnea, who was a year younger than Joel. The fact that the two couples had children who were roughly the same age was one of the main reasons they had started spending time together when they became neighbours seven years earlier. Rebecka, Petri and Joel had moved into the house just a few months before Molly was born.

How had Joel seemed last night? A little low, perhaps, but he and Linnea had gone inside to draw together; she wanted to learn how to do portraits. Her drawing had actually been surprisingly good, though she would never be quite as skilled as Joel.

Rebecka and Ulrika walked home together, Ulrika pushing her mint-green bicycle. She worked on the checkout at Almérs and had changed her hours to fit around the children's schedule. During the week, she didn't begin until nine, though she often took extra shifts at weekends, to boost her hours.

'Is Linnea at school?' asked Rebecka.

'I really hope so.'

Ulrika gave her a concerned look, and Rebecka found herself blurting out all her worries.

'I'm sure he just went in early,' Ulrika told her. 'Come on, this is Joel we're talking about.'

Rebecka's own teenage years had made her think Joel's would be worse, but she had never once caught him with booze. She had never even caught him in a lie.

Rebecka glanced over at Ulrika. She really had enjoyed the barbecue. It had been surprisingly easy for the four adults to spend time together over the past few months, possibly because they had so many similar evenings to fall back on, but it wouldn't work going forward. Not after what Gabriel had done to her. Rebecka seriously doubted he would tell Ulrika about it; he was too weak for that. She personally had no intention of saying anything to Petri.

'See you later,' said Ulrika, turning off towards her house.

Rebecka knew she should head into the studio. She scraped together a living making and selling pottery, and had an order for a fruit bowl to finish off. She also painted watercolours, though she rarely sold any canvases. Deep down, she knew she wouldn't be able to concentrate, so she went into the kitchen instead, and poured herself the last of the coffee. She knew Joel would be angry, but she had no other option:

she called his school, and was put through to the deputy head.

'Is Joel Forslund there?' Rebecka asked.

'Oh, I'm glad you called,' said the woman she had sold a set of teacups to. 'I was just about to get in touch with you. Joel wasn't in school yesterday either. Has something happened?'

Chapter Three

There were no parking spaces outside the station, so Hanna left her car over the road, by the Giraffen Shopping Centre. The drive from the island had only taken her thirty minutes. Kalmar Police Station was clad in dark wood and pale stone, and she could see what looked like two large fingerprints carved into the wall. She stepped inside and told the young man at reception who she was and who she had come to meet.

The seconds ticked away, and Hanna didn't know where to look. The different shades of grey stone on the floor seemed to blend together, and she felt a strong urge to get up and run. Everything would be different now that she could no longer hide away in her new house in Kleva. Her job would force her to interact with people, and some of them wouldn't be particularly happy that she was back.

Hanna tried to breathe through her nerves. She knew there had been no other choice, that moving back to the island had been a question of survival for her.

Her eyes came to rest on the receptionist, who flashed her an encouraging smile. As though that would be enough to convince her everything would be fine.

The door opened, and though it was sixteen years since Hanna had last seen Ove Hultmark, she recognised him immediately. His hair was greyer and his stomach rounder, but his mannerisms and gaze were the same; he was still the officer who wanted to be everyone's friend. His eyes were now framed by a pair of round black glasses, but otherwise his style hadn't changed at all: jeans and a pale blue shirt. For a moment, she was worried he was about to hug her, but instead he held out a hand.

'Hanna, welcome. It's great to have you here.'

She took his hand and nodded. Couldn't bring herself to speak. She followed Ove up the stairs to his office.

The last time they sat face-to-face was in an interview room at the old police station. That building now housed the custody cells, plus a number of fast-food places. They had spoken in one of the more comfortable interview rooms, Hanna on a red sofa and Ove in a chair, and she could still remember word for word what he had said to her. First, he had asked her how she was doing, and when she said that she was fine, he had told her they had evidence. That there was no doubt about it, her father was guilty. As though he had wanted to punch holes in the word she had used. That she was *fine*.

Ove slouched back in his chair and clasped his hands over his stomach. Hanna noticed the hair on his knuckles. During that first interview, he had leaned in to her, picking her apart with his gaze. His body language was more relaxed now, though his eyes still seemed intense. He spent a few minutes chatting about the job and her move back to the island, but then he rocked forward slightly.

'Forgive me for asking,' he said, 'but I can't help myself. Why did you join the force?'

Hanna wasn't sure she knew the answer herself. For a long time, she had nurtured the belief that something had gone catastrophically wrong. That she would become a police officer in order to reinvestigate the crime and bring everything that had been missed or misinterpreted to light. But she wasn't so naive as to not realise that it was also partly down to denial. She simply didn't want her father to have done the things they claimed.

'To understand, I think,' she said.

'And have you? Understood?'

Hanna hesitated. She didn't know quite how honest she could be.

'There's not much to understand, really,' she said. 'People end up in that kind of situation for so many reasons, not just because of cold, hard scheming. Desperation, circumstance. Bad luck . . . And I really do think I can help them. I guess that's why I'm good at getting them to talk.'

Them.

She meant the criminals, of course. The perpetrators. Though most of all, she wanted to help those around them. Their relatives, the victims.

'Yes, your superior in Stockholm said you were a highly skilled interrogator,' Ove told her.

He seemed satisfied with her answer.

Hanna would rather not think about her father right now. She had assumed things would be easier once he was released, but they had actually got worse. She had gone to see him in the old house three times, in the village where no one but his friend Gunnar wanted him. Gunnar was the only person who hadn't abandoned Lars when he took to the bottle, and it was Gunnar who had looked after the house while he was locked up. Seeing him that way had been so painful: a parent in freefall. He hadn't been able to neglect himself like that while he was inside. Without a word, Hanna had stopped visiting him. She had called and written to him from time to time, increasingly sporadically, but he had almost never replied.

The guilt was possibly the worst part, the fact that she hadn't managed to save him. No, she had barely even tried.

'Your boss had lots of good things to say about you, actually,' Ove continued, 'and I'm sure you're going to do a great job here. But before we go through to meet the rest of the team, I'm wondering how you'd like us to handle your background.'

'What do you mean?'

'Well, given your surname, people will wonder. Maybe it's just as well to . . . shine a spotlight on the elephant, so to speak.'

Panic made Hanna's heart race. Did Ove really want to introduce her as Lars Duncker's daughter? She tried to swallow, but her throat was dry. Instead, she forced out the words as though she actually believed them:

'No. It doesn't matter who my dad was.'

Ove leaned forward and studied her, making her feel nineteen again.

'Are you sure?' he eventually asked.

Chapter Four

The morning meeting had been brought forward an hour, and Erik Lindgren climbed the stairs from the cafeteria with his second coffee of the day. He had run ten kilometres that morning, and his thighs were aching. His time had been slightly better than yesterday's, just over forty-seven minutes. Erik was happy with his job here in Kalmar. Three years ago, back in Malmö, his life had been far more stressful, chasing the witnesses and perpetrators of various shootings around the city. He'd barely had time to work out.

Supriya, his wife, had never liked Malmö. She had spent their first year there learning Swedish, but once she was finally granted her licence and began working as a dentist, things had gone downhill. She had struggled with the language and the working culture, and had hated all the conflicts with her colleagues. Erik had tried to explain that perhaps she had just been unlucky ending up where she had, but it was only once she changed jobs that she finally accepted that he was right. Sometimes he wondered whether she still longed for Mumbai, which was where they had lived before moving to Sweden.

Stepping into the investigation room, he saw a woman he

didn't recognise. Erik realised she must be the new detective from Stockholm, and went over to introduce himself. Standing at just over six feet, he was surprised to see that Hanna Duncker was taller than him.

'Have you met Ove yet?' he asked.

The question was hardly a difficult one, but Hanna hesitated before nodding. Erik moved over to his desk – there were five team members working in the room, but he had one of only two standing desks – and put down his cup by his computer. He logged in.

'Did he show you where the watering hole is?'

It was obvious that Hanna had no idea what he was talking about.

'Where to get coffee,' he explained.

She nodded.

'Well, just let me know if you need anything.'

Another nod. Erik glanced at the clock on his desktop. Almost nine thirty. He quickly skimmed through his emails and then logged out.

'Did he tell you where the morning meeting is?' he asked Hanna, who was now sitting at a desk he assumed had been assigned to her.

'Yes,' she said.

As Erik left the room, he thought Hanna had stayed at her desk, but after a few seconds he heard her footsteps behind him, and he stepped into the meeting room just ahead of her. The others were already waiting inside. Ove liked to keep the group small, and aside from Erik there were three other detectives. Four now, including Hanna.

'Good,' said Ove. 'You're all here. This is our new team member, Hanna Duncker. She previously worked as a detective in Stockholm, and she's a fantastic interrogator.'

Something Erik didn't understand seemed to pass through the room. Amer straightened up and gave Hanna a curious glance. Daniel did the same. Carina simply turned to Ove and pursed her lips, the way she always did when she was unhappy about something. Daniel had joined the group from patrol a year or so earlier, and they had all made a real effort to make him feel welcome. Carina slightly more than the others – she was old enough to be his mother.

Hanna raised a hand in greeting and smiled cautiously. Erik hoped Ove wasn't planning to make her say anything, as he pulled out a chair and sat down.

Clearly uncomfortable, Hanna did the same.

Ove studied her for a few seconds. It looked as though he was debating whether to say a few words himself, but eventually made do by asking them all to introduce themselves.

'We've already met,' said Erik.

As ever, Amer made a joke about his surname, Moghadan. He liked to claim that none of the others could pronounce it properly, but Erik still couldn't hear the difference. He was fond of Amer, who was smartly dressed like always, in dark blue jeans and a jacket, his beard neat. Daniel kept things short and sweet, telling Hanna his surname, Lilja. Carina chose not only to mention her surname, Hansson, but also to say that she was from Kalmar and had been working for the police there for over twenty years.

'Thanks, everyone,' said Ove. 'Well, we might as well get started. We need to go back to the beginning with the assault outside the hotel.'

Ove turned to Hanna and explained that the victim had been so badly beaten that he now had to use a wheelchair.

They had been investigating the attack for several weeks, but they still hadn't made much progress, partly because the victim himself couldn't remember what had happened.

'I'll go through all the statements and see if there's anything we've missed,' said Amer.

Since he was the only member of the team who spoke Farsi, he had ended up shouldering most of the burden of the case. Like Amer, the victim had been born in Iran.

'There was a robbery outside the liquor store on Norra Långgatan,' Ove continued. 'A twenty-two-year-old woman who was slashed on her way home from her boyfriend's house. She's in intensive care. Daniel, you talk to the boyfriend and find out if and when we can interview the woman.'

'Sure,' Daniel replied, scribbling in his notepad.

Amer leaned in to Carina and whispered something. Her shoulders relaxed, and she laughed. Of all of them, Amer was probably the one who took most responsibility for the others' well-being, and he had probably also sensed her dislike of their new colleague.

'What was that?' said Ove.

Amer looked up at him with feigned ignorance.

'Would you like to share with the rest of the group?'

But before Amer had time to reply, the door opened and the sergeant popped her head into the room.

'We've got a dead body on Öland.'

Chapter Five

On hearing that the body had been found in the middle of the Great Alvar, the large limestone plain to the south of the island, Hanna slouched down in her chair in an attempt to make herself look smaller. It wasn't the easiest thing to do when you were over six feet tall. She knew she might be the only member of the group who lived on Öland, and she wanted to stay at the station on the mainland. To find her feet before she was forced to head out into the community. Ove had promised not to say anything, but there had been a brief moment, while he was introducing her, when she was convinced he was about to mention Lars.

His eyes moved over her and settled on Erik. *Surfer*, that was the first word that had popped into her mind when she'd seen him. It was only the middle of May, but he was already tanned and looked offensively fit. Dressed casually, in a pair of pale jeans and a black t-shirt, his dirty-blond hair curly. He also happened to radiate the kind of professional friendliness that made her skin crawl.

'Erik, could you head over there and take Hanna with you? She's from the island, after all.'

Take Hanna with you. As though she was something you could shove into your bag and carry away. Or, more accurately, return. Erik nodded and got to his feet.

'What about our meeting?' Hanna heard herself ask.

She and Ove had agreed to reconvene in his office after the morning meeting. She hadn't been given her security pass or her work phone yet. No service weapon either.

'We can do it later.'

The anxiety Hanna felt refused to subside. She hadn't been prepared for just how hard it would be to see Ove again. She wanted to be assessed on her own merits, and was sick to death of allowing herself to be put down by what had happened. The others' eyes were all on her, and the woman called Carina seemed openly hostile. She knew who Hanna's father was, of course. Given how long she had worked for the police, she might even have been involved in the original investigation. Daniel was younger, and though all she could see in his eyes was curiosity, Hanna also found him difficult to look at. With his short, dark hair, he vaguely resembled Fabian, the colleague she had been in a relationship with before she left Stockholm. Amer smiled encouragingly, a little like the receptionist had earlier, and Hanna nodded back.

She got up and followed Erik down to the garage. He didn't try to talk to her. Instead, he pulled out his phone and began tapping away at the screen as he walked, probably trying to find more information about the call they were answering. Without a work phone of her own, Hanna couldn't do the same.

When they reached the armoury, Erik stopped to sign out his Sig Sauer. He gave Hanna a questioning glance, and she shook her head. She had never needed to use her service weapon before, but it still felt strange to head out without one; you never knew what might happen.

'Want to drive?' Erik asked, once they reached the car.

'No.'

'Do you know where Möckelmossen is?' he continued, fastening his seatbelt.

Hanna had vague memories of a class trip there in high school. Rocks, insects and sit mats. The packed lunch she claimed to have forgotten because it was too embarrassing to bring sandwiches without anything in them. Her best friend, Rebecka, had shared her pancakes with Hanna. It was early autumn, and they had gone there to study the cranes resting on their migration south. There were clusters of the long-legged, long-necked birds dotted all over the barren ground, their cries like a dirge of trumpets.

'Yeah, but you should probably use the GPS.'

Not that the roads were in the habit of moving on Öland, but Hanna didn't trust her memory. Why was there a dead body in Möckelmossen, of all places? Perhaps a tourist or mainlander had had a nasty fall by the lake. Hit their head on one of the many rocks there. That felt more likely than a drowning, considering how shallow the water was. During the summer, large sections of the lake dried up completely. How were she and Erik even supposed to get all the way out there? It wasn't like they could drive off-road.

'The body was found next to a rest area,' Erik said, as though he had read her mind.

There went her first theory, though the rest areas were also pretty rocky too.

'So you're from Öland?' Erik asked. 'That explains the lack of a Stockholm accent.'

'I was in Stockholm for the last sixteen years.'

'What brings you back here, then?'

Hanna shrugged. This wasn't something she wanted to talk to him about.

'What did you work on in Stockholm?'

'Investigations,' she replied.

'Aha,' said Erik.

His amused tone bothered her, but she was even more annoyed at herself for not being able to do better than this. She smoothed things over by saying something about how he knew what the job was like; there wasn't such a big difference between the city and the countryside. Erik began talking about the years he had spent working in Malmö.

As they drove up onto the bridge, Hanna turned to look out at the water. There had been a time when she'd had nightmares about crossing the bridge. About it shrinking and swaying the further out she drove, closer and closer to the inevitable climax, when her car plunged towards the dark, swirling waters. She always woke before she hit the surface. But something happened as she drove over the bridge to bury her father and empty her childhood home, and she now found she enjoyed it – at least while she was awake. The only home she had ever had was over there on the other side. And in her world, the bridge had always been there. By the time she was born in 1984, the six-kilometre link between Öland and Kalmar was already twelve years old.

The GPS told them to head south on the 136. Hanna knew that Runsbäcksvägen would be better, but she didn't say a word.

'It's so beautiful out here,' Erik said as he turned south at Resmo and the limestone plain opened up in front of them.

'You've never been to the alvar before?' Hanna asked.

'Nope, this is the first time the job's brought me over here. I've only been in Kalmar for three years, and I've only really been to the north of the island with the family.'

Hanna assumed he had gone to the beach up there, like all the other tourists.

The flat, barren landscape in front of them was beautiful, even with the thin haze hovering over it. But rather than keep quiet and enjoy the view, Erik began telling Hanna about his dream of owning a cottage in the countryside. Of growing his own food and becoming self-sufficient. He was probably more of a tree hugger than a surfer, she realised. Unless he was one of those preppers planning for the end of the world. He finally fell quiet as they pulled up at the rest area.

Forensics were already on the scene, as was the patrol car that had set up the cordon. She assumed that it too must have come from Kalmar. Öland had a local police station, up in Borgholm, but that was at least twice as far away. Erik climbed out of the car and spoke to the officers, introducing Hanna as his new colleague. Fortunately, he made do with her first name.

'Who found the body?' he asked.

'A couple of Germans,' one of the officers replied, nodding over to a parked car. 'I told them to stay until they'd spoken to a detective.'

Hanna felt her phone buzz in her pocket. Until she was given a work phone, she would have to use her own, and she was fairly sure this wasn't a personal message. Sure enough, it was Ove: he wanted her to meet him at the bakery in Färjestaden in an hour. He had to come over to Öland anyway, he wrote, on other business. Hanna sent off a quick 'OK' in reply.

'Could we be looking at a natural cause of death?' she asked.

Now that she was actually working, Hanna felt fine. She knew she was good at her job – her boss in Stockholm had even offered her a serious pay rise when she'd announced that she was thinking about leaving. There hadn't been any suitable positions open in Kalmar, but when she saw that Ove Hultmark was still working there, she got in touch, and he had found a job for her. Claimed they needed another detective anyway. It was only later, once she had said yes, that she realised it meant he would be her new boss.

'No, it definitely wasn't natural,' the officer replied. 'Take a look for yourselves. You'll see what I mean.'

Erik walked over to one of the technicians and repeated the same greetings as earlier. Forensics hadn't put up their tent yet; it wasn't raining, and the stone walls were blocking the crime scene from view. The public wouldn't be allowed into the rest area while the investigation was under way. Hanna glanced out at the flat landscape and shuddered. There was something unsettling about the way the mist seemed to be dancing just above the ground.

The first she saw of the victim was an arm, draped over the collapsed stone wall. Judging by the size of it, it didn't belong to an adult. Hanna took a slow step forward, steeling herself for what was to come.

The victim was a young boy, possibly thirteen or fourteen, though it was hard to tell. He was wearing a baggy hooded sweatshirt, and was leaning back against the rocks. His head, covered by the hood, was close to a sign giving information about the area in German.

It was clear he had been beaten up. One of his eyebrows was split, the eye beneath it swollen. The other was half open.

There was a large bloodstain on his sweater, and a pool of blood on the ground a metre or so from where he was slumped.

There was no doubt about it: this was a murder.

Hanna scanned the ground for the murder weapon, but couldn't see anything. Her eyes came to rest on his right hand, which looked like it was clutching something.

'What's he got in his hand?' she asked one of the technicians, who took a photo of the boy's hand, then struggled to unfurl his fingers.

Inside was a small pink flower that had started to wilt.

The Last Day

Swearing to himself, Joel pops his thumb into his mouth and sucks the blood. How the hell is it possible for a person to be so clumsy that they cut themselves on a cheese slicer?

Molly stops pushing her cereal hoops around her bowl and looks up in surprise. They used to keep an empty jam jar on the cookbook shelf in the kitchen, and anyone who swore had to put a scrap of paper with their symbol on it inside. The jar vanished once Mum realised she was the one who swore most – almost all the pieces of paper had her blue mark on them.

Joel smiles at Molly. It sometimes feels like she is the only person who really sees him. Mum is hunched over a copy of *Barometern* as usual, reading an article about an exhibition at the art gallery in Kalmar. The other local paper, the *Ölandsbladet*, only comes three times a week, so they subscribe to both. Petri's thoughts are elsewhere. Probably on one of the many problems that have cropped up during the renovation. He spent the whole of dinner last night moaning about it.

Joel takes a big bite of his bread and cheese and fishes his phone from the pocket of his jeans. Banning phones at the dinner table is one of the few rules Mum actually enforces, but he has been struggling to breathe since he woke up that morning, and he feels like he is about to start bawling. He needs to speak to Nadine.

Blood spurting across the breakfast table here, he writes.

She replies immediately: *Who got sick of who?*

Joel looks up at his family. He briefly considers inventing an argument between Mum and Petri, but it's just too unlikely. Besides, he doesn't want to jinx it. Doesn't want to be responsible for making something like that happen.

The cheese slicer flipped out on my thumb, he writes.

Nadine replies with a laughing/crying emoji.

'Put that away,' Petri tells him.

Joel sighs and does as he is told. His step-father can really get on his nerves sometimes, but Joel doesn't have the energy to argue with him today.

'I want a pony!' Molly chirps, probably to break the tension she can feel building. She's incredibly perceptive for a six-year-old. Or, as she would put it herself, an almost seven-year-old – even though her birthday is still five months away.

'I'd like one too,' Rebecka tells her, closing the paper. 'But we can't afford it.'

'But what if we can later?'

'Absolutely.' It's a risk-free promise, because it's never going to happen.

Petri gets up and mumbles something about having to head off. His only contribution to clearing the table is to put his crumb-strewn plate and empty coffee cup on the counter. Joel often wonders what his mother sees in him. It's hard to imagine a more narrow-minded person. Petri often throws out opinions about the government that sound worryingly like conspiracy theories. Who knows, maybe he's one of those crazy flat-earthers.

Mum sighs and turns the page, and Joel feels a sudden rush of warmth for her. For everything contained in that sigh. She has been through so much, but somehow she still manages to keep it together. He tells Molly to go and brush her teeth and starts clearing the table, but Mum stops him.

'I'll do that later. You've got a bus to catch.'

The thought comes to him again, as it has so many times over the past few weeks: he should just tell her. He will feel so much better once he gets it off his chest. But how? How is he supposed to tell her that he isn't the person she thinks he is?

Chapter Six

Hanna pushed open the door to the bakery in Färjestaden and only just managed to swallow the greeting on the tip of her tongue. The man deliberating over the bread inside wasn't Ove at all. His haircut and denim jacket had tricked her. She peered out through the window, but couldn't see her superior outside. Should she buy something now, or should she wait? She didn't know whether she was supposed to pay for herself.

The man she had mistaken for Ove paid for his four walnut rolls and left. The young girl behind the counter turned to Hanna, who took a step forward and ordered a coffee and a cheese sandwich. Her breakfast that morning had consisted of coffee and half a bowl of cornflakes, so she was hungry.

The handful of tables inside the bakery were empty, but Hanna chose to head out to the larger seating area outside. She knew she would find it easier to talk if she didn't have to worry about being overheard. There were fleece blankets draped over the backs of the chairs, but Hanna ignored them; the sky was clearer here than it had been in Möckelmossen, and it had to be at least fifteen degrees celsius.

Erik was driving the two German tourists back to the guesthouse in their own car. They had both been too shaken up to get behind the wheel themselves; finding a dead boy was hardly on their holiday itinerary. The plan was for Erik to take their statements at the guesthouse. Hanna would pick him up there after her meeting with Ove.

A group of teenagers walked by, heading towards the harbour. They were laughing, and the lone girl swung a punch in the air after one of the boys. Hanna wondered whether she should have sat inside after all, and was just about to get up when she saw Ove pull into the car park on the other side of the road. He climbed out and raised his hand in greeting. Nerves made Hanna's cheeks flush.

After buying a tea and an almond tart with sliced strawberries on top, Ove came out and sat down opposite her. He had upgraded the old denim jacket he wore sixteen years ago, and was now wearing a black leather jacket. Hanna began by giving him an update on what they had found out in Möckelmossen, and Ove took a large bite of his tart as he listened. Crumbs of shortcrust pastry fell to his lap, and he brushed them away.

'I know you're going to do a great job,' he said. 'I really just wanted to make sure you were OK being thrown straight in at the deep end like this. To be perfectly honest, I feel a certain amount of responsibility for you.'

'Why?'

'Because I hired you, and . . . well, because of what happened with your dad. I'm the one who sent him to prison, after all.'

Hanna stared down at her sandwich, at the glossy slice of cheese. She took a sip of her coffee instead. Part of her wanted to ask whether Ove had ever had any doubts, but she didn't dare. Instead, she said that the only person responsible for her father's prison sentence was her father. Ove seemed noticeably relieved, like he really had been convinced that she blamed him.

'I don't have much to say about the job itself,' he continued. 'You know what's what, and you'll work out how we do things round here soon enough. But don't hesitate to talk to me if you need to. About anything.'

'OK.' Hanna heard how lame her response sounded, but Ove's concern bothered her. She wasn't used to it.

'Do you have much contact with your brother these days?' he asked.

'No, not really. He lives in London now.'

As though his choice of city was the reason she and Kristoffer had drifted apart. Ove had interviewed Kristoffer back then too. More times than Hanna, in fact, since he hadn't been as willing to play ball. Ove fixed his eyes on her now, only letting her go once she forced herself to meet his gaze.

He reached for his bag and pulled out a mobile phone, which he pushed over to Hanna along with a security pass and a sheet of paper.

'Here's your pass, your phone and your login details. Make sure you change your password.'

'Absolutely,' Hanna told him. It was a more enthusiastic choice of word than OK, at the very least. 'And my gun?'

'We can sort that out this afternoon.'

Ove took a sip of his tea.

'We've identified the victim,' he continued. 'He had a bank card and a library card on him, belonging to Joel Forslund, fifteen. We checked his latest ID photo, and it's definitely him. He's from Gårdby.'

He was giving her that look again, searching.

'Is that going to be a problem?'

Hanna shook her head. That was all she could manage. She realised this must be why Ove had wanted to meet. Forslund wasn't a name she recognised, but it was her first day on the job, and she was already being asked to return to Gårdby. As she had locked the door to her childhood home there last autumn, handing the key to the estate agent, she had thought she was finished with the place.

'Joel Forslund had been dead for a few hours at least by the time he was found. The doctor who visited the scene said that rigor mortis had already set in.'

Hanna remembered the technician having to prise the boy's fingers open, but all she could hear was Kristoffer's voice:

You're crazy. You're going to ruin everything.

Ove took out another sheet of paper.

'Here's all the information about his mother – that's who he lived with, plus a younger sister and a step-father. I want you and Erik to go over there and break the news. If possible, also interview her.'

It was only once Hanna was back in the car that she looked down at the information Ove had given her about Joel Forslund's mother. It consisted of an address and a copy of her driving licence.

She stared down at the photo.

At the woman's dark brown hair, which only came down to her shoulders now, rather than her waist. At her eyes and her small upturned nose, both exactly the same as they had been sixteen years ago.

Everything around Hanna seemed to disappear, and it felt as though the ground had opened up and swallowed both her and the car.

Rebecka.

Chapter Seven

The German couple who had discovered the dead body were staying at an inn in Vickleby. The inn was painted yellow, but it was hidden behind so much greenery that Erik almost drove straight past it. He turned off and pulled up by the front door. In the rear-view mirror he saw that Adam and Kirsten Buchner were holding hands – or rather, Kirsten was clinging onto her husband. Erik climbed out and looked around. Between the trees, he could make out a seating area in the large garden. It was just gone eleven, but there was almost no one else around.

'Maybe we could sit down over there?' he suggested, nodding towards the seats.

Erik had studied German at school, but he was far more comfortable speaking English. It was the language he and Supriya used most often at home. Fortunately, the Germans' English was good. Erik had asked a few questions about their lives and their family during the drive over, trying to put them at ease, and had learned that one of their children lived in Canada, another in Australia.

It was obvious the Buchners were still shaken up by what had happened, and Erik was glad he had been able to give them a ride back to the inn. Since Hanna was in Färjestaden, he had plenty of time, and it would probably be easier to take their statements here than at the crime scene.

The seating area in the garden was incredibly quiet, and as they stepped between the trees, it was like the world around them disappeared. All they could hear was the wind in the leaves and the occasional bird chirping. Erik wondered what the rest area at Möckelmossen was usually like. Whether the mist was common. The silence there had felt different, full of undertones.

They sat down at a rickety white wooden table, and Erik asked whether he could get them something to drink. Neither wanted anything, so he took out his notepad.

'Could you tell me how you found the body?' he asked.

'I saw him first,' said Adam. 'I'd climbed over the . . . gate, the thing keeping the livestock in, and when I got to the other side I turned around to help Kirsten.'

Adam paused and glanced at his wife.

'I tried to stop her from looking over there, but I couldn't speak.'

'It was so awful,' said Kirsten. 'That poor boy.'

Erik nodded. Investigations involving the deaths of young people were always the worst. His own daughter would be starting school that autumn.

'And you didn't see anything before that, while you were climbing over the gate?' he asked.

'No,' said Adam. 'The wall the boy was leaning against was in the way. We were looking straight ahead. It's so beautiful out there in the alvar.'

Erik murmured in agreement. It was beautiful, but there was also a bleakness to the place that he hadn't been expecting.

'Did you notice anything in the rest area?' he asked.

'No,' the Buchners replied in unison. Kirsten fell silent again, but Adam continued:

'It was so peaceful,' he said. 'All we could hear were the birds.'

'Were there any other cars there?'

'One, I think.'

That car had still been there when the first officers arrived at the scene.

'It was my sixty-fifth birthday a few weeks ago,' Kirsten explained. 'And I wanted to celebrate my retirement by coming to Öland. My grandmother was from here.'

She had already told Erik the same story in the car, and she smiled, embarrassed, when she realised she had repeated herself. Erik wondered whether it was simply the shock that was confusing her. Adam placed a hand on his wife's knee.

'I've been retired for two years,' he said. 'It's been pretty boring doing everything alone.'

'Did you pass anyone else on the way to the rest area?' Erik asked, trying to steer the conversation back to the dead boy.

'There was a man on a bike,' said Kirsten.

'How far from Möckelmossen?'

Kirsten gave her husband an uncertain glance.

'A few hundred metres,' said Adam.

'What did he look like?'

'Blond, with a thin blue jacket. Around thirty, maybe?'

'And which way was he cycling?'

'Towards us. His face seemed . . . harried, somehow. That's why I remember him.'

'Do you remember what colour the bike was?'

'I think it was red.'

46

A middle-aged woman came out of the guesthouse and began walking towards them. Her thick, grey-flecked hair was plaited, and she was wearing a patterned apron.

'Are you back already?' she asked cheerily.

The Buchners exchanged an uncomfortable look, and Erik chose to pull out his ID and briefly explain what was happening. That they had found a dead body out in the middle of the alvar.

The woman raised a hand to her mouth – a murder just as summer was approaching was hardly what the tourist industry wanted – but then she turned back to the Germans and asked whether they needed anything. A cup of tea, perhaps.

'Maybe later,' said Kirsten. 'I don't think I can manage anything right now.'

The woman left them in peace, and Kirsten placed her palm on her husband's chest.

'I'm so tired,' she said. 'I'd like to go and lie down for a while.'

'We're almost done here,' said Erik. 'How long will you be staying?'

'We got here on Sunday, and the plan was to stay another week,' said Adam. 'But now . . .'

'I'd appreciate it if you didn't leave for a few days,' Erik told them.

Not just for the investigation's sake, but for their own. He thought they would find it easier to process what had happened if they didn't immediately hurry home. He gave them his card and told them to call him if they thought of anything else.

'You might get a few calls from journalists,' Erik continued. 'Or they might come out here looking for you. I'd advise you not to talk to them if they do.'

That was also for both their sake and the investigation's. When people were in shock, they sometimes said things they later came to regret. The news that a boy had been found dead in the middle of the alvar had probably already leaked, but the Buchners knew details that needed to be kept from the press if they wanted to avoid making the police's job more difficult.

Chapter Eight

Hanna fumbled for the steering wheel, gripping it so hard that her hands began to ache. It was years since she had last seen Rebecka, but she had no trouble recognising her from her driving licence. Any wrinkles she might have were barely visible, her age primarily evident in the solemn look on her face. What Hanna remembered most clearly about Rebecka was her laugh. She had been Hanna's one real friend throughout childhood, though her surname had been Karlsson back then.

None of what had happened was Rebecka's fault, but she would for ever be bound up with it.

Hanna's surroundings came back to her, but she still didn't feel ready to drive. She was glad she hadn't looked at the information while she was still with Ove, because there was no way she would have been able to hide her reaction from him. Perhaps she should call him now and let him know, toning down how close she and Rebecka had once been? No. She didn't want to risk being taken off the investigation. Rebecka had always been there for Hanna, and now Hanna wanted to do the same for her. She wanted to try to pay back some of that debt.

She turned the ignition and drove over to the guest-house. Pulling up outside, she shut off the engine and stared down at the copy of Rebecka's licence on the passenger seat. As she put it away, she realised that she still hadn't set up her work phone. She switched it on, logged in and changed her password, dropping it into her pocket and climbing out of the car.

Hanna stepped into the yellow wooden building, passing the various small bedrooms inside. There were chairs everywhere: wooden chairs with striped cushions, wicker chairs, armchairs . . . But they were all empty. At the rear of the house, she found a bar counter. A woman appeared behind it, giving Hanna a questioning look.

'I'm looking for my colleague,' she told her.

'If he's with the police, he's out in the garden.'

Hanna found Erik on a white wooden chair, enjoying a sandwich with his face raised to the sun.

'Decided to take an early lunch,' he explained. 'You eaten?'

Hanna nodded and sat down beside him. Her only connection to Vickleby was that she had once been to a party here, thrown by one of Rebecka's friends. Kristoffer had been there too. All she remembered was throwing up behind a bush and spilling wine on a sofa. That, and the fact that the parents – who were supposed to be in Spain – had come home early and screamed at everyone to leave. It had been a month or so before she graduated from high school. The sofa and the stereo had been ruined, and everyone's parents had been called. She remembered wishing that Lars would shout at her, but of course he didn't – even though she was the one who had spilled the wine, and should really have paid for the damage. That was one of the few times she had complained about them never having any money.

Was that why he had decided to break into the house?

There are consequences to everything we say and do.

'How was your meeting?' Erik asked, his mouth still full.

'Great,' she said, with so much enthusiasm that she hoped he wouldn't ask any follow-up questions.

He didn't. Instead, he brought her up to date with what the Buchners had told him.

'We need to find that man on the bike,' said Hanna.

'Absolutely. And the owner of the car parked in the rest area.'

The car owner would be much easier to find than the cyclist, Hanna thought to herself.

'They've identified the body,' she said.

'Already?'

'Yes, we have to go and break the news to his mother.' She kept her face neutral as she spoke.

'How old was he?' asked Erik.

'Fifteen. Would've been sixteen in December.'

'Older than I thought.'

'Yeah.'

As though it would have made any difference if the boy was a few years younger. Rebecka's son. Hanna felt her eyelids twitch. Fifteen was far too young to be dead. Joel hadn't even started senior high school yet. He likely had other plans for the future than ending up dead behind a wall. Right then, she realised something else, and it shocked her. If Joel was fifteen, Rebecka must have been pregnant during that awful week at the end of high school. Why hadn't she said anything?

'Do you find it hard?' Erik asked.

51

'What?'

'Delivering news of death.'

Hanna nodded, pretended that was what was bothering her. Maybe she should tell Erik, at the very least. Rebecka would recognise her. The last time they'd seen one another was on a Sunday, a week or so after they graduated high school. They had sprawled on Rebecka's sofa, eating ice cream and watching *Friends* on TV. Just a few hours later, Hanna had boarded the bus to Stockholm.

Why didn't you say anything?

The anger and disappointment Rebecka had spat out a few days later, when Hanna called her, still hurt. But if she had shared her plans in advance, she never would have left.

Hanna got up.

'Shall we go?'

Erik shoved the last of his sandwich into his mouth and followed her to the car. Hanna knew where Rebecka lived, so she decided to drive, taking the southern road via Resmo, because it was a slightly longer route. It would give her more time to prepare.

Erik managed to stay quiet for a few minutes.

'You got kids?' he asked.

Please, stop talking, Hanna wanted to tell him. She needed the silence now. But instead she simply shook her head. Her last boyfriend, Fabian, was seven years older than her, and she had felt his longing for kids like he was constantly breathing down her neck. After three months together, he had asked her to move in with him in his suburban terraced house.

Hanna drove through the alvar, past the rest area where Joel's body had been found. The forensic technicians were still processing the scene, trudging around the barren plain in their white overalls. They had finally put up their tent. Was Joel inside, or had they already moved him? The haze was gone, and with the windscreen as protection, there was no longer anything threatening about the landscape.

'I've got a seven-year-old daughter,' Erik went on. 'Nila.'

'Nice name,' said Hanna. 'Is it Sami?'

'Indian. It means "moon" in Marathi and Tamil and probably a whole bunch of other languages.'

Erik was probably expecting a follow-up question, but Hanna didn't have the energy to be nice; it felt like she had already missed her chance to make a good first impression.

As she turned off towards Gårdby, she felt a tug of anxiety in her chest.

'I'm married to an Indian woman,' Erik explained.

'OK.'

Hanna chewed her lower lip. She realised that Erik might think she had a problem with what he had said, which only worsened her anxiety.

'I grew up here,' she told him. 'That's where I went to school.'

Hanna nodded towards the yellow school building. She pictured the scene through his eyes: the blocky building surrounded by houses and trees, the fields beyond, the low stone walls, the clusters of letterboxes by the road. The space. Most of the buildings in Gårdby were residential. Both the petrol station and the supermarket had closed down since Hanna left, and several of the houses looked like they were on the verge of collapse, though many had recently been renovated. Hanna didn't point out her childhood home. A family with young children had bought it around Christmas, and they had already repainted the exterior walls. There was a swing set in the garden now, and the grass was strewn with brightly coloured plastic toys. She wondered whether they knew who had lived there before them.

'What was it like growing up round here?' Erik asked.

'Like anywhere else, I guess,' she said. 'Good and bad.'

It had been good until she turned twelve, when her mother was diagnosed with an aggressive form of leukaemia. She had died just a few weeks later, and life after that had been bad, eventually becoming impossible. Still, there had been two bright points: Rebecka, and Hanna's grandmother.

'Thanks for the exhaustive answer,' Erik laughed.

'Where did you grow up?' Hanna asked, her tone curt.

'Malmö.'

She drove by a burnt-out garage, and her grip on the wheel tightened. Of all the things she had to deal with at work, fires were always the hardest. Her hands relaxed once they passed Gårdby's café and farm shop. The café seemed to have undergone a complete transformation, and now looked like every city dweller's dream of the countryside. Pelle's mechanic workshop was still opposite, looking the same as it always had.

Hanna pulled up outside the house. When she lived in Gårdby, it had been owned by a woman called Sonja. She didn't remember her surname, but it could easily have been Forslund, or possibly something else. Either way, this was the house the children always used to visit first at Easter, begging for sweets. The red paint was flaking, and it was obvious that children now lived there, but little else had changed. There was a pink plastic ball on the lawn.

They walked up to the door, Hanna clutching her left forearm. She wanted to tear back the black material covering her tattoo of a nightingale, the bird that would help keep the darkness at bay.

After her mother's death, her grandmother had given her a small wooden nightingale to keep by her bedroom window. She claimed that because nightingales sing at night, it would help Hanna with her nightmares, but her bad dreams hadn't gone anywhere. When she complained, her grandmother had stroked her cheek and said: *I know those dreams are horrible, but they would be even worse without the bird.* Those words had taken hold, and Hanna had kept the bird ever since – it was on the window sill of her bedroom in Kleva now.

The doorbell didn't work, so Hanna knocked instead. Made an effort to empty her mind of everything other than what she was here to do. The door opened, and Rebecka was suddenly staring straight at her. Hanna had had long hair throughout childhood, but it was now short – her fringe was the longest part, reaching just above her jawline. She was also heavier than she used to be. Rebecka blinked for a moment, but then her expression changed.

'Hanna!' she cried. 'What are you doing here?'

Her eyes flitted over to the ID badge Erik was holding up, and the look of surprise on her face quickly turned to fear.

The Last Day

It is just before eight when Joel gets off the bus outside Skansen School in Mörbylånga. A few steps, that's all he can manage. His throat contracts, his feet refusing to budge. Black spots seem to bounce towards the low red-brick building. Someone laughs. Someone else is arguing in a shrill voice. A shove in the back, followed by: *For fuck's sake, get out the way*. He moves forward, mechanically.

A few metres from the main door, he stops again. He can't handle school today. Listening to all these teachers who think they get it. The only subject he enjoys is art, and he doesn't have art today.

Six months ago, Joel actually used to like school. Maybe *like* isn't the right word, but he could bear it at least. Thought of it as a ticket to something else.

As Joel turns around, he almost walks straight into the deputy head. He mumbles an apology and hurries away. He can feel her eyes burning on his back, but she doesn't say anything to stop him.

Fuck. Life sucks right now. He is desperate for something other than this. The only problem is that he no longer knows what.

Joel takes out his phone and sends a message to Nadine: *Can we hang out today?*

She replies immediately, like always. *Sure. Coffee lunch?*

Lunch is half a day away, and that half-day feels even less manageable than school. Joel's fingers are trembling, making it hard to hit the right letters on his phone. *Can you meet any earlier?*

This time, her message takes a moment to arrive. *Rather not miss any more school. How bad is it?*

Tears begin streaming down his cheeks. Fuck, he hates being like this. He angrily rubs his face with the sleeve of his sweater. Being clingy isn't cool right now. Nadine is always there for him, and the last thing she needs is another dose of his problems.

I'll be OK. Just say where and when.

Sure? asks Nadine. *?? Kullzenska at 11:15.*

Joel replies with a clapping monkey.

What is he going to do until then? The hours are full of obstacles: the library in Kalmar doesn't open until ten, he forgot to put a new sketchbook in his bag, and he's short on money.

Joel heads down to the harbour. He usually likes watching the boats. Dreaming of other places. Imagining that life could be different.

He follows the cobblestones down to the edge. The horizon makes him dizzy, so he stares down at the deep blue water instead. There is barely a ripple on the surface, and it feels so tempting just to take a step out. To vanish into its calm depths.

Chapter Nine

From the corner of one eye, Hanna saw Erik hold up his police ID, but she remained focused on Rebecka.

'Could we come in and sit down?' she asked.

Hanna felt so queasy she thought she was going to throw up. How many times had she done this before – broken the news of a death to someone? Said those exact words and brought yet another world crashing down. But there was no comparing it; this was Rebecka. Standing in front of her now seemed to make the years fade away. She was nineteen again, and had run over to Rebecka's place because what had just happened was going to tear her apart. The way her father, head bowed, had allowed himself to be led away by the police without a single word.

'What's going on?' Rebecka asked.

It was the same question she had asked sixteen years earlier, but back then Hanna hadn't known. It was only later that she found out what Lars was accused of. The years settled like a weight around her heart. Rebecka's son was dead, and Hanna didn't want to tell her. Not like this, not standing in the doorway.

'Could we come in and sit down?'

This time, it was Erik who spoke. Rebecka reluctantly turned and showed them into the living room. While she had her back to them, Erik gave Hanna a questioning glance, but Hanna ignored it.

The living room was much cosier than Rebecka's had been growing up, in a home with a single mother who worked constantly. There was a grey sofa and a retro orange armchair, colourful pictures on the walls. Hanna guessed Rebecka must have painted them herself; she had always been good at that kind of thing. Rebecka sat down on the sofa, and Hanna took a seat next to her.

'So, you joined the police,' said Rebecka.

Fear was practically radiating out of her, mixing with the faint scent of alcohol.

'Rebecka and I were friends in high school,' Hanna explained without looking at Erik.

Excusing herself and leaving wouldn't solve a thing. She couldn't do that to Rebecka. Not again.

'Just say it,' said Rebecka. 'I know it's about Joel.'

'Yes. I'm so, so sorry,' said Hanna. 'He's dead.'

As the last two words left her mouth, tears began spilling down her cheeks. She was powerless to stop them.

Rebecka buried her face in her hands, and Hanna shuffled over and wrapped her arms around her. She glanced over at Erik in the armchair. For the first time, he looked concerned, though it was impossible to know why. Time dragged on. Rebecka made soft whimpering sounds, pressing her hands to her eyes so firmly that Hanna was worried she might hurt herself.

Dead.

There was nothing more final than that.

Rebecka's whimpering transformed into tears. Hanna wanted to take her pain away, but she couldn't.

After a while, Rebecka began to calm down.

'How did you know it was something to do with Joel?' Hanna asked softly.

For the sake of the investigation, they needed to ask these questions as soon as possible. Relatives were sometimes so shocked that they had no choice but to wait, but Hanna thought Rebecka would be able to answer them.

'His bed was empty when I went to wake him up this morning,' she said, lowering her hands. 'And he didn't turn up to school today. Or yesterday.'

'Did he often skip school?'

'No, he wasn't like me.'

Hanna's gaze drifted from Rebecka's bloodshot eyes to one of the paintings. She thought it might represent the sun setting over the sea, though she wasn't sure. Either way, it was beautiful. Beyond the frame, she began to notice the shabbier aspects of the room. The scuff marks on the white walls, the chipped window frames.

'When did you last see Joel?' asked Erik.

'Last night. We went next door to celebrate our neighbour's fortieth birthday. Joel brought Molly home just before nine.'

That explained the alcohol. Rebecka began crying again, though only for a short burst this time.

'Something happened to him,' she sobbed. 'These past few weeks. No, months. He seemed different.'

'Do you . . .'

'No, I have no idea what it was.'

Irritated, Rebecka got to her feet and began pacing around the room. Before long, her footsteps slowed.

'I tried to talk to him, but I didn't get anywhere. Did he ki . . .'

She trailed off, but Hanna knew what she wanted to ask. Joel had clearly been in such a bad place that Rebecka was worried he had taken his own life.

'No, we think he was killed.'

Rebecka abruptly stopped her pacing and stared at her.

'Killed?'

'Yes, in all likelihood,' said Erik. 'But we don't know anything for sure yet.'

It took Rebecka a few seconds to process this new information, but the moment when Erik's words finally sunk in was plain to see. Her hand flew up to her mouth, and she turned and ran away. Through the closed door, they heard her retching, followed by the sound of a toilet flushing. A few minutes later, Rebecka came back into the room and took a seat. She was trembling, as though she was having a shivering fit.

'Why do you think he was killed?'

Hanna chose her words carefully before speaking.

'He had been assaulted.'

Fortunately, Rebecka made do with that explanation. For the moment, at least.

'Where was he found?' she asked.

'Out by the rest area in Möckelmossen.'

Hanna studied Rebecka as she said it, but her friend barely reacted.

'Do you have any idea what might have happened?' asked Erik.

'I don't know. Oh God, I don't know.'

Rebecka was on the verge of tears again, and Hanna placed a hand on her back.

'I know it's hard, but try to shut out the how and why. Who do you think could have done this?'

'Axel.'

There was only one Axel Rebecka could be talking about: Axel Sandsten. He had been in Hanna's class in high school. She had never liked him herself, but he had hung out with her brother. Probably because Kristoffer supplied him with alcohol for his parties. Other substances too, in all likelihood. Axel's family had lived in a huge villa in central Kalmar, and his parents were often overseas.

'Why would Axel—' she began, but Rebecka interrupted her:

'Axel is Joel's father.'

Chapter Ten

'Sorry, but do we have a surname for this Axel?' asked Erik.

'Sandsten,' Hanna told him.

Erik knew who Axel Sandsten was. He ran a consultancy that helped various businesses streamline their operations. Just a few months earlier, he had won an accolade of some kind at the council's business awards.

'Axel isn't who people think he is,' said Rebecka.

'I always thought he was a bully,' Hanna chipped in.

'Yeah, that was obvious.' Rebecka smiled, though it quickly faded.

Erik hovered in the background as the women talked. It was clear that Hanna and Rebecka had been close at one point in time. His new colleague seemed much softer than she had earlier, and he doubted he would have been able to question Rebecka without Hanna present. Not considering the way she had reacted when she found out her son was dead. For a few minutes, she had been completely unreachable.

'Was the pregnancy . . .' Hanna paused.

'No, he didn't rape me,' said Rebecka. 'We were together.'

'When did that happen?' asked Hanna.

'A few weeks before graduation. I was worried what you would think. And then other things got in the way . . . I never managed to tell you before you left.'

A flash of guilt passed over Hanna's face, though Rebecka didn't seem to have noticed. She was too hung up on the past.

'I didn't realise I was pregnant. I thought it was all the drinking that was making me feel sick constantly. And even though I'd started to work out what Axel was like, I wanted to keep the baby. And . . . and I wanted to try . . .'

Rebecka was overwhelmed by such a powerful sobbing fit that she couldn't speak. She pressed her clenched fist to her stomach, and Hanna embraced her again. Erik managed to find the kitchen, and fetched a glass of water and some kitchen roll. On the way back, he almost tripped over a cuddly grey rabbit.

He put down the glass of water on the coffee table and handed a sheet of kitchen roll to Hanna, who passed it to Rebecka.

'We lived with Axel's parents at first,' Rebecka said, blowing her nose. 'And then when Joel was a few months old, they bought us a flat. I guess they were sick of all the screaming. Joel had colic and was barely sleeping at night. But Axel got much worse once it was just the three of us.'

'What did he do?' asked Hanna.

'He was just so jealous.'

'How did he show that?'

'By checking my phone, telling me who I could or couldn't see, that kind of thing.'

'And . . .'

'He hit me too.'

Rebecka was clutching the piece of kitchen roll so tight that it had begun to fall apart in her hands.

'But I still didn't want to give up. Joel was four when I finally decided I'd had enough and moved back to Öland.'

Erik waited for one of the women to go on, but both simply stared straight ahead. Rebecka at the kitchen roll and Hanna at Rebecka.

'So what kind of relationship did you have once you left Axel?'

Rebecka looked up at Erik as though she had only just realised he was in the room.

'He threatened me. I was staying with my mum, and he said he'd burn down the house with us in it if I didn't come back.'

Hanna tensed up.

'Sorry,' said Rebecka. 'But that's what he said.'

Erik didn't understand what she meant.

'And how is Axel with Joel?' he asked.

Rebecka wiped away the tears silently rolling down her cheeks.

'He's a bastard with him too.'

Hanna looked down at the table. It was impossible to tell what was going through her mind.

'In what sense?' Erik pressed.

'He put such impossible demands on him. Like when Joel was five, he locked him in his room because he couldn't tie his shoelaces. Joel was a complete wreck when he got home. I had to coax what happened out of him.'

'So he lived with his dad as well?'

'Only at first. I never knew my dad, so I hoped Axel would get better. But in the end, it just wasn't working. I realised he wasn't good for Joel.'

'Did Axel hit him too?' Hanna asked.

'Only once. That I saw anyway.'

Rebecka was still clutching the ragged piece of kitchen roll.

'What is it?' Hanna asked.

'I had to threaten Axel with sole custody. I said I'd tell them everything he'd done to me if he didn't agree . . . He didn't like that.'

'He kept harassing you?' Hanna asked.

'Yeah.'

'But why would he kill Joel?' Erik spoke up.

'To punish me, maybe?' said Rebecka. 'Or maybe he just lost his temper. That used to happen a lot.'

Erik pictured the boy's bloodied body.

'And the fact that Joel was found in the rest area in Möckelmossen,' said Hanna. 'What do you make of that?'

'I don't understand it,' Rebecka sobbed. 'There's nothing out there.'

Erik got up. He knew there might be things Rebecka would only say if she was alone with Hanna. He nodded towards the door, letting them know he was going out for a while. *Forensics*, Hanna mouthed to him.

Out on the porch, Erik called Ove to arrange for forensics to come to the house, and to let him know they would have to look into Axel Sandsten. Ove didn't sound happy at the news; the Kalmar Police had used Sandsten's firm on a number of occasions. On top of that, the news that a dead teenager had been found out in the middle of the alvar was already being shared on the Öland forum on Facebook – including the exact location, though fortunately no names had been mentioned. Ove had found out when a journalist from *Barometern* called and started asking questions.

After a moment's hesitation, Erik also told Ove that Hanna had gone to school with the victim's mother.

He ended the call and turned around. There was no sign of forced entry on the front door, but the technicians would still have to check the house for any evidence of a break-in. Perhaps people round here didn't even bother locking their doors, Erik thought to himself. Either way, the most likely explanation was that Joel had left the house himself. Abducting a teenager against his will was not something that could be done quietly – not even a teenager as small as Joel. Maybe he had agreed to meet Axel Sandsten. Or someone else. They were still at the very start of their investigation; they couldn't allow their focus to narrow too much.

Erik walked down the steps. At the front of the house there was another, smaller building, and he peered in through one of the windows. It seemed to be a studio of some kind. He could see a throwing wheel in one corner, the shelves around it full of ceramics. He moved to the right and looked into another room. An empty easel and a number of canvases stacked against the wall, facing away from him.

Erik walked around the edge of the main house. To one side there was a swing set and a broken slide. An empty sandpit. There was a seating area to the rear, but the view wasn't at all what he had been expecting. The fields never seemed far away on Öland, yet from where he was standing, all he could see were trees. Through them, he could make out more houses.

He and Supriya had brought Nila to Öland for the first time last summer, driving up to Böda to go swimming. The beaches there were fantastic, the shallow water too, but he preferred this kind of landscape. This was precisely the kind of place he would like to live: in a clearing in the woods, like people had for thousands of years.

'Sorry, who are you?'

A man was peering over from the neighbouring garden. Probably the same neighbour who had just turned forty, given how hungover he looked. Erik walked over and introduced himself. The man's name was Gabriel Andersson, he learned.

'Did you have the Forslund family over for a barbecue yesterday evening?' Erik asked him.

'Yes, we did.' After a brief pause, Gabriel asked: 'Why are you here?'

'I'm afraid I can't say, but I'd like to know if anything unusual happened during the barbecue?'

'No. I mean, like what?'

'I don't know. That's why I'm asking.'

'No, we just ate and chatted. And drank.'

'And the kids?'

'They ran off inside first chance they got.'

'Did you notice anything strange about Joel?'

'No.'

Gabriel seemed to hesitate again, and Erik smiled, but he didn't go on.

'Sorry, I have to go and deal with the laundry,' the neighbour excused himself.

Chapter Eleven

It felt like her consciousness had been torn in two. Half of it was sitting on the sofa beside Hanna, chatting to her as though nothing had happened. Finally sober, having thrown up the last of the alcohol. The other half was floating around the room, desperately searching for a way out. Screaming in protest at everything that was going on.

Joel is dead.

Rebecka tried out the words in her mind, but they didn't sound true.

'Who was Joel's best friend?' Hanna asked her.

Hanna, who had once been Rebecka's very best friend. The only person she could share everything with. And yet Rebecka hadn't told her about the baby she was carrying. Partly because she was ashamed, because she had done the one thing she had always sworn she never would: she had followed in her mother's footsteps. No, worse than that. At least her mother had finished high school before she got pregnant. Hanna had represented sanctuary to Rebecka, and she hadn't wanted to destroy that. With Hanna, she could always pretend that things would change for the better. But then everything with Hanna's dad had happened, and it was too late to say anything. Hanna was suddenly gone. Rebecka wanted to believe that if it hadn't been for the pregnancy, she would have left Gårdby too, but she had hated being abandoned like that. They had tried to stay in touch via phone and letters, but it had fizzled out before Joel was born.

'Nadine,' she said. 'Nadine is probably the only real friend Joel had. They were in the same class until year six, when she moved to Kalmar.'

'Girlfriend?'

'I honestly don't know. I joked about it once, and Joel was furious.'

Was *furious* really the right word? He hadn't shouted or broken anything. He had simply glared at her with eyes that were spilling over with anger and disappointment before turning and heading up to his room, where he spent hours hunched over his sketchpad.

And now he was gone. No, not gone. Dead.

How long had it been since Hanna told her that Joel was dead? Fifteen minutes? Half an hour? Rebecka didn't know. Why? How? She combed through the previous day over and over again, searching for even a hint of an answer. When she'd gone to the kitchen with Ulrika to fetch the birthday cake for Gabriel, Joel and Linnea hadn't just been sketching at the table – they'd been whispering. About what?

'Joel was weird during the barbecue,' she said.

'Weird how?'

'Absent. More than usual, I mean. Molly wanted to tell one of her jokes, but he wasn't listening, and he always listens to Molly. Sometimes I use her to . . .'

How was she supposed to tell Molly? The girl worshipped

her big brother. Or her mother? She was at her new boyfriend's place in Karlskrona. When Rebecka was younger, her mother had always been preoccupied with her own problems, both real and imaginary, but with Joel and Molly, she was a fantastic grandmother.

Rebecka cast her mind back to the day before.

'I was restless all night. It was like I could feel that . . . I should've . . .'

Why was she lying? Yes, she had been restless, but that was hardly because of some maternal sixth sense.

'Stop,' said Hanna. 'This really isn't your fault.'

Hanna's hand tightened around her arm. It was sixteen years since they had last spoken, and so much had happened in that time. She was a completely different person now, no longer the girl who drank witches' brew from a badly rinsed-out shampoo bottle down by the harbour. No longer the girl who thought that everything would be wonderful if she could just make it through school. A sense of disgust rose up in her.

'But if I—'

'No!'

They sat quietly for a moment. Rebecka couldn't drop the thought that this might never have happened if she had just looked in on Joel a second time during the night. Talked to him, if he was awake. She was grateful that the other officer had gone. Hanna had held her tight so many times before. Whenever yet another boy broke up with her, whenever she drank too much homemade cider.

So little had happened. She was almost thirty-five, and she was still making the same fucking mistakes. Choosing the wrong men and getting drunk when things didn't work out.

The deputy head's words came back to her: *Joel wasn't in school yesterday either.*

Why hadn't the school called her? Surely that was their one bloody job if a student didn't show up? They were launching a new system that autumn, Schoolsoft, which was supposed to manage absences digitally, but a simple call from the school might have changed everything. Memories of her begging Gabriel not to leave her flashed through Rebecka's mind. Memories of her humiliating herself. It barely felt real now.

'So what happens next?' she asked.

'We'll investigate what—'

'No, I mean to me.'

'Oh, Rebecka . . .' Hanna swallowed before she continued. 'You'll force yourself through each day. However hard they are. And little by little, it'll get easier.'

'Thanks for the encouragement.'

Hanna's mother had died when she was young, and Rebecka had watched it all from close up. But this wasn't the same. Joel had come from her own body, and losing him was . . .

'Do you want me to call anyone?' Hanna asked her.

'Petri. But not yet, I need to . . .'

Whatever Rebecka had planned to say vanished, and she couldn't find her way back to it. Weariness wrapped around her mind like barbed wire.

'How's Kristoffer?' she asked. 'I haven't heard from him either.'

Sometimes Rebecka couldn't help but wonder what life might have been like if she had chosen Kristoffer instead. But Axel's self-confidence had been so appealing back then.

His money. The promise of another kind of life. In many respects, Kristoffer had been Axel's opposite. Axel might have looked polished on the surface, but he was a mess inside. With Kristoffer, the difficult parts were all superficial. He would never have hit her.

'Good,' said Hanna. 'He lives in London now, works in a fancy hotel. He's married, and he's got a daughter who is almost three.'

Rebecka nodded. She didn't have anything to say to that. Why had she even asked? She felt a sudden urge to put Hanna down. To make her suffer.

'People used to call you my shadow,' she said. 'Do you remember that?'

'I remember,' said Hanna.

She looked away, but Rebecka caught the uncertainty on her face.

'Sorry.'

'It's OK,' said Hanna. 'Like I said, we've opened an investigation. That means a couple of forensic technicians will be here soon, to go through Joel's room. I know it might seem—'

'Just do whatever you need to do,' said Rebecka.

She felt the weariness spread down through her body. Yesterday was becoming increasingly hazy. If only she hadn't drunk so much, and if only she hadn't been so goddamn preoccupied by her own problems, she might have . . .

'Do you know whether Joel was involved in any disputes?' Hanna asked.

Rebecka shook her head. Before long, she wouldn't be able to string a single coherent thought together. She was outside herself again, screaming her protests. From there, she didn't simply feel repulsed by herself. Hanna repulsed her too. She made her chat like nothing had happened. But Joel was dead, and she had nothing to say.

'I want you to leave now,' she said.

A sense of despair rose up in her again. How could Joel be dead?

The Last Day

At five minutes past eleven, Joel is standing by the counter in Kullzenska, ordering two large slices of sticky chocolate cake with extra whipped cream. The little boy behind him in line is staring up at him with wide eyes.

'He's probably already had his lunch,' his mother tells the boy, indifferent to the fact that Joel can hear every word she says.

She probably thinks he should be ashamed of his terrible eating habits. *You don't know anything about me*, Joel feels like yelling, though of course he doesn't.

'Can I have some cake later too?' the child asks.

'No, not today.'

'But I promise to eat up.'

How old is the boy? Four or five? He's younger than Molly, in any case, but he has already learned exactly what to say. Life is full of disappointment, Joel thinks. You may as well get used to that now.

'No,' the mother repeats, far more irritably this time.

She orders a piece of Mediterranean quiche for herself, waffles for the boy. As though waffles with jam and cream are any healthier than chocolate cake.

Joel heads over to their usual table, which luckily happens to be free. He can't deal with any more obstacles today. He sits down on the sofa beneath a portrait of some bearded king, and sends a picture of the cakes to Nadine. *Almost there*, she replies. Five minutes later, she comes charging over, giving him a hug.

'Have you told her?' she asks.

Joel shakes his head.

'I thought maybe that was why things were so bad.'

Joel launches into the same moan he has so many times before. Telling Nadine he isn't happy with a single thing in his life. That he wants to be someone else. To move somewhere else, as far away as possible.

'Things aren't much better in Kalmar,' Nadine tells him.

'I didn't exactly mean Kalmar when I said far away.'

'I know. But I'm not sure things are any better anywhere else either.'

Joel wants to ask what it felt like when she swallowed all those pills. Whether it was easier than slashing her wrists. Probably, because she almost managed it the second time. He wants to tell her how close he came to jumping into the water. If he had kept swimming until he wore himself out, he might not have been able to make it back, even if he changed his mind.

Nadine scoops up some cream on her spoon and pulls it back, aiming at him, but she doesn't fire. Instead, she pushes it into her mouth.

'I've decided to do humanities,' she says. 'At Stagg.'

Nadine has good grades; there's no doubt she'll get in. Mum thinks Joel does too, but that probably isn't true any more. All he can hope is that the teachers take pity on him and don't mark him down too much. It's his last term, after all.

'I guess we won't be at the same school, then,' he says, pulling the corners of his mouth as far down as he can.

'What, you're not picking arts any more?'

'Nah, health and social care.'

'Why?'

Nadine scoops up yet another spoonful of cream, but this time she actually fires it. It hits the king's beard on the painting behind him. Joel glances around, but no one seems to have noticed.

'Lucky for you you missed,' he tells her.

'Seriously though, why?' asks Nadine.

'Because I want a job where I can actually earn money. I don't want to be like Mum.'

'I like your mum.'

'Me too, but without Petri we'd have no money.'

'No, I know,' says Nadine. 'Plus, who wants to rely on some loser man?'

Joel shares his new theory that Petri is a flat-earther, that the reason he is always getting his folding ruler and spirit level out is because he wants to prove the Earth is flat. Nadine laughs so hard she almost falls off her chair. A bald man who must weigh at least 100 kilos pops his head in from the next room and tells them to shut up.

Joel gives Nadine a pleading glance, but there is no stopping her, as usual:

'Shut up yourself,' she snaps.

A few weeks earlier, she had provoked a guy so badly that Joel thought he was going to hit her. It was in the kiosk by the station. Nadine had wanted to buy an energy drink, and got into line behind a guy who was texting someone. She pointed out that he meant *you're*, not *your*, and the guy wheeled around and started screaming at her. This particular man makes do with a shake of his head, but there is a side to Nadine that scares Joel – the way she is always so eager to get hurt.

Chapter Twelve

Hanna let Erik drive when they left Gårdby. She felt drained after their meeting with Rebecka. Despite having been told to leave, she had stayed with her until the forensic technicians arrived. Twenty or so difficult, silent minutes. Rebecka had said she was fine with the technicians searching the house, but whether she really meant it was a different matter entirely. They couldn't risk having her go through Joel's room, hiding things because she thought they weren't relevant to the investigation.

Hanna understood the impulse all too well. How many times had she rummaged through her own house after her father was taken into custody? Searching for evidence that he was the monster they claimed, even though she knew the police had already seized it all.

She was nineteen again, watching the officers lead her father away. That moment was the turning point, and she hadn't been able to cope. She had run off to Rebecka's, and when she got home a few hours later, the police were carrying out a search of the house. One of the officers had given her a ride over to her grandmother's, and she had seen the neighbours watching through the car window. Standing in groups along the edge of the road, heads huddled together. Kristoffer hadn't been home at the time; he had stayed away for several days.

The officers had even searched her room. They hadn't closed the drawer in her desk properly.

'What made you leave Öland?' Erik asked, dragging her back to the present.

'Are you always this nosy?' Hanna countered.

He laughed, but didn't repeat the question. Couldn't he see that she really didn't want to talk about it? Or was he simply trying to provoke a reaction? This time, Erik managed to keep quiet for almost a minute – Hanna was counting.

'Do you really think you should be there when we interview Axel Sandsten?'

There was the question she had been waiting for.

'I haven't seen him in sixteen years, and I never really knew him.'

Erik let that question lie too.

'Do people lock their doors in Gårdby?' he asked instead.

'We almost never did, but that's probably all changed now. I know I lock mine, in any case, even though I live on the outskirts of a place that's even smaller than Gårdby.'

The road beneath the car rose up, away from the ground, and continued across the Kalmar Strait. Hanna always felt a kind of sadness when she left the island now, every single time. Even if it was only for a few hours. She doubted Ingrid locked her doors. It had nothing to do with the size of the village, or even the idea that times had changed. The fact was that she was more afraid now, and the two didn't add up. What did she have left to lose?

* * *

Axel Sandsten's office was on Larmgatan, close to the old water tower. The tower was full of apartments now – or it had been sixteen years ago. Hanna still hadn't managed to get to grips with everything that had changed since she left. The old water tower was yet another place where she had partied as a teen. During her first year of high school, she had been in a brief relationship with a guitar player whose half-sister had an apartment on one of the middle floors. Looking back now, her school days sometimes felt like one long party. Why had she done that? She had never really enjoyed it. Even when she was drunk, she had often felt the fear of getting stuck. Of becoming like her father.

It was probably simply a way of trying to be someone else.

Rebecka's shadow. That was what people had called her, despite the fact that she was almost twenty centimetres taller. Or maybe that was precisely why: she was the gloomy extension of Rebecka, the one who never spoke. Rebecka had always found it so easy to talk to people; she was almost always happy. And it had felt so good to cling onto her.

Being Rebecka's shadow had sometimes bothered Hanna, but when she suddenly became Lars Duncker's daughter instead, she had found herself longing for that period of anonymity.

There was a playground next to the old water tower now, with rubber flooring and an enormous climbing net. Erik found a parking space to one side of it, and the children's voices followed them across the street, to the main door, where an enormous brass sign read 'SANDSTEN CONSULTING'.

Axel always did have delusions of grandeur.

They showed their ID in reception, and asked to speak to Axel Sandsten.

'He's in a meeting right now,' the receptionist told them. She was wearing a snug black skirt and a white blouse, and didn't look a day over twenty.

'We really need to talk to him now,' said Erik.

Ordinarily, showing police ID was more than enough, but the woman still seemed to be hesitating. Eventually, she got up. Hanna peered around the room. Aside from the reception desk, there were two austere armchairs and a small table. The empty spaces were probably meant to make the space feel bigger than it was. The dominant colour was black.

A few minutes later, the woman returned.

'He wants to know what it's regarding.'

The red stress spots on her throat seemed to be pulsing.

'I'm afraid we can't share that information,' said Erik.

'Just go and get him,' Hanna told her. 'That way we won't have to interrupt his meeting and show our ID in there.'

The minute the woman disappeared for the second time, Erik turned to Hanna.

'You really don't like him, do you?'

She shook her head. Axel had always been a bastard. Picking on their most insecure classmates, acting like he was better than everyone else. Using Kristoffer for all kinds of dirty jobs. Still, all that paled in comparison to what he had subjected Rebecka to. It was incredible that more people didn't see straight through him.

A door opened and closed, and Axel Sandsten came striding towards them, closely followed by the receptionist.

'Sorry you had to wait,' he said.

'Is there somewhere more private we can talk?' asked Erik.

Axel led them into a small meeting room, the door barely visible against the wall. There was an oval table inside, surrounded by six chairs, and paintings of local landmarks on the walls: the castle, the cathedral, the old water tower. It felt cheap compared to the rest of the office.

'What is this about?' Axel asked once they were sitting down.

Erik fixed his eyes on him, a calm and steady gaze.

'I'm sorry to have to tell you that your son, Joel, was found dead earlier today.'

Axel closed his eyes for a moment, then quickly opened them again. He looked away.

'Did he kill himself?'

'What makes you ask that?' Erik wanted to know.

'He wasn't doing too well. He was struggling.'

'In what sense?'

'His mother is very controlling,' Axel explained. 'To be honest, I don't think she's doing too well herself.'

Hanna had to dig her nails into her thighs to stop herself from shouting at him, but there was no hiding her reaction. Maybe it wasn't such a good idea for her to be there after all.

'Sorry,' said Axel. 'I don't mean to put the blame on her. I'm in shock. Things are pretty stressful right now, and I've barely slept. I was in the middle of trying to solve a crisis when you showed up. And now this . . .'

Erik gave him a sympathetic smile.

'We understand you and Joel didn't have much contact?'

'Sadly not,' said Axel. 'His mother did her best to keep him away from me.'

Hanna knew she shouldn't, but she couldn't help herself:

'Maybe that's because you beat her.'

Axel turned to look at her, studying her without a word.

'You look familiar.'

'I should, we were in the same class in high school.'

He still didn't seem to have worked out who she was, though perhaps he was just pretending in an attempt to throw her off balance. Considering her impressive height, she couldn't be hard to recognise.

'My surname is Duncker, if that helps.'

'Oh, shit.'

An amused smile. The difference between how he and Rebecka had reacted to the news of their son's death was striking.

'How's your brother?' he asked.

Hanna was sick of everyone asking about her brother – though at least no one had asked about Lars.

'Where were you last night?'

Axel turned back to Erik.

'Why do you want to know?'

'We think Joel was killed.'

With a sigh, Axel reached for the jug of water in the middle of the table. He filled a glass and took a couple of sips.

'I was here, working. Didn't leave until two in the morning. Bit of a crisis, like I said.'

'Alone?'

'Tatjana was with me until eleven, but then she had to leave – she had a childminder.'

'Who is Tatjana?'

'An employee.'

Axel fixed his eyes on Hanna as he spoke, as though he wanted her to challenge him.

Chapter Thirteen

The sound of the children in the playground seemed to hit Hanna as she stepped outside, and she was taken aback by the powerful sense of longing it awoke in her. She shut out their voices, along with the memory of Fabian lying beside her in bed, fingertips grazing her collarbone. Kissing her, his lips slowly moving downwards. Looking up at her and saying that he thought they should start a family.

She pulled out her phone and dialled the number she had been given for Tatjana Edin. The line was busy.

'Back to the station?' asked Erik.

Hanna nodded. She tried Tatjana's number again once they were in the car. This time, the call went through, but Tatjana didn't pick up. Erik glanced over at her with a half-smile.

'What?' she asked. Slightly snappier than intended.

'Today might've been slightly more hectic than you were expecting from your first day, but I swear it's normally much calmer round here.'

'Thanks, but I'm used to it. I was with violent crimes in Stockholm.'

'That wasn't what I meant.'

She knew she should apologise. Blame it on how difficult it

felt that the son of one of her old friends had been killed. Say that it had stirred up so many emotions to see Rebecka again. That was the truth. But her body also felt like it was being torn apart with longing to stop being so damn lonely. When she failed to speak, Erik shook his head and focused on the road ahead.

For once, he kept quiet.

Ove came out of his office as he saw them walk past.

'Ah, Hanna, good. Come in, and we'll get your service weapon sorted.'

The air smelled different in Ove's office, and at first Hanna couldn't identify the scent. Then it struck her: it was some kind of spray to hide the fact that he had been smoking. For all she knew, it could have been there yesterday too; she had been far too stressed to notice.

Ove gave her the name and number of the man she should contact to sign out her weapon.

'None of the searches are finished yet,' he continued. 'Neither the crime scene nor his room. But Joel Forslund's body is on its way to Linköping now.'

'OK.'

She really did need to stop saying that.

'Joel's mother is an old school friend of mine.' There was no way she would be able to hide the link for ever, so she had decided simply to come out and admit it.

'Yes, Erik mentioned.'

Hanna was on the verge of saying OK again, but managed to stop herself in time. It irritated her that Erik had been so quick to talk to Ove. He must have done it when they were still at Rebecka's, because that was the only moment she could think of that they hadn't been together. He should have brought it up with her first.

'Is it a problem?' Ove asked.

'Absolutely not,' said Hanna. 'The opposite, if anything. Rebecka will talk to me.'

'Yes, Erik mentioned that too. But what about Axel? Apparently you also knew him?'

'I haven't spoken to either of them in years,' Hanna quickly pointed out.

In their interview with Axel, she hadn't used their past to her advantage. Ove shrugged. Clearly this part of the conversation was over. Back in Stockholm, she probably would have been taken off the case.

'I just wanted to make sure it wasn't a problem,' he said. 'And that you're doing OK.'

Are you doing OK?

The first question he had asked her sixteen years ago, though she refused to get caught up in that now.

'We need to move forward with Axel Sandsten,' she said, recapping both what Rebecka had said and the way Axel had reacted.

'You know who he is, don't you?'

'Yeah, he's an arsehole. That hasn't changed.'

'Rebecka's word is all we have to back up the alleged abuse. We'll need more than that if we're going to go after him.'

'*Go after him?* Are you serious? We should at least check his phone and emails.'

Hanna regretted her outburst the moment she spoke, but Ove's consideration was like an itchy blanket she wanted to throw off. His choice of words also bothered her. *Go after him.* It was like he thought she had some kind of personal vendetta against Axel.

'I might not have expressed myself very well there,' said Ove, 'but I don't think we should. Not yet.'

When Hanna had first met Ove, she'd got the sense that he wasn't a man who exerted himself unnecessarily. Or maybe that was just what she had concluded afterwards, looking back over their meetings. What she really wanted was to ask him about the investigation into her father, but she held off. She had read almost everything that had been written about it, but she hadn't attended the trial. Her father had forbidden it. Why had she listened to him? There was so much she still didn't know.

'Do we have Joel's phone, at least?' she asked.

Call logs and messages could be requested, but teenagers often used apps to communicate, and for that they needed the phone itself.

'Yes, he had it on him,' said Ove. 'But it's in pretty bad shape, unfortunately.'

Ove's own phone started ringing and, as he reached for it, Hanna took the opportunity to get up and leave. She didn't make it very far: after listening for a few seconds, Ove thanked the person on the other end of the line and hung up.

'That was one of the forensic technicians searching Joel's room,' he explained. 'They've just found some hash.'

'How much?'

'Five grams.'

Five grams was enough for around fifteen joints, depending on how strong you wanted them to be. It was hardly enough to be selling, but the news left Hanna feeling uneasy all the same. This was probably just the beginning. She knew what murder investigations were like. How was Rebecka going to manage all the crap that came to light?

The Last Day

Nadine hurries off to her maths class, but Joel stays behind in the café. Their hour together has helped lighten his mind. The weeks after she told him she was in love with him were some of the worst of his life. That was when she tried to kill herself for the second time, when she almost managed it. But they found their way back to one another, and he never wants to stop being her friend. He can't even imagine a life without Nadine.

It's his head that is the problem. He needs to learn to think differently.

But how easy is that?

Joel scrapes the spoon across the white china plate, raising the last few crumbs of cake to his mouth.

There is a group of teenagers sitting at one of the other tables, clearly bunking off school. Joel has seen them here before. Three guys and two girls. They're loud. Dressed in black, with tattoos and piercings. One of the girls has rainbow-coloured hair like Linnéa Claeson, the ballsy handball player. Why isn't he brave enough to be more like them? To really make a mark. In truth, he doesn't actually like tattoos or piercings. Not on himself anyway. He's too scared of anything painful.

The group are talking about graduation, saying it'll be their turn next year. One of the boys glances over to him, the cutest one. He's blond, with light brown eyes. Just one small tattoo, peeking out from beneath the curve of his top. Possibly a flame, or maybe a flower. Before Joel has time to stop himself, his hand is up on his face. The skin by his nose feels tender; it's going to break out into a spot. The boy doesn't say much, mostly just listening to the others, but his eyes settle on Joel. Worried he is about to start talking to him, Joel gets up and hurries away.

Out on the street, the sun has dipped behind a cloud. It's too early to head back to the island, so he walks down towards the shopping centre instead. Freezes when he sees the man coming out of the bag shop. He tries to escape onto Södra Långgatan, but it's too late.

'Joel!'

He stops. It'll be worse if he doesn't.

'Hi,' he says.

Dad isn't a word he uses with this man, and particularly not to his face. Joel's earliest memory is of Axel shoving his mum into a radiator. He had just turned four, and was convinced she was going to die. There was blood everywhere.

'Shouldn't you be at school?'

'Since when did you care?'

He knows he shouldn't taunt him, but he can't just stand here and pretend everything is fine. Joel is terrible at pretending. Part of him wishes Axel would hit him. Maybe there's something in Nadine's method after all. Maybe physical pain is just what he needs to avoid the other kind. And with so many witnesses, there's no way Axel would get away with it.

'Less of the attitude, please.'

Joel bows exaggeratedly and sees Axel's eyes flash. A second later, he is smiling again.

'I can help you, actually. What do you say about moving in with me when you start senior high? You'll be closer to school that way. Have you decided what your focus is going to be yet?'

This is more than Axel has said to him in months. He calls and texts from time to time, and always sends a birthday present, but Joel never replies.

'I don't know,' he says.

Axel flashes his fake smile again.

'I think you should do natural sciences at—'

'I'll probably go for health and social care,' Joel interrupts.

Axel stares at him like he has lost his mind. Maybe he has, talking to Axel like this. He knows how quickly the man can fly off the handle. But the minute the words leave his lips, Joel feels any hesitation he had vanish. Yes, he loves drawing, but he can't picture himself making a living from it.

'I don't want anything to do with you,' he snaps. 'Do you think I've forgotten what you did to Mum?'

'She's turned you against me.'

'Just leave me alone,' Joel tells him.

He starts walking away, heart racing. The lump in his chest seems to be moving upwards, towards his eyes. Joel blinks back the tears.

'I don't know what you think you remember,' Axel shouts after him, 'but you're wrong.'

No, Joel thinks. *I'm not wrong about you. And if you knew who I really was, you'd probably kill me.*

Chapter Fourteen

The forensic technicians had finally gone. Rebecka pressed her forehead against the front door and closed her eyes. They had taken Joel's computer, the one she had bought second-hand from some guy online. What if there was all kinds of old crap on it and the police thought it was Joel's?

Child porn, for example. That was the worst thing she could think of. When she'd gone to Färjestaden to pick up the computer, the man had been wearing sweatpants and a t-shirt that didn't quite cover his belly. Greasy hair and terrible breath. She tried to dredge up his name from the fog of her mind, but it was impossible. She didn't think she had saved any of their messages back and forth.

Rebecka slowly raised an arm and pressed her palm to the door. It felt like the link between her body and the outside world was coming loose, and she wanted to fix it. Didn't want to lose herself the way she had lost Joel.

The technicians had also taken his sketchbooks, including the one he had refused to let her look inside. He had promised to show her later. Would she ever get to see it now?

What else had they taken? Rebecka didn't know. The technicians had refused to answer her questions.

At first, they hadn't wanted to leave her alone. Kept asking whether there was anyone they could call. In the end, she had forced them to go. Told them her husband was on his way, that she had talked to him, though that was a lie.

Rebecka let go of the door and moved over to the sofa, hugging one of the zebra-print cushions to her body. She had such an ache in her chest that she didn't know what to do. She screamed and threw the cushion away, only just missing the vase on the sideboard. She reached for another.

She really should call Petri. Her mother too. But that would make it all so final. Somewhere, deep down, she was still hoping it was all just a big mistake. That Joel would come striding through the door at any moment and ask why she was so upset.

Tears began rolling down her cheeks again. She was back in the strange meeting with Hanna. It had been such a shock to open the door and see her standing outside. She really had missed Hanna over the years, and had come close to getting in touch several times, but for various reasons it had never happened. Partly because of Axel and Joel, because she would have had to explain all that to Hanna. As though it still mattered that she had kept quiet about it all those years ago.

Rebecka also felt ashamed. How could she have sat there, chatting to Hanna like nothing had happened, after learning that Joel was dead? She should have put a stop to it sooner.

Why did she have so few friends? She had plenty of acquaintances, but barely anyone she actually spoke to – not about anything that mattered anyway. Her family and her small business took up all her time. Ulrika, her neighbour, was probably the closest thing to a friend she had, and she had slept with her husband.

Goddamn Gabriel. Goddamn everything. It was so damn pathetic of her to have been fooled by a pair of bright blue eyes and some defined chest muscles. Beautiful, yet utterly empty words.

Perhaps she should call Ulrika after all? Ask for her help getting Petri back home? Her phone began to buzz on the coffee table, making Rebecka jump. She didn't have the energy to answer, but she reached for the phone anyway, to see who it was.

Molly's school. Shit. Had something happened to her too?

'Hello?' she answered, her voice trembling.

'I just found Molly waiting on the steps. Has something . . .'

Rebecka lowered the phone from her ear and checked the time. She should have picked Molly up over half an hour ago. She pressed a hand to her chest in an attempt to still the panic.

'Sorry,' she mumbled down the line. 'I'm coming now.'

Somehow, Rebecka managed to make her way over to the school. Molly was sitting on the steps with Isak, the teacher who had called. The after-school club was still open, and there was some kind of game going on in the yard, but Molly knew when she was supposed to be picked up, and she didn't like it when things didn't go to plan. Like Joel, she had been more anxious than usual lately. It was obvious she had been crying.

'I'm so sorry, sweetie. I . . .'

That was as far as she got. She couldn't do it. Not here. Isak placed a hand on her arm and studied her, but she shook her head at the question in his eyes. If she said a single word about Joel, she wouldn't be able to make it home.

They left the school yard with Isak's eyes still on them. The journey home suddenly felt like kilometres, and she wanted to call Petri and ask him to come and pick them up, but her phone was still on the coffee table.

'Are you tired?' asked Molly.

Being tired was the excuse Rebecka always gave whenever she had done something she was ashamed of. Shouting at Molly, for example. Or not having the energy to play with her. She nodded.

'I was asleep, that's why I didn't realise the time.'

'In the middle of the day?'

'I know, it's crazy, isn't it?'

But not as crazy as the fact that Joel had been found dead, she thought. That the police thought someone had killed him.

Rebecka bit her lip to fight back the tears, but not even the taste of blood was enough. She wanted to get home. To close the door behind her, crawl into bed and pull the covers over her head. Only waking up when she could handle everyday life again.

'What's wrong, Mummy?'

'I'm feeling a bit sad too.'

'Me too,' said Molly.

'Why?'

'I don't know.'

Rebecka squeezed her daughter's hand.

'That's just the way it is sometimes.'

They were halfway home now, and somehow they had to make it. Fortunately, the only other person they bumped into was Gerd, whose glaucoma meant she couldn't see Rebecka's bloodshot eyes. She nodded in greeting. Rebecka knew she should say something – they hadn't spoken since her garage burnt down – but she didn't trust her voice. Some people claimed Gerd had accidentally started the fire herself, but most seemed to think that someone else was responsible. Rebecka herself was convinced it was the lightning. She had been awake when it happened, counting the seconds between the flashes of light and claps of thunder.

The relief Rebecka felt as she reached the house and closed the door behind her made her sway. She put Molly on the sofa with the tablet and some headphones. Molly grinned, surprised. She often spent the time between getting home and dinner watching TV, but she was rarely given the tablet. An optician had once mentioned that the light from the screen was more damaging.

Rebecka picked up her phone from the coffee table and took it into the kitchen, where she stood cradling it for a few minutes before finally managing to dial Petri's number.

She began crying the minute she heard his voice.

'What's wrong, honey?'

'Come home,' she managed to stutter.

'Why, what's going on?'

'Joel is dead.'

Chapter Fifteen

Erik was in the cafeteria when he felt his pocket buzz. He dropped the teabag into his cup and dug out his phone. It was a message from Supriya, asking what he wanted for dinner. They took turns picking up Nila from school, and making dinner was part of the deal.

Daal? he replied, adding a smiling emoji.

They ate lentils several times a week, and Erik knew Supriya was sick of them, but he couldn't think of anything else. Both he and his wife were vegetarians, though Nila ate meat at school and showed no interest in stopping. She loved all kinds of sausage, *falukorv* in particular.

Erik filled his cup with hot water and moved to one side so that his colleague could reach the cups.

Maybe, Supriya replied, accompanied by an emoji of a man Erik didn't understand. He really should buy her an emoji dictionary.

Both he and Supriya enjoyed cooking, though the stress of their jobs took the fun out of it at times. As a dentist, Supriya's hours were more regular than Erik's, but one of her colleagues had just been signed off sick. Right now, however, he suspected there was also another source of stress in her life.

Everything ready for Friday? he asked.

Her parents were coming to visit from India. They had been over once before, to a damp, slushy Malmö, and still talked about that trip. About how cold and awful the weather had been. How they hadn't even seen any proper snow.

The weather forecast is talking about rain.

Supriya's reply was followed by yet another incomprehensible emoji.

Erik took his cup of tea over to an empty table, sending a laughing/crying face with his free hand.

Not funny, she replied.

He agreed, but he was more worried about her than the weather. About how she would cope with having her parents so close for two whole weeks. They had only stayed a week last time.

And perhaps more than anything, he was worried about what her stress levels would mean for him.

Once his tea had finished brewing, Erik fished out the bag, used his spoon to squeeze the liquid out of it, and put it onto a napkin. It had been a hectic day, and he needed a moment to wind down before he finished writing up the interview report. He was responsible for the interview with Axel Sandsten; Hanna could deal with Rebecka's. He hadn't been there the whole time, after all.

When Erik had gone back inside with the forensic technicians, Rebecka was alone in the living room, Hanna in the kitchen. The atmosphere had felt much more tense than it had when he left, which probably wasn't surprising, given the situation. Rebecka had lost a child. Still, there was something about his new colleague that piqued his curiosity. About the fact that he actually found her difficult. Erik usually got on with all kinds of people. There had to be some kind of history there, he was sure of it. He had asked Hanna whether she wanted to grab a coffee, but she had said no. She was going to try to get hold of Tatjana Edin again.

Erik pictured Joel in front of him. A beaten fifteen-year-old, slumped against a wall in the middle of nowhere. No one should have to die like that, and Erik wanted to help Rebecka find out what had happened to Joel. The prospect of something like that happening to Nila was his worst nightmare. He had been caught up in a similar fear for several minutes when she was born, because she wasn't breathing properly. The doctor had tried to reassure him, but it hadn't worked.

Two of his colleagues came into the cafeteria, fetching coffees and sitting down at the table beside his.

'You remember that murder and robbery case on Öland? Must be fifteen years ago now, at least. The one where the woman was beaten up and burnt to death in her own house?'

'Yeah, over in Åby, wasn't it? My aunt lived in the next village, she knew the ex-husband.'

'His daughter works here now.'

'Who, the ex's?'

'No, the killer's. She joined the force.'

Erik couldn't help but interrupt.

'Sorry, but what are you talking about?'

They filled him in on the drunk who had broken in to Ester Jensen's house with the intention of robbing her. There were rumours she kept money stashed away at home, and according to Ester's daughter, there had been several earlier break-ins for that very reason. But the rumours weren't true, and when the man realised there wasn't any money, he was furious. He had beaten up Ester and then set fire to the house – with her inside.

He claimed she had put up a fight and fallen badly, knocking her head and dying. The fire had destroyed much of the evidence, but not her broken bones. She had almost twenty fractures.

'Who's his daughter?' Erik asked, though he had already worked it out.

'Hanna Duncker.'

Chapter Sixteen

Hanna kicked off her shoes without bending down to untie them. *You'll ruin them*, she heard Fabian's voice telling her. *Untie them properly.* She dropped her keys onto the small chest of drawers in the hallway, and another request from the past suddenly came to mind. This time, it was from her mother: *Would you please move those?* The words were followed by a smile and a *Do it for me*. Her mother had always refused to put keys on any kind of table, and she didn't like it when other people did so either. It was bad luck, apparently. Hanna remembered only the words and her smile, not her mother's voice. That had been the first thing to disappear.

She picked up the keys and hung them on the hook beside the mirror instead, heading through to the kitchen and opening the fridge. She wasn't looking forward to telling Rebecka about the drugs they had found in Joel's room. The conversation they'd had after she told Rebecka Joel was dead had left a sour taste in her mouth. The fact that she had exploited both the shock and their old friendship. Perhaps she shouldn't be the main point of contact with Rebecka after all. Still, however hard it was for each of them, Hanna still believed it was good for the investigation.

She took out a plastic tub of chicken casserole and rice. It was the last portion of the big batch she had cooked on Sunday; she had eaten it every day since.

She shoved the tub into the microwave. Apart from the table and chairs, it was her sole contribution to the kitchen. *Charming* and *authentic* were two of the many words the estate agent had used to describe the place. The floral wallpaper was probably at least twenty years old, and the cabinets were tired and lopsided. Still, she liked it, and had no plans to rip it out and start again.

After tipping the hot chicken casserole onto a plate, Hanna carried it through to the living room. There were four rooms on the ground floor, including the bathroom, and she had decided to make one of them into a dining room – not that she really needed one. The best thing would be to knock down a wall and make herself a decent-sized living room instead. Aside from the TV, all she could fit in the current one was a sofa.

Upstairs, there were two bedrooms. They should probably be knocked through to make one too. Five rooms in total, coming to just under fifty square metres. Strictly speaking, the house was bigger than that, but the sloping ceilings on the first floor reduced the amount of usable space.

When she finished eating, Hanna called her brother.

'Hi,' Kristoffer answered.

His tone of voice felt like a straitjacket around her heart. It was obvious he was still angry with her.

'How are you all?' she asked.

'We're fine. Ella had chicken pox last week, but it's cleared up now.'

'Good.'

Hanna and Kristoffer had both had chicken pox as children – she was ten and he was eleven – but she could still remember how itchy it was. She hoped Ella had suffered less than they had; it was supposed to be milder for younger children. Hanna had only met her niece once, when she was one. She had just learned to walk, and could say *mama*, *dada* and *no*. Could she speak Swedish now? Hanna doubted it. She wanted to suggest that they came to visit, but she suspected Kristoffer never wanted to set foot on Öland again.

'Why are you calling?' he asked.

The question made her airways tighten. He was her brother, but clearly she needed a reason to call him.

'I started my new job today,' she said. 'With the Kalmar Police.'

Kristoffer snorted. He'd had his fair share of dealings with the police before their father ever got into trouble himself. Shoplifting, being driven home drunk, that kind of thing. Their father's arrest and conviction had been a different kind of turning point for him, and Hanna doubted he would ever have got married and found a job in a luxury hotel otherwise.

Fragments of their last conversation came back to her. His anger at her decision to move back to the island.

You always make it so fucking hard for yourself. For me.

All Kristoffer wanted was to move on and leave the past behind, yet here she was, calling to do the same thing again: to drag him back in time.

'I spoke to Axel Sandsten today.'

Kristoffer was silent.

'You remember him, don't you?'

'Of course I do.'

'I thought you liked him,' said Hanna.

'Not any more.'

This time it was Hanna's turn to fall silent. Why had she called? Did she really think Kristoffer would be able to tell her anything relevant about Axel after all these years?

'Why did you speak to him?' Kristoffer asked.

'As part of an investigation.'

'Has he done something?'

'Maybe, maybe not. Did you know he runs a company now? He's a real bigwig in Kalmar these days.'

'Are you surprised?'

'Not really, I just thought he had bigger plans than that.'

'I'm sure he did,' said Kristoffer. 'But life doesn't always turn out how you plan it.'

Hanna didn't speak.

'I have to go,' said Kristoffer. 'We're having dinner.'

'OK, talk soon,' she said, hanging up.

In six months or so, she thought with a hint of sadness. She knew she should make more of an effort with Kristoffer, but she didn't know how. It was like she couldn't do anything right. In a way, their conversation had been a step forward – he hadn't shouted at her, at least.

Hanna missed Kristoffer, almost more than she missed her parents. He was just fourteen months older than her, and they had been so close when they were younger. When their mother died, however, he and their father had reacted in the same way: by letting go. They both started drinking, Dad at home and Kristoffer out with his friends, even though he was only thirteen. Hanna had tried desperately to hold the family together, cooking meals, making sure they had enough money. Her grandmother was living in a flat in Färjestaden at the time, and she had helped out where she could.

Restlessness tore at Hanna. She couldn't bear being home alone and decided to go over to Ingrid's instead. Halfway there, she realised the lights were out and changed her mind: she would drive over to Möckelmossen instead.

When she reached the rest area, Hanna was surprised to see that she wasn't alone. She parked up on the road behind a black Audi with a broken wing mirror and climbed out. The forensic tent had gone, but the car park itself was still taped off and being guarded by two officers. By the cordon, there were a few small groups of people. They had begun laying flowers and lighting candles. A few were talking quietly, but the others were silent.

Hanna scanned their faces for Rebecka, but she wasn't there. She felt an urge to get in touch with her, but she was also afraid of intruding. Or, worse, of being rejected. It felt like she should give Rebecka some space right now.

Hanna stuck to the sidelines so that no one would try to talk to her. Her gaze fell on a blonde woman. She was the only other person who seemed to have come on her own, and there was a desperation in the way she was hugging herself, in the way she was avoiding the others. As though she thought she had no right to be there. Hanna discreetly pulled out her phone and took a few pictures of the woman and the others. Some perpetrators liked to return to the scene of the crime, after all. Maybe this one would be no different.

It was almost nine o'clock, and the sun was approaching the horizon. The light was oddly sharp, but darkness was pressing in from every angle, eager to take over. That included the darkness of the past – the fact that her father had beaten a woman to death, doused her house in petrol and then set it alight.

I didn't mean to, Lars had told her on the sole occasion she had brought it up during one of her visits to the prison. During the ten years he was behind bars, Hanna had made around ten trips to Brinkeberg, but it was hard to have a conversation with someone who could barely even look at you, particularly when that person also happened to be your own father. Hanna had written letters too, about her uneventful life, asking him questions about his. She knew that anything she sent him would be checked, and the fact that other people would read her letters had shaped her choice of words. Communication became an uncomfortable dance around everything they couldn't say.

Hanna looked out across the flat, barren landscape. At the shadows that were growing longer and longer. The feeling was even stronger than it had been that morning: nature was alive out here. Maybe it was just that she was so drained by the day.

Her phone rang, and she cursed herself for forgetting to turn it to silent. She hurried towards her car as she answered.

'Hello?'

All she could hear was breathing.

'Hello?' she repeated, trying to keep the fear from her voice.

There was a click in response.

Thursday 16 May

Chapter Seventeen

In an attempt to avoid any small talk, Hanna planned to stay at her desk until the team's morning meeting began. Another anonymous phone call had woken her that morning, just before six. It had followed exactly the same pattern as yesterday's: her initial *Hello?* was met by the sound of breathing, and her fears had seeped out as yet another *Hello?* It ended with a click when the other person hung up.

A sound from the doorway made her glance up. Daniel, who had been at the meeting the day before, stepped into the room, and she quickly looked down. Too late. A few steps and he was standing by her desk.

'I thought maybe I should introduce myself properly,' he said.

He had a clear Kalmar accent. Hanna couldn't remember him saying anything during the meeting yesterday, but she had probably been too stressed to notice. He looked even more like Fabian close up. Both men cocked their head slightly as they talked.

'Hi,' she said.

'Just let me know if you have any questions or need help with anything.'

'Thanks, I will.'

'Yesterday ended up being pretty hectic, and it's probably—'

But Daniel didn't get any further, because Ove popped his head around the door and nodded for them to come to the meeting room. Hanna got up and followed Daniel. Getting away from Fabian was one of the many reasons she had left Stockholm, but now she couldn't even look at Daniel without thinking about him. She batted away the memory of his fingertips dancing across her collarbone. Of how wonderful it felt to have someone touch her like that.

Two weeks after she told Fabian that she didn't want to move in with him, he had invited her over for dinner at his terraced house in Gustavsberg. She had barely taken a bite of her dessert when he announced that it wasn't working any more. Or rather: she wasn't. The shock had been paralysing. How could he go from wanting to live with her to not wanting her at all in such a short period of time? Without a word, she had stood up and left. It was only later that she had felt angry; that had always been easier for her than grief. Things had been difficult at work afterwards. Seeing Fabian and simultaneously wanting to hit him and throw herself into his arms.

She had made a promise to herself never to get involved with a colleague again.

A new image popped into her head: this time, it was Daniel lying by her side, fingers brushing her collarbone. She paused, only entering the meeting room once the colour had faded from her cheeks.

'I want you to put everything else to one side and focus on the boy found dead by Möckelmossen's rest area,' said Ove. 'The local press aren't the only ones who've found out about the murder – the tabloid vultures have been sniffing about too. The victim's name was being shared on the online forums yesterday afternoon.'

Hanna tried to sit down quietly so that she didn't interrupt his tirade about the media, but her height made it awkward.

Ove smiled and began recapping everything they had learned so far.

'We've got the digital forensics team working on Joel Forslund's broken phone, plus the computer we took from his room. The technicians also took a number of sketchpads full of drawings. They're all very dark, which could suggest that Joel wasn't in a particularly good place mentally.'

'Do we know for sure that he was murdered?' asked Amer.

'Yes,' said Ove. 'According to the pathologist in Linköping who'll be doing the autopsy, the cause of death was probably a stab wound to the stomach – probably caused by a knife. He'd also been badly beaten up. Based on the degree of rigor mortis and the temperature of his body, the time of death was somewhere between twelve and two a.m.'

Hanna scanned the room. Erik looked away, though not quite quickly enough, and her heart skipped a beat as she saw the compassion in his eyes. So now he knew too. He must, because he hadn't looked at her like that yesterday. Though she knew it shouldn't, the realisation upset her. It had only been a matter of time.

'Where did he die?' asked Erik.

'Unclear,' said Ove. 'The pool of blood suggests he had been lying on his stomach, but we haven't been able to determine whether he was moved into a sitting position or crawled there himself. The ground is hard, but a tyre track right by where he was found could indicate that someone stopped to dump him there. There are a number of footprints, but considering how many people pass through the area, that probably won't lead anywhere. We also don't have a murder weapon yet. We'll be lifting the cordon today.'

'Are we tracking his movements through his phone?'

Ove nodded.

'We need to know where he went after leaving the house.'

'Have we identified the driver of the parked car?' asked Amer.

'Yes, his name is Samuel Herngren,' said Ove. 'He lives in Färjestaden and works at the chicken processing plant in Mörbylånga. He's also in the database, suspected of assault, but unfortunately we haven't been able to get hold of him yet.'

'What about the cyclist?'

'Nope,' said Ove. 'Try to dig him out. And talk to the local police, youth groups and known dealers in the area.'

Amer nodded.

'Do we know what kind of flower Joel was holding?' asked Hanna.

She had to say something in order to silence the voice in her head, telling her she shouldn't be there, that she was good for nothing. No matter how much she achieved, she struggled to get rid of the voice, and it often popped up whenever she had been quiet for too long.

'A bloody crane's-bill,' said Ove. 'It's been sent to a specialist.'

'Does it have any particular meaning?'

Ove shook his head.

'I can look into that,' said Carina. 'I love flowers.'

'What you love is taking it easy at your desk.' Amer grinned.

'So what leads are we following?' asked Daniel.

Hanna turned to look at him, and tried to see past his

brown eyes and the way he tipped his head. Was he even thirty?
He was definitely the youngest member of the team, but he
didn't give off the impression of having anything to prove.
If anything, Daniel came across as calm and self-confident.
Hanna wanted to get to grips with the group, the roles they
each played. Amer was clearly the joker, though he was still
highly efficient – most jobs seemed to end up in his lap. Carina
and Ove did as little as possible, which wasn't necessarily great
considering he was the boss. But what about Erik? He was the
person Hanna had spent most time with, but she still wasn't
sure about him. The constant flow of words, the way everything
seemed to run off him like water.

'So far, we only have one real lead,' said Ove. 'Namely that
his father, Axel Sandsten, might be involved somehow.'

'*The* Axel Sandsten?' asked Carina.

'Afraid so, yes. I requested his call logs yesterday. Daniel,
could you take a closer look at him? Give the material to Erik
or Hanna – they'll look after the interviews.'

Ove had seemingly changed his mind about Axel since
Hanna left his office yesterday. At the time, he had been clear:
he didn't think they had enough for measures of that kind.
Tatjana had since confirmed that she had been at the office
with Axel until eleven o'clock, but she denied having discussed
his alibi with him.

Hanna knew she should say something about the pictures
she had taken at the rest area. Mention the blonde woman. She
regretted not pulling her to one side and talking to her there
and then; the woman's grief had seemed different to everyone
else's. More introspective, somehow. Despairing. But Ove was
about to bring the meeting to a close.

The minute it was over, Hanna hurried away. She had to

get in touch with Rebecka. She couldn't put it off any longer. But how?

Hanna locked herself in the bathroom so that she could gather her thoughts in peace. Eventually, she sent a message:

I'm so sorry about everything. I've been thinking about you non-stop.

Rebecka called her back right away.

'I've been thinking about you too. I'm glad we met again, but . . .'

Her voice sounded gravelly. It wasn't clear whether that was because she had been crying or because she had taken something – possibly both.

'I know how hard yesterday must have been,' said Hanna. 'And I don't just mean finding out, but all the questions too. I—'

'Don't worry,' Rebecka told her. 'You were just doing your job.'

It didn't sound like she quite meant what she said.

'I actually have another question for you,' said Hanna. 'The police officer in me has to ask.'

'OK.'

'Did Joel smoke hash?'

The silence that followed seemed to quiver with anger.

'Who said that?'

'No one. Forensics found some hash in his room. The tests will be able to tell us whether he used it or not.'

'Did you have any other questions?'

'No, not right now.' Hanna wanted to show Rebecka that she didn't just care because of her job. 'I went to the place where Joel was found yesterday. There were quite a few people there.'

'People have been coming here too,' said Rebecka. 'But no one has knocked. They just leave things at the gate.'

'Honestly, isn't that quite nice?'

'Yeah.'

Hanna stared at the toilet door. There was a blue line down the middle of it, as though someone had started to do some graffiti and then lost their nerve.

'Is your husband at home?' she asked.

'No, he's just started working for a friend's carpentry firm, and they've got a job they need to finish before June. But I don't actually want him here right now anyway. Sonja is looking after Molly today, and she's filled the fridge with food.'

'Sonja?'

'Yeah, the lady with the sweets is my mother-in-law now.'

'I didn't realise she had kids.'

'She adopted Petri when he was thirteen. You and I were already eleven by then.'

The two women listened to one another breathing for a moment. Hanna was struggling to tear her eyes away from the blue line. Maybe it wasn't even deliberate, maybe someone had accidentally drawn it when they opened the door. She didn't really want to ask, but she knew she had no choice:

'What about your mum?'

'Yeah, she's still alive, we've got a good relationship now. She lives in Karlskrona, but she booked a ticket as soon as I called her. She's arriving tonight.'

Hanna heard footsteps, pausing outside the door.

'Listen, I need to go,' she said. 'But I promise I'll call every day.'

'There's only one thing I want you to promise.'

'What?'

'That you'll find whoever killed Joel.'

Hanna knew that was the kind of promise she should never make, but this was Rebecka. She had no choice.

'OK,' she said. 'I promise.'

The Last Day

Joel is sitting at the very back of the bus, his face to the window. They are nearing the highest point on the Öland Bridge, and he feels like his body is about to burst. Like there isn't room for him inside it. Or on the bus. Anywhere. He wants to scream at the bus driver to pull over and let him out. To throw himself from the bridge and end it all. He hits his forehead against the glass.

The woman in the row in front turns around and glares back at him. He should tell her to mind her own bloody business, but instead he gives her an apologetic smile. As usual. Mum won't believe him if he tells her how dark and ugly he is inside. She won't believe what he is thinking about doing. Everything he has already done. But he's so tired of acting. Of pretending to be someone he isn't.

Joel turns to look outside again. For a few seconds, the bus seems to float between sea and sky, but then it continues downwards, and it becomes easier to breathe.

It's so typical of his bad luck that he ran into Axel of all people. If only he'd left Kullzenska a few minutes earlier or later, he could have avoided it.

The shove into the radiator isn't the only abuse Joel remembers, but it was definitely the worst. There was just so much blood. He was sure she was going to die. Mum says Axel also hit him, but he has no memory of that.

When Joel was ten, he agreed to spend a weekend with Axel. He was so desperate for a father – one who didn't just have eyes for Molly – and he had also been promised a bike. A mountain bike. At the time, he hadn't seen Axel in over a year.

Joel doesn't remember what started it, but he recalls Axel raising a fist to him and screaming: *You ungrateful brat!*

Axel didn't hit him that time, but Joel never stayed at his place again. He never got his bike either.

In truth, he has tried to stay away from him ever since.

Joel takes out his phone and scrolls through his feed. It does nothing for his anxiety, but it does help to pass the time. He spends several minutes watching a video of a cat attacking its own reflection, only managing to tear himself away from it when Nadine sends him a snap. It's a picture of the graffiti on her desk, accompanied by the words: *School sucks. You're not missing a thing*.

Sucking is what someone has scrawled they want to do to Sigge, Nadine's incredibly hot woodwork teacher.

You're just trying to cheer me up, Joel replies.

Is it working?

Yup.

Joel closes Snapchat and sees that he has a new message on WhatsApp. He opens the app and stares down at the words that make the darkness open up and swallow him whole:

You're fucking dead. It's you or her.

Chapter Eighteen

Erik's training left him constantly hungry, so he went downstairs to grab a couple of bananas. He had run another ten kilometres that morning, albeit at a slower pace than yesterday.

Supriya had watched as he tied the laces on his running shoes. She was still wearing her dressing gown, a coffee in one hand. Smiling mockingly: *Aren't you going to admit defeat soon?*

She had enrolled him in an ironman competition as his Christmas gift, probably because he had been so negative about the atmosphere in town during the competition, comparing it to religious ecstasy. The fact that Erik, who had never even run a marathon before, was now supposed to do just that after first swimming 3.84 kilometres and cycling 180 kilometres, was slightly terrifying. But he would show her.

Erik planned to take the bike ferry over to Öland at the weekend, combining his training with their search for the ideal place to build a cottage. He would never be able to convince Supriya to live somewhere like that permanently, but he hoped he would be able to sell her on the idea of a summer house. Then he realised just how unrealistic his plans were – he couldn't just run off like that when her parents were visiting.

The book he had ordered from Amazon had finally arrived yesterday: *The Knowledge: How to Rebuild Our World After an Apocalypse*. It wasn't that Erik thought the world was about to go under – at least not during his own or Nila's lifetime – but the book contained all kinds of information about how to begin growing and preserving food, how to build waterways, generate electricity, and so on.

He returned to his desk and opened the latest email. It was from Daniel, forwarding a summary of Axel Sandsten's call logs. As he wolfed down his first banana, he scanned through the list, searching for the time frame when they'd visited Axel's office.

'What've you heard?'

Erik turned around and found himself staring straight at Hanna's blank face. The woman really was hard to read. He held up the call logs to her.

'Axel called Tatjana right after we left him,' he said, though he suspected that wasn't quite what she meant.

'No. About my dad.'

'A couple of people were talking about him in the cafeteria yesterday.'

'And what did they say?'

'That he was a drunk who broke in to a woman's house, beat her up and then burnt down the house with her in it.'

Hanna's face softened slightly. It had been the right decision not to lie.

'Listen,' Erik continued. 'I don't care what your dad did.'

'But I do.' She turned around and strode out of the room before he had time to say anything else.

Well, that went well, Erik thought to himself as he munched on the second banana. It was Hanna who had spoken to

Tatjana yesterday, but he suspected she needed time to calm down, so he made the call himself this time.

'Are you at work?' Erik asked after introducing himself as a police officer.

'Yes,' said Tatjana Edin.

'Then I'd like you to take your phone somewhere you can't be overheard.'

Axel Sandsten was really the only person he didn't want to hear their conversation, but Erik was reluctant to mention his name.

'Hold on.'

He heard the click of heels against a parquet floor, followed by the sound of a door closing.

'Yesterday, you told my colleague that you were at work until eleven p.m. on Tuesday. Do you stick to that statement?'

'Yes,' Tatjana said quietly.

'Axel called you at 14:02 yesterday. What did he want?'

'I don't remember.'

'Come on, I'm sure you do. It was right after we spoke to him, so I'm assuming that was what your conversation was about.'

Tatjana was quiet. Erik thought he could hear her pulse down the line.

'I need you to tell the truth,' he said.

'Axel will fire me . . .'

'This is a murder investigation, and I think you know you can't withhold information from us.'

Tatjana made a noise that sounded like it was part sigh, part sob.

'Axel went out at lunch on Tuesday,' she said. 'And he was so agitated when he got back that I asked what had happened.'

'What did he say?'

'That he'd run into his idiot son.'

'What happened?'

'He didn't say.'

'But this is what he told you not to tell us?'

'Yes.'

As soon as Erik hung up, he went over to see Ove, knocking and opening the door without waiting for an answer. He found his boss slumped in his desk chair, head tipped back, snoring. Another loud knock made him jolt awake, wiping his mouth with his arm, even though he hadn't been drooling.

'Christ, I'm tired,' he apologised. 'We were babysitting Penny last night, so I didn't get much sleep.'

Penny was Ove's only grandchild, and knowing what Ove was like, Erik guessed she had been allowed to eat what she wanted and stay up until she crashed on the sofa.

'How old is she now?'

'Turned one in January.'

Erik recapped what Tatjana had said about Axel Sandsten's meeting with his son.

'So what do we do now?' he asked.

'Check whether Daniel has found anything on Sandsten,' said Ove.

'And then?'

'Bring him in for questioning.'

Erik had already turned to leave when Ove continued:

'Take Hanna with you.'

Erik wanted to argue, but he couldn't do that without revealing what had just happened between him and his colleague, so he held his tongue. In order to give Hanna a little more time, he began by tracking down Daniel. As ever, he was sitting at his desk, reading something on the screen. Being a detective was a sedentary job.

'You got anything on Axel Sandsten?' he asked.

From the corner of one eye, Erik saw Hanna step into the room and walk towards her desk.

'All I've found so far is a load of praise,' said Daniel. 'And I'm guessing that's not what you're after?'

'Ideally not.'

Erik made his way over to Hanna, who was slumped in her chair, staring at her phone as though it had just given her a telling-off.

'What's wrong?' he asked.

She glared up at him. 'I just called Tatjana. Imagine how stupid I felt when I realised you'd already spoken to her.'

'Sorry,' he said. 'I should've told you.'

He should have, of course, but Erik still thought she was overreacting. Misunderstandings happened, and he doubted Tatjana really cared.

'What did you want?' Hanna snapped.

'We're bringing in Axel Sandsten for questioning.'

Hanna reached for her black bomber jacket and got to her feet. Both it and her blue jeans looked like they came from the men's section. Her body language seemed different now; she was probably looking forward to the interview a little too much.

Chapter Nineteen

Without a word, Hanna pulled on her jacket and began making her way down to the garage. Erik was one step behind her the whole way, and took what felt like an eternity to sign out his gun, unlock the car and climb in behind the wheel. It was like he was deliberately trying to provoke her.

'Do you want to talk about it?' he asked as he adjusted the rear-view mirror.

Hanna shook her head. Now wasn't the right moment to start bickering about the fact they had both called Tatjana. They were going to pick up Axel Sandsten, and she needed to prepare herself mentally. Larmgatan was only a seven-or-so-minute drive away.

Erik seemed to have got the hint, but his silence only lasted a few minutes.

'This thing with your dad . . .'

'Stop.'

Her father was the very last thing she felt like talking about.

Hanna peered out at the buildings flashing by: Jenny Nyström School, the courthouse. If anything, they should be preparing for the interview, but she didn't have the energy – not with Erik.

This time, he managed to keep quiet until they pulled up by the playground outside the water tower.

'Ready?' he asked.

Hanna nodded and climbed out.

The same woman was behind reception, and the smile that she had turned on as the door opened faltered as she recognised them.

'Wait here, I'll go and get him,' she said, walking away.

This time, she returned immediately with Axel Sandsten.

'Do you have news?' he asked.

'We need you to come with us,' said Erik.

'Can't we do it here?'

'Afraid not.'

For a moment, Hanna thought Axel was about to refuse, but then he turned to the receptionist: 'Cancel my meetings until three.'

The woman nodded and began tapping away at the keyboard. Hanna had no doubt: it was Axel who was making her nervous, rather than their presence. You could say what you liked about Ove, but there were definitely worse bosses out there. There was no sign of Tatjana.

'If you'd like to have a lawyer present, you should call them now,' Erik told Axel as they walked towards the main door.

'Am I a suspect?'

'Formally, we don't have any suspects yet. This is purely for information purposes.'

'Well, I can't be bothered to wait for that slacker,' said Axel. 'I haven't done anything wrong.'

During the drive back to the station, Axel played with his phone. In the rear-view mirror, Hanna could see that he was writing something, but she couldn't see what. He looked up and smiled at her, and she forced herself to hold his gaze.

As they walked through the station, Axel greeted several other officers, and when he reached the interview room, he looked more like he was going to a job interview – one where he already knew he would get both the job and a serious pay rise. He sank into the chair, knees spread.

Hanna enjoyed interviewing people. She typically had a clear picture of what was driving her: a desire to understand. But with Axel, there was nothing to understand. She had worked out exactly what he was years ago: a narcissist with zero empathy for anyone but himself. No matter what came out about him, he wouldn't think he had done anything wrong.

'You saw Joel on Tuesday,' said Erik. 'What happened during that meeting to upset you?'

'Who says I saw Joel?'

'Just answer the question.'

'If Tatjana—'

'You were surrounded by people,' Erik interrupted him. 'Did you really think we wouldn't find out?'

That was all true, but Hanna doubted it would save Tatjana's skin. She would probably admit exactly what she had told the police the minute Axel put any pressure on her. In the short term, losing her job was obviously a bad thing, but ultimately she would probably be better off for it.

'I wasn't particularly upset.'

'OK,' said Hanna. 'So what was it about meeting Joel that annoyed you?'

'The fact he wanted to take health and social care at school. Such a waste of talent.'

'So you thought he was talented?'

'Of course I did. He was my son. It just needed bringing out.'

'And how were you going to do that? With your fists?'

Hanna knew she was being too aggressive, but there was something about the way he was looking at her that was pushing her ever closer to the edge.

'I've never hit my son,' he said.

'What about Rebecka?'

'Rebecka is only good at one thing, and that's lying.'

Hanna leaned back in her chair and smiled. She needed to pause and rein herself in, if possible.

'Come on,' Axel continued. 'You of all people should know that.'

'And what is she supposed to have lied to me about?'

The minute the words left her mouth, Hanna saw the fault line: Rebecka had been pregnant and hadn't said a word. But not being able to tell someone you were having a baby wasn't the same as lying. Axel fixed his eyes on Hanna and smiled mockingly.

'Rebecka never liked you,' he said. 'Why do you think she started pulling away during graduation? She was sick of all the drama.'

A sense of grief washed over Hanna, practically knocking her down. She didn't want to allow her thoughts to return there, but they rushed backwards anyway. It was true that Rebecka had been acting differently those last few weeks of school. Hanna had noticed it, wanted to talk about it, but she hadn't managed to. Lars was drinking more than ever, and Kristoffer was almost never home. They had been a family racing towards catastrophe, and once it finally happened, they had been torn apart. With a father being held on suspicion of murder and a brother who drank until he blacked out, ending up in hospital, she hadn't been able to talk about anything. She must have been awful to be around back then. Everything had revolved around one single thing: what was going to happen to her father.

'Do you have a sore arm or something?' Axel asked.

'What?'

'You keep rubbing it.'

Hanna let go of her left arm as though it was on fire. Seeking comfort from the tattoo wasn't always a conscious decision. Axel turned to Erik, seemingly convinced he would understand.

'Rebecka wasn't good for Joel. She—'

'Did you see him again, after work?' Erik cut him off.

'No.'

'And yet you told your colleague to lie about it?'

Hanna had been hoping Erik wouldn't drag Tatjana into it, though clearly it was the fact that Axel had told her to lie that made him look suspicious in the first place. A large chunk of Hanna was still back in those weeks before graduation. Rebecka might have pulled away because she had just found out she was pregnant, but Hanna was fairly sure that wasn't the only reason. Her hand began making its way to the nightingale again, but this time she managed to stop herself. The pain of everything she had lost was making it impossible to focus.

'I didn't tell Tatjana to lie, just that she should leave that part out.'

'Why?'

'Because I don't have time for this. I'm in the middle of a stressful project right now. I knew how you'd see it.'

'When did you leave the office?' asked Hanna.

Her grief had finally passed, leaving behind a huge sense of weariness. At the fact that she had allowed it to get to her, and that what had happened would never go away.

'Around two.'

That was the same time Axel had told them previously. Interviews largely revolved around finding contradictions or gaps in what was being said, prising your way through to the truth. Once they were done, Hanna would ask one of the technicians to search for CCTV footage covering Axel's office.

'Anyway, Shadow,' he said. 'Who do you think came up with your nickname?'

It was as though he could feel that he had lost his grip over her. Was he suggesting it was Rebecka who had thought up the name? Hanna had no intention of handing him control by replying.

'You didn't seem particularly sad when we told you your son was dead,' said Erik. 'Why is that?'

'I barely got to see the kid.'

Hanna studied Axel. He wasn't even trying to look sad now. Joel had meant nothing to him, but was that purely because he was incapable of love, or did he also have some kind of reason in his sick head?

Find the lies, one of the tutors at police college had told them during a session on interview technique. It was good advice, but interviews were just as much about sifting through the noise to find whatever wasn't being said.

What was Axel Sandsten not telling them?

Chapter Twenty

The sweat made her clothes cling to her body, and Rebecka felt like she couldn't breathe. She threw back the duvet and sat up. That was as far as she got in her attempt to get out of bed.

After her conversation with Hanna, she hadn't known what to do with herself. She had gone up to her bedroom, closed the blinds and crawled beneath the covers. The news that Joel had smoked hash was too much to take. How could that have passed her by? It also left her worried. Worried about what else might come out.

On the bedside table, her phone buzzed. Petri had been in touch several times, asking how she was. It was nice that he cared, of course, but his concern felt just like her clothes right now: itchy and uncomfortable.

Sonja had come to pick up Molly that morning, and planned to spend the day spoiling her. As though ice cream could make up for a dead big brother. Rebecka had held off telling Molly until Petri got home the evening before, and the memory of the little girl clinging onto her as she sobbed desperate, silent tears, made her gasp for air. They had sat there like that for several minutes, and Rebecka hadn't known what to do. Or say. Molly's hamster had died six months earlier, and they had read a picture book about a group of children who start a funeral parlour for animals, but Rebecka hadn't wanted to bring up the stupid little hamster as though it was comparable. In the end, Molly had let go of her and thrown herself at Petri instead.

Her mother had come over for a few hours yesterday evening, and was coming over again that afternoon. Right now, Rebecka couldn't deal with her either. It was as though she could only see her old mum. The one who had thought Rebecka was putting it on when all she really wanted was to be seen. Her mother had been twenty-one when she had her, dropping out of university and moving home, finding a job to support herself and her baby. Her parents had refused to help her. What Rebecka was most proud of after she had Joel was that she had never made him feel like a mistake – or she didn't think she had anyway.

She turned on the light above the bed and reached for her phone. But the message wasn't from Petri, it was from Axel:

Stop telling the police all this bullshit about me.

Rebecka slumped back into bed. All the police had told her about Joel's death was that he had been beaten up. Had Axel hit him? She hoped not, mostly for Joel's sake. She didn't want the last thing he saw to have been his father raising his fist.

It's not bullshit, it's the truth, she wrote back.

She knew what Axel was capable of. He had broken her ribs, given her bruises all over – though he had always been good at avoiding her face – split her eyebrow . . . Not by using his fists, but by throwing her against a radiator. The awful cry Joel had let out when he saw her was seared in her mind.

But killing someone? No. Rebecka didn't want to believe

that, for her own sake as much as anything. Because of what it said about her. The mistake had never been Joel; it was trying to make things work with Axel.

Her phone buzzed again: *I bet your perverted boyfriend did it. Maybe I should tell the cops.*

Perverted? What did he mean? She knew Axel was trying to provoke her, and she couldn't let it get to her. Petri was the calmest, most considerate man she had ever met. Possibly *too* calm.

They hadn't spoken much about his childhood, though she knew it had been hard. His parents, Finns living just outside of Stockholm, had died in a car accident when he was just nine, and Petri had spent a few years moving between various care homes and institutions, forgetting Finnish and learning plenty of other things, before ultimately ending up with Sonja. About as far from the big city as he could get.

Rebecka couldn't think of a better adoptive mother than Sonja, and Petri certainly seemed to have taken after her in many respects. But was it really possible to make it through a childhood like that unscathed? When they'd first started dating, she had been hesitant; she had heard the rumours about him, the whispers that he liked to drink and fight. But she had quickly realised they weren't true.

What Rebecka had done to Petri was awful. Unforgivable. The first time she and Gabriel had slept together was during the harvest festival last autumn, and she felt physically sick when she thought back to the way they had behaved like teenagers, having sex in his car. She might have been able to explain away that first time by saying they were both drunk, but not the fact they had done it again just a week later. She had told Petri she was going to meet a friend, another artist, but instead she had gone away with Gabriel. And she had allowed it to continue, month after month, choosing to shrug off any blame. Instead, she blamed Petri, claiming that his calmness was boring, that he couldn't give her what Gabriel could. That she not only felt like Gabriel really saw her, but also that he worshipped her. It was the spring festival at the weekend, and he had sent her all kinds of messages about how incredible she was.

That was why it had come as such a shock when he told her he wanted to end things on the night of the barbecue. She knew she shouldn't have been so upset, that she should have been happy. Looking back now, she felt numb when she thought about her reaction. Joel's death had changed everything.

It was her guilty conscience that eventually forced Rebecka up out of bed. She went downstairs, to the kitchen, and filled the kettle. Took out a cup and reached for the jar of instant coffee.

Petri was more than she deserved. Kind, stable. He didn't get worked up for no reason, and he meant everything he said. Just like Sonja. Molly was better off there than here with her. Or in school.

Did Molly really understand what had happened? Rebecka wasn't sure. The girl had cried desperately because Joel would never be coming back, but that morning she had also talked about his absence as though it were only temporary.

The sound of the phone ringing made Rebecka jump. She doubted Axel would call, but maybe it was Petri. The number wasn't one she recognised, and after hesitating for a moment, she picked up.

'Hello. My name is Veronika Krans, I'm a reporter calling

from *Expressen*. I was wondering if—'

Rebecka hung up before she had time to hear what Veronika Krans was wondering. What it was like to have your son murdered, perhaps? Your drug user of a son. Or to suspect that it was his father who had killed him? Everyone in the village knew what had happened by now, and even those who didn't must have seen the mountain of flowers outside. *Barometern* had published an article about it that morning. *Ölandsbladet* too.

Rebecka slumped to the floor, she didn't have the energy to make it to a chair. She had experienced Axel's anger so many times, and it was usually something stupid that set him off: the fact that he had heard her talking to Kristoffer, that she had burnt his dinner, that she was wearing the wrong shade of lipstick. She had threatened to leave him once, and that was when he threw her into the radiator.

No matter how desperately Rebecka wanted someone else to be responsible, the awful truth was that Axel had no limits.

Chapter Twenty-One

The last Hanna saw of Axel Sandsten before she left the interview room was his self-confident smile, and the sense of relief she felt as the door closed behind her was physical.

'You OK?' asked Erik.

'Let's have a quick chat with Ove,' she said.

Hanna had no intention of apologising for almost losing control during the interrogation. The latest meeting with Axel had been far more unpleasant than the last. She had been off balance from the very start, and he had used that fact against her. Hanna didn't know how he got away with behaving the way he did, why more people didn't see straight through him. In all likelihood, he knew full well when it was safe to let the mask slip or not; he was far more polished now than he had been sixteen years ago.

Another thought struck her: Axel might have made more of an effort at the station than in his office because he felt under more pressure here. It was almost like he was trying to shift the focus from himself to her. But if he was guilty, he wouldn't get away with it for long.

Ove was on the phone, and his tone of voice as he said *I love you* and ended the call led Hanna to the conclusion that he must be married. She realised she didn't know a thing about his life outside of work.

'So?' he said.

Erik gave him a quick recap of what Axel Sandsten had said.

'That's not enough to hold him,' said Ove. 'But I'm guessing you knew that already?'

'Shouldn't we at least take it to the prosecutor?' asked Hanna.

Ove shook his head.

'So what do we do now?' asked Erik.

Ove's computer pinged, and he momentarily lost his focus. He brought up a message that made him laugh out loud.

'Sorry,' he said. 'What were you thinking?'

'We need to get a better idea of who Joel was,' said Hanna. 'I think we should start by going to see his friend Nadine. Rebecka thought she was his only real friend.'

'Do it,' said Ove. 'I'll let Axel Sandsten know he can go.'

Hanna wondered what Ove would say to Axel, but she was relieved not to have to see his smug face again. She called Nadine, and found out she had stayed home from school. Her flat was on Klockhusgatan in the Skälby area of Kalmar.

She and Erik didn't speak on their way down to the car, and for once the silence troubled Hanna. It felt like she had forced it on him. She wondered whether they would ever reach a stage where they could chat comfortably with one another. In Stockholm, she had often worked alongside a man who talked constantly, about everything under the sun, but he had never shown any interest in what she thought or felt. Someone else would have to listen to him now, she realised with an unexpected sense of melancholy. Life would have gone on as normal after she'd left the capital. Her time there had barely left a mark. Fabian had moved on just a few weeks after he dumped her, finding a petite blonde preschool teacher who would probably jump at the chance to move in with him. Hanna had bumped into them once, outside the station. Her father had died the very next day, and she had immediately known that she would have to return to Gårdby, alone, to sort everything out.

Back in Stockholm, Hanna had barely socialised with her colleagues. She had gone for the occasional beer with them after work, but always as part of a group. She didn't want to live like that any more. She was desperate to build relationships with people, but it was like she didn't know how.

'Does Ove have a family?' she asked.

She knew she should defuse the tension by apologising for the way she had reacted, both to the fact that Erik had called Tatjana and that he had found out about her father. Possibly also for her behaviour during the interview with Axel.

'His wife's name is Birgitta, they live in a villa in Lindsdal. They've got three daughters, but only one of them is still at home. The eldest has a little one-year-old girl. Anything else you'd like to know?'

Though she didn't know why, Erik gave her an amused glance.

'Thanks, that'll do.'

As he drove over to Skälby, he told her a little about the other members of the group. Amer had a wife and two small children, the youngest just a few months old. He had performed at the Park Hermina comedy evening once, representing the local talent, and the top brass had been annoyed that he joked about life in the police force. Carina had been married twice, no kids, and could talk about her garden for hours. Daniel lived alone, and his life seemed to revolve around work and the gym.

So Daniel was single? Hanna felt the familiar flush in her cheeks.

'I don't think Carina likes me,' she hurried to say.

'Who wouldn't like you?' Erik replied.

Hanna couldn't quite tell whether it was a joke, and the uncertainty made her circle back to Ove, blurting out the first question that came to mind:

'Why doesn't Ove wear a wedding ring?'

'I doubt there's any juicy story behind it,' Erik laughed. 'My guess is that his fingers got too fat.'

Erik parked the car between the low concrete buildings on Klockhusgatan. Nadine answered the door wearing a pair of sweatpants and a ripped t-shirt. Her forearms were laced with scars. Most looked old, but a few had fresh scabs on top. A couple were also considerably bigger than the rest.

'Yes, I like cutting myself, and I've failed to kill myself twice,' she said, giving them a defiant look.

'So have I,' said Hanna.

Nadine turned around and walked into the flat.

'If I'm going to talk to you, I need to smoke,' she said, leading them out onto the balcony. 'That's so the cat can't jump off,' she explained when she saw them studying the netting around it. 'Guess he's a bit suicidal too,' she added with a smile.

On the small, rickety metal table, there was an overflowing ashtray. Nadine sat down and lit a cigarette. She held up the carton to them.

'Either of you want one?'

Hanna shook her head. From the corner of one eye she saw Erik do the same. He had probably never smoked in his life. She herself had given up when she applied to police college, though her smoking career had only ever amounted to the cigarettes she had managed to bum at parties. She had never been able to afford them herself.

There was only one free seat, and Hanna took it.

'Sorry,' said Nadine. 'There are just two of us here. Me and my dad. Plus the cat.'

She took a long drag on her cigarette. Turned away and exhaled. Erik leaned against the railing, pushing the cat net out slightly.

'What can you tell us about Joel?' he asked.

'He was perfect,' said Nadine, her eyes welling up. 'Smart, funny, considerate. Not like all the other idiots in this dump.'

'Were you in love with him?' asked Hanna.

'Yeah, for a while. But I got over it. He never felt the same way about me.'

Hanna got the impression that she wasn't over it at all, though there were so many things that seemed confusing after a person died.

'Do you know who did it?' asked Nadine.

'I'm afraid we can't comment on the investigation,' said Erik. 'Sorry.'

'His dad's an arsehole,' said Nadine.

'Why do you say that?'

'He used to beat up Joel's mum. And he's so fucking slimy and manipulative.'

'Did he ever do anything to Joel?' asked Hanna.

'Other than try to make him into a mini-Axel, you mean? No.'

'How was Joel doing?' Erik spoke up.

Nadine took another drag on her cigarette and then slowly blew out the smoke. This time, she didn't bother turning away.

'So-so,' she said. 'It was like he couldn't get it into his thick head how great he was.'

'What was making him feel so bad?'

'Everything, nothing,' Nadine replied, looking Hanna straight in the eye. 'Do you always know why you feel like crap?'

Hanna shook her head. She got the impression that Nadine knew far more about Joel's state of mind than she was letting on, but she also knew that there were certain things that would need time to come out naturally. If they put too much pressure on Nadine now, she would probably clam up. Hanna took out her phone and showed the teenager the picture of the blonde woman she had taken at the rest area.

'Do you know who this is?'

Nadine studied the image for some time.

'Don't have a clue, sorry.'

'Do you know if Joel had fallen out with anyone?' asked Erik.

'Other than his dad, no.'

Hanna nodded towards the cigarette, and Nadine lowered it to the ashtray and tapped off the ash.

'We mostly talked about the future,' she said. 'What we were going to do once we got out of here.'

'And what was that?'

Hanna shifted on her uncomfortable plastic chair.

'Whatever we wanted,' said Nadine. 'We'd finally be free.

It's like people round here are allergic to anyone who sticks out.'

'What stuck out about Joel?'

There was a flash of something in Nadine's eyes, and she took another drag on her cigarette before she replied:

'He wanted more from life than playing football and floorball, drinking beer and driving a tractor.'

'Did Joel have any other friends?'

'Linnea, I guess. She's a year younger, but they're neighbours. Were neighbours . . .'

Nadine looked straight at Hanna, and a wave of black grief hit her like a wall of hot summer air.

'Where did Joel get his hash from?' asked Erik.

'An old classmate, I think. The kind who likes beer, football and tractors.'

The Last Day

Joel gets off the bus in Färjestaden and jealously watches all the people heading off in different directions. People who know where they're going. He has to learn a poem by heart for his Swedish class on Friday, and has been trying to memorise Karin Boye's *In Motion*. It's going OK. His days are so far removed from the ones she writes about, where the way is the labour's worth. Where a new day shows its light.

Maybe he should find another poem, but that would require energy he doesn't have.

All Joel wants is to go home, slump onto the sofa and watch Netflix. Eat toast and drink chocolate milk. He is halfway through a documentary about those idiots who genuinely believe the Earth is flat. The Flat Earth Society. Listening to their arguments and watching them do experiments, tying themselves in knots to make excuses for the results, is incredible. One of the men involved actually had to cut all ties with his family because they argued so much.

But Joel can't go home yet. The school day isn't over. That's the downside of having a mum who works from home.

His phone makes him uneasy, but he pulls it from his

pocket anyway. He doesn't have enough battery to watch Netflix, and he forgot to bring a charger.

He hasn't received any more death threats.

Joel starts walking towards Ölands köpstad. It's a pathetic excuse for a shopping centre, but he can kill a few hours there before catching the bus home. He doubts his mum knows his timetable that well, and if he has to, he can always say that his last class was cancelled. There is a slight risk he might run into Petri – the carpentry firm where he works is just behind the shopping centre – but he thinks his step-father is on a job in Kastlösa today. Besides, he isn't too worried. It happened once before, and Petri didn't snitch on him.

His hand reaches for his pocket. *You're fucking dead. It's you or her.*

Should he reply? No. The idiot can write whatever she wants. He's been expecting this since last week.

Joel cuts across the car park and hears a couple of guys making their way back to their car talking about what they are doing at the weekend. They must be at least thirty, and it's insane that they haven't got further in their lives. They're talking about beers and birds and what happened in high school. Joel refuses to end up like them. He needs to get away, go somewhere else, the only problem is he doesn't know where. Once he finishes high school, he'll move to Stockholm and find a job. Maybe he'll keep studying. But how easy will that really be?

The sign for the supermarket makes his stomach rumble, but he doesn't want to waste his last few kronor on food. It's only a few weeks since he got his monthly pocket money, but he has already spent most of it on sketchbooks, charcoal and hash.

His thoughts turn back to the message. Is he wrong to be taking it so seriously? He couldn't bear it if anything happened to her. Joel will have to talk to her once he gets home.

Chapter Twenty-Two

'Lunch?' Erik asked as they left Nadine's building on Klockhusgatan.

Hanna shrugged, her eyes on the ground. He wondered whether she had been telling the truth when she told Nadine that she too had tried to commit suicide. Maybe it was just a way of trying to strike up a rapport.

'How should I interpret such overwhelming enthusiasm?'

His new colleague didn't answer.

'There's a restaurant round the corner that serves traditional potato dumplings,' he continued.

Erik was ravenous, and if he didn't get something down within the next few minutes he would probably either collapse or start rambling incoherently. Being this hungry couldn't be healthy. Perhaps he should use his parents-in-law's visit to skip training at the weekend. Hanna finally turned to look at him.

'Sorry, I was miles away. Dumplings sound good.'

Erik would have loved to know where she was, but he didn't ask. His concentration levels were dipping, and it wasn't like she would have told him anyway. With trembling fingers, he unlocked the car. It felt ridiculous to drive just a few hundred metres, but they needed quick access to the car in case anything happened.

He turned the corner onto Arvid Västgötes gata and parked opposite the restaurant, Kroppkakan. Erik had been there once before, with Nila, so that she could try a better version of the dish they were often served at school. She'd had the traditional version of the dumplings, with meat, and she had loved them. Erik had ordered the vegetarian alternative. He should bring his parents-in-law here, he thought. Two weeks was a long time to keep them entertained. Supriya would be taking a few days off, but not the whole time. She had written lists of things her parents could do on the days she had to work.

Hanna ordered the dumplings, but Erik went for the potato pancakes, without bacon.

'I'm a vegetarian,' he explained, though she hadn't asked.

One of the tables in the small outdoor seating area was free. It was no more than twelve or thirteen degrees, and it was cloudy, but it was quieter out there. The only other people outside were a woman and a young boy, who looked like he might be too unwell for preschool. One of his nostrils was blocked with yellowish-green snot, and he seemed more interested in lowering his head to the table and sleeping than anything else. Erik had been keen to have more children, but Supriya was four years older than him, and though they had tried, it had never happened. They'd had some tests when they came to Sweden, followed by three inseminations, but Supriya was too old for IVF. They had also felt like they'd had enough of the treatments. That they were simply meant to be a family of three. Erik didn't consider himself religious, but he still believed there was some kind of inexplicable higher power guiding everything.

'I think we should go and see Linnea after lunch,' said Hanna.

'Sure,' said Erik. 'That sounds good.'

He preferred to put work to one side at lunch – his brain needed a decent break in order to be able to keep going – but it was nice to hear Hanna say more than a few words. He shovelled pancake into his mouth and listened to her talk about the blonde woman and the way she had been behaving at the rest area. How she had avoided the others and showed a sense of despair that could have been down to guilt. Hanna was convinced she was important, and that they needed to identify her.

Hanna's phone started ringing, but she hesitated before answering. After saying *Hello?* and *Stop calling me*, she hung up.

'What was that all about?'

'I don't know,' said Hanna. 'Someone keeps calling me, but they never say anything.'

'On your work phone?'

'Yeah.'

'Have you mentioned it to Ove?'

'I will if it keeps happening. This was just the third time.'

She ate a mouthful of dumpling. Erik was fairly sure she had no intention of saying anything to Ove, no matter how many calls she got. But Ove needed to know.

'Why did you move back here?' he asked.

He had asked the question before, unsuccessfully, but he was even more curious now that he knew about her father.

'Because I felt like it,' Hanna replied.

'You weren't happy in Stockholm?'

'It was OK, I guess.'

Erik smiled. It really wasn't easy to get any personal information out of her.

'Why did you move here?' she countered. An attempt to avoid talking about herself, of course.

'Because I wanted to get away from Malmö,' he said. 'It was too stressful there. And I managed to convince my wife that we should try living somewhere smaller. She thinks the Swedish countryside is exotic. My job was the only reason we ended up in Malmö after India, and it didn't feel right. I'd rather move forward than back.'

The focus Hanna was giving her glass of water made Erik realise that she had taken his words as criticism. After several long sips, she put down her glass.

'Where do you live now?' she asked.

'Varvsholmen.'

Hanna raised an eyebrow slightly. 'That's hardly the countryside.'

'It is compared to Mumbai and its twelve million people.'

Both focused on their food for a few minutes. Hanna used her fork to scrape clean her plate, pushing it into her mouth.

'What? It was tasty,' she said when she noticed him watching her.

'Did you ever have someone who used to make you dumplings?'

'My granny. These weren't quite as good as hers, but almost.'

'Is she still alive?'

'Yeah, but she has dementia, so she's in a home. Last time I saw her, she thought my shoe was a cat.'

Her face was so solemn, but Erik felt like both laughing and offering his condolences.

'My grandfather had Alzheimer's,' he said. 'Towards the end, he kept thinking I was a burglar and trying to hit me with his stick. He was in the police too.'

Hanna smiled softly. 'What does your dad do?'

'Retired policeman. There was a real lack of imagination behind my choice of career. Two of my siblings are in the force too.'

'How many do you have?'

'Three. Two brothers and a sister.'

'And you're the youngest, right?'

'Yeah,' said Erik.

He had been told he was a stereotypical youngest child before – an adventurer who wanted to have fun in the here and now; easy-going and relationship-oriented – though he had always pushed back against that kind of simplification or generalisation.

Erik knew he shouldn't, not considering how it had gone last time, but he just couldn't help himself. He was too curious, and choosing to take the cautious route had never been his thing. Besides, it felt like Hanna had relaxed a little, and they were already on the topic of families.

'It must've been tough with your dad,' he said.

Hanna looked up at him and her expression seemed to flatten. He would get through her shell, somehow. She got up.

'I'm going to get a coffee. Want one?'

Erik nodded and watched her walk into the restaurant. He had met so many relatives through his work, of both victims and perpetrators. They all shared a sense of grief, but the perpetrators' families almost always tried to mask it. He suspected he knew why: their anger was different, and they were ashamed. Still, he thought it would make him a better policeman if he could just talk to Hanna about it. He also thought he could help her. Though maybe he was just being naive. And insensitive. How would he have reacted if one of his parents had committed a crime it was impossible to forgive? There was no imagining it.

Chapter Twenty-Three

Hanna filled two chipped mugs with coffee and added a splash of milk to one. She tried to ignore Erik's conceited smile. They had been having a good time until he suddenly brought up her father – again. It felt like she had become his hobby project: the broken cop who needed to be fixed. The only problem was that she wasn't broken, or at least not in the way he seemed to think. She also doubted that laying bare her private life to him would make her feel the least bit better.

She slowly carried the mugs back to their table. The milky coffee sloshed over the edge of the cup as she put it down in front of Erik, but she let him deal with the mess. As she waited for her coffee to cool down, she called Linnea's mother, Ulrika. Erik had already had a brief conversation with her father, Gabriel, but they needed to go through the evening with both parents.

'I understand the Forslund family came over to your house for a barbecue on Tuesday? How long did they stay?'

The times Ulrika gave matched Rebecka's. She confirmed that Joel and Molly had gone home around nine, Rebecka and Petri a few hours later.

'Did anything unusual happen that evening?'

'No, we just ate and talked and . . .'

'And?'

'Nothing. It was nice, but it feels so awful now, considering everything with Joel.'

'How did he seem that evening?'

'The same as ever. The kids snuck away as soon as they could. He and Linnea went into the kitchen to draw.'

'We'll need to talk to Linnea too.'

'Absolutely,' Ulrika replied, as though she were giving Hanna permission.

The fact was that Linnea was over fourteen, and she wasn't a suspect, so all Hanna needed was her phone number. Once she had it, she thanked Ulrika and hung up. Her daughter, Ulrika had said, was at school.

Hanna drank a few sips of her coffee before dialling Linnea's number. She felt Erik's eyes on her the whole time, but she ignored him.

'Oh, I'm glad you answered,' Hanna said, introducing herself as a police officer. 'Are you at school?'

'Yes, but I'm on my way home.'

'If you wait there, we can give you a lift,' said Hanna.

'Why?' The question was no more than a whisper.

'We need to talk to you about Joel.'

Linnea released her anxiety like a sigh.

'I've been thinking I should get in touch with you,' she said.

'Why is that?'

'Can we talk about this later?'

Hanna fully understood why Linnea might not want to say whatever it was over the phone. Some things were just easier to talk about in person. Hanna herself wasn't particularly fond of phone calls, but she always did whatever was necessary when she was at work.

'We need to go,' she said to Erik.

'Mmm, I got that.'

He drained his cup as he got to his feet.

'I'll drive,' said Hanna.

Not simply because she knew Öland better than Erik, but also because he was a little too keen to stick to the speed limit. It was the only part of him that seemed to diverge from his stereotypical youngest-child behaviour. Hanna herself was a youngest child, but Kristoffer had always felt more like he was the same age than an older brother. For the most part, they had got on well, but there had been a period when he had wanted to be left alone with his friends, and had forbidden her from coming any closer than ten metres when they were outside the house. Hanna hadn't even been allowed to take the same bus as him. And then their mother died, and he hadn't been much of a brother at all.

The traffic moved freely for the first ten or so minutes, but they ran into a jam just before the turn-off from the bridge. A red Fiat seemed to have broken down, and a queue had formed behind it. Hanna used her blue lights to get past.

'What?' she said. 'Linnea has something to tell us, and there's a risk she might not hang around if we take too long.'

'I didn't say anything.'

Once they were off the bridge, Hanna continued to Mörbylånga. She had no trouble finding Linnea. The girl was standing directly opposite the school on Ölandsgatan, right where she had said she would be, wearing jeans and a dark blue hoody that was several sizes too big for her. The style reminded Hanna of the one Joel had been wearing. Her strawberry-blonde hair was tied up in a bun.

No one said much on the drive back to Gårdby. Hanna liked to be able to read people's body language during interviews, and Erik clearly felt the same way.

Hanna glanced out at Rebecka's house as they passed. The blinds were down, but there was a car on the drive that hadn't been there yesterday. Petri's, perhaps. Or possibly Rebecka's mother's.

She pulled up onto Linnea's driveway a little too sharply, scraping up against one of the bushes to the side. Erik tensed, but he didn't say a word. Probably because Linnea was with them. A few weeks after Hanna first got her driving licence, she had rammed Rebecka's letterbox. Her licence had represented freedom to her, and still did. It was as though all her inhibitions disappeared the minute she got behind a wheel. Her grandmother had paid for her driving lessons as an eighteenth-birthday present.

The front door opened and Ulrika came out. She stood awkwardly, waiting for them, unsure of what to do with her hands. Linnea squirmed away from her attempt at a hug. Though they didn't want the mother to be present during their interview, Hanna was glad Ulrika was home. The girl might need her support afterwards. Fourteen was such a sensitive age.

They sat down in the kitchen, purely because it had a door they could close. Linnea filled a glass with water and quickly drank it down, refilling it and taking a seat.

'So, tell us,' said Hanna. 'What was it you thought we should know?'

'Something happened last week,' Linnea replied, gripping the glass.

They waited for her to go on, but she didn't speak.

'What happened?' asked Erik.

'I went with Joel to pick up Molly from school. His mum couldn't do it. That happens sometimes, when she can't leave the studio.'

'OK, and what happened?' Erik asked.

It was clear Linnea was going to need help saying everything she wanted to say.

'Fanny pushed Molly up against a wall. It looked really nasty – she had her arm on her throat, and Molly's face looked so strange. Like she couldn't breathe.'

'Who is Fanny?'

'A girl who used to be in Joel's class. Her gang hangs around Gårdby School sometimes. They're not doing well in high school, so I guess terrifying the little kids makes them feel big.'

'Very mature,' said Erik, provoking a smile from Linnea.

Like so much else in Hanna's life, there was a before and after when it came to school. She had been happy in primary and middle school, but her high-school experience had largely revolved around hiding the fact that Lars was drinking. She had borrowed clothes from his wardrobe when she grew out of her own, pretending they were what she wanted to wear. She had behaved in class and made sure she got good grades in an attempt to prevent anyone from asking how things were at home; Kristoffer caused enough trouble for the both of them. After her mother's funeral, she'd had just one aim: to make it look like what was left of the family wasn't on the verge of collapse.

She had even lied to her grandmother, despite going to stay

with her some weekends, whenever she needed a break. She used to love waking up and tiptoeing out into the kitchen to sit on the old-fashioned wooden daybed. Listening to the radio with Granny, waiting for the bread to bake.

'What happened then?' she asked.

'Joel ran over and pulled Fanny off her, and she went completely crazy. Started hitting him and yelling that he'd regret it.' Linnea let out a sob. 'I don't know how he dared. Joel is practically the same height as me, and Fanny's so much bigger. One of the teachers eventually came out and broke it up.'

'Why did Fanny attack Molly?' asked Hanna.

'She's always doing that kind of thing. Molly cried almost the whole way home.'

'And the teacher just let everyone go?' said Hanna, unable to hide her agitation.

'Yeah, why wouldn't he? No one told him anything.' Linnea shook her head.

Hanna remembered what school was like, of course – the name-calling and the fighting, the teachers who saw but didn't care. It was just that she had assumed things must have changed since then.

'What's the teacher's name?' she asked.

'Isak Aulin. But he's cool.'

Hanna wasn't done with the subject, but Erik got in before her:

'It's good that you're telling us this.'

Linnea nodded, but she seemed to be struggling to believe him.

'Fanny was really pissed off with Joel afterwards,' she said. 'She probably thought he'd messed up her image or something.

Anyway, it was like she'd decided to break him. I know she'd threatened Molly too.'

'Did Joel mention any of this on Tuesday?'

'No. I could see something was bothering him, but he ducked the question when I asked. I should've . . .'

Hanna reached out and placed her hand on Linnea's, quickly removing it when she realised the girl didn't appreciate the gesture. Instead, she took out her phone and brought up the image of the blonde woman from the rest area. Linnea claimed not to recognise her.

'Does Fanny sell hash?' asked Erik.

'I don't think so,' said Linnea.

'Do you know anyone who does?'

'No.'

The glass of water in her hand shook as she took a sip.

'What are you so afraid of?' Hanna asked.

Linnea glanced at the door, pausing before she answered.

'I think Fanny might come after me now.'

'Why?'

Linnea took another sip of water.

'Because I was there when she was threatening Joel. That's the only reason she needs.'

Chapter Twenty-Four

As Erik opened the kitchen door, Linnea's mother took a quick step back in the hallway, mumbling an apology about wanting to ask how it was going. It was obvious she had been trying to eavesdrop, but if she had managed to hear anything, she would hardly have been loitering outside as he and Hanna made to leave. They let her go in to Linnea.

'Just leave me alone!' Erik heard the girl hiss as they left the house.

'We need to talk to Molly,' said Hanna. 'If you call Ove, I'll ask Rebecka where she is.'

'Sure,' said Erik.

There was a hedge separating the two properties, and Hanna walked down to the road and around it. Erik moved the car over to Rebecka's driveway, wanting to keep an eye on the house. So that he could act quickly if Hanna needed help. There was no sign of movement behind the closed blinds, and Erik dialled Ove's number. He saw an elderly woman approaching, a red rose in one hand. She hesitated when she saw him, but then stepped forward and laid the rose on top of the other flowers by the gate. When Ove picked up, Erik recapped what Linnea had said, and told him they were planning to talk to Joel's little sister.

'Good,' said Ove. 'Sounds like things are moving forward.'

Erik murmured in agreement.

'I'll ask one of the others to look into this Fanny girl,' Ove continued. 'What's her surname?'

'Broberg.'

'Nothing new to report on this end, I'm afraid,' said Ove. 'But I'll let you know if anything changes.'

'So we still haven't tracked down the owner of the car from the rest area?'

'Sadly not. We've left messages on his phone, but he hasn't called back yet. He's on leave from work, not due back until Monday.'

'And the cyclist the Germans saw?'

'Amer hasn't managed to identify him yet.'

Hanna re-emerged from Rebecka's house, and Erik ended the call as she opened the driver's side door.

'It's better if I drive; I know the way. Molly's at her grandmother's. I can't remember the exact address – I just know who used to live there.'

'And who was that?'

'A religious studies teacher who should've become a priest instead.'

Erik walked around to the passenger side.

'Rebecka didn't recognise the blonde woman either,' Hanna told him as he climbed in.

A few minutes later, she pulled up outside a small red house. Its brown front door was to the right of a large window with a green frame, and for a brief, confused moment Erik was sure he had been there before. Then he realised that the memory came from a children's book his mother had read to him until it fell apart. The house was the spitting image of the one Little Red Riding Hood's grandmother had lived in.

Hanna was quicker out of the car than he was. A woman with grey hair opened the door. Erik explained who they were and why they had come, but her eyes were fixed on Hanna.

'I recognise you,' she said.

'I was at school with Rebecka.'

'Are you Lars Duncker's girl? I heard she was back.'

Hanna nodded uncomfortably, but Sonja was already done with the subject.

'Molly is inside.'

Sonja showed them into a living room that was far removed from the pared-back style of Erik's childhood book. The wooden furniture was just as simple, but there was more of it, and there was also a pale grey sofa dotted with colourful cushions. Molly was sitting on the floor, surrounded by a ring of paper printouts of various animals, mostly birds, that she was hurriedly colouring in. Her fingers were streaked with ink.

'It would be good if you could stay here with us,' Erik turned to Sonja, raising a finger to his mouth to show her not to speak.

Whenever they interviewed someone as young as Molly, they needed a witness. Strictly speaking, it was supposed to be someone without a connection to the girl, and if they were being particularly picky, the person who did the interview should also be a specialist in dealing with children. In practice, however, the situation always determined what happened. Molly was a child who might have information that was vital to the case, and they needed to get to that information as quickly as possible. Hanna dropped to her knees beside the six-year-old.

'Hello, my name is Hanna.'

Molly glanced up and said hello, immediately turning her attention back to the wings of the parrot she was colouring purple.

'I'm friends with your mum, but I'm also a police officer.'

The girl's colouring stopped.

'Are you going to find the person who hurt Joel?'

'Yes, I'd really like to do that, but I need your help. What happened when Joel and Linnea came to pick you up from school last week?'

Molly began colouring again.

'Do you mean with Fanny?'

'Yes,' said Hanna. 'What did she do?'

'She was choking me.'

'Why?'

Molly looked up at Sonja, who gave her an encouraging smile. Erik kept to the background, keen to avoid disrupting the rapport Hanna had with the girl. After a brief pause, she continued:

'Fanny wanted money. Some of the others steal money from home and give it to her. Then she doesn't hit them.'

'Why did you say no?' asked Hanna.

'Mummy always says we don't have enough money. I get pocket money, but I'm saving it.'

'What are you saving up for?'

'A rabbit. I really want a horse but I can't save that much. It'll take years.'

'Has Fanny ever done anything else to you?'

Molly picked up an orange pen and began filling in the

parrot's breast feathers. For a while, Erik was sure she wasn't going to answer.

'She says mean things, but she hasn't choked me again.'

'What does she say?'

'That she'll kill me if I tattle-tale. Or if Joel doesn't do what she wants.'

'And what does she want Joel to do?'

'I don't know.'

Molly dropped the pen and looked up at Hanna. Erik didn't know how she could stay so calm. He was simmering with rage. He would never be able to work with kids.

'I'm scared she's going to choke me now that Joel is gone.'

'I'll talk to Fanny, I promise,' said Hanna. 'And after that she won't dare hurt you. Or any of the other children.'

Molly threw herself at Hanna, almost knocking her over, hugging her tight.

'Thank you,' Hanna said. 'You've been a huge help. Is there anything else you want to tell us?'

Molly shook her head.

'Or do you have any questions?' Hanna continued.

'Do you want to draw with me?'

'I love drawing,' said Hanna, reaching for a butterfly that still hadn't been coloured in.

After she had coloured the body blue, she handed the sheet of paper to Molly.

'Maybe you can choose the colour for the wings; I have to get back to work now.'

Molly put the parrot to one side and chose a yellow pen to fill in the butterfly's wings. Sonja followed Hanna and Erik out onto the porch.

'What a monster,' she muttered.

'I know,' said Hanna. 'But it's vital you let us deal with this. Please don't mention what you've heard to anyone but Molly's parents.'

'Of course,' said Sonja. 'I'm not like the other gossips round here.'

Sonja held Hanna's eye, and Erik suspected she wasn't simply talking about the present. There must have been plenty of talk about Hanna and her father back in the day, and the fact she had returned to the island had probably stirred it up again. He felt a sudden pang of guilt at having pressed her.

Hanna nodded to Sonja, who closed the door.

'What do you think?' Erik asked.

'That whatever was going on between Joel and Fanny was about more than her strangling Molly. We need to find out what Fanny wanted Joel to do.'

Chapter Twenty-Five

Rebecka wiped down the kitchen counter for the second time. There was a stubborn orange spot that was refusing to disappear, possibly from the bolognese sauce she had made on Sunday. She scrubbed harder.

'Would you please sit down?' her mother, Annette, begged.

With a sigh, Rebecka wrung out the dish cloth and draped it over the tap. Spotting a lone breadcrumb clinging to the yellow cloth, she snatched it up again and rinsed it under the tap, eventually tossing it into the sink.

'No, Mum, I can't.'

She couldn't find peace anywhere in the house. Joel was everywhere she looked. All the thousands of dinners they had eaten in the kitchen. All the spills she had wiped up. All the weekday evenings she had tried to get him off the sofa and up to bed. All the times she had stood outside his door and he had actually been in there, on the other side. In bed, or sitting at his computer.

Oh, Joel. Why did you sneak out?

Rebecka was convinced he had left voluntarily. That he had

got mixed up in something he shouldn't have. No one could have broken into the house and dragged him away without anyone noticing – particularly not when she had been awake at the time.

The forensic technicians had examined both the front door and the patio door. She had checked them herself afterwards, and hadn't seen any sign of forced entry. There were no new marks on the windows either. Besides, it was only May – they didn't leave any of the windows open yet.

Joel must have crept down the stairs and headed off to meet someone, but who? She just couldn't make sense of it. Particularly not considering where he had been found. Should she call Hanna and ask what they knew?

Hanna had actually been over a little earlier. It seemed Linnea had said something that meant the police needed to talk to Molly. She was still at Sonja's, and Rebecka had said no to going over there with them – it was enough that Sonja was there.

She had been too scared to ask what it was all about.

Hanna had seemed different. Harder, somehow. And she had claimed that Joel smoked hash. Should Rebecka have gone with them, for Molly's sake? She repressed her maternal guilt. If she had been there, Molly would probably have refused to say a word.

'Rebecka.'

The pleading in her mother's voice was like nails on a chalkboard. She wanted her to sit down and talk about Joel, about all the wonderful things they had done together, but Rebecka didn't want to talk about him like he was gone. She wanted him back. Why had Hanna shown her that photo of the blonde woman? She hadn't asked about that either.

'The police found hash in Joel's room,' she said.

'Oh?'

'Is that all you have to say?!'

'No, it's just . . . You got up to that kind of thing too, at his age.'

'I didn't do any bloody drugs.'

'It's more common among teenagers now. I read—'

'I need to get some air,' Rebecka interrupted her.

She hurried over to the back door, opening it on her second attempt, stepping out onto the porch and filling her lungs. She stayed close to the wall so that none of the neighbours would be able to see her; she didn't have the energy to talk to anyone right now, particularly not Ulrika and Gabriel.

Joel was out there too, she realised. How many evenings had they spent sitting on the pine furniture she had found for free online? Barbecuing, lingering. Playing *kubb* in the garden. Joel had filled the small plastic paddling pool and let Molly splash around in it. And later, once she had learned how to run, he'd had water-balloon fights with her, deliberately missing on his shots and letting her hit him.

How was Molly going to cope without her big brother?

Rebecka peered through the trees. The new houses on the other side of the wood were too far away for her to be able to see properly, but she thought she could make out a dark silhouette moving between the trunks. Someone pottering about in their garden, perhaps. She took in her own overgrown garden. Cutting the lawn occasionally was about the only gardening they ever did. No, not they – Joel. And only ever when he was desperate for money.

Her eyes scanned left, towards Ulrika and Gabriel's house. It was two days since they had grilled flank steaks on the enormous barbecue Ulrika had bought and since stashed away in the garage. Two days, but a different life. Rebecka had pressed her leg against Gabriel's beneath the table, and he had pulled away. At the time, she had assumed it was because he thought she was being careless, but he had probably already made up his mind. Just a few hours later, she had been on the floor of her studio, clinging to that same leg, physically trying to keep him there with her. He had told her to stop acting like a fucking child, and she had crawled into the cramped toilet and thrown up.

When she eventually got back to her feet, he was gone.

What if it was Axel who had killed Joel after all? Her thoughts hopped around like birds hunting for seed. She hadn't heard from him again. The fact that she had fallen for someone like Axel now seemed completely incomprehensible. *Money doesn't make anyone happy, but it helps.* That was what her mother always used to say as she played her scratch cards on a Friday. Not that she ever won anything.

Rebecka headed back inside.

'Sorry,' she told her mother, who was still sitting at the kitchen table.

'You've got nothing to apologise for.'

Rebecka hadn't eaten since breakfast, so she opened the fridge door, but quickly closed it again. There was no way she would be able to keep anything down.

'Do you want me to make you something?' her mother asked.

'I'm fine, thank you.'

'I can throw an omelette together.'

'I said I'm fine.'

Her mother's sigh cut right to the bone. Rebecka knew she

should be handling the situation better, but she just couldn't do it.

'It was nice to see Hanna again,' her mother said.

'Yeah.'

Her mother had always liked Hanna. She was everything Rebecka wasn't: calm and conscientious, good at school. Strong.

Rebecka turned to rescue the dish cloth from the germs in the sink. Through the window in the gable end of the house, she saw that Gabriel was standing in his driveway, gazing over to her house. He looked sad, which brought her a hint of satisfaction, considering how he had humiliated her. He had come to the studio with a bottle of wine, and he hadn't brushed her off when she'd caressed him. It was only once they had emptied the bottle that he'd dared tell her he no longer wanted to see her. Not like that.

She quickly stepped to one side so that he wouldn't spot her. Rebecka had only bothered to fit blinds on the front of the house, since that was where it was most overlooked. Neither Ulrika nor Gabriel had been in touch, and that bothered her, though she could understand why he might want to stay away. What had she ever seen in him? He had said all kinds of things he probably didn't mean in order to get what he wanted: sex. Telling her she was both funny and beautiful, fulfilling her need to be seen. But things were never quite that simple. He had made her laugh. Talked to her like she wasn't just some housewife.

Still, in comparison to Joel, he was nothing, and Rebecka felt like wiping Gabriel from her memory, pretending they had never had a relationship at all. But what about Ulrika? Rebecka both wanted and didn't want her to get in touch.

Rebecka felt like she needed to see the place where Joel had been found. She might never know what had happened to him, might never get any closer to the last few moments of his life than the rest area. The police couldn't even tell her whether that was where he had died.

The simplest option would be to ask her mother to drive her over there, but the thought exhausted her. She didn't want her mother's reproaches and worries there beside her.

'I'm sorry,' she said, 'but I think I need to be on my own for a while.'

'Stop apologising,' said her mother, getting to her feet.

Rebecka let her mother give her a long hug.

'You know where I am if you need anything,' she said as she disappeared through the front door.

Petri had taken the Volvo to work, but they also had a rusty old Saab that Rebecka sometimes used when he wasn't home. She knew that driving over there herself was out of the question, that she would probably end up in a ditch if she tried. She could wait until Petri got home, of course, but she wasn't patient enough for that.

Maybe she could send Hanna a message asking her to tag along, but she wasn't sure she could handle that either. Besides, she didn't want to bother her, didn't want to risk slowing down the investigation.

The place itself would never be enough. Rebecka needed to know what had happened to Joel.

The Last Day

Joel is the last to board the 102 bus to Gårdby, and he heads straight for the back seat as usual. He wants to be able to keep an eye on things, doesn't like having people behind him.

There are no more than ten other people on the bus, but he avoids their gaze. Most of them pay no attention to him anyway. Tilde, from Linnea's class, is there, with another girl he doesn't recognise. They're huddled together, laughing at something on Tilde's phone. A few weeks earlier, Tilde had tagged along to the cinema in Kalmar with him and Linnea; she didn't have anyone else to go with. She glances up at him now with an incredibly guilty look on her face. But why the hell should she feel bad? It's great that she's managed to find a friend. Without saying a word, she looks back down at her phone.

Joel reaches his seat without having to speak to anyone, and as he slumps down into it, he feels like he'll never be able to get up again. Just a few seconds later the anxiety returns, tearing away at him. He'll be stuck with these nagging thoughts for a whole half hour.

The bus pulls away and he takes out his phone and checks

the screen. The battery is down to eight per cent.

Nadine has sent him a message: *What you up to?*

It feels so good to have someone who really cares. His mum does too, of course, but it often seems as though she has some kind of glass wall around her. Joel is pretty similar in that regard.

On the bus to Gårdby, he writes. *Phone's gonna die soon*.

He adds a few crying emojis, and Nadine replies with the same.

Joel watches the trees racing by outside, the sunlight filtering through the gaps between their trunks in a dusky dance. The bus route goes right up to Algutsrum before turning off towards Gårdby; it would take half the time in a car. Joel's eighteenth birthday is just two and a half years away, and he wants to take his driving test as soon as he can. Ideally get a car too. But in order to afford that, he'll have to find a job. He doubts his mother will want to pay for any of it. She had been reluctant even to send off his application for a provisional licence, as well as the forms allowing both her and Petri to teach him.

How can he get hold of enough money?

He has had so much else on his mind lately that he hasn't managed to find a summer job. Once he finishes the first year of senior high, he can get a paid work-experience job through the council. Nadine will be selling ice cream for a few weeks outside a café. He could pick strawberries again, that'll bring in a bit of money, but the question is whether it's really worth it.

A moped would be much cheaper, but they've never really felt like his thing. Maybe because Fanny has been driving around on one since she was twelve.

Joel's phone buzzes, and he looks down at the screen.

Come to the woods at midnight.

He feels like telling Fanny to go to hell. He's so sick of her. Why can't she use her muscles and her brain for something other than beating people down?

Fanny is actually a bit like Axel: they both think they can take and take without ever having to give back. They both think the world is theirs for the taking.

But if Joel writes anything Fanny doesn't like, Molly will be the one who pays, and Joel has to protect her. He has no other choice but to go to the woods. He knows there isn't any point asking what will happen once he gets there.

She's probably planning to beat him up.

I'll be there, he writes.

172

Chapter Twenty-Six

Hanna turned back to face the red house. Through the window, she saw Sonja open a kitchen cabinet and take out a can. Inside, the house looked nothing like it had on the one occasion she had been there previously. It was brighter, with more modern furniture. Back then, it had been full of heavy wooden furniture, and there had been an unpleasant smell. Their religious studies teacher, Jakob, had invited the entire class over for coffee and to talk about God's forgiving nature, though he had explained that in order to be forgiven they would first have to confess their sins.

His words, or perhaps the way he had said them, had frightened some of the children, and there had been a real outcry from the parents. That had brought an end to any future class visits. Jakob should never have become a religious studies teacher. For him, Christianity was the only faith.

'Could you drive?' Hanna asked.

Erik nodded and took the keys just as his phone started ringing. Hanna knew it must be Ove, and considered taking back the keys so that they could get going, but she really didn't think she was capable of driving right now. Besides, Ove might have new information for them, something that was more urgent than going to see Fanny.

Hanna climbed into the passenger seat and looked out to the house again. She wondered what had happened to Jakob. It was only much later that she realised he must have had some kind of mental illness. The village could be pretty accepting of things like that, providing it stayed within certain boundaries.

But frightening children was not OK.

Nor was killing anyone.

More than anything, it was the gossip that had driven Hanna away from Öland. The way everyone suddenly felt free to talk about the things she wanted to lock away in a dark room: the fact that her father had killed. Maybe Kristoffer was right, and it was selfish of her to have come back. The phone calls she was getting suggested that at least one person was particularly upset by it. That they were coming to her work phone wasn't something she attached much importance to – that number was far easier to get hold of than her private one.

Her phone buzzed, and Hanna brought up a message from Rebecka:

Will you come to Möckelmossen with me?

She stared down at the words. She wanted to say yes, but the car she was in belonged to the Kalmar Police. She could always ask Erik to drop her off once they were done, but then she would need to work out both how to get home and how to get into work tomorrow. Her own car was still parked outside the station in Kalmar. She didn't have the energy to go after work, and she also doubted Rebecka would be able to wait that long.

'Ove said IT have managed to restore WhatsApp on Joel's phone.'

174

Erik looked at her as though he was expecting a drum roll, starting the engine and pulling away.

'And . . . ?'

'Fanny sent two messages to Joel on Tuesday. The first was at 14:05: *You're fucking dead. It's you or her.* The second was at 15:12: *Come to the woods at midnight.*'

'Let's go and talk to the monster, then,' said Hanna.

Erik didn't seem to react to the fact she had used Sonja's words.

'He also just sent over everything they've got on Fanny,' he said. 'Seems like she's well known to both us and social services.'

Hanna sent a message to Rebecka telling her she would be in touch later. That she could go out to Möckelmossen with her. Now that Rebecka had actually asked for help, she would have to work it out somehow. She opened the file Ove had sent over.

'Turn there,' she said, pointing to Snegatan. Fanny lived just outside of Gårdby, in Övre Ålebäck.

Hanna's phone started ringing as they drove, and she answered without checking who it was, convinced it must be Rebecka. Hearing the silence on the other end of the line, however, she realised she had been wrong. Almost immediately, the silence was broken by the sound of crackling, quickly growing in volume. Something was on fire. Hanna wanted to tear the phone from her ear, but it was as though it were glued to her. She felt Erik's eyes on her, and knew she should pretend to be talking to someone so that he wouldn't work out what kind of call it was, but she couldn't even manage that. A scream down the line seemed to loosen the phone from her ear, enabling Hanna to end the call.

Erik pulled into the yard, where Fanny was on her knees, tinkering with her moped. She was wearing ripped jeans and a black t-shirt, and her short hair was black – though the growth at the roots gave away that it was dyed.

Was the fire a recording? It must have been, from a film or something, but the pain in the scream had sounded so real.

Erik parked right alongside Fanny. She looked up, then continued tightening something on the moped. According to the files from Ove, she had turned sixteen that January. Her previous dealings with the police involved shoplifting, drinking, public damage and more – there was one case of assault, plus an attempted fraud, where she had tried to trick people out of their money on an online marketplace. Both the police and her school had reported their concerns to social services on multiple occasions.

Hanna and Erik introduced themselves and showed her their ID. Fanny got up and held out an oil-flecked hand, grinning when they declined to shake it. Though she was only sixteen, she must have been at least five foot nine.

This could have been me, Hanna thought to herself. *If I'd reacted to Mum's death the way Kristoffer did.*

Unlike Hanna at that age, Fanny didn't deal with her height by hunching. Back in Stockholm, Hanna had hired a personal trainer to help her strengthen her back and shoulders. To become better at standing tall. For the most part, she now stood straight, though she occasionally forgot and fell back into old habits.

'Are you home alone?' asked Erik.

'Yeah,' said Fanny. 'But don't worry. I can handle talking to you without my mum being here.'

'That's big of you,' said Hanna.

The crackling fire and the piercing scream were still fresh in her mind, but she knew she had to let go of the call. She had a job to do. Hanna looked down at Fanny's hands. She couldn't see any cuts or bruises, but that could easily be because of the grease and the dirt.

'Isn't it.' Fanny bowed to Hanna. 'Lady Brienne of Tarth.'

'What are you talking about?'

Erik snorted: '*Game of Thrones.*'

Hanna rolled her eyes. She hadn't seen a single episode of the TV show, and had no intention of starting.

'We want to talk to you about Joel Forslund,' said Erik.

'I wish I could say it's sad he's dead,' said Fanny, 'but I'm not surprised.'

'Why is that?'

'Because he kept sticking his nose in.'

'Into your little side earner, you mean?' said Hanna.

'What side earner?'

'Stealing money from children.'

The teenager laughed until she noticed their expressions.

'That was just a bit of fun,' she defended herself. 'I didn't need the bloody money.'

The moped was a red Honda, but that meant nothing to Hanna. It was obviously well cared for, and Hanna was willing to bet it was also souped up. She peered around the messy yard. There was a main house and two side buildings, a pile of junk in front of one of them – including a broken bed frame and a couple of chairs. An old tractor was parked in front of the other, the same kind that had dominated the countryside when Hanna was younger.

'I don't give a damn about your intentions,' said Hanna. 'You're going to stop.'

Fanny shrugged.

'That's not enough. If you don't stop, I'll see to it that you get locked up.'

'Fine. Chill out, woman.'

Fanny raised her hand in a salute. Hanna was on the verge of drumming the message into her again, but Erik spoke up before she had time:

'You sent Joel a couple of messages on Tuesday,' he said.

'Yup.'

'Do you remember what you wrote?'

'More or less, but I'm guessing you know the exact words?'

Erik read the messages to Fanny, who sighed.

'That was just to scare him.'

'Did you meet Joel in the woods?'

'Yeah,' she admitted without hesitation.

'Where ar—'

'Behind Gårdby School,' Hanna interjected.

'Brienne here knows what's what,' said Fanny, giving her another bow.

Hanna felt a strong urge to reach out and slap her.

'What did you and Joel do in the woods?' asked Erik.

'We just talked,' said Fanny. 'We convinced Joel to mind his own business.' She emphasised the word *we* so that they would understand she wasn't alone.

'Who else was with you?'

'Lukas and Tilde.'

Hanna asked for their surnames, and jotted down both in her notepad.

'Did you use your fists while you were talking to Joel?' asked Erik.

'Nope, just our mouths.'

The way Fanny smiled at her own joke made Hanna realise that the girl was probably coming down from a hash high, at the stage where the giggling and chatter transitions into a confident sense of calm. That would explain why she didn't seem the least bit nervous that they were asking her questions about Joel. Hanna studied her pupils. The girl's eyes were so dark it was hard to make them out. The whites, however, were bloodshot.

'Did Joel buy hash from you?' she asked.

Fanny hesitated for slightly too long, and during the pause, Hanna finally caught sight of her nerves.

'No, he didn't.'

Chapter Twenty-Seven

It was with a certain sense of reluctance that Erik left Fanny's house. He was convinced she was lying about both the hash and not hitting Joel, and thought they should at least run a drugs test on her. That way, they could use the results to make her talk. But Hanna seemed to be in a hurry to get away. After holding out a card that Fanny refused to take, she put it on the ground and turned back towards the car. Erik felt like he had no choice but to follow her.

The call that had come through on the drive over had clearly unsettled her.

Though maybe that wasn't what the hurry was about at all. They now knew that Joel had met three people in the woods on the night he died. Perhaps Hanna simply thought that talking to the others would be more fruitful. Erik closed the car door, ready to discuss it with her, but she had already pulled out her phone and was busy writing a message. With one last glance out at Fanny, he started the engine and drove away. The girl didn't even look up.

'Could you drop me off at Rebecka Forslund's?' Hanna asked him.

Was she really planning to hang out with the victim's

mother? Right now? They had to follow up on what Fanny had told them. Though maybe it was Rebecka who had called, in a hysterical state. Erik thought he had heard a scream. But in that case, Hanna should have said something.

'Why?'

'She wants to see where Joel was found, and I think it could be good to get some more photos out there today. Plus, she might be able to tell us more about him.'

Not a word about their relationship, nor the call she had received.

'Sure. I can call Lukas and Tilde to see whether their version of what happened matches Fanny's. I'll talk to Amer about the hash too. He can check with the youth team to see what they know about Fanny Broberg.'

For a moment, Erik considered offering Hanna the car, but he wasn't particularly keen to catch the bus back to Kalmar, no matter how bad he felt for her – especially not now that she had dumped all this work on him. It was his turn to pick Nila up today, which made it even more important that he got back to the station in good time.

'Call the teacher, Isak Aulin, too.'

Erik nodded. Hanna was cooler since he'd asked about her father, but he could deal with that. What he didn't like was that she wasn't being completely open with him: failing to admit that the visit to Rebecka's was also about their friendship, and the fact that she had been threatened again.

'Anything else?'

Hanna shook her head and climbed out.

Erik set off for the station. He spent more time driving in Kalmar than he had in Malmö – the area was bigger, and much less densely populated – and it was always more enjoyable when there was someone to talk to. Today, he used the time to think about what he was going to make for dinner. The simplest thing would be to take Nila to the supermarket and let her choose. Suggest pizza or pasta or something else they wouldn't have for a while once his mother-in-law took over the kitchen.

When he got back to Kalmar, Erik headed straight to the cafeteria to grab a piece of fruit. All the thinking about food had made his stomach rumble. He polished off his apple in a few quick bites and then went up to the office. Amer had the standing desk opposite his.

'Did something happen?' he asked Erik.

'What do you mean?'

'You look so gloomy.'

'I'm just tired,' Erik told him.

He didn't want to air his irritation with Hanna, or discuss the fact that he thought she was making strange decisions. Amer studied him for a moment, clearly not buying Erik's explanation.

'Have you got the names of any dealers?' Erik asked.

'Ten or so. Why?'

'Is Fanny Broberg one of them?'

'Nope.'

'Could you ask the youth team if they've got anything on her?'

'Sure.'

Erik checked his emails, then settled down to make some calls. Lukas first, followed by Tilde, but he struggled to get either of them to say much. That was one of the limitations of phone calls. In the end, they both confirmed Fanny's version of events: they had met Joel behind the school at midnight, and they had just talked – no violence. After roughly fifteen minutes, Joel had left. They claimed not to know anything about the dispute between Joel and Fanny; they had gone along purely because she asked them to. Erik gave them his spiel about how serious it was to lie to the police, particularly during a murder investigation, and Tilde seemed noticeably stressed, but she stuck to her original statement.

Erik had been hoping for the smallest of openings at the very least, something he could use to prise their stories apart, but even without that, it felt like they had taken a big step forward. Joel had left the house voluntarily to meet Fanny at midnight, and just a few hours later, he was dead. Were Fanny and her minions the last people to see him alive? Depending on what happened in the investigation, they could put more pressure on the three teenagers tomorrow.

Ove came over to talk to him. 'Could you come with me a minute?'

Erik logged out and followed him.

'First, I just wanted to let you know that we've got Axel Sandsten on CCTV leaving his office at quarter past two on Wednesday morning.'

Ove seemed relieved that Axel couldn't have murdered Joel. Erik felt the same. He always struggled to deal with parents who hurt their own children. The hardest investigation he had ever worked on had involved a two-year-old who had been beaten to death by his father. The fact that a child had died was obviously the worst part, but the way the father had talked about it – claiming the little boy was so difficult that he just couldn't help himself – was also awful. As though it were the child's fault somehow. Axel seemed like the type who resorted to using his fists whenever he lost control. The idea that he had hired someone to kill Joel didn't feel particularly likely.

'How has Hanna Duncker been today?' Ove asked.

So that was what he really wanted to talk about. Erik had no idea what to say, because he wasn't quite sure what he thought. The frustration he had felt earlier had softened slightly, though he knew this might also be his chance to mention that someone had been making harassing phone calls to her.

'Good,' he eventually said.

'I suppose you could say that she and I have history,' Ove continued. 'So I'm keen to make sure she settles into the group.'

'She's a good officer,' said Erik. 'Maybe not the most talkative, but that doesn't really matter.'

Ove smiled.

If Erik was honest, it was only really him that Hanna seemed to clam up around. She hadn't had any trouble talking to anyone else they had met all day – she had actually been fairly friendly with several of them. To an extent, he only had himself to blame. Erik knew he could be a bit much at times. It was perfectly possible to manage the job without being friends with your colleagues, but he didn't like working that way.

'No, I see that,' said Ove. 'Her father—'

'Surely it doesn't matter what her dad did,' Erik interrupted him.

'So you know about it?'

'Yes.'

Erik studied Ove, trying to work out what he was getting at.

'It left a real wound when it happened,' said Ove. 'And there are a lot of people who still remember that.'

Erik didn't speak.

'It would've been easier if she'd changed her surname,' Ove continued.

'Maybe.'

'We had quite a bit to do with her brother too. But he seems to have turned his life around . . .' Ove trailed off. Perhaps he realised he had gone too far.

'Was there anything else?' asked Erik.

'Just keep an eye on Hanna,' said Ove. 'Make sure she's doing OK. And come to me if there are any problems.'

Erik nodded and walked away. He felt slightly confused by Ove's request. Was it purely down to concern? He sent a message to Hanna telling her the news about Axel, then he sent a second message, to Supriya this time.

I love you.

She replied immediately, with a monkey emoji. Probably because she thought it was cute.

Her parents' visit was stressful for Erik too. He didn't like how Supriya was when she was around them.

He glanced at the clock. He had to pick up Nila from preschool in the next half an hour, so he returned to his desk and called Isak Aulin, the teacher who had interrupted the fight between Fanny and Joel. As he listened to the phone ring out, he brought up the investigation log.

The results of the trace on Joel's phone had just been uploaded to the system. According to the report, it had never left Gårdby. What did that mean? That he had been in Gårdby when he died?

185

The Last Day

Through the studio window, Joel can see his mum at the throwing wheel. Sneaking past without her noticing is a piece of cake. She is usually in a world of her own while she's working, and it's hard to get through to her, even when he wants to.

That is what Joel loves most about drawing: the way it makes everything else fade away, until all that exists is him and the paper.

Maybe he should do some drawing now? No, he isn't in the mood. It wouldn't work.

The first thing Joel does when he gets inside is to run upstairs and plug in his phone. The second is to roll a joint. He never normally smokes at home, particularly not when Mum is in the studio, but he needs it now, to dampen his anxiety.

He opens the window looking out onto Linnea's house, and checks that no one is watching before he lights up. He smokes half, then stubs it out and closes the window. He doesn't want to get too high. Can't run the risk of Mum noticing.

His anxiety has shrunk to a rumbling pain in the background. Joel has a small buddha incense holder on his window sill, and he lights it for a few minutes. Carries it around the room to disperse the scent. He then goes down to the kitchen and mixes a glass of chocolate milk, cutting a few thick slices of cheese to put onto some bread. He slumps down on the sofa and switches on Netflix.

He manages to finish the documentary about the flat-earthers and gets halfway through another about the moon landings being faked by the USA. He switches it off as the front door opens.

'Oh, you're home already,' says Mum. 'I'm going to get Molly now, so could you hide the evidence?'

For a split second, Joel thinks she is talking about the joint, but she nods to his empty glass. He wonders whether he should offer to pick up Molly himself, but then he realises that it would be better if Mum caught Fanny red-handed. Molly has made him swear not to say anything, but he still checks in with her every day after school. On a few occasions, he has asked whether Fanny has been mean again, but she always says no. Joel is pretty sure she isn't telling the truth.

'We're going next door for a barbecue tonight, by the way.'

She means Linnea's house. They often go over there for dinner. Their other neighbours are a couple in their seventies. He and Molly walk their Golden Retriever sometimes, and get cookies and milk in return, but they never hang out with them otherwise.

'Why?'

'It's Gabriel's fortieth birthday, so Ulrika wanted to throw him a surprise party.'

'Couldn't you have mentioned it a bit sooner?'

Ordinarily, Joel would be thrilled at the prospect of hanging out with Linnea, but he doesn't think he has the energy even for her tonight.

'I only found out myself a few hours ago. Come on, it'll be nice.'

Joel mumbles something in reply, as Mum slams the door behind her and disappears.

Doubt makes him tremble. Maybe he should forget all about going to the woods tonight. Whatever Fanny has planned is hardly going to end well for him. But if he doesn't go, nothing will change. The past week has been awful, and this whole thing with Fanny can, at least, be resolved.

He takes his glass and plate to the kitchen and loads them into the dishwasher. He then returns to the sofa, but doesn't switch on the TV. Instead, he closes his eyes and tries to think about nothing at all, but it only half works. How can Fanny be so confident? Joel has no idea who he is or how he should act in this messed-up world. Maybe that's why he finds these documentaries so fascinating. So many people who just can't handle the truth, tying themselves in knots to deny the obvious. Joel himself doesn't doubt for a second that the Earth is round and that the Americans landed on the moon.

The door flies open.

'Joel!' Molly cries, running into the room.

He can tell from her voice that Fanny hasn't bothered her today. That he can put off talking to her until tomorrow. Maybe he'll be able to straighten out everything with Fanny tonight.

'Shoes off!' Mum shouts after her.

Molly takes off her shoes and tosses them towards the hallway.

'Molly!' Mum protests, but she leaves it at that. She's probably had an OK day too.

Molly slumps onto the sofa beside Joel.

'We're having a barbecue tonight! And cake, because it's Gabriel's birthday.'

'Cool,' says Joel.

Molly shakes her head at his lack of enthusiasm.

'Want to play Go Fish?' he asks.

Molly nods and runs off to fetch the cards. The ones with the wild animals on them. Mum pops her head into the room and mouths *thank you* to him, but he isn't doing it for her. He needs to distract himself, and that is always easier with Molly around. He isn't a freak in her eyes.

After a few rounds, they switch to Carcassonne instead. The game was his Christmas present to Molly, but he wrote *To everyone* on the label so that he didn't have to come up with something for Petri. His step-father had given him a pair of jeans, but it was Mum who actually picked them out.

Molly doesn't care about roads, monasteries and fields; all she wants is to build cities. To her, making them big and beautiful is more important than winning, and she always tells stories about the people living in them. This time, she starts talking about a wizard called Ruben.

'No, actually, it's a witch called Lisa.'

Petri gets home, giving Molly a hug and Joel a nod. His eyes seem to linger on Joel's. He must know that he smokes. Joel forces himself to smile, and Petri heads off into the kitchen to see Mum. Judging by her giggling, it sounds like he must have grabbed her bum. Seems like Petri had a good day too.

Petri is much nicer than Axel ever was, but Joel sometimes gets the feeling that Mum has settled for him. That she could find someone better if she wanted to. He barely does anything around the house. Joel once asked her about it, why she doesn't make him do more. *He does lots of things you don't see*, she had replied. And then she said that tidying up helps her to think.

Joel knows what it's really about: Petri brings in the money.

'Your turn.' Molly nudges him.

But before Joel has time to draw a new tile, Mum appears from the kitchen.

'We're leaving in fifteen minutes, so go and get yourselves ready.'

'I am ready,' says Joel.

'I'm going to wear my cat dress!' Molly announces, running up to her room.

Everything feels a shade darker without her around. Joel tidies the game away and feels a pang of anxiety at having to sit through an entire dinner with the neighbours, being nice. At whatever Fanny has planned too. Going up to his room and smoking a little more feels incredibly tempting, but he doesn't dare risk it. Linnea would notice, and she has already been pestering him for more as it is. He regrets ever letting her try it, because he doesn't like her when she smokes. It makes her angry, somehow. It just calms him.

Right then, Joel realises that there is another risk he can't afford to take: showing up to meet Fanny empty-handed. He'll need something to defend himself with.

Chapter Twenty-Eight

Her hand paused above the doorbell. It was less than twenty-four hours since Hanna had last tried to ring it, and it hadn't worked. She felt a sudden sorrow at the passing of time. All the years she and Rebecka had been friends. From the organised playdates of early childhood to their teens, when they had gone round to each other's houses almost every day. They had never bothered to knock back then, simply opening the door and charging inside. Both were almost always home alone. Lars and Kristoffer would be out drinking, doing God knows what, and Rebecka didn't have any siblings. Her mother often worked nights, and occasionally took evening classes in order to find a job she actually enjoyed. The list of professions she had tried was long: cleaner, shop assistant, saleswoman, personal assistant . . . She had also worked at the chocolate factory until it shut down in '98.

Hanna knocked instead, firmly, a meaningless protest at how everything had turned out. She waited a few seconds, then opened the unlocked door. Rebecka was almost there.

'How are you doing?'

The answer came in the form of a despairing, sobbing cry,

and Hanna wrapped her arms around Rebecka.

'Let's sit down.'

She led Rebecka over to the sofa in the living room. It may have been unnecessary given the state her friend was in, but she had used the question as a way of getting her to open up. She wanted Rebecka to be able to offload some of the pain welling up inside her.

'Is there anything you can tell me?' Rebecka pleaded once she had composed herself somewhat.

'About the investigation, you mean?'

Rebecka nodded. Hanna knew she shouldn't, but she didn't want to disappoint her again.

'Axel wasn't on Öland when the murder took place.'

'So it wasn't him?'

'No.'

He had enough money to pay someone to do it, of course, but Hanna doubted that was what had happened. He didn't have a motive, and planning your own child's murder was very different to beating them to death because, for some terrible reason, you were so angry you couldn't stop yourself.

The news made Rebecka sob again, but her tears were different this time. Quieter. She didn't ask any more questions, and Hanna was grateful for that. Sonja would probably tell her what Fanny had done to Molly, but her mother-in-law didn't know about the interaction between Fanny and Joel. About the threats she had sent, the meeting in the woods.

'Why?' Rebecka sobbed. 'I just don't understand why someone would want to do this to Joel of all people.'

'Neither do I.'

Hanna rubbed her friend's back, feeling all the years that had passed. Shapes that had filled out. Rebecka had always been so thin during their teens. Hanna felt a sudden sense of longing pulse through her. Both for what she and Rebecka once had and for what Fabian had meant to her. Someone to touch and be touched by. Why hadn't she let him in? If life was going to be different here, she was going to have to start finding the courage. To refuse to let herself be paralysed by setbacks. Fabian hadn't known anything about her father; she had told her previous boyfriend, and he hadn't been able to handle the news, interpreting everything she said and did differently afterwards.

'Do you know who Brienne of Tarth is?' Hanna asked.

'Yes, why are you asking me that?'

'Someone said I looked like her.'

Rebecka snorted, somewhere between a laugh and a sob.

'There's something in it,' she said. 'Hold on, let me show you.'

Rebecka brought up a picture on Google. There were certain likenesses, in their height, hair colour and style, but Hanna wasn't as broad-shouldered as the actress, and her face was longer. Both did seem to have the same crease between their eyes, however. Rebecka put down her phone, and Hanna felt a pang of anxiety at the look she caught in her eyes.

'Are you getting any help?' she asked.

Rebecka immediately tensed.

'What do you mean?'

'Are you talking to anyone?'

'Like who?'

'Petri? Your mum? A psychologist? A yoga teacher?'

Rebecka laughed at her awkward attempt at a joke.

'Petri has mostly been staying away. Mum would love to talk, but I just can't bloody do it. It feels like everything she's

193

done for me these past few years never happened. I just can't cope with her right now.'

Hanna wanted to say something that would make a difference, but there was nothing to say. Nothing she could think of anyway.

'Shall we go?' she asked instead.

Rebecka headed up to her bedroom to get changed and wash her face. Hanna's work phone buzzed with a group message from Ove, and she had to read it twice to process what he had written. A bloody knife had been found in a ditch just a few hundred metres from the rest area in Möckelmossen. A runner had seen it flash as they ran past, and had the presence of mind to immediately call the police without touching it first. Hanna closed her eyes. This was great news – just what she needed right now. Rebecka came down the stairs and Hanna hurried to put her phone away.

'What is it?' Rebecka asked.

'Nothing.'

'Stop. I can see it's something.'

Hanna replied by ushering her into the kitchen and forcing her to eat a banana. She doubted her friend had eaten all day.

'I don't have a car,' said Hanna. 'So I hope yours is working.'

'And I hope you're a better driver than you used to be.'

One of the few advantages of having an alcoholic for a father was that she had been able to lay claim to the car – at least whenever Kristoffer didn't get in there first – but the demolished letterbox wasn't the only incident. Just a few months after passing her test, Hanna had driven into a snow-filled ditch. Unless the snowplough had been out, it wasn't always easy to see the edge of the road in winter. She hadn't been able to afford a recovery truck, so one of the neighbours had helped her pull the car out with their tractor. She had given them one of her father's bottles of vodka as thanks.

The two women drove over to Möckelmossen. As before, there were a few people dotted around, but since the area was no longer cordoned off, it was easier to find a place to park. Hanna left the car right outside the rest area.

Rebecka gripped her arm, clutching it so hard that Hanna grimaced.

'I don't know if I can do this.'

'You don't have to,' said Hanna. 'But I think it could be good for you. Let's stay here for a minute, then we can see how you feel.'

They sat in silence for a moment. Axel's words came back to Hanna: *You of all people should know that.* Hinting that Rebecka had lied to her.

'Did you talk to Axel about me?' Hanna asked.

'What do you mean?'

Hanna hesitated, reluctant to repeat what Axel had said.

'Come on,' said Rebecka.

'Axel said you didn't like me.'

Rebecka stared at her with a look of shock and anger before opening the door and climbing out. Hanna hurried after her, following her into the rest area. She wanted to apologise, but couldn't make the words come out.

Why had she asked about Axel here? When it came to Rebecka, her defences had always been weak.

There were now considerably more flowers and candles than there had been the day before, clustered up against the wall where Joel had been slumped. Hanna wondered how people could have known his location with such accuracy. The small crowd kept a respectful distance.

Had they done this for Ester too? The woman her father had murdered. He claimed she had fallen and hit her head, that that was what had killed her, but it didn't fit with her injuries.

The candles flickered in the breeze. The wall was providing some shelter, but a couple had already blown out. The remaining flames failed to light up the grey afternoon, and the faces all around them were bathed in shadow. The grey haze felt compact out in the middle of the alvar. It no longer seemed living, it was dead – and, if it was possible, even more threatening.

'I should have brought something,' said Rebecka.

'Drop that thought right now.'

'But . . .'

'No.'

Rebecka bit her lower lip, only just managing to hold back the tears. A few heads turned in their direction, but they quickly looked away when they realised who she was.

Hanna scanned the crowd for the blonde woman, but she couldn't see her anywhere. Still, she took out her phone and snapped the crowd as discreetly as she could. It was as she was taking a picture of the flowers and candles that she noticed them: the bloody crane's-bill flowers. They hadn't been left as a bouquet, but were growing in the crack between the ground and the wall. Rebecka noticed her taking pictures, but didn't ask why. Without a word, Hanna put her phone away.

Right then, an elderly woman came forward.

'It's such awful news,' she said. 'I'm so sorry for your loss.'

On hearing her voice, Hanna recognised her: the woman

had been their art teacher in high school. One of the better ones, though Hanna couldn't recall her name. She gave Rebecka a hug.

'It's wonderful to see you back here,' she said, squeezing Hanna's elbow.

She sounded like she genuinely meant it.

The art teacher walked back to her car, and Hanna turned to Rebecka to see whether she'd had enough. A few metres away, she noticed a woman who was staring straight at her. The look in her eyes was so full of hate that Hanna found herself taking a step back.

It was Maria.

Ester's daughter.

Friday 17 May

Chapter Twenty-Nine

Hanna was the last member of the team to arrive for the morning meeting. Being late was starting to become something of a habit for her, but this time it wasn't intentional, and she was embarrassed. She was also wearing the same clothes as yesterday, considerably more crumpled than they had been the day before. It was probably fairly obvious that she hadn't managed to get much sleep.

Daniel smiled. Hanna didn't like the feelings his smile woke in her, and simply nodded in reply.

Fabian had smiled at her as she stood in the garage beneath the station in Stockholm, waiting for the lift. Starved of that kind of attention, she had smiled back. That was how it had all begun.

'Nice of you to join us,' said Ove.

Though comments like that had always been directed at other people, the feeling of being back at school washed over Hanna, and she sat down and tried to stop her cheeks from flushing. Even Carina was smiling now, though hers was more openly malicious than anything.

Hanna hadn't been prepared for the shock of bumping into

Ester's daughter yesterday, nor for the suspicions it had raised in her. Could it be Maria who was making the anonymous calls? She hadn't dared go over to ask. Hadn't wanted to risk causing a scene. She was there for Rebecka, after all.

Hanna had gone home with Rebecka afterwards, and ended up staying so late that she slept over in Gårdby. Petri had seemed relieved to have her there; it was obvious he had no idea how to deal with his wife's grief. Rebecka's mother had called, but Rebecka had asked her to stay away. Sonja had also brought Molly over for a while, but she eventually took her home again. The little girl was going to sleep in the fort they had built. Petri had anxiously asked if it was outside, but Sonja reassured him it wasn't.

There was a certain amount of fear on Öland that the perpetrator might kill again. In cases like this, people reacted with their hearts rather than their minds, and the media had painted the entire case as a mystery. The beaten boy who had been found in the middle of the alvar. The evil lurking in the darkness, ready to strike again. Hanna was sure they were wrong, and that there was some kind of connection between the victim and the perpetrator. Then again, she also had more information than they did. The media didn't know about the knife, for example, but it was only a matter of time. Still, regardless of how sure she was, she couldn't guarantee that there wouldn't be more victims.

'Did you find out anything else from Rebecka yesterday?' Erik whispered to her.

Hanna shook her head. What did he think of her? That she would use the visit to the rest area to put pressure on her friend? Then she remembered that that was the exact reason she had given for going over there, and blushed.

In truth, she and Rebecka had spent the evening wallowing in memories, both shared and individual; Rebecka's memories of Joel. Hanna felt she had a better picture of him than before, though she hadn't learned anything that needed to be followed up. She was also less worried about her friend now. Rebecka had more people around her than Hanna ever had. Neither of them had said a word about Maria, probably because Rebecka hadn't recognised her.

Maria had given several interviews after her mother's death, and Hanna had read them after one of her visits to Lars in jail. It had been a good visit, full of talk about their fishing trips to Grankullavik. About Pippi Longstocking. Hanna had always loved hearing about her as a girl. But when she got home that day, she felt as though she needed to be reminded of what he had done. That he couldn't be trusted.

She was back there again now, in those same thoughts. Was it Maria who had been phoning her? Hanna had received yet another call that morning, following exactly the same pattern as yesterday: a fire taking hold, then a scream. It had made her even more certain it was a recording. But from where?

Ove was watching her with a frown. She met his eye as steadily as she could, and after a few seconds he looked away, across the room.

'I've pushed forensics for the test results,' he said. 'We're their priority, but nothing is ready yet. They've promised to try to check the knife today.'

Hanna would have been surprised if any of the results had come in already. It was only the third day of the investigation.

Ove had pinned up a picture of the knife, and said that he would task someone with trying to trace it. It was made by

Mora, and was the type used for all kinds of activities: outdoor life, carpentry, hunting, and so on.

'Things went better with the medical examiner,' Ove continued. 'Joel died of a single stab wound to the abdomen; it ruptured his spleen, and he bled to death. Aside from that, he had a broken rib and contusions all over his body. The blood tests revealed hash, and the examiner also found DNA in the wound on his face. Saliva.'

This was another piece of good news: the DNA probably came from whoever had killed him. With both the knife and the DNA, Hanna wanted to believe that this was a perpetrator who was unlikely to get away.

'Should we get a DNA swab from Fanny Broberg?' asked Erik.

'Not yet,' said Ove. 'Let's run it through the database first. But given the threat she sent him, she's still our main lead. Not to mention the fact that she and the others saw Joel that night.'

'What about Axel Sandsten?' asked Carina.

'You'll have to log in and read the updates on the system.'

His words made Carina's face darken.

'He's been ruled out,' Amer explained. 'He didn't leave the office until two fifteen in the morning, just like he said.'

'The other two kids backed up Fanny's account of what happened when she met Joel,' said Erik. 'But I'll see whether there's anything that contradicts that.'

'I think you should interview the three of them again,' said Ove. 'Ramp up the pressure.'

Both Erik and Hanna nodded. She felt guilty for having abandoned him yesterday, but she doubted it had affected the investigation.

'Do we have any other leads?' asked Daniel.

'I was looking into the bloody crane's-bill flower,' said Carina. 'The flower itself doesn't seem to symbolise much, but if we look at the number and the colour, it means "You are my everything" and "I love you and promise you fidelity."'

'I don't think it means anything,' said Hanna. 'I was taking some photos at the rest area yesterday and noticed that they grow wild there.'

'But couldn't it suggest that it's some kind of romantic drama?' Carina insisted.

Love was often a motive, particularly when it was unrequited, but Hanna had trouble seeing Nadine as the perpetrator here. Particularly not the kind of perpetrator who cared about the symbolism of flowers. She was just about to say as much, but Ove got in before her:

'OK, keep looking into it, Carina,' he said. 'Amer, how's it going with the cyclist?'

'Haven't managed to find him yet, I'm afraid.'

'Let's increase our efforts on that,' said Ove. 'Given where the knife was found, he might have tossed it there.'

'Isn't it weird that the driver, Samuel Herngren, seems to have been swallowed up by . . . the ground?' asked Hanna.

She had been about to say fog. That was how it had felt while she was at Möckelmossen yesterday, like she could walk out into the haze and disappear.

'Maybe something happened to him,' Erik suggested.

'Or maybe he's our killer,' said Daniel. 'And now he's lying low. He was suspected of another assault, after all.'

'Either way, we need to track him down,' said Ove. 'I'll request a location on his phone. Can you dig deeper into that old assault case?'

Daniel nodded.

* * *

After the meeting, Hanna went to the cafeteria to grab a coffee. She hadn't had time beforehand. Hearing quick footsteps behind her, she turned around. She had been sure it would be Erik, but was surprised to see Carina.

Hanna paused, assuming Carina must have something she wanted to discuss with her, but her colleague simply walked by, turning and glaring at her with the same expression as Maria the day before.

In an alternative universe, Hanna would have marched after her and demanded answers. Instead, she fixed her eyes on the floor. Evasive and weak. The same way she had handled Maria.

Hanna had always struggled to deal with people who didn't like her, particularly when the reason was her father. She decided to clear the air with Erik at the very least.

Chapter Thirty

Once the meeting was over, Erik hurried back to his desk. Supriya was picking up her parents from the airport that afternoon, and the weather forecast was making her nervous – there was now a chance of thunder. Erik had promised her he would buy a few extra duvets, not that he knew when he was meant to find the time. According to Google, Ikea was his best bet.

Hanna came over to his desk with a cup of coffee.

'I can cope with the investigation, despite my history with Rebecka.'

'Good,' he said. 'Though I never thought otherwise.'

At first, Erik couldn't understand why she had spoken up, but then he realised that she must have misinterpreted what he said during the meeting. All he had wanted to know was whether Rebecka had said anything useful. Or maybe it was to do with yesterday, with the fact that she had run off with her friend. He was just about to get up and follow Hanna, who was already halfway back to her own desk, when reception called. Tilde, one of Fanny's friends, was down there with her mother, and she wanted to talk to him.

'On my way,' Erik said, slamming down the receiver.

He hurried over to Hanna's desk and explained what was going on. Surely she would see that he thought she was a good cop now: he wanted her in there with him.

'I'll get us an interview room,' she said.

Erik opened the door to reception. Tilde was standing by the window, looking out at the parked cars. She was wearing a pair of tight white jeans and a blue sweater. Her mother was sitting on the sofa behind the colourful plastic animals that were big enough for children to ride. Erik was fairly sure he had seen her before, at the local bank on Norra Långgatan. In fact, she was dressed as though she was on her way there now. Both turned to face him, and Tilde failed to hide her fear. The look on her face gave Erik a jolt of hope about what she had come to tell him.

'You can wait here,' he told Tilde's mother.

'That's fine, I already know what she's going to say.'

'Come with me,' he said to Tilde.

After a quick glance at her mother, she did as he said.

In the interview room, Hanna started the tape recorder and explained who was present and why. She then turned to Tilde.

'So, what did you want to tell us?'

'I lied yesterday,' she said. 'When I talked to you.'

Erik explained for the tape that Tilde had nodded towards him.

'What really happened when you met Joel in the woods?' he asked.

Tilde's nerves were starting to get the better of her. She was tugging at the ragged sleeve of her sweater, her eyes darting around the room. Beads of sweat had begun to glisten on her forehead, which was bumpy with foundation-caked spots.

'We hit him,' she whispered.

Her body seemed to slump with a confused mix of relief and fear over how they might react.

'What do you mean by "hit"?' Erik asked softly. 'Could you elaborate?'

'Fanny punched him a couple of times.'

'Where?'

'In the head and the stomach.'

'Anything else?' asked Hanna.

'He fell over, so we started kicking him too.'

'All three of you?' asked Erik.

'Yes,' said Tilde. 'But mostly Fanny.'

Considering how small Tilde was compared to her friend, Erik didn't find it hard to believe that Fanny had been the ringleader. The kind of abuse the teenager was describing didn't involve a knife, but before he asked her about that, he wanted her to give them her full version of what they had done to Joel.

'Go on,' said Erik. 'What happened next?'

'Joel got up and walked off.'

'Are you lying again now?' asked Hanna.

For the first time, Tilde looked straight at them.

'Please, we didn't kill him. He got up and walked off. You have to believe me. We'd messed him up pretty badly, but he could still walk.'

'Did any of you use a knife?' asked Erik.

Tilde began sobbing.

'You need to tell us exactly what happened,' said Hanna. 'This is a murder investigation.'

'Joel went totally crazy after he got up,' said Tilde. 'He pulled out a knife and started waving it around, screaming that he'd cut us. But I swear, he got up and walked off.'

Erik produced a picture of the knife they had found and showed it to Tilde.

'Was this the knife?'

'It was so dark, but I think so.'

'What were you fighting about?' asked Erik.

'Money.'

'Money for what?'

'I don't know.'

'Hash?'

'No idea.'

Erik asked her to take them through the assault again, and nothing she said caused either him or Hanna to react. Tilde's hands were clasped in her lap, and he asked her to hold them out. She didn't have any cuts.

'Who spat on Joel?' asked Hanna.

Tilde jerked, as though a gob of spit was even worse than a clenched fist.

'I didn't see anyone do that.'

'So what did you do after Joel left the woods?'

'We stayed there.'

'All three of you?'

'No, Fanny left after maybe ten minutes, but Lukas and I stayed and talked. About Fanny and all the stuff she does.'

'Why did you lie about beating up Joel?' asked Erik.

'Because of Fanny. She'd kill me if . . .'

'Did you see which way Joel went after he left you?' asked Hanna.

'No, it was dark, and we were behind the school.'

At that moment, Erik realised what Tilde was so afraid of.

'Do you think Fanny killed Joel?'

Her eyes seemed to scream that she wanted to say no, but she didn't.

'Yeah. Who else could've done it?'

Erik ended the recording and led Tilde back down to her mother. She walked into her mother's open arms and buried her face in the grey coat.

'What happens now?' the mother asked.

'It's too early to say, but it's good that Tilde told us the truth.'

Erik headed back to the interview room, where Hanna was waiting.

'What do you think?' he asked.

'It was pretty obvious from the outset that they'd beaten him up.'

'Maybe, but if they'd killed him, shouldn't his body have been behind the school?'

'Yeah,' said Hanna. 'It seems more likely that Fanny followed Joel and then killed him herself. What did the teacher say, Isak Aulin?'

'It's all in the report I wrote yesterday.'

'I haven't had time to read it,' said Hanna. It almost looked like she was smiling.

'He confirmed that Fanny is a troublemaker and that they've been having problems with her at school, but I don't think he understands just how big the problem is. He didn't have a clue what was going on when Molly was being choked.'

'There's one thing I still can't make sense of,' said Hanna. 'Why did Joel end up all the way out in Möckelmossen?'

'Maybe Fanny dumped him there to lead us astray,' said Erik. 'Right now I can't see any other plausible explanation.

Though the question is how she got him out there, given she only has a moped.'

'She could've got hold of a car,' said Hanna. 'I was already driving at her age. Should we go and talk to Lukas?'

Erik didn't think they had time. 'I'll call him.'

Once Lukas realised that Tilde had been to see them, he also confessed to beating up Joel. Like his friend, he said that Joel had pulled out a knife and walked away. That Fanny had left a while later. All Lukas knew about the conflict was that it was over money, and he was insistent that the only reason he had gone along that night was because Fanny had asked him to. There was just one point on which their accounts differed: Lukas had seen Fanny spit in Joel's face.

'We need to run this past Ove,' Erik said once he ended the call. 'Then we need to find Fanny and confront her with what Tilde and Lukas have told us.'

The Last Day

'I think we should sing for Gabriel!' Ulrika shouts.

Some of the red wine sloshes from her glass as she stands up, and Joel tries to catch Linnea's eye. They've joked about this before, about how embarrassing people are when they drink. How smoking is so much better. But that was before it made her flip out.

'No, please.' Gabriel shakes his head.

'Yes!' Mum eggs her on, despite hating it when people sing for her.

Petri starts, the only one of the adults who can actually hold a tune. His voice is deeper than when he talks, much nicer to listen to. He actually sang in a choir for a while, but quit because he didn't think he had time. He hasn't drunk much either. Joel can't remember ever having seen him drunk.

'Happy birthday, honey,' Ulrika says, kissing Gabriel on the lips.

Elias makes gagging sounds, and Molly giggles in embarrassment. Joel cuts off a piece of chickpea burger and smothers it in Béarnaise sauce before lifting it to his mouth. He gazes longingly at the steaks the others are eating as he chews, but

Linnea is a vegetarian and it wouldn't feel right to sit next to her and eat a bloody lump of meat.

'I want to tell a joke,' says Molly.

'I think that's enough now,' Mum says as Petri gives her an encouraging smile.

Molly chooses to respond to his smile, and tells the same incomprehensible joke about a German, a Dane and a Swede called Bellman that she has already told twice. Something about a cork that ends up all the way in China. Joel usually manages to listen, but he just can't do it right now.

'Can we leave the table?' Elias asks once Molly is done.

'Of course,' says Ulrika. 'I'll shout for you when it's time for the cake.'

The adults are talking about how great the new barbecue is, and Joel feels the pressure mounting in his chest. This isn't the kind of future he wants. Sitting around, talking about possessions as though they actually mean anything. Still, it's better than when they talk about politics. Ulrika once got so angry with Petri that she threw him out.

Linnea tilts her head towards the house, and Joel nods. They excuse themselves and head inside. Elias and Molly are watching TV in the living room. Some children's horror show about a kid who walks around whistling in a white mask. Molly had been so scared by an episode she'd seen at home that she'd had to turn off the TV.

'Can you teach me to draw portraits?' asks Linnea.

'I can try, if you get some paper and pencils.'

'Shhh!' Elias hisses, eyes locked on the screen.

'Yes, baby boss.'

Elias sticks out his tongue at her.

* * *

They sit down in the kitchen, mostly so they can get some peace. Joel starts by sketching Linnea, describing the process step-by-step as he goes. She then draws him, and the final image is much better than he expected. You can almost tell it's supposed to be him, though the eyes aren't quite right. They look far too happy.

'Has something happened?' asks Linnea. 'You seem sad.'

'No,' Joel tells her.

He doesn't have the energy to talk about Fanny, not with Linnea. Though maybe he should call Nadine.

Ulrika and Mum come into the kitchen with a stack of plates each. Linnea holds up her drawing, but Mum is the only one who pays her any attention. She heaps her with so much praise that Joel feels embarrassed. Why does she always have to be so over the top?

'Time for the cake,' says Ulrika. 'Can you help us set the table?'

Linnea immediately gets up, but Joel takes his time. Why can't Gabriel and Petri help? At least Gabriel usually does. Whenever Joel stays for dinner, it's often Gabriel who cooks. He makes really good Asian food. Ulrika takes out a shop-bought *prinsesstårta* from the fridge, and Mum begins taking down plates.

'Not those ones,' says Ulrika. 'We'll use the good china.'

Joel can see that Mum is annoyed, but she puts back the plates without a word. Linnea goes over to the glass cabinet and takes out the right plates.

Elias and Molly start clapping as the cake is carried outside. Petri's eyes look glossy, and his cheeks are flushed.

Has he been drinking? Fighting? Both?

* * *

The minute they finish eating, Mum tells Joel to take his sister home and put her to bed.

'But it's not even dark yet!' Molly protests.

'It's almost nine o'clock,' Petri tells her. 'This time yesterday, you were already fast asleep.'

'And no story tonight,' says Mum. 'Straight into bed.'

'Please?' Molly pleads.

'No.'

Mum looks at Joel as she says it, and he nods.

'Of course we'll read a story,' Joel whispers to Molly the minute they are out of earshot.

The setting sun has turned the sky pink.

'It looks like it's on fire,' says Molly.

'It does, doesn't it.'

Joel lets Molly skip brushing her teeth and lies down next to her. She has an extendable bed, and they recently pulled it out to its full length. Not that she needs it, but because she wants to feel big. Sadly, it doesn't extend width-wise.

Joel reads her the first chapter from a book about a beggar boy called Tam.

'One more chapter, please?' she begs, though she can barely keep her eyes open.

They have already read the entire series before, and both know that Tam eventually becomes a dragon rider.

'OK,' says Joel.

'One more,' Molly mumbles once he finishes. Her eyes are no longer open.

'No, that's enough now,' he says, getting up from the bed.

He pulls her unicorn duvet up to her chin, kisses her on the forehead and leaves her room.

* * *

Joel lies flat out on his bed. Just to be on the safe side, he sets the alarm on his phone, though he knows he won't be able to sleep. He stares at the wire of the lamp hanging from the ceiling. Petri keeps promising to get him a ceiling rose, but he never actually gets round to it. The house is full of things he has promised to fix, though he probably doesn't want to spend his spare time doing more of the same stuff he does at work.

Being a handyman is one of the last things Joel would ever want to be. He knows that a job in the healthcare system will be difficult, but at least he'll be able to work with people there, to help them.

It makes him nervous that Mum and Petri aren't home yet. What if they stay out past midnight?

Over an hour passes before Joel hears the sound of the door. He quickly turns out the light and crawls beneath the covers. Mum and Petri stomp up the stairs, making no attempt to be quiet. As expected, she pops her head around his door, and he makes a real effort to breathe heavily. Fifteen minutes later, once the sounds from outside have died down, Joel gets up and moves over to his computer to pass the rest of the time.

At ten to twelve, he pulls on a hoody. He doesn't want to have to rummage through all the jackets downstairs. He opens the bottom drawer of his desk and takes out the knife he keeps hidden beneath an empty notepad. Pulls it out of its sheath and gently touches the sharp edge. The blade is made of stainless steel, the handle some kind of rubber. He pushes it back into its sheath and then stashes it in the pocket of his sweatshirt.

Joel tiptoes downstairs, avoiding all the creaky floorboards. He pauses when he reaches the front door. He could still change his mind. Turn towards the kitchen and drink a glass of milk instead. Go back up to bed and sleep through the rest of the night. Hope that it all works out for him and Molly. That Fanny wasn't serious with her threats.

The only problem is that Joel is sure she is, and that he needs to make her back down somehow. He opens the door and steps out into the night.

He glances over to his bike, but decides not to take it. Instead, he begins walking along the road.

Joel doesn't want to get there too early. Doesn't want to have to wait anxiously like some nervous little kid.

Gårdby is almost completely dark. It's hours since the sun went down, and the moon is hidden behind a cloud. Jesus, he hates the darkness, so much so that he still sleeps with a nightlight on. And, like the idiot he is, he didn't think to bring a torch. He'll have to make do with the light on his phone instead.

The sound of grasshoppers fills the air. They aren't crickets, as some people think. He is freezing. It's much colder than when he took Molly home, and the wind has picked up.

A bird begins chirping, singing with bright, fast tones. At first, Joel is surprised, but then he realises it must be a night singer, a nocturnal bird of some kind. Possibly a nightingale. Or a marsh warbler. It's as though it is singing to make him turn back, and there it is again: the thought that it isn't too late. That he could turn back and pretend he simply went for a walk, if anyone is up. But this time, the thought is nothing but an echo of what he felt inside the front door, so he keeps walking.

He has no choice.

Chapter Thirty-One

'There's always a chance they're lying,' said Ove, giving the drawer in his desk a look of such longing that Hanna came close to getting up and opening it for him. 'Tilde and Lukas could have come up with this story to shift the blame onto Fanny.'

'Yeah, and three people would definitely find it easier to move a body,' said Erik.

What a turncoat, Hanna thought to herself. It seemed far more likely that Joel had walked off on his own, as both Lukas and Tilde claimed, and that Fanny had followed him – something Erik had said he agreed with just a few minutes earlier. Fanny had a history of violence, and Hanna didn't think Tilde was capable of lying like that, not based on their interview with her. Still, they couldn't afford to narrow their focus too much.

'I'll send forensics to the woods behind Gårdby School,' said Ove. 'That may be where Joel was killed. Find Fanny, and put more pressure on her.'

Ove was talking unusually quickly. Probably because he was eager to get rid of them.

'Can we get her DNA?' asked Hanna.

'Absolutely. Get her prints too.'

Hanna and Erik didn't even have time to leave Ove's office before he pulled out the drawer and they heard the sound of a plastic wrapper being torn from a carton of cigarettes.

'I think we need to pay Fanny another visit,' said Hanna. 'She's hardly going to come down to the station voluntarily.'

'I agree,' said Erik, 'but I'll try calling her anyway. See if you can get hold of her mother.'

They split up, Hanna returning to her desk. Neither of them had managed to speak to Fanny's mother yet, and Hanna got no further than the answer machine again this time. Fanny's father, Hans Broberg, was registered at the same address, and had been released from prison six or so months earlier after serving a two-year sentence for smuggling narcotics. There were no details about what he was doing now, nor where he was currently living, and the mobile phone registered in his name was switched off.

Erik came over with one of the technicians in tow.

'Fanny didn't answer, and according to her school she hasn't been in all week. I think we should go over there and try our luck. I'm guessing you didn't manage to get hold of her mother?'

Hanna shook her head and got to her feet.

In the car, Erik explained that Ove wanted them to join the technicians at Gårdby School, and to liaise with the staff there. They crossed the bridge in file: a patrol car, the technicians' van, plus their unmarked car.

Pulling up by the school, Hanna told the others to wait outside. The yard was empty, and the moment she reached for the white wooden handrail to the side of the steps, she felt a pang of longing. Life had been good here. It was only when she moved into year six that everything had changed. In the years that followed, she had occasionally returned to Gårdby School in an attempt to cling onto everything that had once been good. Perhaps that drive was the same as Fanny's, just expressed in a different way: Hanna had dragged Rebecka to all kinds of jumble sales and plays there.

She pushed open the green door. It was almost twenty years since she had last set foot inside, but the building smelled the same as ever. There was no one in the office, so Hanna knocked on one of the classroom doors and asked the teacher to step out into the corridor.

The teacher was far too young to have worked at the school while Hanna was a student. He was probably around her age, in fact, wearing jeans and a knitted sweater, with a small goatee. He was also taller than her. He introduced himself as Isak.

'Isak Aulin?' she asked.

'Yes, I spoke to one of your colleagues yesterday. What is this about?'

'Our forensic technicians need to search behind the school.'

'Can I ask why?'

'Afraid not.'

'Have you spoken to the head?'

'No.'

'Then I'd like to call and let her know.'

'That's fine.'

'Could you keep an eye on the children while I'm gone?'

Isak laughed when he saw the look on Hanna's face.

'Don't worry, I'm not asking you to go in. Just standing here will be fine.'

Hanna nodded as the familiar damned redness spread across

her cheeks. There was a window in the door, and she moved over so that she could peer into the room. She could see around twenty children inside, all juniors. Hanna had no specific memories from her first few years at the school, nothing but the sense that she had been happy here. What she did remember was the woods, and how she and Rebecka had pretended to be astronauts landing on alien planets.

A child appeared in the window, pulling faces at her. Hanna stuck out her tongue. She regretted it almost immediately as Isak came around the corner, but he just smiled and waved for the girl to sit down.

'How long can you wait?' he asked.

'Why?'

'The head doesn't think the children should be here during the search. She's given them the rest of the day off, but some will need to be picked up, and that'll probably take a little while.'

'I don't think we can wait,' said Hanna, 'but I'll talk to the technicians. The area they need to search is set back from the school itself, in the woods.'

Isak thanked her and stepped back into the classroom. Just a few seconds later, she heard the children cheer.

Without warning, a memory came flooding back to her: Hanna was sitting in a classroom just like this, and their teacher had told them that school was over for the day. The power had gone out, and didn't seem to be coming back. On another occasion, the school had closed because there was so much snow no one could actually get to it.

An unknown number flashed up on Hanna's phone. She didn't want to answer, but knew she had no choice. It could be something to do with the investigation. This time, the fire barely had time to take hold before she ended the call. What was next? Would they start a real fire?

With another quick glance at the classroom, Hanna headed outside and let the technicians know what was happening. They didn't look particularly happy to learn that dozens of children were about to come charging out of the building, but their investigation would probably take some time, and they obviously couldn't keep the children locked inside while they worked. Announcing their arrival in advance hadn't been an option either – that would simply provide an opportunity to remove or plant evidence. Hanna didn't bother asking whether they could wait; that was just something she had told Isak because it was easier than saying no.

She followed the technicians around the building and showed them into the woods, which weren't particularly big. She pointed out the rough area Lukas and Tilde had given her, and the uniformed officers began setting up the cordon. It was the only way to keep curious eyes away.

Hanna and Erik made their way over to Fanny's house. This time, the yard out front was empty, possibly because it was a few degrees colder than it had been the previous day. The sky was grey.

'Come in!' Fanny yelled as they knocked on the door of the main building.

Erik opened it, and they stepped inside, over a pile of shoes. They found Fanny on the sofa, watching TV.

'Why don't you answer your phone?' asked Hanna.

The mess in the living room reminded her of the second half of her childhood. The part she never wanted to revisit. Empty bottles, overflowing ashtrays, mountains of clothes on the floor. Hanna had often tried to keep the place neat and tidy, but she hadn't always managed. Social services had paid a couple of visits because of concerns about Kristoffer, and she had always made sure to tidy up beforehand. Forced Lars to stop drinking. It had been the same whenever Granny came over, though she always noticed anyway. Once, after a visit to Gårdby, she had asked whether Hanna wanted to come and live with her instead, telling her she didn't have to take responsibility for those two.

Hanna repeated her question: 'Why don't you answer your phone?'

'Don't feel like it.'

It was obviously an attempt to sound cocky, but it failed. Fanny was sitting with her knees drawn in to her chest, hugging them tight. She was wearing the same black t-shirt as before, but had swapped the jeans for a pair of grey sweatpants. Her self-confident veneer was gone, possibly because it had been easier for her to stand up to them outside, while she was working on her moped, though that was hardly the only reason. Her hands were cleaner now, and Hanna could see that several of her knuckles were split.

'Tilde and Lukas have both given us a different version of what happened in the woods.'

'Well, whatever they said, they're exaggerating,' said Fanny. 'They always do.'

Her eyes didn't leave the TV for a second. On the screen, a couple of teenagers were standing by an enormous window, peering down at a planet. Perhaps Fanny had dreamed of being an astronaut too. Erik moved over to the TV and switched it off.

'Hey, what the hell?' Fanny snapped.

Her tone was uncertain again. She sounded more afraid than angry.

'They both admit that you hit him,' said Erik. 'And that the three of you kicked him once he was on the ground.'

'Yeah, we slapped him around a bit, but that's it. It really wasn't a big deal.'

'So why did you lie about it?'

Hanna moved a shoebox from an armchair and sat down, but Erik chose to remain standing.

'I'm not stupid. I knew how it would look.'

'Did you spit on Joel?'

'Who said that?'

Once Fanny realised that neither of them planned to answer, she continued:

'I might've spat a bit when I was talking to him.'

Hanna leaned forward in her chair. 'What happened after Joel pulled out the knife?' she asked.

'He was waving it about and screaming like a total psycho, so we let him go.'

Erik showed Fanny the picture of the knife.

'Was this it?'

'Don't know.'

'Where did you go once you left?' asked Hanna.

'Home.'

'Can anyone confirm that?'

'Well, my mum definitely can't. She has to pop pills to get to sleep.'

Hanna assumed that Fanny used both her parents to get hold of drugs to sell.

'Where is your dad?' she asked.

'I don't fucking know. Haven't seen him in months.'

'Is it his hash you've been selling?'

Fanny stared at her. The pleading look in her eyes tied a knot in Hanna's stomach.

'I don't sell hash,' she said. 'Anyone who says I do is a liar.'

'Did you see Joel again on your way home?'

'No.'

'Are you sure about that?'

'Yeah.' Fanny turned to Erik. 'Is she always this thick?'

Erik replied by taking out the DNA kit, and the teenager finally lost out to her fear.

'You're not putting that fucking stick in my mouth!' she shouted.

'You don't have a choice,' said Hanna. 'If you don't do this voluntarily now, you'll have to come down to the station with us.'

Fanny reluctantly agreed to be tested, but as Erik put the DNA kit away and took out the fingerprint kit, her fear turned to panic.

'No!' Fanny roared. 'You fuckers are trying to frame me for this!'

Chapter Thirty-Two

The lump of clay looked like a fat old man who couldn't dance, but it kept twirling round and round on the wheel as though it owned the world.

Rebecka lifted her foot from the pedal and the lump of clay came to a halt.

She had been working on a fruit bowl for someone from Norra Möckelby, but the woman had just called to say she no longer needed it. Joel's name hadn't come up, but Rebecka knew that was the real reason: she wasn't expected to be able to work now that her son was dead. It was true, she couldn't. Everything she did came out wrong. Uneven and lopsided. After the phone call, she had thrown the rough bowl at the wall.

The woman had been so happy when she ordered it, telling Rebecka she was going to give it to one of her grandchildren as a wedding gift. But phoning up to cancel the order, she had sounded nervous.

Rebecka poked at one of the fat rolls on the lump of clay. It was supposed to be a teacup. She had decided to build up her stocks of those instead. There was a sign advertising her ceramics business down by the road, and both islanders and tourists came to buy from her. The cups sold best, followed closely by bowls and small jugs. Her plates sold pretty well too.

You should have a proper website, Mum.

That was what Joel had told her a few weeks earlier, even offering to set one up for her. Claiming it wasn't difficult if you used a pre-existing design. *Template* was the word he had used, explaining it to her when she didn't understand.

Kind, wonderful Joel. Rebecka grabbed the lump of clay and hurled it across the room. It hit the wall with a damp thud and dropped to the floor, landing not far from the broken fruit bowl.

Molly was at Sonja's again. Her grandmother was still keeping her off school, and while Rebecka was relieved that Molly wouldn't have to listen to people talking about Joel there, she also knew she couldn't stay home for ever. Sonja had told her what Fanny had done to Molly, and Rebecka felt like driving over there and giving her a good slap. Forcing some answers out of her. Had Fanny done anything to Joel? Could she have killed him, even? Sonja had said there was nothing to suggest she had, and that they had to let the police do their job.

Rebecka knew that she should have Molly back by now – it was pathetic not to be able to take care of her – but the girl was also much too clear a reminder of what they had lost. Rebecka had also noticed the way Petri looked at their daughter, how grateful he was that she was still alive. She felt the same way, of course, it was just that she wanted *both* her children.

Things had been OK between Joel and Petri, though he had never really been a proper father to him. It was only once

Molly was born that Rebecka had finally understood that, realising that Petri treated Joel with a kind of awkward benevolence and Molly with genuine warmth. She had brought it up with him, and though he didn't agree with her, he had made an effort to treat them more equally.

But I'm not his father, he had said.

And Sonja's not really your mother, Rebecka had thought, though she hadn't dared say it aloud. She was far too afraid of being left on her own for that. She knew it wasn't a rational fear, but it still paralysed her. Compared to Axel, Petri was so much better.

Rebecka reached for her phone. She found herself compulsively checking it now, skim-reading the messages she received, trawling online forums and newspapers.

She wanted to know what had happened to Joel, but things seemed to be moving so slowly with the police. With Hanna. And they weren't talking to her.

Axel's face stared up at her from the *Expressen* homepage. He was sitting in a black leather armchair – probably in his office, because she could see his framed awards in the background – and not a single hair on his head was out of place. His blue eyes were looking straight at the camera. Rebecka's hand began to shake so much she could barely click the link, but the image assaulted her again once she did, accompanied by a huge pull quote: *The sense of loss is awful.* She only managed to read two sentences before closing the tab.

Anger dragged her up from her chair. She came close to ripping down the shelf of cups from the wall, but managed to restrain herself in time. It would only make things harder for her, not him.

Where did he get the fucking nerve?

She wanted Axel to suffer, for him to grieve for Joel, but she doubted he meant a single word of the interview.

There was a knock on the window, making Rebecka jump, but she relaxed when she saw Ulrika outside, waving at her. So, she had finally dared come over. Gabriel had been at the rest area in Möckelmossen yesterday, and he had seemed far more upset to see her than she had to see him. He had actually avoided even looking at her. The man was a coward, a complete fake. None of what he had said to her was true. Right now, Rebecka could only handle seeing his bad sides.

She rinsed the clay from her hands and stepped outside.

'I'm so, so sorry,' Ulrika told her. She looked like she was on the verge of tears, though her sense of relief that death hadn't struck her family was also tangible. 'I should have come as soon as I heard, but I . . . I didn't want to bother you.'

Rebecka nodded but didn't step forward to give Ulrika a hug. She didn't have the energy to smooth over her neighbour's shortcomings. Getting in touch was the very least Ulrika should have done. Her friend paused, at a loss for what to say. She glanced over at her own house.

'Elias went in ahead of me, and you know, there's always the worry that—'

'Elias is home already?'

'Yes, the school called to say we should pick up the kids. The police are there, doing some kind of search in the woods.'

Ulrika's mouth kept moving, but Rebecka had stopped listening the minute she said the word *search*. Did the police think Joel had been killed outside the school?

Ulrika placed a hand on her arm, trying to catch her eye. 'I just thought you should know.'

'Thanks.'

Rebecka felt like screaming at her to leave, but Ulrika kept talking about how sorry she was that she hadn't come sooner. That what had happened was so awful. That Rebecka only had to say if she needed help with anything.

I slept with your husband.

For a split second, Rebecka worried she had said it aloud, because Ulrika was staring at her, but it was just another thought she hadn't dared share. No, she didn't want to say it. On the whole, Ulrika was a decent person, and she didn't deserve what Rebecka and Gabriel had done to her. How could she have been so dumb and so selfish? The thought that what had happened to Joel was a punishment of some kind flashed through her mind, but she quickly batted it away.

'Linnea has taken it all so hard,' said Ulrika. 'She's not eating or sleeping.'

Do you think I care? Rebecka felt like screaming, but instead she made do with a nod.

'Gabriel too,' Ulrika continued.

Her eyes seemed to bore into Rebecka, as though she wanted her to say something about Gabriel. What did she suspect?

'He's . . .'

The sound of a door opening made Ulrika trail off. Elias was standing on the porch, shouting that he wanted a biscuit.

'I have to go,' said Ulrika.

'You do that.'

The minute Ulrika stepped into her house, Rebecka hurried down to the school.

Chapter Thirty-Three

'What a dump,' Erik muttered.

He fastened his seatbelt before starting the engine, the stench of the house still lingering in his nose. Old sweat and cigarette smoke, plus a hint of something worse: vomit and urine. It was obvious that Fanny was not in good shape, but they had eventually managed to get her fingerprints.

'Having a drug user for a parent is no excuse,' said Hanna. 'Or an absent parent, for that matter . . .'

'Of course not, but sometimes it can be part of the explanation, at least.'

A drunk. That was what his colleagues in the station cafeteria had called Hanna's father. Erik's curiosity had led him to google the murder – he couldn't access the investigation itself without leaving a trace – and he had learned that Lars Duncker had spent ten years in jail before returning to Öland, where he died four years later. That was probably how long it had taken him to drink himself to death. An article published just after the trial mentioned his two children, but said nothing about a wife.

'Do you think we should get in touch with social services?' he asked.

'It hasn't helped so far,' said Hanna. 'I didn't count, but they've been contacted on at least twenty occasions.'

He wanted to ask her what she thought *could* help, but they were in the middle of a murder investigation. Their first task was to work out what role Fanny had played in Joel's death. Her current state of mind might have more to do with guilt than her home environment.

'Should we have brought her in?'

'Not yet,' said Hanna. 'Not until we've got more evidence.'

She took a breath like she planned to go on, but no words came out.

'I'll stop off at the school so we can see how forensics are getting on,' he said.

'OK.'

The school was virtually empty by the time they arrived. There was no one in the yard out front, but a child's face appeared in one of the windows, pressing her nose to the glass until a teacher came to lead her away. At one side of the building there was an officer in uniform keeping watch. For once, Erik didn't know his name, but he and Hanna said hello and then walked round to the woods.

The technician working closest to the cordon was called Klas, and he came over when he spotted them. He had been part of the forensics team that went out to Möckelmossen when Joel's body was first found.

'How's it going?' asked Erik.

'We've found the place where Joel Forslund was beaten up,' Klas told him. 'Come through, I'll show you.'

They followed him over, pausing a few metres from a den that looked like a tipi. Nila would have loved playing here,

Erik thought. She had really inherited his love of nature. Through the sparse trees, he could make out a corn field. It was no more than twenty or so metres from the school, which was the only building he could see.

'It was a few metres further back,' said Klas, pointing to another clearing. 'Over there.'

'Are you able to tell us any more about what happened?' asked Erik.

'We can see that the victim was on the ground.'

'So do you think this is where he was killed?' Hanna asked.

'Probably not. There are quite a few blood spatters, but no more than that. There was more blood in the rest area, so I'd say he probably died there – or at some point on the way there, though that seems less likely. If you ask me, he was stabbed somewhere else entirely.'

The dead don't bleed, that was the fact the technician was basing his assumptions on. Joel's injuries suggested he had been bleeding for some time, and the blood at the rest area could easily have transferred from his sweater. Aside from the stab wound, Joel had bruises, a broken rib, and a gash on his temple. Erik guessed that the blood on the ground here had probably come from the latter.

'Anything else?'

'We've collected some rubbish. A few sweet wrappers and a cigarette butt, among other things, but I doubt it'll lead anywhere. There have been a lot of kids playing round here since that night. We've lifted a few shoe prints, but we skipped the ones we decided were too small. We'll be packing up and finishing off soon.'

Just then, they heard shouting over by the building. A woman's voice cut through the air.

'You have to let me go over there. He was my son!'

'Shit. It's Rebecka,' said Hanna, hurrying over to her.

By the time Erik arrived, Hanna had led her friend away from the cordon. Erik told the officer by the blue-and-white tape that the technicians were almost done.

He looked around. It seemed Fanny and the others had been telling the truth when they said that Joel had got up and walked away, but where had he gone? The road in front of the school went just two ways. His home was to the north, but Joel had never made it back there. Instead, he had been found a few kilometres to the south-west.

Had Fanny attacked him again?

Erik glanced over at Rebecka Forslund. She was still agitated, but Hanna seemed to have the situation under control. She was standing in front of her, her outstretched hands gripping Rebecka's upper arms. Speaking so quietly that Erik couldn't hear her, even though he was just a few metres away.

His phone rang.

'Forensics just confirmed that the knife was the murder weapon; the blood on the blade is Joel's,' said Ove. 'We've also managed to identify the fingerprints, which come from two people: Joel and Axel Sandsten.'

The Last Day

There are two mopeds parked outside Gårdby School, and Joel wonders who Fanny has dragged along this time. Probably Lukas. He's pretty sure the other moped is his.

Joel shoves his phone into his pocket and trudges around the back of the building. He sees their beams of light bouncing around between the sparse, black trunks, but there aren't two of them there, there are three. As Fanny hears him approaching, she shines her light straight in his face. The icy hatred in her eyes makes Joel want to turn around and run.

He doesn't know what he was thinking, how this is going to solve anything, but it's too late for that now. He can't turn back.

Lukas is grinning behind Fanny, Tilde standing by her side. The sight of her makes Joel's stomach lurch. What is she doing here? He has only ever been kind to her. Linnea told him that someone had locked Tilde in a cupboard in the school gym, and that she rarely has anyone to hang out with – that was why he suggested inviting her to the cinema.

Though her being here now explains why she looked so guilty on the bus.

Joel walks up to Fanny. She is the only one he needs to convince. The others are just noise.

'I want my money,' she tells him.

'No.'

'What d'you mean, "no"?'

'I already paid you.'

'Not for all of it.'

'I only had one bag.'

'Nope, you had one and Linnea had two.'

'You're lying, and even if—'

Fanny's fist slams into his temple, making the world spin. His head snaps to one side, a branch scratching his eye. Joel hunches over, gasping for air, and Fanny shoves him to the ground. This was clearly the signal the others were waiting for, because all three are soon kicking him. For some reason, Fanny's blows are the only ones that hurt. Someone must have dropped their torch, because the beam is shining straight into his eyes.

Should he pull out his knife? If he does, it will just make Fanny angrier, and she is so much stronger than him. Instead, Joel curls up with his arms over his head. If he protects his head, he might be OK.

Kick after kick hits his arms.

'You're gonna pay,' Fanny hisses. 'And you're going to stop sticking your nose in where it's not wanted.'

The rage that surges through Joel wipes out any pain.

'You're fucking crazy!' he roars, struggling onto his knees. 'You're an inbred fucking freak.'

Fanny is so shocked that she takes a step back. Joel fumbles for his knife, but doesn't have time to pull it out before she steels herself and kicks him in the chest. Joel falls backwards, and feels a crack. He tries to scream in pain, but all that comes out is panting. The panting is also all that is left of his anger.

He curls up again, shielding his head with his arms.

'That's enough now,' says Tilde. Lukas murmurs in agreement.

Joel almost hates them more, the pathetic tag-alongs. Maybe because they're much more like him than they are Fanny. They go along with things, but they have no idea what they actually want.

Fanny bends down over him.

'Your pathetic little outburst didn't help, you hear me? You're gonna pay, and you're gonna stop butting your nose in.'

Joel searches for his anger again, but all he can find is fear. He wraps his arms tighter around his head. The only thing he can do now is stay still and take it. A small part of him tells him he deserves this, imagining that it might make him feel better, help him hate himself a little less.

Fanny's next kick hits one of his hands, tearing it away from his head. Joel isn't quick enough: this time, her foot strikes his temple. Blood starts running down into his eye, and he imagines his mother standing in front of him. Her face is covered in blood, as is her top and her hands.

The fear is immediate: *Am I about to die?*

Fanny kicks him again.

'You're still the same little shit,' she hisses. 'The only freak is you, faggot.'

She spits at him, and Tilde grabs her arm.

'For God's sake . . .'

Joel doesn't know whether it is Tilde or Fanny who says it. Everything sounds warped, like maybe Fanny's kick knocked something out of place in his ear. He can hear rushing, clicking.

They step back. Joel can no longer see them, the light from the torch still blinding him. He struggles up onto all fours, reeling with dizziness. The pain in his chest is the worst. One of his ribs must be broken.

He wants to get away as quickly as he can, but he forces himself to stay still until the world stops spinning.

'What are you doing up?' Fanny asks.

Joel finally manages to pull the knife out of its sheath.

'Don't come any closer!' he roars. 'I'll cut you.'

The three of them are now staring at him. Joel is standing above the light of the torch, no longer blinded by it. The moon comes out from behind a cloud and their faces look oddly enlarged. Even Fanny looks scared, though he knows her anger will flare up again at any moment, and when that happens he doesn't want to be there to see it. Joel slowly backs away. When he bumps up against a tree, he turns around.

Chapter Thirty-Four

The words seemed to hover in the air between them. Hanna spoke, but nothing she said cut through. She couldn't get Rebecka to look at her. She tightened her grip on Rebecka's arms, repeating the same words again:

'I'm sorry, but I can't tell you why we're here.'

Rebecka pulled away, her gaze still stubbornly locked on the school building.

'Is that where he . . .'

'No, we don't think so.'

For the first time, Rebecka met her eye.

Hanna sighed to herself. She might have said more than she should, but she desperately wanted to soothe Rebecka's pain, the thing making her upper lip tremble. Besides, it wasn't as though she was stupid. Why else would they be searching the woods behind the school?

'So what do you think? Was it this Fanny girl who . . .'

'I'm sorry.' Hanna didn't say any more.

Rebecka turned to look at the school building again, as though it could provide her with answers. Hanna shouldn't be talking about what they did or didn't think. Not until they knew for sure what had happened. Assumptions were so fleeting. Anything that leaked had the potential to impact the investigation, and that wasn't all: people might also suffer. Children. If their suspicions about Fanny became widespread and it turned out she was innocent after all, she might never recover. That was why Hanna wanted to wait until they knew more before bringing her in.

She saw Erik approaching, and knew from his face that something had happened. Rebecka noticed it too.

'What's going on?' she asked.

'Hanna and I need to get back to Kalmar.'

'Why?'

'I'm afraid I can't say.'

Rebecka gave Hanna a pleading look, but Hanna simply shook her head. Rebecka closed her eyes. When she opened them again, they seemed completely different. They were dark with frustration and anger.

'You can't do this!' she shouted.

Hanna wanted Erik to leave. It was harder to manage Rebecka with him standing right there, watching everything. She didn't want him to question her. But she couldn't exactly say any of this, so instead she simply did her best to shut him out.

'How did you get here?' she asked Rebecka.

'You can't do this!' Rebecka repeated. 'I can't fucking cope with this.'

'Did you walk?'

Rebecka had often had outbursts as a teenager, but they rarely lasted long. Back then, the best way to make her anger subside had been to ignore it, but that didn't work as well now; her anger was mixed up with so much else.

'Yes, I walked,' she hissed.

'We'll give you a lift home,' said Hanna.

Rebecka reluctantly allowed Hanna to guide her over to the car, casting one last glance back to the school before climbing in. Hanna got into the back beside her.

'Do you want me to call someone?' she asked.

'Like who?'

'Like Petri, or your mum?'

Rebecka replied by turning away and shrugging off the hand Hanna had placed on her arm.

No one spoke as they drove the few hundred metres to her house, and the silence slowly expanded, transforming into something else. When Hanna had turned down a last-minute week in Greece because she hadn't wanted to leave her father and Kristoffer alone, Rebecka had refused to talk to her for three days. She hadn't gone on the trip herself, nor had she asked anyone else.

In truth, her father and Kristoffer had only been part of the reason. Though Hanna had saved enough to be able to afford the holiday, she wanted to hold onto the money until she really needed it. She had used it to pay for her bus ticket to Stockholm, and had also been able to afford a couple of weeks in a youth-hostel dorm. She had left for Stockholm without any real plan, and had come close to giving up after a few weeks. That was when her grandmother had stepped in and given her some money, and a day or two later, Hanna had found a job in a restaurant. Before long, she had even managed to find a sub-let flat of her own. Just a year later, she was admitted into the police academy.

Erik pulled up outside Rebecka's house, and she climbed out of the car without another word, slamming the door behind her. Hanna had an urge to follow her. It felt like something between them had broken, and she desperately wanted to fix it, but she couldn't. Her job was to investigate Joel's murder. She also doubted Rebecka would put up with her company right now. So she climbed into the passenger seat instead.

'OK, fill me in,' Hanna said the minute Rebecka had closed the front door.

'The blood on the blade was Joel's, and there were only two people's prints on the handle: Joel's and Axel Sandsten's.'

'But what about the CCTV footage?'

'The film came from Securitas, but we've got a new technician examining it in Ove's office.'

'Why Ove's office?'

'To keep it isolated. Ove thinks the footage might have been tampered with. He's going to get people going house to house in the area, and he's sending the technicians to examine the verges between the school and Joel's house. Fanny's too. We need to know where Joel went after he left the school.'

Hanna was so shocked she didn't know what to say. She turned to look at Rebecka's house. How was she supposed to look her in the eye and tell her about this, about Axel? About how she might have been wrong when she said he wasn't on the island when Joel was killed.

Chapter Thirty-Five

The sky above the Kalmar Strait was dark grey, and it felt like it was bearing down on them. Over on the mainland, Erik could see large black patches amid the grey. He hoped there would be some kind of release before his parents-in-law landed.

He glanced over at Hanna in the passenger seat. She hadn't said a word since they'd left Rebecka's house, and though he wanted to respect her silence, he couldn't. They needed to go through the new developments in the case before they got to the station.

'What do you make of the fingerprints?' he asked.

'It feels like there's no point thinking anything before we've checked the surveillance footage. I'm wondering about Fanny and Axel Sandsten. Do you think there could be some kind of link between them?'

'Like what?'

'Like maybe Axel has been selling Fanny hash.'

'Are you serious?'

The words came out with a laugh, and considering what Hanna had interpreted as criticism earlier, Erik was surprised she didn't react.

'Yes. Axel was into drugs in high school.'

Erik's phone began ringing, Supriya's name flashing up on the screen.

'Sorry, I need to take this,' he said. 'Could you put it on loudspeaker?'

Supriya was incredibly stressed ahead of her parents' visit, and if Erik didn't answer her now, things would only get worse. Hanna hesitated for a moment, then did as he asked.

'I'm on my way to the airport,' Supriya announced.

'Already?'

'Yeah, their plane lands in less than an hour, and I can't risk not being there.'

'*Pappa!*' Nila called from the back seat.

Clearly they were on loudspeaker too. Nila switched effortlessly between three languages, meaning Erik was *Pappa* and Supriya was *Aai*. Supriya actually spoke Hindi as well as Marathi, but they had decided that was probably one language too many for the young girl.

'Hi, honey. Are you excited?'

'Yes! *Aji* is bringing me a new dress. A pink one!'

Aji was Supriya's mother. Nila still hadn't quite grown out of the pink princess stage.

'Did you manage to buy the duvets yet?' Supriya interrupted.

Erik realised he should tell her she was on loudspeaker and that his colleague was in the car with him, but he decided not to. Hanna seemed to have frozen, and he guessed she didn't want to make a sound. He feverishly racked his brain for what he had told Supriya about Hanna – but why would she start talking about her now?

'Not yet, sorry,' he said. 'But I'm working on it.'

Erik had switched back to English. He often did. English

when he spoke to Supriya and Swedish with Nila. His wife sighed unhappily. He thought he could hear the patter of raindrops in the background. It must be raining over there.

'I'll get them, I promise.'

He ended the call.

'Why do you need to buy duvets?' Hanna asked. 'It's May.'

'My parents-in-law are coming to stay for two weeks, and my wife is worried they'll be cold.'

For once, his words actually made Hanna smile.

Erik wondered if this was an opening. He had taken a step back, but he still wanted to talk to her about her father, to show her that he didn't care about it the way she seemed to think he did. That there was no ill will in his curiosity. On the other hand, he was also fairly sure she wouldn't appreciate a direct question. Maybe he could take a roundabout route instead.

'You know, Ove asked me to keep an eye on you.'

For a second or two, Hanna tore her eyes from the windscreen and turned to look at him.

'Did he now?'

'Yeah, but I told him it was obvious you're a great cop. Because that's what I think – if that wasn't clear already.'

'Thanks, I guess.'

It didn't seem like Hanna had anything else to say on the matter. Erik had assumed she would be furious; it must be awful to be questioned because of something one of your parents had done. Strictly speaking, Ove had simply said he wanted to make sure Hanna was doing OK, and Erik felt a little guilty at having twisted his words in an attempt to make her talk.

'Honestly, I think he meant well.'

Just stop talking.

He could see it in her eyes and hear it in his own head, but still he couldn't do it.

'Did you know Ove before you came back? I got that impression.'

Hanna turned to look out at the water again. For a moment or two, Erik didn't think she was going to reply.

The first raindrops hit the windscreen as the car left the bridge.

'He led the investigation into my dad.'

'Oh, shit.'

Erik searched his memory, but he was fairly sure he hadn't read any statements from Ove; they were all from a police spokesperson. If Ove's name had cropped up anywhere, he would have remembered it. The investigation seemed to have been wrapped up quickly, and the press had been more focused on the crime itself. On how it had affected the small community. How it had brought back memories of previous fires.

They were fifteen minutes out from the station when the heavens finally opened. A flash of lightning cut across the grey sky.

Erik parked in the station garage and they hurried up to Ove's office. Erik opened the door without knocking, and closed it behind him. Ove was standing by the window with his arms folded, clearly unable to sit still.

'Hi, I'm Melina.'

The woman cast a quick glance at Erik and Hanna, her fingers still racing over the keyboard.

'Hi,' said Hanna, introducing herself with her first name.

Melina was in her late twenties, a Kalmar native, and she was the technician Erik got on best with. Primarily because she liked to try out new things. Just a few weeks earlier, she had dragged him to a tae kwon do taster session, but it wasn't something he planned to take up. All that kicking wasn't really his preferred type of workout.

'Well?' said Ove.

'Take it easy, I'm almost done,' said Melina. 'OK.'

She pressed Play, and Erik took a step forward so that he could see the screen. The same surveillance video they had watched earlier was playing: Axel Sandsten walking along Larmgatan outside his office, but the timestamp was different. He had left the office just after Tatjana.

'Shit,' Ove muttered. 'Was it manipulated here or not?'

'Hold on, let me call my contact at Securitas,' said Melina.

Just a few minutes later, she had the answer:

'That's the film that was sent over to us.'

She nodded to the screen, where Axel Sandsten and a 23:14 timestamp were frozen.

'I want Axel Sandsten in an interrogation room now,' said Ove. 'And I want the technician who received the CCTV footage in another one.'

'Who was it?' asked Erik.

'Benjamin Karlstedt,' Melina replied, a dogged tone to her voice.

Erik pictured Benjamin: a short, dark-haired guy in his early thirties. Quiet and efficient. His father had been in the force too. Why had he risked his job like this? Erik just couldn't understand.

Chapter Thirty-Six

The front door opened and Molly called up to her. Rebecka had felt so drained when she got back from the school that she had gone straight upstairs and climbed into bed, pulling the covers over her head. Trying to shut it all out: the police in the school yard, Hanna refusing to say what was going on. She had dozed off for a while, and now felt even more exhausted than before. She wanted to get up and go downstairs, but she couldn't seem to move. The footsteps on the stairs were Petri's, not Molly's.

He sat down on the edge of the bed and switched on the bedside lamp. Rebecka turned away from the glare.

'How are you doing, honey?'

How the hell do you think? she felt like screaming at him. He must have been able to see it on her face, because he stiffened and leaned back slightly. His entire body seemed to be quivering with indecision. He glanced longingly towards the doorway, and Rebecka felt like screaming again, for him to go this time. But he composed himself and stroked her cheek.

'Sorry. Obviously I know you're not OK.'

In that moment, Rebecka hated him and all his goddamn

awkwardness. Hers too. Petri glanced over at the door again, and she really did think he was about to get up and leave. Instead, he turned back towards her. His eyes were far too close together, and his nose much too big for his face. No, he was nowhere near as handsome as Gabriel, and she hated herself for being so superficial.

'But can't you talk about it? How you're doing, I mean?'

'Why?'

'Because I think it'd do you good.'

Sonja must have talked to Petri when he went to pick up Molly, sharing her concerns about how Rebecka seemed to be doing. Encouraging him to give her more support. After all, Petri always did as Sonja said. Who would he even be without her? No one. At times, it felt like Rebecka had married Sonja, not Petri.

'It hurts so much I wish I could disappear. Is that what you want to hear? Huh? Do you think I feel even a tiny bit better now?'

'Please, keep your voice down.'

Petri's words made Rebecka realise she had been shouting, and that started the tears flowing instead. At the fact that Joel was gone. At the fact that she didn't know what to do. At the fact that she was being so unfair to Petri. At least he was trying now. It wasn't entirely his fault that their relationship was the way it was. That they almost never really talked. That they only lived together to fool themselves that they weren't alone. That she had been having an affair with their neighbour for months.

Petri hesitantly placed a hand on her arm, and Rebecka pulled it to her. She could see that it hurt, but he let her press his hand to her heart until she had calmed down enough to talk.

'The police were looking for something in the woods behind the school today. But Hanna said that it's not where Joel died.'

'Yeah, I heard,' said Petri.

Rebecka noticed the hesitation in his voice and dragged herself up into a half-sitting position.

'What else have you heard?'

'They've been knocking on doors, asking if anyone noticed anything around midnight on Tuesday.'

'What do they think happened then?'

'I have no idea.'

The hesitation in his voice was still there.

'What else?' she demanded.

'They've been combing the roads.'

They heard a knock on the door, and Petri got up and hurried downstairs. Probably to prevent Molly from answering it. Rebecka followed him down. It could be a journalist who was sick of their calls being ignored, wanting a few words from the grieving mother, not just the despairing father. The police were the only people Rebecka wanted to talk to right now. She wanted to force answers out of them. But it wasn't the police. It was Molly's friend Vera and her mother.

'I'm really sorry about your brother,' said Vera, holding out a plastic tub. 'Mummy and I made chocolate balls.'

Vera's mother peered through to Rebecka.

'We were so sorry to hear the news, all of it. Vera asked what she could do, and this was the only thing I could think of.'

'Thank you,' said Molly. 'I love chocolate balls.'

'I know,' said Vera. 'Me too.'

'Do you—' Molly began, only to be interrupted by Vera's mother.

'We'll go now,' she said. 'We have to get home and make dinner.'

Rebecka still hadn't managed to say anything, but she nodded in a way she hoped came across as appreciative. In all likelihood, she looked horrendous. Molly gave her friend a hug and asked whether she could try one of the chocolate balls the minute the door closed.

'After dinner,' said Petri.

'When will that be?'

'Soon, but the food will cook quicker if you help me make it.'

Molly seemed OK at the moment. Sonja had sent a few pictures of her during the day, all happy ones, but she had also written that Molly's moods seemed to be more up and down than usual. That she could be laughing one minute and crying the next. Had she finally understood that Joel would never be coming back? Rebecka still wasn't sure.

Never was too big a concept for Molly.

Molly and Petri headed into the kitchen, and Rebecka turned back to the stairs. The darkness of the bedroom was calling to her, tempting her with its false promises of forgetting, but she forced her body to follow what was left of her family instead, sitting down on a chair in the kitchen. Petri had already started cooking, and judging by the ingredients on the worktop, he was planning to make mango chicken. He cut the chicken fillets while Molly sliced the leek. A little too quickly for Rebecka's liking, but she didn't have the energy to say anything.

Petri glanced over at her, and the corner of his mouth twitched. He probably knew exactly what she was thinking: that Molly wasn't being careful enough with the knife.

She smiled at him, mouthed *sorry*, and he nodded.

Words weren't everything in a relationship. She and Petri had been living together for over ten years now, and they had so many shared memories.

'Are you hungry, Mummy?' asked Molly.

'Yes,' said Rebecka. This time, she really did feel like she would be able to eat.

Chapter Thirty-Seven

From the moment Hanna first learned that Axel Sandsten's fingerprints were on the knife, it had felt as though she was on a downward slope. During the drive back to the station, and while Melina was working on the CCTV footage, she had slipped further and further down.

The rest of the team had come to Ove's office for a quick debrief while Axel Sandsten and Benjamin Karlstedt were brought in for questioning. The technician was thirty-two, and had been working for the Kalmar Police for nearly three years. According to Ove, he had barely taken a day off sick, and had done his job without any complaints, either from him or his superiors.

'Erik and Hanna, I want you to question Axel Sandsten,' said Ove.

'No.'

'Why not?'

Hanna grappled for an answer. There was so much that was niggling away at her. The fact that she had told Rebecka that Axel wasn't on Öland when Joel died. How much she disliked him. But plenty of other things too that had nothing to do with the investigation: the fact that someone clearly didn't want her there. She couldn't find any good answer.

'OK, you take him instead,' Ove said to Amer. 'Hanna and Daniel can question Benjamin.'

'Wouldn't it be better if I did it?' Carina turned to look at Hanna as she spoke, almost as though she was challenging her with her gaze.

'No,' said Ove. 'Hanna has never met Benjamin. Have you had much contact with him, Daniel?'

'Almost none,' he replied.

Carina was about to argue, but Ove received word that Benjamin was waiting for them in interview room three. During the short walk down there, Hanna recognised yet another thing that was gnawing away at her: jealousy of Erik's family. The fact that he had a partner and child and parents-in-law he clearly didn't mind coming to stay. Hanna had only her grandmother and her brother, and barely even that. Granny's dementia was so severe that she no longer remembered who Hanna was, and Hanna had only been to see her once since she'd moved back to the island. She knew she should visit her again soon, but it was just so painful to see how little of her was left. As ever when Hanna thought about her grandmother, her hand sought out the tattoo on her arm.

She had tried to repair the relationship with her brother. That was why she had gone to London when Ella was one, but it was as though Kristoffer didn't want it.

As though all he could see in her was their father.

She also had another set of grandparents, on her father's side, but she hadn't seen them in around fifteen years. They hadn't even come to the funeral. That was how they had always dealt with problems on that side of the family: by trying to smother them with silence. When they eventually grew so large they could no longer be ignored, you ran away. Her father's parents now lived in Norway.

Granny hadn't been that way at all. She had kept Hanna's mother alive through her stories, and she had forced Hanna to talk about her father. She had tried to do the same with Kristoffer, but she had never managed to get through to him.

Hanna couldn't interrogate Axel, because no matter how much she wanted to deny it, he was a link to Kristoffer. To everything that had happened.

'You OK?' asked Daniel.

Hanna felt his presence like a heat by her side. Somewhere she could draw energy from if she would just open herself up to the possibility, though she doubted she would ever dare.

'I'm just tired,' she said.

'You sure?'

Hanna nodded. She wondered how much Daniel knew about her father. It was a given that Carina must have told him who he was, but all she could feel radiating from him was kindness – none of Erik's intrusive curiosity. Kindness, and eyes that dragged her right back to Fabian.

Daniel opened the door to the interview room, and Benjamin Karlstedt looked up at them.

'Why do you want to talk to me?' he asked.

His grey shirt had already turned dark beneath his arms.

Hanna felt herself slide even further down the slope. She was worried about what this would mean for Rebecka. For her.

They sat down, and once Daniel had started the tape recorder and gone through the formalities, he got straight to the point:

'You found the CCTV camera on the street outside Axel

Sandsten's office, and you went to collect the footage from Securitas.'

'Yes.'

Benjamin ran a hand through his dark hair. It was as though he had just come across himself doing something inappropriate, because he then placed both hands on the table in front of him and stared down at them.

'When did Axel Sandsten leave his office?'

'I don't remember the exact time.'

'Roughly, then.'

'Around two o'clock.'

The minute the words left Benjamin's lips, Hanna knew he was the one who had tampered with the film.

'Except that's not quite right, is it?' said Daniel. 'He left the office at quarter past eleven. Why did you change the timestamp?'

'I didn't,' said Benjamin.

He glared down at his hands, as though they had acted without his knowledge.

'You gave us the wrong time,' Hanna said calmly. 'But the film you got from Securitas had the correct timestamp on it. So far, that's the only evidence we've got that you manipulated it, but it's only a matter of time, as you know. Help us now, by not wasting any more time – this is a murder investigation.'

Benjamin looked up, to the door behind them. Hanna decided to try a different approach.

'How do you know Axel Sandsten?' she asked.

'Through my wife.'

'What's her name?'

Hanna was struck by a sudden fear that it would be someone

from her past. But Benjamin was only thirty-two, and his wife was probably even younger.

'Ylva. Ylva Karlstedt.'

Hanna had never hung out with anyone called Ylva.

'Her company hired Axel's, and the costs spiralled out of control. She hasn't managed to pay off the debt yet.'

Benjamin's eyes darted between them. The man clearly felt conflicted. He both wanted and didn't want to confess.

'Who suggested that you should keep an eye on any investigations where Axel Sandsten's name popped up?'

'No, that's not what happened,' said Benjamin.

'So what did happen?' asked Hanna.

'We never talked about it. But when I saw Axel on that film, I thought maybe I could use it to write off Ylva's debt.'

'How much does she owe?' asked Daniel.

'Seventy thousand,' Benjamin sighed. 'We don't have much money. We want to start a family, but the treatment costs so much.'

Bringing up their longing for children was clearly an attempt to provoke sympathy, but it didn't change a thing for Hanna. Though she did feel sorry for his wife, who would also suffer.

'And you didn't stop to think that maybe you would be helping a murderer?' Daniel continued.

'No. People like Axel always get away with things, so I felt like it didn't make much difference.'

'You're a police officer.'

'I know, but . . . I really don't think it was him.'

Benjamin was trying to shrug off all responsibility, but his pained face suggested it wasn't working.

'Did you talk about Joel?' Hanna asked.

'No,' said Benjamin. 'I honestly didn't want to.'

'How did you change the timestamp on the video?' asked Daniel.

Benjamin explained the process, and Daniel ended the interview.

'So what happens now?' asked Benjamin.

'I don't know,' said Hanna. 'That's up to Ove and the prosecutor.'

'Can I call my wife?'

'Not yet.'

Hanna and Daniel left Benjamin in the interview room, asking one of their colleagues outside to keep an eye on him. They couldn't take any risks with someone who might want to hurt themselves, or others.

'The cyclist the German couple passed was blond and in his thirties,' said Daniel. 'Could be Axel Sandsten?'

'Maybe,' said Hanna.

She was dubious for many reasons. Joel had been dead for several hours by the time he was found, and she also struggled to imagine Axel on a bike. Still, he could have had some reason to come back without his car.

'I'll get in touch with the Germans to check,' Daniel told her.

Hanna nodded and walked towards the video room, next to the one where Axel Sandsten was still being interviewed. She needed to see him, to see the man who had, in all likelihood, killed his own son.

The Last Day

Joel keeps an ear out behind him the whole time. He can't handle any more of a beating. It doesn't sound like Fanny is following him. She is the only one he's really afraid of; he finally understands just how dangerous she is.

When Joel reaches the road, he turns north and slowly makes his way home. He wonders why he didn't bring his bike – not that he is sure he would be able to ride it in this state. He doesn't have the energy to light the road up ahead of him with his phone, but he is moving so slowly that he can find his way without it. The moon is still out, and the porch lights are shining on some of the houses, yet the darkness seems so compact that nothing can really touch it. God, he hates the dark. When he was younger, he was convinced there were monsters in the jet-black gap between his bed and the wall.

Monsters don't exist, Mum had comforted him. Except they do.

Faggot.

That's what Fanny and her gang of hangers-on had called him throughout primary and middle school, but the hatred in her voice had been stronger this time. Maybe that was what her anger was really about, more than the money and the fact he had shoved her away from Molly. Fortunately, the nickname hasn't followed him to high school. Some of his classmates there are the same, but a lot of them are new.

Yes, Joel likes boys, but he has never got any further than kissing. His heart flutters when he remembers Sebbe's warm lips and cautious smile in Nadine's kitchen. She had invited Sebbe to her birthday party purely because she thought Joel would like him – and he had – but it never came to anything more than their kiss that evening and a coffee at Fiesta. Maybe Sebbe could feel Joel's insecurity. There is so much he just doesn't understand. How can you love someone when you don't even know who you are?

The pain muddies his thoughts. His side is the worst, and Joel is convinced something must be broken. There's another kind of pain there too: what has Linnea done? He doesn't think Fanny was lying about the drugs. She doesn't know that he let Linnea try it, after all. But why didn't Linnea let him know how desperate she was for more? Why did she go straight to Fanny?

Funny, lovely Linnea.

The money thing must have been a lie. Linnea can't have said he would pay.

Joel replays everything that happened in the woods in his mind. The punches. The kicks. The way he curled up like a terrified baby. How he flipped out. Everything he should have said to Fanny: that she's a loser who picks on little kids. That he will never give in.

He gingerly reaches up and touches his brow. It's sticky, but it doesn't seem to be bleeding any more.

How is he going to explain this to Mum? Tell her that he

strolled out through the front door in his sleep and fell over in the driveway? He used to sleepwalk when he was younger, but it must be at least five years since he last did it now – that time he thought he was in the bathroom, and ended up peeing all over an armchair.

Joel reaches Gårdby Church and sits down in the bus shelter. He needs to rest, and he wants to check just how bad his face is. He notices that his jeans are muddy and that he has a hole in one knee. The jeans Petri gave him for Christmas.

Do you think we're made of money?

He can practically hear the disappointment in Mum's voice. Petri probably won't say a thing.

Joel takes out his phone and realises that the screen is cracked. Damn it, not that too. Mum will never agree to fork out for a new phone. He eventually manages to get it working, and holds the camera up to his face, but the light is too poor. He takes a picture with the flash instead, studies the image. His face looks terrible. He'll have to wash when he gets home, and in the morning, he'll have to steal some of Mum's make-up to cover the worst of it.

The blood and dirt will rinse off, but he is certain he'll have a real shiner around his left eye. His lip has swollen to twice its usual size, and no amount of make-up will be able to cover that. Cooling it with ice might help.

As Joel shoves his phone into his pocket, he almost cuts himself on the knife. He should put it back in its sheath, but he just doesn't have the energy. Instead, he tips his head back against the wall of the bus shelter and closes his eyes.

The air around him suddenly seems full of noise. When Mum finally managed to convince him there were no monsters under his bed, he became afraid of ghosts instead, and there are now just a few small buildings between him and the graveyard. There has been a church here for over a thousand years. How many people must have been buried during that time?

The chill he can feel on his skin is them whispering.

Joel wants to get up and go, away from the dead. But then he hears the low hum of an engine, and decides it will be safer to stay put if it's Fanny. He sits still, breathing as quietly as he can. The hum quickly grows in volume. Why is it so loud?

Chapter Thirty-Eight

Hanna found Ove standing by the screen in the room next to the one where Axel was being interviewed, Carina lying back on one of the blue sofas. She told them that the technician had confessed to changing the timestamp on the surveillance video, messaging the same information to Erik as she spoke. She watched on screen as he picked up his phone and read the message before turning and showing it to Amer.

'What has Axel Sandsten said so far?' Hanna asked.

'That he gave Joel the knife for his fifteenth birthday. He claims that must be why his prints are on it.'

Ove took off his glasses and used his shirt to rub the greasy marks from the lenses.

'So how did he explain the manipulated timestamp on the CCTV footage?'

'They haven't got to that yet. Erik just asked when he left the office, and Axel Sandsten is sticking to his story that it was quarter past two in the morning.'

Ove put on his glasses again. Hanna studied Axel on the screen. He looked comfortable, leaning back in his armchair. His lawyer, sitting beside him, was on an ordinary chair.

Both were wearing suits, but Axel's was slightly lighter in colour.

I would never murder my son, he said.

My client has given a perfectly credible explanation as to why his fingerprints were found on the knife, the lawyer interjected. *An explanation that, I might add, can also be backed up with the receipt.*

A receipt that proves your client bought the murder weapon, said Amer.

His face was blank, but Hanna could hear the smile in his voice.

Yes, said the lawyer. *A week before his son's birthday. It was a gift.*

It's not just a matter of the knife, Erik said to the lawyer. *The CCTV footage showing your client leaving the office has been manipulated.*

For a split second, the lawyer lost his composure. Hanna had met plenty of people like him before, in interrogation rooms in Stockholm: polished on the surface, but with very little going on beneath. In all honesty, some lawyers were different. She had met them too. But she hadn't liked her father's lawyer either. She had only ever spoken to him once, and it had been clear that he thought her father was guilty. Was that because Lars had confessed to him?

Erik turned back to Axel.

Can you explain why the CCTV footage was manipulated?

For the first time since Hanna had stepped into the room, Axel looked annoyed. Was that his way of showing that he was stressed?

The technician got in touch, he said. *He offered to deal with it.*
So why did you agree?

Because I don't have time to be dragged into a murder investigation.

Axel glanced at his lawyer, but it was clear the man had no intention of stepping in to help him.

What did you do when you left the office? asked Erik. *Just after eleven.*

I can't say, said Axel.

Why?

I promised I wouldn't.

That answer won't cut it, Erik continued. *Don't you see how this looks?*

I don't have time for this, Axel Sandsten told him, moving to get up. Both his lawyer and Amer told him to sit down. Instead, it was Amer and Erik who left the room.

'Come on,' said Ove, hurrying towards the door.

'What do we do?' Erik asked as they met in the corridor outside.

'I'll call the prosecutor,' said Ove. 'It's not ideal, but we don't have any choice but to hold him. Tell Daniel we'll debrief in your room afterwards.'

Daniel was working on something at his desk, possibly the report from the interview with Benjamin Karlstedt. Carina headed straight for the conference table, pulling out her phone as she sat down. Hanna didn't have the energy to try to break through Carina's dislike right now, so she chose the furthest seat from her she could: her desk.

It was fifteen minutes before Ove came back, and everyone hurried over to the table.

'Sorry that took a while,' he said, slumping into a chair and opening his laptop. 'A few new things have come to light.'

'Axel?' asked Erik.

'Yes, he's being held in custody, so he'll spend the night in a cell. Question him again in the morning, see whether he's ready to talk then.'

Daniel told the group that the Buchners had returned to Germany. He had sent them a picture of Axel Sandsten, but neither had been able to say whether he was the cyclist they had passed.

Ove began wiping his glasses again, though they could hardly be dirty already.

'I heard from IT,' he said. 'That's why it took a while. It seems Joel always deleted his search history, but they've managed to recover it, and it paints broadly the same picture as his sketchbooks: that he wasn't doing well emotionally. He googled suicidal thoughts and methods of suicide, for example. He also seems to have been confused about his sexual orientation.'

'Was he gay?' asked Daniel. 'There's nothing in his sketchbooks to suggest he was.'

Axel's homophobia had always been clear during high school. At one of the many parties Hanna had been to at his parents' house, he had punched another boy for touching his bum. Hanna didn't for a moment think it had been intentional – no one would be stupid enough to grope Axel. This was the first thing resembling a motive they had found: the fact that Axel couldn't bear to have a homosexual son.

'Unclear as yet, like I said. The IT guys are working on it. They promised to have more for us tomorrow. They've also managed to save a few photos from his broken phone. This is the last one Joel took.'

Ove brought up an image on the computer and turned it to show them.

Joel's bruised, bloodied face stared out at them from the screen. It looked like a selfie, and he was clearly still alive.

'This was taken at 00:34,' said Ove.

'Where is he?' asked Hanna.

'We've sent the picture for analysis.'

'Pass the computer.'

Ove pushed it over, and Hanna zoomed in on the photograph, focusing on different areas of it. Joel's face took up almost the entire shot, but along one edge she could just about make out glass. Or plastic. Behind that, the background was green.

'I think it's a bus shelter,' she said.

'Are there still buses at that time of night?' asked Erik.

'Hardly,' Hanna replied. 'Not during the week anyway.'

'Do you know where it is?'

'I think there's only one bus shelter in Gårdby, by the church.'

'OK, I'll let forensics know,' said Ove, massaging the bridge of his nose beneath his glasses.

'I've got another candidate for who the cyclist could be,' said Amer. 'A forty-two-year-old birdwatcher from Stenåsa. I've left a message telling him to get in touch.'

'What about the owner of the car?' asked Daniel.

'No news, I'm afraid. Samuel Herngren's phone hasn't been switched on since Tuesday.'

'Isn't that strange?' asked Hanna. 'Do we know any more about the assault he was suspected of?'

'He hit another man over the head with a bottle, but he also filed a conflicting report claiming the other man started it.'

'I think we should be doing more to track him down,' said Hanna.

'Like what?' asked Ove.

'Like talking to his family.'

'OK,' said Ove. 'But Axel Sandsten has to be our priority right now. Unfortunately, forensics were hindered by the bad weather, which has probably destroyed any evidence at the side of the road. So far, the door-to-door hasn't thrown up anything either, but we'll continue with that tomorrow. Hopefully we'll also have the results of the DNA test then. Who can come in tomorrow?'

Daniel was first to volunteer. Hanna wasn't quite so quick, but that was simply because she had assumed everyone would be coming in.

'Sorry, I can't,' said Amer. 'It's my son's fourth birthday. But I can come in on Sunday if you need me.'

'Tomorrow doesn't work for me either,' said Carina. 'I'm seeing my cousin.'

'I can,' Erik said after a brief pause that Hanna assumed was linked to his parents-in-law's visit.

Hanna was too afraid of the answer to ask the question, but she did it anyway.

'Can I tell Rebecka?'

'No,' said Ove. 'Not tonight. We'll reassess after the interview tomorrow.'

Chapter Thirty-Nine

It was just after six on Friday evening when Erik finally stepped through the front door. Nila came running towards him in her new dress. It was pink and glittery and everything she loved. Hard to wash too, in all likelihood, though that was something his parents-in-law didn't have to worry about.

'It's beautiful, isn't it? I'm going to wear it to Sally's party!'

Sally was turning seven next weekend, and had invited her friends to a party at Leo's Soft Play Centre. Possibly not the most practical outfit for somewhere like that, but Erik hoped that was something she might realise herself. Providing her clothes were weather-appropriate, he and Supriya always let her wear whatever she wanted. She had gone to preschool in pyjamas on several occasions, but when she tried to go in a swimsuit, Supriya had forced her into a pair of trousers. Nila had started at the Lindö School in the autumn, and generally made do with leggings and a sweater.

Right now, Sally was Nila's best friend, but just a few weeks earlier Nila had come home in tears because Sally had said that her arms were brown. *But they are*, Erik had replied, repeating the same thing he had in similar situations before: that everyone looks different, and that no one is better or worse than anyone else. That anyone who claims otherwise is wrong.

Did Sally say anything else? he had asked, but Nila simply shook her head.

Still, the tears suggested she had interpreted her brown skin as something negative.

Supriya came into the hallway with her parents, and nodded happily when she saw what he was carrying: two down duvets. The plastic wrappers were dotted with tiny raindrops. It felt like it had been raining constantly for the past few hours, and Erik's body was aching as if he had actually been out hunting. He had very nearly decided not to bother buying the duvets at all, but he didn't have the energy for Supriya's reaction when things didn't turn out how she'd planned.

That was the one part of their relationship that didn't quite feel balanced. She had far more opinions and requirements of him than he did of her.

I'm just tired, he thought.

Aavika and Yadu greeted him with a hug and a kiss on the cheek. They had always seemed to like Erik. Still, he had trouble believing they were happy that their only daughter had moved so far away. Supriya's two younger brothers still lived in India.

'How was your day?' Yadu asked. 'I hear you're investigating a murder.'

Erik nodded.

'That poor boy,' Aavika exclaimed. 'But I'm sure you'll find whoever did it.'

Erik didn't share Aavika's unfaltering optimism, but he liked how it made him feel when his in-laws talked about his work.

'Hopefully,' he said.

Erik could smell the heady aroma of cooking from the kitchen, and Aavika excused herself to return to whatever she was making.

He took off his wet coat and carried the duvets through to the master bedroom. His parents-in-law would be sleeping there during their visit, while he and Supriya squeezed into Nila's room.

In the living room, Yadu and Nila were playing chess. Though Erik couldn't understand what they were saying, he could work out what was going on: the old man was trying to teach her the rules, and Nila was making up her own. Supriya made a brief, half-hearted attempt to help out in the kitchen, then she and Erik went out onto the balcony with a glass of Chardonnay each.

The balcony was Erik's favourite part of the flat. He loved the views out over the Kalmar Strait, being able to hear the waves and the seabirds. The storm was moving away and the sky had brightened, the rain and the gentle breeze all that were now troubling the surface of the water. Being so close to the water was what had convinced Erik to compromise on where they lived, but he still couldn't get over his dream of a place in the countryside, somewhere he could start growing his own vegetables. Having an allotment didn't feel like enough, because he didn't just want to grow things, he also wanted to try out some of the ideas from the book he was reading. If he could just find a little summer house or crofter's cottage for sale, they might be able to afford it without having to move.

'You'd think she would be tired after such a long flight,' Supriya said in Swedish.

'Just thank her and accept her help,' Erik replied.

They usually ate pizza on Fridays, because neither of them had the energy to cook. And whenever Erik's parents came to visit, they spent all their time with Nila and only came through to the kitchen to eat. He sometimes thought it would be nice for them to live closer, but they had no plans to leave Malmö.

'I have to go in to work tomorrow,' he said.

'Yeah, I thought you might. We'll be OK,' said Supriya. 'Nila wants to show them the castle. Besides, my parents will be more impressed by you toiling away at work than traipsing around with us.' She leaned forward and gave him a kiss. 'Plus, Sunday will probably be more than enough,' she continued, switching back to English. 'You're not planning on working then too, are you?'

There was a sudden sharpness in her voice. An entire weekend with her parents so close was more than Supriya could handle. Her mother was very similar to her and liked to share her opinions on how she thought things should be done.

'No,' Erik replied, hoping that was the truth.

'How's it all going?'

'Moving forward.'

Supriya laughed, but no matter how much he wanted to talk about the case, he knew he couldn't. Her laugh was actually the first thing Erik had noticed about her. She had laughed at the look on his face as he tried to push through the crowd at a literature festival in Jaipur, and she and her friend had decided to help him.

'How about your new colleague?'

'Good.'

'But . . .'

'She's a bit difficult.'

'In what sense?'

'She doesn't really say much.'

Supriya laughed again. 'Since when was that a problem for you?'

Erik found himself spilling the entire story about Hanna's father. How he had served time for a brutal, heavily publicised murder, and then drunk himself to death. How Ove had been the one who'd led the investigation.

'Brave of her to move back here,' said Supriya.

'Or stupid.'

'Some people need the place where they grew up.'

She took another sip of wine.

'Fix it,' she said. 'Like you always do.'

'How?'

'Invite her over tomorrow night. And try to be tactful about it.'

This time, it was Erik's turn to laugh.

'You just want more of a buffer against your parents.'

'Maybe, but does that matter?'

Chapter Forty

Hanna took a detour to the Möckelmossen rest area on her way home from the station. There were still a large number of flowers and candles in front of the wall where Joel had been slumped, but this time she was the only person there. Possibly because it was Friday, and everyone else had better things to be doing – eating tacos or pizza with the family, settling down in front of the TV with a bag of crisps or cheese puffs. It was quarter to seven, and the sun was dipping towards the horizon, but it would be another two hours before it set for good.

Summer had always been Hanna's favourite time of year, more because of the light than the heat. You often had to be able to find shelter in order to enjoy the heat, and the flat island had few natural places to do that, but by the middle of June, the light triumphed for sixteen hours a day.

Samuel Herngren's car still hadn't moved from the rest area. He was the only person registered at his address in Färjestaden, but Hanna had managed to speak to his mother, who lived in Rälla. She claimed that he liked to go off grid from time to time, and that it wasn't usually cause for concern.

Hanna had now given her reason to worry, without even

mentioning the fact that his car was parked at the rest area where a boy had been found dead; the simple fact that the police were looking for her son was enough. The woman hadn't known that he had once been suspected of assault. According to her, he had never been violent.

Hanna peered down at the small patch of blood that was still visible on the ground. Life went on, but it was hard to get a sense of that here. Joel belonged to the dead now, the people Hanna often visited: Mum, Dad, Ester. And Granny. Hanna often thought of her as dead, because in essence she was. It was more than five years since she had last been able to have a proper conversation with her. In truth, her grandmother was stuck in some kind of transition zone; in the dusk she had always loved talking about.

Granny had been full of stories like the one about the nightingale that could sing evil away. Hanna had googled it without much success. Maybe it was just something her grandmother had made up as a counter to all the dark stories she told.

Hanna shuddered. She didn't want to be here as dusk fell. No nightingales would help her then. She dropped to her knees and pressed her palm to the damp stone. The rain had finally stopped, but it was probably only a temporary respite.

What happened to you, Joel?

So far, all they knew was that he had been beaten up in the woods behind Gårdby School. That he had got up, waved a knife, and walked away. Probably headed home, given the bus shelter by the church was in that direction. They knew that Fanny had climbed back onto her moped, that she may have followed him. That at some point after 00:34, Joel had been stabbed, and that Axel Sandsten's fingerprints were on the knife.

Hanna desperately wanted to talk to Rebecka, but she couldn't. Particularly not now Ove had said no.

Why had she asked?

After another few minutes, Hanna returned to the car and drove home. She saw her neighbours gathered in their kitchen as she passed, and though it was only a fleeting glimpse, she imagined they were talking, laughing. She considered driving on, towards Ingrid's house, but turned off at her own instead.

She slumped onto the sofa with her phone and brought up Rebecka's number. She wanted to fend off the feeling that had been lingering in her since they'd parted ways earlier that day, that something between them had broken, but nothing she could say now would help. Eventually, she sent a message:

Just so you know, we're not taking the weekend off. We're still working hard to solve this.

The reply came a few seconds later:

Thanks. I'm sorry for how I acted earlier.

Don't be, Hanna wrote. *I've seen worse.*

From me?

That too.

The three little dots showed that Rebecka was writing, but the seconds passed and her reply never came through. Was she angry?

Hanna got up and made her way into the kitchen. Her phone buzzed.

I hate Axel. He's got a sob story all about his grief in Expressen, but he didn't care about Joel. He's just looking for sympathy.

Hanna wanted to call Rebecka, but she couldn't do that without sharing what she knew.

What an arsehole, she wrote instead.

After several minutes of waiting for a reply, she wrote that she was going to make dinner and promised to get in touch again tomorrow.

Hanna had finished the last of the leftovers, so she cooked some pasta and heated a jar of shop-bought tomato sauce instead, grating Parmesan over the top. She searched the cupboards for some black olives, but couldn't find any.

As she ate, she watched an episode of *Outlander*, a series about a British woman who goes on honeymoon to Scotland in 1945 and is transported back in time to 1743. To a love far greater than anything she has ever experienced before. Hanna lapped up the woman's love as though it was enough to save her. The lush green hills of Scotland made her feel calm.

She carried her empty plate over to the sink. The kitchen didn't have a dishwasher, but Hanna had no plans to get one. Yet again, the thought of going over to Ingrid's popped into her head, but she didn't have the energy for it tonight. No, she didn't feel like it. She was happy in her little house. Instead, she poured herself a glass of red wine and tried to read, giving up after just a few pages. Hanna was all alone, but she didn't feel particularly lonely, and though there were plenty of things that were troubling her about being here, she knew it had been the right decision to move back to the island.

Hanna's phone started ringing, and she reached for the remote control. She saw Kristoffer's number flash up on the screen, and swallowed before she answered.

'Hi,' he said.

That one word was all it took for her to hear that he was drunk, and she didn't speak. Simply waited for him to go on.

'I've been thinking about Axel since you called.' Kristoffer took a sip of something. 'He really was a bastard. Ice-cold. I saw him punch a guy once, and the guy lost his sight in one eye. Whatever you think Axel's done, he probably did it.'

He practically sighed the last few words.

'Was the guy gay?' she asked.

'Don't think so, why?'

'I can't get into it, sorry.'

The silence that followed was charged with Kristoffer's desire to hang up and keep drinking, but Hanna didn't want to let him go. Not yet.

'How's the family?'

'They're fine, I guess. Visiting Bethany's parents in Colchester over the weekend.'

'You didn't want to go with them?'

'I have to work.'

From his tone, Hanna suspected there was more to it than that. Or maybe it was just the booze.

'Hotels, you know,' he continued.

'Listen,' she said, because once she had started, she would have to follow through.

'What?'

'Everything with Dad . . . do you ever wonder if it was really like the police said?'

'Why are you asking me that? Has something happened?'

His voice was so cold he sounded almost sober.

'No, it's just . . .'

It was the violence she wanted to talk about. All the injuries Ester Jensen had sustained.

'You know what?' said Kristoffer. 'I'm not interested. You'll have to keep obsessing over him on your own.'

'I—'

But Kristoffer had already hung up. Hanna hugged the

phone to her chest, sitting motionless for several minutes until she felt a message come through, buzzing against her. She was sure it must be Kristoffer, apologising for his behaviour, but she didn't recognise the number. She opened the message.

You should've stayed away.

Saturday 18 May

Chapter Forty-One

Hanna eventually managed to doze off towards the early hours, but it was a fitful sleep, full of dreams about her father. At first, she wanted to linger in them. She wanted to keep looking at the sea trout he had caught, watching it writhe about on the rock, gasping for air. She wanted to feel the wet, salty squalls on her cheeks and nose. Her father had taken them fishing at Grankullavik on the northern tip of Öland when she was twelve. Later that evening, he had told them their mother was ill.

A sound tore her from the beach just as she was about to cast her line. Confused, she looked around in the soft dawn light and registered the drowsy thought that there was someone else there. But Hanna wanted to keep fishing. As she tried to make her way back to the rocks, she found herself in a house she didn't recognise. It was incredibly dark, but she could hear someone opening cupboards and drawers. Rummaging around inside. A glass fell to the floor. She could hear footsteps drawing ever closer, and barely dared breathe. Before long, they reached her. Arms gripped her, knocked her over. The man – his face was only a dark shadow, but she was sure it was a man – kicked and hit her until it felt like every bone in her body was broken. He then poured something over her, making her skin and lungs burn. Petrol. The sound of the match being struck against the box was like thunder.

Hanna sat bolt upright, panting. She patted herself down, convinced she was on fire. Convinced that the man was standing over her, watching it happen. Little by little, she took in the room. The grey light on the sloping white ceiling boards. The chest of drawers, the only other piece of furniture apart from the bed. She was alone, but the lingering emotions from the dream sent tears spilling down her cheeks. Not out of fear at having come close to death, but out of trembling grief.

Her father should be impossible to love, so why couldn't she help herself? Why couldn't she be like Kristoffer, simply forgetting and moving on?

You should've stayed away.

Yes, she should have.

It was only five o'clock, but Hanna got up and moved over to the window. Rolled up the blind, which had been a terrible purchase because it didn't fit properly. She remembered the drowsy thought that had come to her as she woke, that someone had woken her. That she wasn't alone. Hanna peered out of the window, her fingertips brushing her grandmother's wooden nightingale. The fields stretched out as far as the eye could see, and she could only just make out the treetops on the horizon.

No, she was simply spooked by the message. And the calls.

She decided to go on a longer walk than usual. Getting some fresh air and exercise was the only thing that would really calm her down. She had lived close to the Nacka nature reserve in Stockholm, and had often gone walking there. Today, she followed the path south, towards the water. The sky was full of heavy grey clouds, and the wind whipped at her face. The weather had been bad that day in Grankullavik, but it hadn't made a difference.

I should get a fishing rod, she thought. As though she could recreate that one last day of happiness. If her niece ever came to visit, she would make sure to buy one.

The heavens opened as she was halfway to Mörbylånga, and she turned back. The trees provided some cover, but Hanna was soon drenched, and any lingering trace of the dream was washed away.

She was just a few hundred metres from home when the rain finally stopped. Ingrid spotted her through the window and hurried out.

'It may be wonderful that it's raining, but why on earth are you out walking in this weather, woman?'

Ingrid had told Hanna she was hoping for rain. The past few summers had been hot and dry, causing difficulties for her son, who had taken over the family farm.

'It wasn't raining when I left,' Hanna protested. She tugged at her damp jeans. The denim peeled away from her thighs with a sucking sound, but quickly clung to her legs again.

'Such awful news about the murdered boy from Gårdby,' said Ingrid. 'Are you working on the case?'

Hanna nodded and glanced over at her house.

'I'm not so slow that I can't take a hint,' said Ingrid, 'but I just want to say one thing. About the boy's father.'

'Oh?' said Hanna, a sense of panic drumming in her chest. Had the fact they were holding Axel already leaked?

'He's up to something in Grönhögen.'

'Up to something?'

'It was my son who told me. His wife works for the council.'

'Do you know any more?'

'No, but I can ask my son.'

'Don't do that.'

Hanna shivered.

'Go in and get yourself warmed up,' said Ingrid.

'I will, but . . .' Hanna peered over to her house again. Maybe this wasn't the right time to ask, but she knew the perfect moment would probably never arise. 'How much are people talking about me?'

'In relation to your dad, you mean?'

Hanna nodded.

'The old biddies at stitch and bitch have been talking a bit, but they've got nothing better to do.'

'Stitch and bitch?'

'My sewing circle, then. Though I don't like that name.'

'But you haven't heard anyone else saying anything?'

'No. It was all so long ago now, and they know you're not him.'

'Thanks,' said Hanna.

'What for?'

'I feel a bit better now.'

Though she was drenched, Ingrid gave her a hug.

'I saw that there'd been a fire in Gårdby,' said Hanna. 'Do you know anything about that?'

'The garage, you mean?'

'Yes.'

'There were rumours it was deliberate, but my money is on lightning.'

'Oh, by the way, did you win on the horses on Wednesday?'

'Fifty-four kronor,' Ingrid said with a smile. She turned and walked back towards her house. 'Stay inside next time!' she called over her shoulder.

Hanna nodded again.

When she got home, Hanna peeled off her clothes and took a long, hot shower in the tiny cubicle on the ground floor. If she knocked together a couple of rooms downstairs, as she'd thought about already, she could have a much bigger bathroom, with a tub too.

Once she was done, she got dressed, ate a hearty breakfast, and set off for the station.

Should she show someone the message she had received?

For some reason, it felt a little worse than the calls. It might also be traceable. She had googled the number without success, and there wasn't much more she could do on her own. She needed to put a stop to this before it escalated into something worse.

Hanna knocked on Ove's door. Since she was convinced there must be some kind of link to her father, she didn't want the others to see it.

'You should've stayed away.'

Ove read the words aloud. It almost looked like he was swilling them around in his mouth, tasting them like a vintage wine.

'This could be linked to the investigation,' he said. 'One of the people you've spoken to.'

'Most of them are fifteen or sixteen. I doubt they'd write something like that.'

'Maybe not, but we can't rule it out.'

'So what do we do?'

'I'll pass the number on to IT, they can look into it.'

Ove picked up a paper bag full of pastries from his desk and waved it in the air.

'I brought a special treat for the morning meeting. It's Saturday, after all.'

Aside from Ove and Hanna, Daniel and Erik were the only other people in the office, so they had the meeting at the table in their room. Daniel was dressed more casually than usual, in jeans and a t-shirt, and Hanna realised she preferred that look on him. It made him appear softer, and less like Fabian. This time, she reciprocated his smile. She couldn't keep him at arm's length just because he happened to look like her ex. Ove bit off a chunk of his Danish pastry.

'The cyclist the Germans passed wasn't Axel Sandsten,' he said. 'Amer managed to get in touch with him yesterday. He didn't see anything as he cycled past the rest place. He's a bird-watcher, and the reason he was in such a hurry was because there'd been a sighting of a black-winged stilt.'

'So why didn't he just drive?' asked Erik.

'His car's in for a service.'

Ove took another bite of his pastry before he continued:

'Forensics also confirmed that the DNA we found on Joel's face belongs to Fanny Broberg.'

'Not surprising considering she more or less admitted to spitting on him,' said Hanna. 'But the selfie Joel took proves he was still alive after they beat him up. And now we've got Axel Sandsten's fingerprints on the knife.'

'Maybe we should still bring Fanny in,' said Daniel. 'In case Axel is telling the truth about the knife being a birthday present. Fanny beat up Joel, so isn't it more likely that she followed him?'

Ove pushed the last piece of pastry into his mouth and chewed as he made up his mind.

'Let's hold off on Fanny. Her prints weren't on the knife.'

Erik nodded.

'I think we should look into whether there's a link of some kind between Fanny and Axel Sandsten,' Hanna spoke up.

'Why?' asked Ove.

'Because of the hash. Axel smoked a lot in high school, and I think he sold it as well.'

'OK, then let's ask Fanny about that too.'

'When are we interviewing Axel again?' asked Erik.

'In a few hours. I've put the whole of forensics on tracking his movements after he left the office on Tuesday.'

'I want to tell Rebecka,' said Hanna.

'Hold off until after we've interviewed him,' Ove told her.

'But it's going to end up leaking – if it hasn't already.'

'No,' said Ove.

'What should I do?' asked Daniel.

It was obvious he wanted to defuse the tension, and Hanna found herself wondering whether he had a lot of siblings. It would explain why he behaved like a typical middle child. If she and Kristoffer had had another sibling, things might have been different between them. But no, a third child would have just been yet another person to look after once their mother died.

'Look into hate crimes in southern Öland,' said Ove. 'Particularly homophobic ones.'

'Do we know for sure he was gay?'

'I spoke to IT again, and they found a forum for LGBTQ people that Joel was active on. They've contacted the admins to ask for his login details, so that might be something worth looking into. It's also something Erik and Hanna can talk to his family and friends about.'

Hanna wanted to argue. It didn't feel like that type of crime would happen in the middle of nowhere in the middle of the night. It was far more likely that the perpetrator knew Joel. Though the two weren't mutually exclusive, of course, particularly not if Axel was who she thought he was. She had heard him say that gay people were paedophiles on more than one occasion.

Ove rounded off by telling the others about the message Hanna had received, and she avoided meeting their eyes. Didn't want to know what they thought.

'Was the message from the same number as the calls?' asked Erik.

Ove turned to Hanna so suddenly that he almost knocked his mug of coffee over.

'What calls?' he demanded.

Erik didn't even try to look sorry for having mentioned them. Could the man never shut up? Hanna had to grit her teeth to stop her anger spilling out.

Chapter Forty-Two

For a few seconds after Rebecka woke, she felt happy, but reality quickly caught up with her.

Joel was gone.

She felt like screaming, and had to press her knuckles to her mouth to stop herself. Didn't want to give Petri yet another reason to worry. Did he even miss Joel? It didn't seem like it.

She reached for her phone on the bedside table and checked the time. Quarter past nine. She must have managed to get a couple of hours' sleep after all. There were a few new messages from people in town, from old friends and relatives, all saying they were thinking of her. It was so strange to see who got in touch and who didn't. She was still getting calls from journalists, but nowhere near as persistently. Perhaps they had finally worked out that she didn't want to talk. Then she remembered Axel's interview. That must be it: they had already found their grieving parent.

Still no word from Gabriel.

The only message Rebecka cared about was the most recent one, sent by Hanna a few minutes earlier: *Call me*.

She was about to do just that when the door opened and

Molly came padding into the room in her unicorn dress. Her face lit up when she saw that Rebecka was awake.

'Are you getting up now?'

'Soon.'

'Daddy's making pancakes.'

Petri had probably sent her up. He knew the chances of Rebecka coming down to eat were higher that way. It was the same trick she had used on Joel, and she felt a jolt in her chest.

'I'll be down in a minute,' she said. 'I just need to make a call.'

'I'll wait here.'

'No, sweetie, I need to be alone.'

Her daughter's face crumpled with disappointment, and Rebecka hurried to say that she wanted a hug first. Molly ran over, and Rebecka buried her nose in the well-worn fabric, breathing in her scent.

'You can let go of me now!' Molly giggled.

Rebecka waited until she heard her footsteps on the stairs, then dialled Hanna's number.

'Do you have any news?' she asked. 'Do you know who killed Joel?'

'Not yet, unfortunately,' said Hanna. 'But there's something I need to ask.'

Hanna paused, and Rebecka felt her anxiety levels shoot up: had they found something illegal from the previous owner on Joel's computer, or had he done something awful himself? Something far worse than smoking a bit of hash. It felt like she was at the start of something she didn't want to get to the bottom of.

'Was Joel gay?'

Rebecka needed a few seconds to breathe through the

terrible scenarios that had begun playing out in her mind.

'Why are you asking me that?'

'I'm sorry,' said Hanna, 'but I can't say.'

Rebecka searched for a good answer, but drew a complete blank.

'I don't know,' she replied as the tears began to roll down her cheeks.

Hanna sensed some of what her tears conveyed. 'But you suspected he was?'

'I thought he could be.'

'And you never talked to him about it?'

'No, I assumed he would bring it up when he was ready.'

Hanna kept quiet, which Rebecka took as criticism.

'I know I should've—'

'No,' Hanna interrupted. 'Stop that. There's nothing you could have done that would have changed what happened. So far, we have no idea what the motive could have been. Or whether there even was one. But we have to turn over every last stone.'

The firmness in Hanna's voice was slightly reassuring.

'I promise to let you know whatever I can if anything changes.'

'Thanks.'

Rebecka had to compose herself for a moment before she went down to Petri, Molly and their pancakes. Yes, she had heard some of the other children call her son faggot, but they had done it before Joel could really have felt that kind of attraction either way. She also remembered the nicknames from her own school days. They were all so cruel, and with such shaky connections to reality. Joel had always been on the small side. And beautiful. So incredibly beautiful . . .

Rebecka raised her palms to her cheeks. She couldn't start crying again now. She would never make it out of bed if she did.

Molly's face lit up as Rebecka stepped into the kitchen.

'I thought you'd gone back to sleep, but Daddy said I wasn't allowed to go upstairs again!'

Rebecka kissed her on the temple and sat down beside her. Petri could see that something was bothering her, but she shook her head. Not yet.

I bet your perverted boyfriend did it. Axel's words came back to her, but she forced herself to ignore them. It was insane that he could still knock her off balance like that. And why did he write boyfriend when he knew they were married?

Petri meant more to her than Axel ever had.

Rebecka raised a forkful of pancake to her mouth.

'You forgot the jam!' said Molly.

'Uh oh. Maybe you can help me?'

Rebecka smiled at her daughter, who squeezed a sticky blob of jam onto her pancake in return.

'Look, it's a rabbit!' Molly chirped.

Rebecka's phone began ringing, and she answered without thinking.

'Hello, this is Veronika Krans again, from *Expressen*. Joel's father, Axel Sandsten, is currently being held in custody on suspicion of murder. Do you have anything to say about that?'

Chapter Forty-Three

After her call with Rebecka, Hanna took one of the leftover pastries and went out to the coffee room. Last night's lack of sleep had finally caught up with her, and she needed an energy boost. Both from the sugary pastry and from a moment or two to herself.

Five minutes. That was how long her break lasted.

Erik came up the stairs from the cafeteria with a coffee in one hand. Hanna suspected he had taken a different route to make it seem like he wasn't following her. She could sense that he wanted to be alone with her. Maybe even apologise. Right now, she didn't have the energy to keep stoking her anger.

Erik sat down in the chair next to her and sipped his coffee.

'You look tired,' he said.

'You too.'

'Yeah, bit of a late night yesterday. We've got Supriya's parents staying. And then I got up early to go for a run.'

Hanna glanced over at him. If this was an apology, it wasn't a particularly good one – though maybe she was the one who should be making more of an effort. Speaking more, being more friendly and relaxed, making herself easier to like. But how? Asking him questions about his parents-in-law would just sound strange, and she really wasn't interested in his workout routine. Back in Stockholm, that had been yet another thing that had separated her from the others. After her year with the personal trainer, she had continued going to the gym in order to stay in shape for work – both physically and mentally – and she had enjoyed that. The fact that physical exertion seemed to help calm her mind. But she had zero interest in talking about weights or reps.

In the end, Hanna chose the easy way out, simply getting up and walking away. Telling herself it was because she needed to make some more calls.

Stop overthinking, she thought irritably as she got back to her desk. That had been easier in Stockholm. Back there, she hadn't cared in the same sort of way, but she didn't want to be that person any more. Distant and shut off, somehow.

Hanna started with Linnea, who told her that Joel had been called a faggot when he was at Gårdby School. She had no idea whether it was true or not; she had never thought it was important, because she had never seen him as anything but a friend. Linnea sounded blunt.

'Has something happened?' Hanna asked.

'My friend is dead.'

'Aside from that.'

'It's just my parents fighting.'

'What about?'

'Stupid stuff.'

'So it doesn't have anything to do with Joel?'

'Why would it?'

'I don't know.'

'No,' said Linnea. 'They're screaming at each other about a

couple of sheets that turned pink in the wash.'

In the silence that followed, Hanna tried to make out the argument, but she couldn't hear a thing.

'Is there anything else I should know about Joel?'

'No.'

Hanna thanked her and hung up, closing her eyes and taking a few deep breaths before calling Nadine.

The teenager exhaled as she answered, and Hanna assumed she must be smoking on the balcony.

'I'll get straight to the point,' she said. 'Was Joel gay?'

'Why?'

There was a clattering sound, and Nadine swore.

'I just knocked my cup over,' she hissed. 'Got boiling tea all over me. Surely it makes no difference if Joel was gay?'

'Probably not, but we need to know everything about him if we're going to solve this.'

Hanna heard clinking as Nadine picked up pieces of broken mug, and she had to stop herself from telling her to be careful. The last thing Nadine wanted was for someone to start mothering her.

'Sorry,' Nadine sighed. 'I can be a real bitch sometimes. I just really fucking miss him.'

'You're still in love with him, aren't you?'

'Yeah, but I tried to repress it so we could still hang out.'

'Was he gay?'

'If you're asking whether he liked boys, the answer is yes. But it was messier than that.'

'In what sense?'

She heard Nadine take a drag on her cigarette.

'Pff, forget it. I'm just blabbering.'

Hanna drew a question mark in the notepad she always

kept to hand whenever she made phone calls. There was something in this, she was sure of it. She remembered the flower, and Carina's theory that the murder was the result of some kind of dramatic love affair. Maybe she had been too quick to dismiss the idea.

'What do you know about Joel's relationships?' she asked.

'Not a lot. It was hard for us to talk about that kind of thing because of . . . well, my feelings.'

Hanna wanted to prise open Nadine's brief answers.

'What was the little you knew?'

'I tried to set him up with a guy called Sebbe once, but it didn't work.'

'Full name?'

'Sebastian Bianchi.'

Nadine took another drag on her cigarette. Hanna wondered how many she got through a day. The girl was only sixteen.

'How are you doing?' Hanna asked.

They were Ove's words, but unlike Hanna, Nadine didn't reply that she was doing fine.

'Like shit. But I promise I'm not about to throw myself off the balcony.'

'Good,' said Hanna, ending the call.

She was convinced there were things Nadine wasn't telling her, but she also knew she wasn't going to get anywhere right now. Maybe the perpetrator was someone they hadn't even considered so far, and they would have to dig deeper into Joel's personal life. Hanna still doubted the flowers had been chosen for their symbolism, but she couldn't see that Carina had added any updates to the report log. It would have to wait until Monday; she had absolutely no desire to bother Carina on a Saturday.

Hanna called Fanny next, to ask about Axel, and when she failed to answer, she tried her mother's number instead.

'Yeah?' a drowsy voice answered.

'Hello, my name is Hanna Duncker and I'm calling from the Kalmar Police. I'm glad I caught you.'

She used her cheerful voice, because it was always more constructive than her admonishing one. Her surname didn't seem to have provoked any kind of reaction. She was always slightly hesitant when she said it, but introducing herself by her first name only felt unprofessional. Besides, she didn't want to feel ashamed.

'What's the little brat done now?'

'Pardon?'

'It's Fanny you're calling about, right?'

'Is she at home?'

'Fanny!' the woman roared. It sounded as though she was moving through the house. 'Nope, her bed's empty,' she said.

'Where were you between Tuesday night and Wednesday morning?' Hanna asked.

'Why?'

'If you could just answer the question, please.'

Her cheery tone had started to falter, but in this case it probably didn't matter. She doubted Fanny's mother was susceptible to that kind of nuance.

'I was here, asleep in bed. Hold on a second . . . You don't think I killed that kid, do you? I know you've been asking around.'

'Were you alone?'

'Fanny was here too.'

'Did you see her?'

'I told you, I was asleep. Are you thick or something?'

'You didn't wake up and—'

'No, what? Do you think it was Fanny? That she . . .'

'Right now, we don't think anything. We're just asking everyone what they were doing that night.'

Fanny's mother muttered something about the police being useless and slammed down the receiver. There wouldn't have been any point telling the woman that her daughter had beaten up Joel on the night he died. That was one of the very few things they knew for certain. But then he had walked away, and at 00:34, he had taken a selfie in the bus shelter by Gårdby Church. Hanna could see herself in Fanny, the person she could have become if it hadn't been for her grandmother, and maybe that was why she felt such an urge to protect her. It wasn't easy to recover from being a murder suspect. Even harder than having one as a relative.

Hanna hit redial, but this time the mother didn't answer.

Chapter Forty-Four

There was just one bite of pancake left. Rebecka raised it to her mouth, broke it down between her teeth, and swallowed. She had to keep it together, for Molly's sake, but the journalist's words were racing around her head like trapped rats. Increasingly panicked, they had begun gnawing their way out. Petri was busy filling the dishwasher, but he kept glancing over to her. Molly too, despite having long since finished her breakfast. Her lips were moving.

'What was that, sweetie? I didn't hear,' Rebecka asked her.

'Do you want another one?'

When Rebecka said no, Molly leapt up and ran off to watch TV. Petri put down the jam-smeared plate he was holding and took Molly's seat at the table.

'What's going on?' he asked. 'Tell me.'

Both his voice and his face were full of pleading, and his fears of being shut out made Rebecka anxious. It was another responsibility she didn't need right now; she had enough on her plate as it was. She also didn't understand it. Where had this new eagerness to talk come from?

'That call, it was a journalist,' she said. 'Axel is being held on suspicion of murdering Joel, and she wanted to know what I thought.'

Petri reached out and touched her shoulder, and she had to make a real effort not to shake off his hand.

'You need to call Hanna,' he said.

'I just spoke to her, before I came downstairs. She didn't say a word about any of this.'

Petri's hand moved up to her neck, his fingers brushing her hairline. Rebecka usually loved it when he did that.

'Maybe the journalist was just trying her luck? To see what you knew?'

Rebecka's anger and fear had to go somewhere, and she unleashed both on him.

'Why the hell would she do that?'

Petri chose to duck.

'What did Hanna say when you spoke?'

'She asked if Joel was gay.'

'And what did you tell her?'

'That I thought he might be, but that we'd never talked about it.'

Petri turned towards the window. He seemed so focused that Rebecka wondered what he could be looking at out there, and was surprised to see that there was nothing outside.

'What is it?' she asked.

She sounded more annoyed than she'd intended, but it was so obvious that he was grappling with something. Was it Joel's sexual orientation? Was that why he had never really been able to love him?

'Come on,' she pushed him.

'There's something I need to tell you,' said Petri, his grip on her neck tightening.

He may as well have thrown a bucket of icy water over her, because she felt a paralysing chill. This time, she was the one who felt like pleading with him: *Don't. I can't handle any more.* Why had she put pressure on him? She didn't want to be here. She wanted to be back beneath the duvet.

'I saw Joel with a man in Färjestaden. It caught my attention because the other guy was much older and I didn't recognise him. They seemed angry with one another too. Or Joel seemed angry anyway.'

'Why didn't you say anything?'

'I spoke to Joel about it, and he told me not to mention it to you.'

'Why?'

Petri shook his head in resignation. Rebecka felt like hitting him, like roaring that he shouldn't have listened to Joel. If he had just told her, she might have been able to prevent all this. She couldn't shake off the feeling that there was a chain of events leading up to Joel's death, and that it could have been broken somewhere along the line.

That it didn't have to end up this way.

Everything had come crashing down, and she was left with a pile of fragments she didn't know what to do with. Her anger boiled over.

'You should have said something!' she shouted, pulling away from him.

'I was trying to be a father to Joel, like you wanted me to.'

He glanced uncertainly towards the living room, but not even the thought of Molly could help Rebecka control herself now.

'He's dead! Don't you understand that everything changed the minute he died?'

'Yes – it felt wrong that I didn't tell you right away. Plus I have trouble—'

'*It felt wrong*,' Rebecka cut him off, mimicking his voice.

'Stop,' Petri hissed. 'I've been trying to talk to you, but it really hasn't been easy.'

'You can't fucking blame me because you didn't manage to say anything sooner.'

'You could have said something too.'

'What the hell is that supposed to mean?'

'Do you think I'm totally fucking blind?'

Petri's voice was still no louder than a hiss, but the rage spilling out of his narrowed eyes scared her more than anything she had ever seen in him before.

'I knew there was someone else,' he said. 'But do you know how it felt to go over there on Tuesday and realise it was Gabriel?'

Chapter Forty-Five

Sebastian Bianchi was a new name to Hanna, so she ran a quick search on him. There was nothing in any of the police databases, but he was an active user of social media, where he came across as an outgoing young man who liked partying and films. She wondered how far that image corresponded with reality.

Hanna didn't have a Facebook or Instagram account in her own name. What could she possibly upload there that wasn't a complete lie? Besides, she couldn't think of a single person who might want to follow her. Aside from Kristoffer, perhaps. He occasionally uploaded pictures to Facebook. That was why Hanna had created an account with a fake name, to watch Ella grow up. In the latest image, the little girl was sitting in one of the armchairs at the hotel where Kristoffer worked, mimicking her father. She had a brochure in her lap and was pretending to write in it. The look of concentration on her chubby little face was fantastic. Hanna hadn't been able to get enough of it. Ella looked just like she had at that age.

Nadine had given her Sebastian's number, and she called it now. After a few rings, a gruff voice answered. It was Saturday, and he was a teenager. She had woken him, of course.

'We just kissed once,' Sebastian explained after Hanna asked whether he and Joel had been in a relationship.

'What was he like?' she asked.

She was annoyed by how vague her question was – obviously she didn't want to know what Joel was like as a kisser. Sebastian laughed, but before she had time to clarify, he answered her real question.

'He was sweet. Smart. Considerate. I know those sound like empty words, but they're not. Most people are ugly, crazy and egotistical.'

Sebastian's words painted a fairly gloomy picture of humanity, but Hanna thought there was probably some truth in it.

'But your relationship never went anywhere. Was that because he didn't want it to?' she asked.

'Honestly, I don't know. He seemed pretty unsure about most things.'

Hanna would have liked to meet Joel. The realisation took her by surprise. She felt that way not just because he was Rebecka's son, but because she wanted to shake that uncertainty out of him. To tell him that he should stop caring what other people thought or said. That he should just be himself – something she often struggled with herself.

Sebastian yawned. 'What time is it anyway?'

'Almost ten thirty.'

'It's so fucking sad, what happened to Joel. But I really need to go back to bed.'

Hanna couldn't think of anything else to ask, so she let Sebastian go back to his sleep. After a quick glance at the clock – she had just over half an hour until they were due to question Axel – she went over to Daniel's desk to fetch Joel's sketchbooks. They wouldn't be returned to the family until the team could be sure they weren't relevant to the investigation.

As she reached the low partition wall in the middle of the office, she paused. From this angle, Daniel really could be Fabian. Looking at pictures of Ella wasn't the only thing Hanna had used her fake Facebook account for; she had also used it to keep track of Fabian and how he was moving on from her with his new preschool-teacher girlfriend. Daniel looked up, and the spell was broken.

'Did you want something?' he asked.

'Joel's sketchbooks,' Hanna managed to stutter.

He passed them to her, and she hurried back to her desk. Joel's sketches were all in black, mostly done in charcoal – or so she thought – and there was a real darkness to the drawings themselves. One depicted a head that seemed to be opening up at the back, a hand stretching out from it. It was incredibly well done, but she didn't like the way the image made her feel. As though, beneath the calm, polished surface, there was something fighting to get out.

Hanna picked up another pad, half empty this time, and decided it must be his most recent. It was full of comic strips about someone Joel called Mr Man and Miss She, who poked fun at male and female stereotypes. Her phone rang, and she reluctantly answered. It felt like she was touching upon something important here.

'Hi, this is Petri Forslund . . . Rebecka's husband,' he added when Hanna didn't immediately respond. It was fear that had made her hesitate.

'Has something happened?' she asked.

'Yeah, I guess you could say that. A journalist just called

Rebecka and asked for a comment on Axel Sandsten being held in custody.'

A series of expletives coursed through Hanna. She had known this would happen. Why hadn't she said something?

'Can I talk to her?'

'No,' said Petri. 'She was so upset I had to give her a sedative. So it's true?'

'Yes,' Hanna admitted after a brief pause.

She wanted to explain that being held wasn't the same as being guilty, but if she did that she would also have to get into why and how, and she knew she couldn't do that right now.

'Tell Rebecka she can call me,' she said. 'Any time.'

'I will, though I'm not sure she wants to talk to you.'

His words stung like a physical blow. Petri sighed, and Hanna waited to be given a telling-off over how she was doing her job.

'I saw something I should've mentioned right away.'

'What did you see?'

'Last Thursday, when I was heading home from the office in Färjestaden – I guess it must have been around four thirty – I saw Joel.' He sighed again.

'Go on.'

'I went into the shopping centre to pick up a few things, and I saw Joel there with a man. It looked like they'd fallen out. Joel was upset, and the man was trying to calm him down. I saw him grab Joel's arm.'

'Did you hear what they were saying?'

'No, I was too far away.'

'Where exactly was this?'

'They were standing outside the shoe shop, Sko Dej.'

'Can you describe the man?'

'He was around forty, and he had short, light brown hair.'

'Did you notice anything else?'

'What do you mean?' Petri raised his voice slightly, as though he had interpreted her question as an accusation.

'You said Joel was upset. Did you notice any other emotions?'

Petri was quiet for a moment, and Hanna didn't rush him.

'Rebecka said you think Joel was gay.'

'Yes.'

'I don't know why I didn't mention this to Rebecka,' he eventually said. 'Maybe because he was so old. But afterwards, I asked Joel whether he and the man were in a relationship.'

'And what did he say?'

'He denied it, but there was something about the way they were interacting that felt really intimate.'

Chapter Forty-Six

What was his family doing right now? Erik sipped his coffee. Aavika might be in the kitchen, making brunch. Nila and Yadu could be in front of the TV in the living room. His parents-in-law had both been up when he left for work that morning – Mumbai was four and a half hours ahead of Sweden, after all – but both Supriya and Nila were still asleep. Nila usually woke up at nine at the latest, but it was always a struggle to get Supriya out of bed on Saturdays.

The thought of Aavika cooking dosas with coconut chutney made his stomach growl, and he silenced it with another sip of coffee.

Erik glanced down at his phone screen. No messages from the family yet. He had kissed Supriya on the cheek that morning, both when he woke and when he got back from his run. She hadn't even stirred the first time, but on the second she had mumbled something inaudible and then rolled over.

His laptop had gone into standby mode, and as Erik woke it, he realised he had just twenty-four minutes until the interview with Axel Sandsten. Moving quickly, he logged out and gathered his things. He needed to speak to forensics before he went down to the cells to pick up Axel.

Glancing over at Hanna, Erik saw her put down the phone with an odd look on her face.

'What's up?' he asked.

She met his eye, and her features seemed to reset. He felt as if he had caught a glimpse of something she didn't want him to see.

'I just spoke to Rebecka's husband,' she said. 'She got a call from a journalist asking about Axel. They know he's being held here.'

'Shit.'

'I know, and now she's refusing to talk to me. Her husband also saw Joel arguing with a man outside Sko Dej at the shopping centre in Färjestaden.'

'When?'

'Thursday last week, around four thirty. He said the man was in his forties, with short, light brown hair. He also seemed to think they had some kind of relationship, but Joel denied it when he asked.'

'A forty-year-old?'

'I know.'

'I need to speak to forensics about what they've found on Axel Sandsten before I interview him,' said Erik. 'I can ask them to search the CCTV footage from the shopping centre too.'

Hanna nodded and looked down at her keyboard.

Erik wanted to say something. Supriya would be disappointed if he didn't bring Hanna home with him that evening, but if he didn't even ask her, she would be angry instead. The problem was that she had also told him to be tactful, and this didn't feel like the right moment.

He walked away, over to Melina's desk. She was hunched in her chair, staring at the screen, listening to something that was making her bob her head. Noticing Erik, she pulled out her headphones. The music spilling out of them sounded like it had been made by a two-year-old playing with a synthesiser.

'Derrick May,' she told him. 'It's a techno classic.'

Melina was the same age as Daniel, but unlike him, she had the ability to make Erik feel ancient. He decided not to mention the music, and instead explained what they were looking for from the CCTV. When and where, and who should be in the shot.

'Sure,' said Melina. 'I'll put someone on it. I have to keep looking into Axel Sandsten.'

'Have you found anything yet?'

'Afraid not.'

Her eyes didn't leave the screen for a second as she spoke. Erik could see a road, softly illuminated by streetlights. Nothing but darkness around it, with the occasional car passing through.

'By the way, do you know how it's going with the threat someone sent to Hanna Duncker?' he asked. 'Were you looking into it?'

'Yeah, but I couldn't trace it. It came from a burner phone.'

Since he had inadvertently told Ove that Hanna was being harassed by someone making anonymous phone calls, he wanted to help her get to the bottom of it. But that wasn't the only reason. He had received a few threats of his own over the years, though they had always been directed at him as a police officer. This felt far more personal. He was sure it must be something to do with her father.

'Have you tried calling the number?' he asked.

Melina smirked. 'Of course I have.'

Erik asked her for the number and tried calling it himself. When no one picked up, he sent a message instead:

I know you're hurting, but I'd really like to talk to you.

He was just about to leave when a shout from Melina stopped him in his tracks. She pointed at the car on the screen.

'That's Axel Sandsten's car crossing the Öland Bridge at 23:30 on Tuesday fourteenth of May.'

Chapter Forty-Seven

It took Hanna no more than fifteen minutes to throw together a report on Petri Forslund's call. She stared at the closing words, at Petri's description of the man he had seen with Joel. Rebecka still hadn't called, and all Hanna wanted was for the interview with Axel Sandsten to be over and done with. Maybe then she would pluck up the courage to call Rebecka, particularly if Axel confessed. She couldn't help but hope, despite knowing, deep down, that he never would, no matter how guilty he was.

Erik came running over to her desk and slapped down a couple of printouts in front of her. The first was a black-and-white photograph of a car.

'Aren't you supposed to be in the interview now?' she asked.

'Soon.' He nodded towards the car. 'There's Axel Sandsten driving over the Öland Bridge on Tuesday fourteenth of May. After he left his office that evening.'

Hanna picked up the image and studied it. A shifting gradient of darkness and light. The car's registration plate was clearly visible. She grabbed the second image. It was an enlargement of the car's windscreen, and she could see Axel

Sandsten staring out from behind the glass. There was no doubt about it: it was him, and she felt a sudden, trembling longing – a longing to call Rebecka and tell her that she knew how Joel had died.

'I want you in the interview with me,' said Erik.

'But—'

'Yes,' he interrupted her. 'I've already discussed it with Daniel, and Ove agrees. I think there's a chance Axel will talk to you.'

Hanna wasn't quite so sure, but she didn't say anything. She wanted to join the interview. Time would pass much quicker there than it would waiting at her desk, and she also wanted to see Axel's face when confronted with the images.

'I've booked the video recording room, but maybe it's best if I go and get him myself?'

Hanna nodded and got up. The window was open, and she could smell a hint of petrol on the breeze, casting her back to last night's dream. This time, she was slightly removed from the action, and the man was no longer simply a dark shadow – it was her father. She saw him looking down at the bloodied, beaten body lying motionless on the ground before dousing it in petrol and setting the house alight.

Hanna had to steady herself against the desk to stop herself from collapsing.

'You OK?' asked Erik.

'Just a bit dizzy,' she replied. 'I stood up too fast.'

Erik took a deep breath, and Hanna thought he was about to demand that she told him what was going on in her head.

'Do you have any plans this evening?' he asked instead, smiling at her.

'Why?'

She slowly let go of the desk. Did he really want to make small talk about her free time right now? They had an interview to do.

'My wife wants to know if you'd like to come over.'

Panicked, Hanna desperately tried to think of an excuse.

'Me too, obviously,' he continued. 'Supriya's mum cooks so much food, we can't eat it all. And I thought that . . . after today . . . pff, never mind. So, what do you say?'

She knew exactly what he was thinking, and it had nothing to do with food – it was about getting to know one another. She and Erik had been working closely over the past few days, and that would probably continue going forward. Hanna knew she should make more of an effort, but there was just so much else going on right now. Besides, she still thought he was an idiot for telling Ove about the threatening phone calls.

'I can't tonight, actually,' she told him. 'I'm having dinner at my neighbour's.'

A lie. She had no plans at all, but she didn't dare admit that she just didn't have the energy.

'Shame,' said Erik. 'Another time, then.'

'Absolutely.'

He managed to keep quiet all the way to the corridor. A distance of just a few metres.

'Who's the neighbour?'

Was he trying to scrutinise her lie? Hanna batted back the suspicion.

'Her name's Ingrid.'

'What does she do?'

'She's retired now, but she used to be a farmer.'

Erik turned to look at her, and she realised that he might

actually think she was joking. But about what?

'That's something I want to hear more about sometime,' he said, heading off towards the cells.

Hanna got the interview room ready, then sat down to wait in one of the armchairs. Erik arrived a few minutes later with Axel Sandsten and his lawyer. Axel's right arm seemed to twitch, as though he wanted to reach out and shake her hand. Instead, he sat down in the other armchair.

'Nice to see you again,' he said.

Hanna met his eye. 'I'm afraid the feeling isn't mutual.'

Her words made him laugh, though his lawyer didn't seem anywhere near as amused as he took a seat on the hard wooden chair to one side of his client.

'I hope you realise this can't go on,' he said.

Hanna ignored him, her eyes still on Axel.

'Did you have a good night?' she asked.

He wasn't wearing the same clothes as yesterday, so she assumed his lawyer must have brought him a fresh change. Axel didn't look like he had struggled to sleep, but he seemed to appreciate the question.

'I've had better,' he said.

'Any epiphanies overnight?'

'A few,' said Axel. 'But none concerning guilt, if that's what you were hoping for. I didn't kill Joel. He was my son.'

'What did you do after you left the office on Tuesday?' asked Erik.

'I'm afraid I can't say.'

'Not good enough. I thought you would have understood that by now.'

'No, it's you two who don't understand.'

'This thing you were doing, whatever it is you don't want to talk about,' said Hanna. 'It didn't by any chance take place on Öland, did it?'

Axel's eyes narrowed, but before he had time to say anything, Hanna held up both pictures. One second: that was all it took for his lawyer to request a moment with his client. Hanna and Erik left the room.

'Daniel could have done this, you know,' said Hanna. 'Or you.'

'Yeah,' said Erik. 'But it felt good, didn't it?'

She nodded. Proof was the only thing that might work on Axel Sandsten.

After a few minutes, the lawyer popped his head out into the corridor and told them they could come back in.

'OK, let's try this again,' said Erik. 'What did you do once you left the office?'

'I drove to Mörbylånga,' Axel replied.

'And what did you do there?'

'I met the chair of the local housing committee.'

Hanna felt like something had come crashing down inside her, the certainty of Axel's guilt that had filled her as they waited outside. Surely he wouldn't lie about something that could be easily contradicted? Hanna stopped the collapse by clinging onto the one remaining glimmer of hope: that the chair of the housing committee might have some reason to give him a fake alibi. After all, one of their own technicians had voluntarily manipulated CCTV footage for him.

'In the middle of the night?' she asked.

'Yes, there was a bit of a crisis. I've bought some land in the south of Öland, and I'm planning to build a resort there.'

'And why couldn't you tell us that?'

'It would put the entire project at risk.'

Hanna felt a sudden wave of frustration at Axel's nature.

'Your son is dead,' she said. 'Surely the most important thing should be helping us with our investigation?'

'Exactly, he's dead, and nothing can change that. I had to save the project.'

'Is the land you bought in Grönhögen?'

Axel studied her with pursed lips.

'How do you know that?' he eventually asked.

'I've got my sources.'

Hanna smiled as she thought about Ingrid, which seemed to trigger Axel.

'This can't get out,' he said, leaning forward. 'Not yet. It could ruin everything.'

The lawyer placed a hand on his arm, and Axel sat back in his armchair.

'What's the name of the chair of the committee?' asked Erik.

'Göran Olander.'

'Sit pretty while we give him a call.'

'Fine,' said Axel, though he didn't sound happy about it.

As Erik called Olander, Hanna leaned back against the wall outside the interview room. She could see the answer on his face before he even spoke:

'Göran Olander confirms that he met Axel Sandsten in Mörbylånga at midnight. The meeting went on for over two hours.'

Hanna searched for some hope to cling to – Olander could still be lying – but she couldn't find anything. Instead, she walked off to the bathroom. She needed to be alone.

Chapter Forty-Eight

What Rebecka really wanted was to go back upstairs and crawl beneath the covers, shutting out the world and its demands. The pill Petri had given her had made her drowsy, but it had also left most of her worries intact. Molly was the only reason she was forcing herself to stay downstairs, on the sofa. She couldn't leave her, not after what she had put her through.

The girl had come into the kitchen just as Petri hissed that Rebecka was a selfish slut. Too terrified to say anything, she had frozen in the doorway, watching them argue. When Rebecka noticed her standing there, she had rushed over to her and their argument had fizzled out – or perhaps it had simply been pushed back.

Rebecka no longer felt angry, she was just tired.

She glanced down at her daughter, who was curled up beside her with her cuddly rabbit. Her face was calm and relaxed as she followed Hiccup and Astrid and the other dragon riders on the screen. Suddenly, she giggled, and turned to Rebecka.

'Did you see that, Mummy?!'

Rebecka smiled and nodded, though she had no idea what

Molly was talking about. No, it wasn't just for her sake that Rebecka had resisted the urge to flee upstairs: sitting here made her feel better too. Molly loved everything to do with dragons, and Joel had often read to her about Tam the dragon rider. She had asked Rebecka to continue the story last night, but Rebecka hadn't been able to bring herself to do it. Petri had stepped in instead.

Her phone started ringing, but when she saw Hanna's number, she refused to answer. She doubted she would ever want to talk to Hanna again. It buzzed with a message a few minutes later, and Rebecka's first instinct was to ignore it. But she needed to know.

Axel is free to go. This is how it goes in investigations. Being held doesn't mean someone is guilty. That's why I didn't say anything. We're sure it wasn't him.

Rebecka wrote a quick reply:

As sure as you were last time?

She stared at the words for a moment or two, then deleted every last one and put down the phone. Molly turned to her.

'Are you sad, Mummy?'

'Yes, a bit. Are you?'

Rebecka wiped away the tears that had begun running down her cheeks. She had no control over them.

'Yes, but not right now.'

For a few minutes, Rebecka managed to follow the action on screen without thinking about either Joel or Hanna, but she couldn't make sense of the plot. One minute Hiccup and Astrid were flying around, searching for something, then suddenly they were in a cave.

On Saturdays, Rebecka usually came up with something fun to do with Molly. Last weekend, they had gone to the indoor water park in Kalmar. She had asked Joel if he wanted to come along, but he had said no, claiming he had a headache. Neither she nor Petri had the energy to entertain Molly now. Things had been harder on him than she realised, and the tears started flowing again when she thought about how he had said nothing, despite knowing about her affair. Yes, she had noticed he was drinking more than usual on Tuesday, but she hadn't for a second thought that it might be because of her. Because of what she had done. She had been too preoccupied with Gabriel, with finding ways to be close to him, oblivious to the fact he was already drifting away.

Petri came out from the kitchen and asked if she wanted anything. From his face, she couldn't tell what was going on inside.

'Some tea would be good,' Rebecka replied. Mostly because she couldn't deny him anything right now.

He returned a few minutes later with tea for both Rebecka and Molly. Molly's cup was at least two-thirds milk, and probably contained a few spoonfuls of sugar. He had even brought them a couple of biscuits on the tray, and the girl wolfed them down one after another. Maybe she thought they would disappear if she didn't hurry.

Rebecka took a sip of her tea and put down the cup.

There was a knock at the door, and Petri went to answer. Rebecka heard Ulrika's voice over the TV. People were still laying flowers at their gate, but almost no one actually dared knock.

Ulrika stepped into the living room. 'Want to get some fresh air?' she asked.

Rebecka's suspicions were immediately raised. Could Petri have called Ulrika to tell her about the affair? It didn't seem to fit with the calm anxiety of Ulrika's question. If Petri had called her, it would be more out of a warped sense of concern. Because he thought Rebecka would feel better if she got up and about. Sleep, eat, get a bit of exercise, and everything will be fine. But the idea of parading through the village wasn't appealing in the slightest.

Particularly not with Ulrika.

'We could just go out back?'

Rebecka nodded and got up. Ulrika might have heard something.

'You'll have to watch the dragons with me instead,' Molly said to Petri, who sat down in Rebecka's seat.

The two women went out to the porch at the back of the house. The wooden chairs were hard and cold, but Rebecka didn't fetch any cushions. Ulrika was watching her, and for the first time, Rebecka noticed the dark circles beneath her eyes.

'Are you OK?' she asked.

'I'm the one who should be asking you that. It's why I came over.'

'Maybe, but I don't have the energy to think about it.'

Ulrika peered over to the small cluster of trees and sighed. 'We're actually having a bit of a tough time right now.'

'You and Gabriel?'

Ulrika nodded. Rebecka didn't ask any follow-up questions, afraid that the answer might touch upon the affair. Afraid that Ulrika, like Petri, had put two and two together on Tuesday. But would she really be here if she had? She probably just knew he was having an affair, not who it was with. Maybe that was why she had organised the barbecue, in an attempt to win him back. If that was the case, it had worked. He had ended things with Rebecka. What could possibly have gone wrong since?

Another suspicion struck her: perhaps Petri had invited Ulrika over because he thought Rebecka should confess to sleeping with her husband. She felt a headache building. Trying to analyse other people's behaviour was exhausting.

'Gabriel . . . he . . .'

Ulrika didn't seem to be able to look at her, and Rebecka realised she would have to put a stop to this.

'Listen, I don't have the energy . . .'

It bothered her that Ulrika only seemed to have come over to talk about her cheating husband. Any concern for how Rebecka was doing had been forgotten a little too easily.

'No, you're right,' said Ulrika. 'It's not me we should be talking about. Are you getting any information from the police?'

'So-so, actually.'

'I heard that Axel—'

'They let him go.'

'Why?'

'Hanna loves telling me they can't reveal any details of the investigation.'

'Hanna?'

'Hanna Duncker, yeah. She's from round here. We went to school together. Didn't you know?'

Ulrika shook her head. She was originally from Borgholm, and had attended a different school, but Rebecka saw the moment the penny finally dropped.

'Duncker . . . So was it her dad who beat up and burnt that woman?'

'Yes,' Rebecka replied, irritated, swallowing the impulse to defend Hanna.

'Sorry,' said Ulrika. 'I just didn't know you were friends.'

'We were, but we barely spoke after she moved away.'

'Why did she come back?'

'I have no idea.'

The two women sat quietly for a moment or two. Rebecka hadn't thought to bring a jacket out with her, and she began shivering softly. She glanced back to the porch doors.

'It must be awful having a dad who—'

'Yeah,' Rebecka interrupted.

She couldn't deal with Ulrika right now. Couldn't she just get the hint and leave?

'Do you know what the police think happened?' Ulrika asked.

'Not really, but the latest thing is that they've started asking whether Joel was gay.'

Ulrika looked shocked. 'Was he?'

'I don't know,' Rebecka told her, bursting into tears.

Ulrika hugged her.

'Why didn't he say anything?' Rebecka sobbed. 'Did he think I wouldn't accept him?'

Chapter Forty-Nine

As Erik watched the drizzle through the window, he again found himself wondering what his family were doing. It was almost eleven thirty, so they had probably just arrived at the castle. Maybe they had left the car, and were running over the drawbridge towards the defensive walls. A sudden longing to experience another Indian monsoon welled up in him. The dry greyness exploding into colour, children splashing in puddles, people laughing.

'Why are you smiling?' asked Hanna.

Erik didn't think he would be able to explain.

'My family's visiting Kalmar Castle today,' he said. 'And Supriya is stressing about the weather. She thinks her parents are going to freeze.'

Hanna got up and closed the window. They were sitting at the table in their office, waiting for Ove and Daniel. The morning meeting was the only time they ever booked a proper meeting room. Erik had called Ove after speaking to Göran Olander, and Ove had suggested they have a quick debrief. The forensic IT specialists had seemingly managed to extract more information from Joel's computer and telephone.

Supriya wanted them to visit Mumbai next year, possibly

even travelling up to Jaipur so that Nila wouldn't forget it. Erik didn't want his daughter to forget either, he wanted her to add new experiences, but he found it difficult to put the sense of conflict that provoked in him into words. He simply didn't think they should be flying.

Hanna had withdrawn into surly silence, and Erik couldn't understand why. Perhaps she thought it was pushy of him to have invited her over for dinner – they had only been working together for four days, after all – but he had invited people over in less time than that before. Just last year, for example, he had run into a couple of lost Indian tourists outside the cathedral, and when he heard them speaking Marathi, he had gone over to say hello. He quickly ran out of Marathi phrases and switched over to English, but they had ended up going home with him all the same, and had enjoyed a pleasant evening together.

'Back to square one,' said Hanna.

'Come on, that's unnecessarily pessimistic. At least we know it wasn't him this time.'

'Do we?'

'Yeah,' said Erik. 'Why would someone like Göran Olander lie for Axel Sandsten?'

'Now you're being unnecessarily naive.'

Hanna looked away, almost as though she was ashamed of her words, but she did have a point. Their work largely revolved around uncovering lies, but there was nothing to suggest that Olander was lying.

'We need to talk to Fanny again,' she said.

'Yeah, we'll head over to Öland after the meeting.'

Daniel came into the room with a laptop, Ove just behind him.

'Ah, good, you're both here,' said Ove. 'Have either of you come across the name Markus Johansson?'

'No,' said Erik. 'Why?'

'Joel was chatting to someone by that name on the LGBTQ forum. The chat itself doesn't seem to contain much of note – Joel was torn about his sexuality and who he was, and Markus gave him support. It was the age difference that caught the analyst's eye during the initial check. Markus mentions that he has a son around Joel's age, so he must be at least twice as old as Joel. They also arranged to meet.'

'Do we know who he is?' asked Erik.

'I'm working on it,' said Daniel. 'There are around ten Markus Johanssons in the Kalmar area.'

'Are any of them around forty?' asked Hanna.

Daniel tapped away at the keyboard.

'There's one living in Oxhagen who's forty-three. He's married but separated, and has a son who attends Katrinelund High School in Gothenburg.'

'Do you have a picture?'

'Hold on.'

A few minutes later, Daniel brought up a photograph for them. The man in the image had light brown hair, and could easily be the man Petri had described.

'He's the store manager at Teknikmagasinet in the Giraffen shopping centre.'

That was just over the road from the station.

Erik dialled the number for Teknikmagasinet and was informed by the woman who answered that Markus Johansson wasn't working today.

'I think we should go over and talk to him,' said Hanna.

'Prioritise finding Fanny Broberg,' said Ove. 'When I called the prosecutor about Axel, I was told that we can do a search of her home.'

It was obvious Hanna didn't like his decision, and Ove noticed.

'She assaulted Joel that night,' he continued. 'They live close to one another, and it's highly likely that she caught up with him on her way home.'

'I'm not saying we shouldn't talk to her,' said Hanna, 'but isn't a search of her house a bit much? Considering where Joel was found, it feels more likely that someone else picked him up.'

'We can swing by Markus Johansson's place on our way to Öland,' Erik suggested. 'We'll only lose fifteen minutes or so.'

Ove turned to Daniel as though looking for back-up, but Daniel kept quiet.

'Fine,' he said. 'Go and chat to Markus Johansson, but I want Daniel to follow the patrol car out to Fanny Broberg's place. And if she's there, I want them to hold her until you arrive.'

The Last Day

The rumbling of the engine seems to make the bus shelter tremble. Joel holds his breath and closes his eyes. Not because he thinks it will be enough to make him invisible, but because he can't bear seeing. He focuses on the cold, hard bench beneath him. Rather that than the darkness beyond. The churchyard and its dead.

The rumbling stops suddenly. Joel opens his eyes and finds himself staring straight into the moped's headlight. He doesn't look away. Through the glare, he can just about make out Fanny's face. His heart is racing so fast he feels queasy, and he makes a real effort not to show it.

He doesn't want to provoke her into beating him again.

In the end, he can't do it any more. If he wants to avoid bawling, he'll have to do something.

Slowly, he rises to his feet. Pain shoots through his body, making him gasp. He hears Fanny snort mockingly, but Joel turns away from the light and begins walking along the road.

Fanny drives behind him at a crawl, and Joel feels grateful that the sound of the engine is drowning out his thundering heart.

Why isn't she saying anything? Why isn't she doing anything?

Probably because she knows how terrified he already is.

Joel comes close to asking about Linnea simply to break the silence. He still can't quite take in what she has done.

For a while, he definitely had feelings for her. There is something bright and simple about her that he finds himself drawn to – probably because he doesn't have those qualities himself. He tried to explain it to Nadine once: that they are too dark for one another, that that's why they can't have that kind of relationship.

Maybe he should give Nadine a chance after all? Linnea isn't the person he thought she was, but he is really fucking sick of relationships right now. Of not knowing who he is.

Tina.

Her name crosses Joel's mind, but he doesn't want to stay there. It's too painful.

The moped skids on the gravel, and Joel almost cries out, but manages to bite his tongue. He regrets not telling Nadine about Fanny, but he was worried she would do something stupid. As though things could be any worse than this.

He doesn't want to die.

Joel is halfway home, and in order to convince himself that he will actually make it, his thoughts turn to what he is going to do once he gets back. He'll pop a couple of painkillers. His body is hurting all over, but he is pretty sure he will be able to sleep. He has never been this exhausted before.

Snegatan, where Fanny needs to turn off, is close now. The moped illuminates the road for Joel, and he stares at the small black flies dancing in its beam. Repeating the thought like a mantra, that she will have to turn off soon.

Five metres to go, then four, three . . . The engine revs like
a predator poised to pounce.

Chapter Fifty

A sense of failure followed Hanna as she got behind the wheel. She should have done more to stop the raid on Fanny's house. Given the consequences it could have on the girl, it was far too early. Particularly now that the investigation had taken another turn. Hanna still hadn't dropped the idea that there might be a link between Fanny and Axel Sandsten, but right now she was convinced that Markus Johansson was the lead they should be chasing down.

'Idiots,' she muttered as she saw the headlines outside a newsagent.

AXEL SANDSTEN IN CUSTODY

She hated it when suspects were hung out to dry like that, especially when they had already been released. The press was always one step behind. Yesterday afternoon, while their headlines were focused on Axel's grief, he had been in custody. She wondered what they would write tomorrow. Axel would no doubt turn things in his favour. In fact, that was probably one of the reasons he hadn't immediately given them his alibi.

In the passenger seat beside her, Erik was on his phone. First with Supriya and then the caretaker of the building where Markus Johansson lived.

'There's no code,' he said. 'The door should be open.'

Hanna parked up on Drottning Kristinas väg, outside a building with glazed, red-framed balconies. They walked around the corner and entered through the first door. The lower half of the walls were painted dusty pink, and there were two birds painted in the same shade on the white upper section.

The building didn't have a lift, so they took the stairs to the third floor and rang the buzzer. Markus Johansson answered in a pair of chinos and a white t-shirt. Barefoot. Though he was only around five foot seven, there was something about his body that made him seem gangly. Hanna thought he looked vaguely familiar, but she couldn't place him. They identified themselves as officers, holding up their badges, and he welcomed them in, showing them through to the kitchen.

'Have we met before?' asked Hanna.

Markus studied her for a moment or two before shaking his head.

'We want to talk to you about Joel Forslund,' said Erik.

'Yes, I thought you might.'

They had found the right Markus, but Hanna didn't feel any sense of relief. She was still trying to work out where she could have seen him before. Was it before she left the island? He was eight years older than her, so she doubted it.

'Were the two of you in a relationship?'

Erik's question was too blunt and to the point for Hanna. She would have preferred to begin with a more open-ended question, giving them a chance to hear Markus talk about who Joel was. She glanced over at Erik, trying to tell him to calm down, but he didn't meet her eye. Maybe he didn't think they had time. Yet again, Markus didn't seem surprised by their question.

'No, absolutely not. Joel wasn't doing particularly well, and I wanted to support him.'

'Where did the two of you meet?'

'In an online forum.'

'An LGBTQ forum, correct?'

'Yes.'

Hanna had no choice but to let Erik continue. She peered around the room. The only objects on the worktop were a fruit bowl and a pot of utensils. There were no curtains at the window, and just one solitary green plant on the window sill. The table they were sitting at was painted white, the chairs too. She was struggling to make sense of both Markus and the room. Older men rarely made contact with young boys online purely to support them.

'How would you define your sexual orientation?'

Markus sighed, possibly at the roundabout way Erik had asked the question.

'I'm married to a woman,' he said. 'So what do you think?'

'Where is your wife?'

'We've chosen to live apart. She has her own flat nearby.'

'Why?'

'Because when we lived together, we got on one another's nerves far too much. We both have a great need for time alone.'

Hanna had never lived with a partner, and it bothered her that she hadn't been brave enough to move in with Fabian. She might never get the chance again: to try out a life where she wasn't alone. But somehow, deep down, she also knew that it wouldn't have worked in the long run, no matter how she felt about him. He had wanted too much, for everything to happen *now*; they had only been together three months when he suggested she move in.

Erik turned to Hanna, probably irritated by her silence. She ignored him and focused on Markus.

'Did Joel have feelings for you?' she asked.

'No,' said Markus. 'I would have noticed if he had.'

His answer was too quick, too certain. As though all he wanted was to get rid of them. Hanna tried to find another way in.

'Why was Joel struggling?'

'Being a teenager isn't easy.'

'No, but it was more than that for him, wasn't it?'

Markus gave a resigned shrug.

'What happened to Joel is awful, but we only knew one another for a few months. I can't tell you any more than I already have.'

'What did the two of you talk about?' Hanna asked.

'Books, TV shows, documentaries. But mostly about how hard it is to find your place in the world. About how it shouldn't matter who you love or what you identify as.'

His answers were still irritatingly vague, so Hanna tried a different angle:

'How is your relationship with your son?'

'What does that have to do with anything?'

'Just answer the question,' said Erik.

'It's been difficult,' said Markus. 'But things are getting better.'

'Why is he at school in Gothenburg?'

'It's a hockey school.'

Markus seemed to change as he talked about his son. His

face was telling a different story to his mouth, indicating that things hadn't improved at all, and Hanna spotted an opening to cling onto.

'Is your son the reason you joined the forum?' she asked.

'To an extent.'

'Go on.'

'I've always struggled to talk to him, but it's easier with others. I really feel like I can help them.'

'Is your son gay?' she continued.

'No. Or at least not as far as I know.'

'So why an LGBTQ forum?'

'I used to work for a support line for people considering suicide.'

'Where were you between Tuesday night and early Wednesday morning?' asked Erik, who seemed to have grown weary of Markus's evasive answers.

'I was here, asleep. I went to bed early, around ten.'

'Is there anyone who can confirm that?'

'No. I spoke to my wife on the phone, but that was just after nine.'

'When were you last on Öland?'

'A few weeks ago. I went to see a friend in Färjestaden.'

Hanna and Erik left Markus Johansson, telling him to get in touch if he remembered anything else they should know about Joel.

'Do you have Markus Johansson's registration number?' asked Hanna.

When Erik shook his head, she called a colleague and asked them to check. They were walking towards the building's car park, and quickly found the black Audi with the right plates.

Hanna got the same feeling she had when she saw Johansson for the first time: that she had seen it before. The left wing mirror was broken, and there was a long scratch down one side of the car. She peered in through the windscreen. The car's interior was much tidier than her own. Not a single thing visible, not even any scrap paper. She also thought she could make out the smell of cleaning products.

'What do you think?' asked Hanna.

'It looks like someone's angry with him.'

Chapter Fifty-One

As Hanna drove over to Öland, Erik called Ove to give him an update. The line was busy, so he sent a message telling him to call back. He was still looking down at the phone in his hand when a picture came through from Supriya. Nila and Yadu were standing by a set of prison bars, pressed up against them as though they were trying to escape.

He was never like that with me, Supriya had once said about the way Yadu played with Nila. As a girl, she had been expected to keep quiet and do as she was told. While she helped her mother with whatever their maid hadn't managed, her brothers were free to do what they liked. Still, her parents had encouraged her in her studies, worried that she would never get married, and then welcomed Erik with open arms. Before they retired, Yadu had run his own liquor business, and Aavika had been a chef. Just as Erik sent off an emoji to his wife, Ove called him back.

'How's it going?' he asked.

'Speaking to him just strengthened our suspicions,' said Erik. 'You should probably get someone to do a thorough search on Markus Johansson. Find out whether he has been in touch with any other boys around Joel's age on that forum? Or other forums. He mentioned that he used to work for a suicide prevention line.'

'Already done. How far have you got?'

'We're on the bridge,' said Erik. 'Was Fanny at home?'

'Sadly not, but given the state the house is in, the search is going to take a while. She might still turn up.'

Erik doubted Fanny would return to the house while the police were rummaging about inside, but he didn't say that. Instead, he felt a sudden urge to laugh. It was as though Hanna's pessimism had rubbed off on him. She seemed unusually sulky today.

'I want you and Hanna to do a loop of the area looking for her,' Ove continued.

Once they hung up, Erik recapped what they had been asked to do.

'OK,' she said. 'If the kids still hang out in the same places they did when I was younger, I know where we should check. We'll start with the school.'

The traffic on the bridge was heavier at the weekend than it was during the week, but still nowhere near as bad as it could be in the summer months.

'It feels like there's something about Joel that no one wants to mention,' said Hanna.

'Yeah, but what?'

'I don't know.'

Hanna took the exit onto the 136 at far too high a speed, and Erik had to grab the door handle to stay upright. She gave him an irritable glance, but he ignored it and kept his eyes fixed on the windscreen. On the yellow and green fields, the solitary trees flanking them. It was so bleak round here.

Just as the thought came to him, they passed a small cluster of houses and a windmill. Hanna turned off towards Gårdby, and the road narrowed.

'What were you like at school?' he asked.

'How is that relevant?'

'Were you like Fanny?'

'No,' said Hanna. 'More like Joel if anything.'

Did she mean she was gay? He couldn't exactly ask, so he stayed quiet instead. Though on second thoughts, why not? It shouldn't be any more charged a question than asking someone's shoe size.

'Are you gay?'

'No, are you?'

'I have a wife.'

Hanna snorted.

'I know,' said Erik. 'That doesn't mean anything.'

As they approached Gårdby, he began keeping an eye out for Fanny, though he didn't see anyone who looked like her. Just people working in their gardens and a couple of women out with buggies.

Hanna parked up by the school. One quick lap of the main building was enough to establish that there were no teenagers anywhere nearby. A couple of younger children were playing on the climbing frame in the yard.

'Are you from the police?' they called after them.

Just a week ago, that probably wouldn't have been their first guess. Erik raised a hand in greeting.

'Where now?' he asked.

'The harbour.'

The harbour proved to be further away than he expected, and they had to drive through another small village to get there, past another row of houses and more of the ever-present fields.

Erik climbed out of the car, the Baltic stretching out in front of him. He felt the same sensation he had earlier, but much more powerfully this time: it was so bleak round here.

Without saying a word, Hanna moved towards the water's edge and stood with her back to him. Erik did a quick lap of the harbour. A few small huts were the only buildings to speak of, and though he doubted Fanny would be hiding in any of them, he tried their doors and peered in through the windows anyway. On one of the jetties, he saw a man around his own age, fishing with a casting rod.

'Are they biting?'

'Nope,' said the man. 'The water's getting too warm.'

Erik knew nothing about fishing, but nodded as though he did.

'How long have you been here?' he asked.

'Couple of hours.'

'Have you seen anyone else while you've been here?'

'Just Henrik, working on his boat.'

Erik nodded again, as though he knew who Henrik was. He glanced over at the few boats that were tied up. Simple motor-boats for the most part, plus a couple of rowing boats.

'No teenagers?'

'Nope.'

Erik thanked him and headed back over to Hanna. The man had shown zero interest in who Erik was, despite the fact that he was snooping around the huts. Back in Malmö, he wouldn't have been able to ask questions like that without receiving thousands of counter questions in return. The man had probably realised he was from the police.

His phone started ringing; a call from the same number that had sent the threatening message to Hanna. He held up the screen for her to see, and told her about the message he had sent.

'Want to take it?' he asked.

'I really don't.'

If anything, she looked like she wanted to grab his phone and toss it into the water. Hanna's anger surprised him, but he didn't have time to process it: he had to answer before they hung up.

'How can you claim to understand?' an angry woman's voice asked him.

'I—'

But the woman had no intention of letting him speak: 'You have no idea what it was like to see her round here again. Her dad killed my mum. He . . .'

She struggled to catch her breath for a second or two before hanging up.

Erik met Hanna's eye. It probably wasn't the phone she wanted to throw in the sea; it was him.

'Did Ester have a daughter?' he asked.

'Yeah. Maria.'

'Well, she's the one who's been threatening you.'

Chapter Fifty-Two

Hanna had suspected as much, but suspicions are easily ignored, and she hadn't been prepared for how she would feel once she knew beyond all doubt. Everything was unravelling. Even the anger that had flared up at Erik once again; the fact he had sent a message without discussing it with her first.

He gripped her arm, led her over to the car, and pushed her into the passenger seat. She wanted to tell him she didn't need any help, especially not his, but she couldn't utter a single word. The door swung shut, and he walked around the car to climb in beside her.

'It's not OK for her to do this to you,' he said.

Hanna turned to look out at the Baltic. Whenever she hadn't been able to cope with things at home, this was where she had come.

'Maybe not, but do you know what he—'

'Yes,' said Erik. 'You don't need to tell me.'

Hanna's eyes were locked on the waves. Of course he had looked up what happened the minute he found out her father was a murderer. Everyone always did. It was the same impulse that made people slow down and gape out of the window whenever they passed a car crash.

A handful of the officers in Stockholm had recognised her name, but very few people outside the force ever did. She had brought it up herself on three occasions, but no one could ever handle it, unable to separate her from her father. Until now, it had always been a case of creating distance, but a line had been crossed. Maria actually wanted to harm her.

Hanna had worked on several investigations where hatred had been directed towards the perpetrator's relatives. She remembered the wife of a man who had raped and killed a young woman. Someone had put stones through her window, and she was injured by the glass. The harassment went on for so long that she had ultimately been forced to move.

'What's Maria's surname?' asked Erik.

'Jensen.'

Erik tapped away at his phone.

A lapwing landed a few metres from the car. Probably a male, she thought. The feathers on its back were shimmering and green. It stared up at Hanna with an accusing look in its eyes: *What are you doing here? You should have stayed in Stockholm.*

In Stockholm, she'd had the chance to become someone else, but her life there had been a half-life – if that. She'd had her job, but that was pretty much all. The odd relationship and friend had fluttered by, but she hadn't managed to hold on to anything. Still, it wasn't the city that was the problem, it was her. Her half-hearted attempts had always been doomed to fail, because she wasn't like Kristoffer. She couldn't shake off their past. If she was going to move on, she needed to understand what had happened. Really process it. It was just that it had taken a long time for her to realise that.

'Maria Jensen lives in Norra Sandby,' said Erik. 'I think we should go over there.'

Hanna already knew where Maria lived. She had looked her up after seeing her at the rest area in Möckelmossen.

'We've got work to do,' she said.

'Do you have any other ideas about where Fanny could be?'

'At Tilde's? Or Lukas's?'

'Do you really believe that?'

'No.'

Considering what both Tilde and Lukas had said about Fanny, they probably wouldn't let her in even if she did show up. She could easily have other friends, they just didn't know who to ask. Her mother was hardly going to know.

'OK, then I think we should go to see Maria,' said Erik. 'We can do another lap of Gårdby afterwards. Ove might seem a bit slow sometimes, but he's not, and he's basically a decent guy. I'll send a message to explain.'

Before Hanna had time to reply, he sent his message and started the engine, pulling away without waiting for Ove's response.

At several points during the journey, Hanna felt a sudden impulse to ask him to turn around, but she let it pass every time. She gazed feverishly out through the windscreen instead, desperate to spot Fanny and put a stop to what was about to happen.

It became harder to breathe the closer to Norra Sandby they came. She might even have begun making a noise, because Erik cast an anxious glance in her direction. Still, if he was really worried, he wouldn't be doing this. Hanna let go of her left forearm. She had been gripping her tattoo so tightly it hurt.

Erik pulled up outside Maria's little stone house, and Hanna somehow managed to convince him to stay in the car. The garden was incredibly neat and tidy, and she felt like staying there. May had always been her favourite month, with greenery exploding to life everywhere you looked. Hanna knew a lot about plants and animals – before her mother died, her father used to drill both her and Kristoffer on their knowledge – but there was a lot here she didn't recognise; Lars had always preferred the wild to the cultivated. Hanna's fingertips brushed a lilac that was on the verge of blooming. A wasp lifted off and buzzed away.

She walked to the door, and after touching the nightingale on her arm one last time, raised her finger to the bell. The muted sound echoed through the house. The lights were on inside, but she was hoping Maria wouldn't be home.

The door swung open, and when Maria saw who was standing outside, every muscle in her face seemed to tense.

'Please, don't close the door,' Hanna begged her.

Maria's hate-filled eyes looked Hanna up and down, tearing and clawing at her. Eventually, she turned and walked away, though she left the door open. Unsure what to do, Hanna followed her in, closing the door behind her without looking back at Erik.

'Why did you come back?' asked Maria.

She was standing on the rug in the open-plan kitchen and living room, her arms tightly folded. There were many answers to that question: the fact that Hanna had never really been able to breathe in Stockholm; the fact that she hadn't managed to forge a single meaningful relationship there; that she had constantly felt like something was missing; that the way she had been forced to leave the island was wrong. The fact that she felt a bond to Öland that went way deeper than her family. But she had no idea how to explain any of that.

'I wasn't happy in Stockholm,' she said.

'You weren't *happy*?' Maria practically spat the last word.

'I know what my dad did was . . . unforgivable. But I'm not him.'

'So how do you feel about him now?'

The smart thing would have been to lie and say that she hated him, but Hanna just couldn't do it. When she was younger, Lars had been a fantastic father. He had read to her, played with her, explained the world to her. Taken her and Kristoffer on adventures. Walking, camping, fishing. It was just that all that had disappeared when Mum died. Tears began spilling down her cheeks.

'I think you should go.'

Maria's words and body language were as hostile as ever. Hanna no longer knew what she was doing there. She should never have let Erik talk her into coming. But she also couldn't go. Not yet.

'Have you been calling me?'

Maria simply stared at her.

'Not saying anything, but playing—'

'No.'

Hanna felt a sudden urge to get out of there, and as she turned, she spotted the photograph on the chest of drawers: Maria and Carina, standing in front of a blooming rosebush, both in matching sunhats. The photo couldn't be much more than five years old, and Carina had a look on her face that Hanna had never seen at the station: she seemed relaxed, happy.

She hurried outside.

'How did it go?' Erik asked as she climbed into the car.

'Fucking awful. Just drive.'

Erik started the engine and pulled away, but he didn't have enough sense to stay quiet for long.

'You have to—'

But that was as far as he got.

'I don't have to do anything,' she hissed.

Erik jumped, turning to look at her.

'What exactly happened in there?' he asked.

Not *what's wrong with you?* His calm compassion lit the anger towards him that had been smouldering away inside Hanna all day.

'What the hell is your problem?' she spat.

'My problem?'

'Yeah. You're constantly undermining me. First, you blab to Ove, then you send Maria a message without checking with me first. It's such bad fucking style. Then you decide it's a good idea for me to go and see her.'

Erik pulled over to the side of the road and came to a halt. His hands were trembling on the wheel. They were almost back in Gårdby.

'I'm sorry,' he said, his face dogged. 'But you've not exactly been easy to deal with yourself.'

'I'm not my father.'

'And I never said you bloody were. You misinterpret everything I say. Everything I do.'

Hanna stared at Erik, at how wounded and upset he seemed, and turned away. She repressed the urge to get out of the car. She didn't want to be here, but she also knew that it wasn't him she was most angry with, it was her shitty life. In her mind, she was back at Maria's place. Maria knew Carina, and she had probably been telling the truth when she said that she hadn't made the calls. That meant they must have come from someone else, but who?

They sat there by the side of the road for several minutes until Hanna eventually broke the silence.

'Sorry,' she said.

Erik glanced over at her, seemingly weighing his words.

'I'm the one who should apologise.'

Hanna fixed her eyes on the lock on the inside of the door, blinking back the tears. She knew she should explain, but how?

'I know I don't always think before I speak,' Erik continued, 'but I really don't mean any harm.'

'OK,' said Hanna. 'I . . .'

That was as far as she got. After a few minutes, Erik started the engine.

'Go south,' said Hanna.

'Why?'

'Fanny might be in Möckelmossen.'

Chapter Fifty-Three

A small group of people were gathered in front of the pile of flowers. Many of the bouquets had started to wither, but new bunches were being added all the time. There was still no sign of Fanny, nor the blonde woman Hanna had seen that first evening, but she pulled out her phone and took pictures of the crowd anyway.

Erik nodded – an approving nod, she thought, though she wasn't sure. They hadn't said a word since she had failed to explain herself.

Once Hanna had finished taking pictures, they returned to the car. There was no reason for them to stay.

The image of Maria and Carina kept coming back to her, and she didn't know what to do with it. Or with the fact that someone other than Maria was behind the calls. Or that she had completely lost control and shouted at Erik. He started the engine and guided the car out of the car park.

'I'm starving,' he said. 'We should get some food.'

Hanna turned to look at him.

'What?' he said. 'Arguing works up an appetite. Besides, it's gone two already.'

She swallowed back the tears trying to escape.

'Let me just call Daniel to see how the search is going,' she said. 'They might need us there.'

There was no answer from Daniel, so she called Ove instead. He revealed that the search was still under way, and that there had been no sign of Fanny. Her mother was there, and claimed sarcastically that her daughter had gone to the Maldives. When Hanna explained that they hadn't managed to find Fanny either, he told them to come back to Kalmar.

She hung up, wondering whether she should have mentioned what had happened at Maria's. The fact that the calls had come from someone else. Or the photograph. Deep down, she knew she couldn't talk to Ove either. She needed to find out what kind of relationship Maria and Carina had first. No one could do anything about the threats so long as they remained anonymous.

'Ove wants us back at the station,' she told Erik. 'I didn't bring any food, so maybe we can stop somewhere on the way.'

She made a real effort to keep her tone light and friendly.

'What do you feel like?' he asked.

'Don't mind. You choose.'

As they reached the mainland and turned off the E22, Erik took a right towards the Scandic Hotel instead of the station. He pulled up outside a charcoal grill restaurant called Dilan.

'Eat in or takeaway?'

'I'd prefer takeaway,' said Hanna.

She didn't know where she stood with him right now, never mind herself, and the thought of sitting opposite him for an entire meal was just too much. Back at the station, she hoped there might be someone else in the coffee room for him to talk to. As luck would have it, there wasn't, and when she failed to speak he began telling her about the apocalypse book he was reading. Saying that according to its author, the way she lived was better than the way he lived. If a large percentage of humanity was wiped out, the towns and cities would quickly become uninhabitable; they weren't built to function without modern infrastructure. Plus, they would quickly fill up with the dead.

'I thought you were an optimist,' said Hanna.

'I am, I just think it's an interesting subject.'

Hanna hurried back to her desk as soon as she had finished her lamb skewer. She ran a search on Maria, but couldn't find anything that explained her relationship with Carina. She didn't dare search the database for any information about her colleague.

She was finding it difficult to concentrate, her mind constantly returning to the meeting with Ester's daughter. There was a chance she might leave Hanna in peace now that she had said what she needed to say, though Hanna doubted it. That kind of hatred didn't just disappear. But what about the calls? Those probably had nothing to do with grief and anger over what her father had done, but were directed at her personally. Someone felt threatened by her return to the island.

Hanna tried once more to force herself to focus on the investigation. Aside from Fanny, Tilde and Lukas, who else knew that Joel would be walking through Gårdby that night? All the evidence suggested that Fanny was guilty, but Hanna didn't want to believe it. She would prefer a forty-three-year-old perpetrator to a sixteen-year-old girl.

She opened the investigation and began reading through the interview notes, call logs, and the few forensic reports that had come in, but she couldn't find any new leads. Someone else was looking into Markus Johansson, but they hadn't uploaded anything to the system yet, and probably wouldn't before Monday. Just to be on the safe side, she sent a quick message to Ove:

Any news on Markus Johansson?

He replied immediately:

Nope. You'll know as soon as that changes.

'Have you changed your mind?' asked Erik.

Hanna looked up from her phone, confused. Had he seen what Ove had written?

'About what?'

'Coming for dinner. I'm leaving now.'

Was he joking? Hanna searched his face for a sign, but drew a complete blank.

'Do you really want me to come?' she asked.

'I can handle being shouted at,' said Erik. 'Believe me, I've been called far worse.'

Yet again, Hanna was tempted to use dinner with Ingrid as an excuse, but she knew he probably wouldn't believe her. To her annoyance, she felt herself blush, and stared intently at her screen. What she had found out at Maria's had shaken her, and she probably wouldn't be able to breathe calmly tonight, even in Kleva. She might be able to invite herself over to Ingrid's, but unlike her neighbour, Erik had actually asked her to come. That had been before she'd shouted at him, yes, but she really did need to stop being so pathetically weak. And she still wanted to explain herself.

'OK,' she said.

The look of surprise on Erik's face made Hanna panic. He had probably asked purely because he thought she would say no, but the emphasis he put on the word *cool* helped to dampen her fears to a manageable level. She logged out and stood up.

It was just before five when they stepped into Erik and Supriya's apartment in the Varvsholmen area of Kalmar. His daughter, Nila, came running towards them in a pink dress.

'Hello! Who are you?'

'I'm Hanna. I work with your dad.'

She heard quick footsteps, probably drawn towards the unfamiliar voice. Supriya's head only came up to Hanna's chest, but she pulled her into a hug anyway.

'It's so nice to meet you.'

Erik gave his wife a disapproving glance, possibly thinking she was overreacting. Hanna had been under the impression that Supriya didn't speak Swedish, but she did – albeit with an accent, occasionally muddling her word order.

Hanna greeted Supriya's parents, shaking their hands. For some reason, she had assumed they would be wearing traditional Indian clothing, but the only hint of India she could see was the shawl draped over Aavika's shoulders. Hanna never liked being reminded of her prejudices; the only time she had ever left Europe was on a week-long package holiday to Morocco.

Nila went off to play chess with her grandfather while Supriya's mother headed back to the kitchen to cook. Hanna was left in the living room, unsure where to turn. Erik and Supriya had disappeared.

'Come on,' Erik told her when he returned, leading her out to the balcony.

Supriya handed her a glass of white wine. Hanna's car was

still parked outside the station, but she had decided to take the bus home.

'Thanks,' she said.

The view from the balcony was incredible. Being able to see the sea was the one thing she missed in her house, and it was the main reason she walked down to the beach every morning. Yes, she saw the water as she drove across the bridge, but it wasn't the same if you couldn't hear the waves or taste it in the air.

Hanna sat down with Erik and his wife, sipping her wine and nibbling nuts. They managed to talk among themselves, meaning Hanna didn't need to speak, but she still found herself struggling to relax.

'How long have you been living in Sweden?' she eventually asked, in an attempt to prove she could do something other than listen.

'Almost five years,' said Supriya.

The look in her eyes changed, and Hanna saw a wave of longing pass over her. It felt like she had touched upon something. Erik didn't seem to notice.

'And you work as a dentist, right?' Hanna continued.

'Yes,' said Supriya. 'It's probably not as exciting as your job, but today I helped a kid who had knocked out a tooth.'

'Your work is important too,' said Erik. The look he gave his wife was brimming with love.

A sudden realisation struck Hanna: she would probably never get to experience that kind of love. Far more often than she wanted to admit, she found herself wondering what life would have been like if she had said yes to Fabian. They might still have been together, though she doubted they would have been particularly happy. It often took her a long time to realise certain things, but she now knew that it wasn't Fabian she had been in love with; it was the thought of having someone to share her life with.

She looked over to Supriya, who smiled back. Hopefully her longing wouldn't become unbearable.

Hanna's phone rang, and when she saw that the number was withheld, she hesitated before answering. This time, what she heard on the other end was neither silence nor flames, but a distorted male voice saying: *Get out of here. If you stay, you'll die.* She hurriedly hung up.

'Is she still calling?' Erik asked.

Hanna shrugged dismissively. She knew this might be her opportunity to tell him what she had realised at Maria's place, but she just couldn't do it. Supriya excused herself, saying she had to go to the bathroom, probably in an attempt to give them a moment. Hanna searched for the right words, but no matter how encouragingly Erik seemed to be looking at her, she couldn't manage a single one. He put up with her silence for just under a minute.

'There's something you should know about Daniel,' he said.

'What do you mean?'

'He's gay.'

'OK . . .'

'It's just I've seen the way you . . .'

'Thanks, that's enough.'

Hanna took a sip of her wine, resisting the urge to press the cool glass to her hot cheeks. Had Daniel noticed too? That was the worst part – the fact that she had been yearning so openly. In a way, it was a relief that he was gay. She had known from the very outset that the attraction was purely physical, because of his similarities with Fabian, but she really knew nothing about him, which was now painfully clear. As she tried to smooth over the silence with another sip of wine, Supriya came out and told them that dinner was ready.

At the table, everyone switched to English. Hanna's was much rustier than she would have liked, and she felt a little ashamed, though the others didn't seem to care. The food was fantastic, and nowhere near as spicy as she had assumed it would be. She mentioned that to Supriya's mother, who laughed.

'I add less spice so that Erik can eat it.'

Everyone laughed. Even Erik.

Supriya's mother began asking questions about Hanna's family, and seemed to feel sorry for her when she learned that she lived alone. That the only family she had was her grand-mother, who lived in a home, and her brother, in London. Hanna talked up their relationship, claiming that they spoke every week. She managed not to mention her paternal grand-parents.

Before long, the wine started to go to Hanna's head. It mixed with the sense of release from her outburst earlier, and with the latest call. Her family too. It was all just too much.

'I should be heading off,' she said. 'I have a bus to catch.'

It was an exaggeration – her bus didn't leave for another hour, but she was banking on Erik not knowing that.

The station building was closed, so Hanna sat down to wait in the bus shelter. It was hard not to think about Joel. About the photo he had taken of his bruised, bloodied face.

What had happened next?

She leaned back and closed her eyes. The voice from the

phone immediately came back to her, telling her that she would die unless she left. The problem was that she had nowhere else to go.

She opened her eyes in an attempt to get away from the voice. It had confirmed the suspicions she had spent so many years trying to repress: that something wasn't quite right. The fragments she had heard didn't seem to fit. The excessive violence, what little her father had said. She needed to find out what really happened that night sixteen years ago.

Hanna sent a message to Ove asking whether she could read the investigation into her father.

The Last Day

The moped engine roars, and Joel's body reacts instinctively, convinced Fanny is about to mow him down. Either that or pull up in front of him so she can hit him again, never stopping this time.

There is nothing he can do about it.

Instead, Fanny tears by, kicking out as she passes. Her foot doesn't hit him particularly hard, but it's enough to make Joel lose his balance. He stumbles towards the ditch, only managing to raise his arms halfway. His left elbow takes the brunt of the impact, his cry drowned out by the roar of the engine. Joel is lying on his side in the longish grass. Curled up like he was in the woods, protecting his head with his arms.

Without slowing down, Fanny cuts across the road and turns off onto Snegatan.

Joel doesn't dare believe she is actually gone, and he lies quietly in the darkness, waiting. Listening. But the pain is all he can hear. The throbbing of his ribs.

He has only ever broken a bone once before, when he fell off his bike and landed on his arm, but he doesn't remember the physical pain. All he remembers is the rest of it: Axel telling him to stop whining. Saying that only girls whine.

How old was he then? Eight? Old enough to have started school, at the very least, because he remembers the other kids drawing on his cast. No, not kids. The girls. They were the ones he spent most time with.

His life is one big mess. How did it end up like this?

Joel has no idea how he is supposed to straighten everything out. He already talks to Nadine, but that isn't helping, possibly because there is a limit to what he can tell her. Some of the things he shares make her feel bad, that's obvious from a mile off. But he understands that. It's Joel she has fallen in love with.

Joel knows he should call Tina. That he should try to apologise and explain himself – though he doesn't know whether he can ever be forgiven.

Tina was so upset.

A cold gust of wind makes him shiver, and he crawls to his feet. Fanny really is gone. Joel is on the verge of crying tears of relief, and he realises for the first time just how tense he was. Still, he doubts she will leave him and Molly in peace going forward. Not before she gets her money.

He should talk to Mum about this too.

Ask her for help.

The darkness quickly eats up his sense of relief. However bad it was to have Fanny behind him, the worries about what she was going to do, at least the moped illuminated the road.

'Almost there,' he says aloud in an attempt to fight back the ghosts in the dark.

He is just a few hundred metres away from warmth, from his bed.

Joel takes out his phone to turn on the torch and send a message to Tina. A sorry will do right now. Any explanations can wait. But this time, his phone refuses to show a single sign of life.

Chapter Fifty-Four

It was quarter to twelve when Hanna stepped off the bus in Kleva. They had arrived a few minutes early, so the driver sat at the bus stop to wait while she began walking along the side of the road. The man who had left the bus with her seemed to head off in the other direction. She was roughly halfway home when the bus finally passed her, driving south towards the final stop in Mörbylånga with its handful of passengers.

The sun had set an hour or so earlier, and it was pitch-black, so Hanna pulled out her phone to light the way. She really would have to get herself a small pocket torch for exactly this type of situation. As she came around the bend and saw the streetlight illuminating the village road, she felt a sudden sense of relief.

She could still feel the wine in her system – she had drunk almost three glasses, which was more than she was used to – and was longing to get home. She would drink a big glass of water and then settle down in front of the TV for an hour. Drown out the knowledge that Daniel was gay with an episode of *Outlander*. After that, she would go to bed.

Hanna sped up. She would never admit to being afraid of

the dark, but she had forgotten how different the darkness was here. So compact and heavy compared to Stockholm. It felt like there was nothing beyond the edges.

Her heart skipped a beat as she heard something rustle behind her. Had the man from the bus come the same way after all? She turned around, though she couldn't see anything. So what if he had? Maybe he lived in the village too?

Hanna couldn't calm herself. She was convinced the man was after her, that he might even be the person who had been threatening her. All she had to defend herself was her own strength, and that wouldn't count for much if he had a weapon. She had taken a course in disarming techniques, but that was in a brightly lit gym hall, not on a pitch-black country road after three glasses of wine.

She decided to do the only thing she could: she began running.

Her pace was far quicker than it should have been, considering she couldn't even see where she was putting her feet, but so long as she stuck to the tarmac, she should be OK. Her eyes were locked on the streetlight that seemed to be bobbing up and down; that was where she needed to get to. She tried to listen out behind her, but all she could hear was the sound of her own feet on the road, her pulse roaring in her ears. She strayed too far towards the edge of the road and stumbled. In desperation, she staggered forward, convinced she was about to fall, only just regaining her balance at the last moment. Hanna knew she should slow down, but couldn't actually bring herself to do it. The turn-off was only ten or so metres away now.

The sense of relief Hanna felt as she turned into the village made her sob. There were more lights here, and most of the people who lived in the village still seemed to be up. More importantly, she could both see and cry for help if she needed to. She paused for a long moment, looking back, but if the man was following her, he must have stopped too.

Hanna walked quickly through the village. She didn't want to run in case anyone saw her, didn't want to give them any reason to gossip. To be known as the crazy policewoman who sprinted home as though she had the devil breathing down her neck.

Before long, she reached her dark house, but couldn't bring herself to go inside. What she needed right now was to be with another living person. Someone who could reassure her that her scars weren't real. The lights were on in Ingrid's house, so she made her way over there and rang the bell.

Ingrid peered out through the kitchen window, and Hanna raised her hand in an awkward wave. The door swung open. With Ingrid, it was always best to simply come out and say whatever was on your mind:

'I just got the bus from town, and it felt like someone was following me. I didn't dare go home.'

'Come in,' said Ingrid. 'I was just about to get ready for bed, but that can wait.'

Hanna cast a quick glance over her shoulder. The night was full of dark spots and shifting shapes, but it was impossible to tell what was creating them. She stepped inside and locked the door behind her.

'Want a whisky?' Ingrid asked.

Hanna hesitated. She shouldn't really have any more to drink, but right now she needed the alcohol to calm her nerves.

'Yes, please.'

'I found some Japanese whisky at the Systembolaget in Kalmar.'

'Sounds good.'

Ingrid told her to sit down in the living room, and after rummaging around in the kitchen, came through carrying a tray with two glasses and a bottle on top. *Nikka*, Hanna read from the label. She took a big sip from her glass. It was good whisky. Deep, and not too smoky, just how she liked it.

'So, what's going on?' Ingrid asked.

Hanna's fears had already begun to soften at the edges, but she told Ingrid anyway. About the man who had left the bus with her, how she thought he had been following her.

'What made you think that?' Ingrid asked once she finished.

Hanna's eyes began to well up. Her grandmother had often done the very thing Ingrid just had: trying to get to the bottom of whatever Hanna was saying, rather than simply accepting it. Because even if she had imagined the man was following her, the voice on the phone hadn't been all in her mind.

'I've been getting threats,' Hanna told her. 'Someone calling me, among other things. At first I thought it was Ester's daughter, Maria, but I realised today that it must be someone else. All I know is that it has something to do with my dad.'

Ingrid sipped her whisky. 'Why would someone threaten you because of him?'

'Because I . . . I don't think the truth came out back then, and I need . . . I need to find out what actually happened.'

'You think your father was innocent?'

'Maybe, I don't know . . .'

Hanna fell silent, trying to sort through the chaos of her mind. She just couldn't do it. Ingrid watched her for a moment, then dug up the weak point in her argument.

'Does anyone else know that you're planning to find out what happened?'

'No.'

Not even an hour had passed since she sent her message to Ove asking to see the investigation, but she had been receiving calls since Wednesday. Did someone really feel threatened just because she had come back to Öland? Hanna couldn't make sense of it. Not until a sudden realisation struck her like a punch to the face. Her father might not be innocent, but what if he'd had an accomplice?

Monday 20 May

Chapter Fifty-Five

It was just before seven when Hanna reached the overturned rowing boat on the beach at Kleva. The sky above the Kalmar Strait was clear and blue, the temperature already twelve degrees. She hadn't checked the weather forecast, but it looked like the heat was on its way.

Supriya's parents would be pleased, though perhaps the early Swedish summer still felt like winter to them.

Hanna had gone into the station yesterday, primarily to pick up her car. Since none of the others from her group were there, she had driven straight back to Öland, taking a detour through both Gårdby and Möckelmossen.

She had been hoping to find Fanny, but the girl seemed to have gone up in smoke. Whenever Hanna called, she went straight to voicemail.

Hanna had spent the afternoon with Ingrid, who had come over to see how she was doing. The rain had been torrential, so they had sat on Hanna's little porch and enjoyed it from there, drinking tea and eating Ingrid's home-made biscuits. For the most part, they had talked about Ingrid. She was anxious because her son had called that morning and suggested she move into sheltered accommodation; he thought she was no longer capable of looking after herself. Ingrid had also touched upon the grief that she found harder to put into words: that time was marching on.

Having a neighbour Hanna enjoyed spending time with was a huge change from Stockholm. Back there, it had never even occurred to her to try.

As evening approached, Hanna realised that she had forgotten to call Rebecka, and sent a message saying she was thinking of her. Not a word about the investigation, about Fanny Broberg or Markus Johansson. Nor the fact that a forty-three-year-old man may have exploited Joel's insecurities and struggles.

Did Rebecka know they had searched Fanny's house? Probably. There likely wasn't a person in town who didn't.

Her answer was brief: *Thanks.*

Hanna filled her lungs with sea air one last time, then turned and headed back to the house.

Forty-five minutes later, she stepped into the office with a mug of filter coffee in one hand. So far, the commute to the mainland wasn't a problem, though that would probably change once more tourists began to arrive. She remembered the tailbacks from childhood. One of the old men from town used to take his deckchair to the end of the bridge, where he sat and glared at the drivers passing by. More lanes had been added to the bridge since then, but there was also more traffic, so she wasn't sure it had really made much difference.

Erik came into the office just behind her.

'Thanks for the other night,' she told him.

He smiled. It really did feel like something had changed

between them, though perhaps that was just because Hanna had finally relaxed. She had a tendency to make things unnecessarily complicated at times, but she didn't feel like she needed to explain herself now.

Instead, she made her way over to her desk to check her emails and the investigation log. She paused, still a few metres away. Leaning against her keyboard was a brown paper folder. She sat down at the desk and stared at it, eventually opening the cover and reading the top sheet. It was a copy of the report into the murder and robbery of Ester Jensen.

Hanna had somehow managed to forget asking for it, possibly because she hadn't received any threats the day before. She was still convinced she needed to get to the bottom of what actually happened sixteen years ago, but right now she needed to focus on the promise she had made to Rebecka: that she would find Joel's killer.

She opened the top drawer of her desk and placed the investigation folder inside.

The latest update to the investigation log was a report saying that the owner of the car that had been parked in Möckelmossen had finally called back. He had gone hiking for a few days with his phone switched off, and had only realised something had happened on Sunday evening, when he got back to the rest area and saw the flowers. After listening to the anxious voicemails from his mother, he had reached the messages from the police, and immediately got in touch. He had nothing to add to the investigation, he said, and Hanna saw no reason to question that.

At ten past eight, she called Markus Johansson. It was early, but she wanted to speak to him before the morning meeting.

She could hear voices in the background, and assumed he must be at work.

'Hold on,' he said.

She heard him moving, the background noise growing quieter and eventually disappearing entirely as a door closed.

'OK. How can I help?'

'Did you think of anything else to do with Joel?'

'No.'

'It might be useful, even if you don't think it's important.'

'I don't have anything else to tell you.'

'How did you get those scratches on your car?'

The silence was filled by the sound of Markus breathing, and Hanna's body reacted by making her heart race. The man who had called to threaten her had upset her sense of calm. Did he really think she would just pack up and leave? What would he do once he realised she had every intention of staying?

Carina and Daniel entered the office together, walking towards their end of the room. Daniel nodded to both Hanna and Erik, but Carina ignored her. Seeing Daniel gave Hanna a sudden pang of embarrassment.

'Why is that important?' Markus eventually asked.

'I'm afraid I can't say.'

He sighed.

'Some man lost his temper in a car park. He kicked the wing mirror and then dragged something sharp along the side. A key, maybe. I don't know.'

'Why?'

Another pause. As it stretched out to several seconds, Hanna repeated the question. Gently, without any accusations.

'I have no idea,' Markus told her. 'It was dark, and he was drunk. I guess I'd done something to annoy him.'

'Was this man Joel?'

'Absolutely not!'

The force of his denial piqued her interest.

'Thanks,' she said. 'I'm guessing we'll be in touch again.'

Chapter Fifty-Six

Rebecka watched as Molly wolfed down her cereal hoops. Last night, her daughter had announced that she wanted to go back to school. That she missed her friends, especially Vera. Petri had immediately said that he thought it was a good idea, but Rebecka was sceptical, and that same uncertainty had forced her out of bed when her alarm went off that morning.

'Have you changed your mind?' she asked.

She wanted nothing more than for Molly to say yes, but the girl shook her head eagerly. Molly was wearing her cat dress, the same one she had put on for the barbecue on Tuesday.

'I have to go to school so they don't forget about me.'

'They won't forget you that quickly.'

Was this about Joel? Did Molly feel like she had already started to forget him? Rebecka didn't dare ask, and glanced at his empty chair. She could just picture him hunched over his usual cheese sandwiches. She could even hear the sound of him chewing. But when she tried to remember how he smelled, it was the baby scent that came back to her. That sweet mix of talc and milk that had lingered for so long.

Axel had talked about the baby and toddler years in his

awful interviews. About how fantastic Joel had been. Rebecka hadn't been able to resist reading them. He was now the poor grieving father who had been falsely accused of murdering his own son, and the media loved him. It was like they couldn't get enough. Just last night, he had been on a live news broadcast. The only thing he had said about Rebecka was that they didn't get on, though he had made it perfectly clear that it was all her fault.

'But I want to play with Vera!' said Molly.

Petri popped his head around the kitchen door.

'You can. Run up and clean your teeth, and I'll take you down there.'

He avoided looking at Rebecka. They had barely spoken since their fight on Saturday, but the silence between them felt different now. Not quite stale, but utterly draining. Though he was flat-out at work with his new renovation job, he had stayed home to take his daughter to school, and Rebecka loved him for that. But she also realised what she was most afraid of: the moment when Petri came home, and they were left alone. Without anyone to upset with their shouting.

Like her, he had struggled to sleep last night, but she hadn't asked why. Hadn't wanted to dredge up anything that couldn't be stopped. In the end, he had drifted off, and she had lain awake in the darkness, listening to the sound of his breathing.

Molly came down the stairs and gave Rebecka a pleading look. 'I want Mummy to take me.'

'OK.'

Rebecka got up, but Petri stopped her in the doorway. His eyes were locked on the doorframe to the right of her.

'Are you sure?' he asked.

She nodded, though she wasn't. Neither that Molly should

be going to school, nor whether she would be able to handle bumping into any of the other parents or teachers. But she also knew that she couldn't say no to Molly.

As they left the house, Molly reached out and took her hand. It was clear she was nervous.

Rebecka glanced down at her clothes. She had managed to put on a clean top and a pair of jeans, at the very least. Her own shoes this time too. It suddenly struck her that she hadn't washed her hair in several days, and she raised her hand to the back of her head and tried to comb through her greasy locks. Her irritation with Petri reared its head again. Why hadn't he said anything?

Spotting a few people up ahead, Rebecka slowed down. She didn't want to catch up with them.

'What's wrong?' asked Molly.

'Nothing,' she said with a smile.

They reached the school yard and, to Rebecka's relief, Vera was already inside. She ran over to Molly and hugged her, dragging her off to play. There was still ten minutes before the first class of the day.

'Bye, Mummy!' Molly shouted over her shoulder.

Rebecka waved, but she had no voice to call back with. Instead, she walked over to Isak, the teacher she trusted most. It was obvious that he liked his job and that he took the children seriously. He had only been at the school for a few years, so he had never taught Joel. Rebecka didn't need to say a word.

'I'll keep a close eye on Molly today,' he told her. 'And I'll call you if anything comes up.'

'Thanks.'

'I'm so sorry for your loss. I know how hard it is to lose someone.'

'Thanks,' she said again.

She quickly turned away, a knot of tears like a hedgehog in her chest. *Hodgeheg*, that was what Molly had called them when she was younger. Rebecka felt like she had just walked straight out into the middle of a motorway and left Molly there. She desperately wanted to turn back, grab her daughter and run.

But she didn't.

With every step, the knot in her chest seemed to loosen slightly, and she even managed to say hello to the people she passed. She walked slowly, because she didn't want Petri to be there when she got home. Fixing the problems in their relationship was more than she could handle right now.

It struck her that she should have asked Isak who he had lost. Maybe Ulrika knew – though she probably would have said something if she did. Ulrika loved gossiping about everyone in town.

When she reached the house, Rebecka saw that Petri's car was still parked in the driveway, and felt an urge to turn around. But where would she go? Perhaps she could sneak into the studio and wait there until he was gone. Thoughts of the studio made her glance over to Gabriel and Ulrika's house, where she saw Gabriel sitting on the steps. He turned away from her, but she noticed that his eyes were red and puffy. A small part of her wanted to go over and ask if he was OK, though there was a risk he would simply start whining about his and Ulrika's problems. Could Gabriel have finally confessed to the affair? It all felt so stupid now. She didn't know what she had ever seen in him. The despair she had felt after Gabriel dumped her was nothing compared to the utter darkness the loss of Joel had thrown her into.

Gabriel was nothing to her. He never had been, and she didn't even have the energy to be angry at him for building a castle in the sky and tempting her inside. But how could she make Petri understand that? Did she even want to?

The answer came to her like a sudden hot flush. She had experienced them occasionally while she was pregnant with Molly. Yes, there was nothing she wanted more. Petri had never deceived her. He had always been there for her, and put up with her mood swings. On top of that, he loved their daughter more than anything. She wouldn't be able to move forward without him.

Petri opened the door and stepped outside. The determined look on his face scared Rebecka, making the certainty she had just felt falter. After a moment's hesitation, she moved towards him.

'We need to talk,' he said. 'There's something I need to tell you.'

Chapter Fifty-Seven

On his way out of the morning meeting, Erik got such bad cramp in his calf that he had to pause for a moment. He knew he had probably pushed himself a little too hard on his run that morning, but doing things half-heartedly had never been his thing. When he first started learning Marathi, he had spent a few hours a day on it for several weeks, but his progress seemed so slow that he eventually gave up entirely.

He took a step to one side to allow Amer to pass.

'You OK?' his colleague asked.

'Think I've been taking the Ironman a bit too seriously.'

'The real trick is doing the race without any training.'

'Are you kidding me? Is anyone crazy enough to do that?'

'My brother,' Amer laughed. 'A few years ago. He couldn't walk for days afterwards.'

'How about you? Don't fancy it?'

'I'd rather swallow fire on *Sweden's Got Talent*.'

'You can swallow fire?'

'Maybe. We'll find out.'

Erik's cramp had begun to wear off, and he limped down the corridor. Perhaps he should just admit to Supriya that he was sick of the training. That would cheer her up. Her parents were planning to explore Kalmar on their own today, and Supriya was worried about what they might get up to. That they would keep calling her, constantly asking for help. Erik found her moaning hard to take; it was so out of character.

Either way, Supriya had been right about one thing: inviting Hanna over to dinner had been a good idea. Erik had been slightly worried when she got up and left so abruptly, and had wanted to send a message to check she was OK, but Supriya had said it was unnecessary. And Hanna had seemed perfectly happy when he'd said hello to her that morning.

During their meeting, different emotions had taken over. They were in a position where all they could really do was wait, and the meeting hadn't lasted long. A jacket with blood on one sleeve had been seized from Fanny's house and sent off for analysis. The girl herself seemed to have gone to ground, a fact Ove interpreted as a sign of guilt, though it could just as easily be down to fear. Erik remembered the look of panic in Fanny's eyes as she roared that they were trying to frame her.

Ove wanted them to focus on Fanny, and he had put out an internal alert for her. Erik hadn't argued, despite being convinced that Markus Johansson was a more likely perpetrator. They were still busy gathering information on him, and Carina was supposed to be checking through everything they'd collected so far: bank statements, call lists, background information. There was something about the so-called friendship between Markus and Joel that just didn't sit right.

In Erik's view, it was high time they started reinterviewing people, with a focus on those closest to Joel Forslund. Sometimes you had to allow the initial shock over a person's death to settle before their relatives and friends could really talk about the deceased.

His phone buzzed with a message from Supriya:

It's only nine o'clock and Mum's already called me twice. Where are the keys? Where's the nearest ATM? I'M GOING CRAZY.

She had explained everything to her parents the day before, but clearly none of it had sunk in. They were getting old, and they were in an unfamiliar environment, though Erik didn't write any of that. Instead, he sent his sympathy.

He logged in to his emails and discovered a new message from Melina. She had checked the CCTV footage from the shopping centre in Färjestaden and thought she had found what they were looking for. He clicked on the attached file.

The film was from a camera positioned diagonally above, and showed Joel walking past in jeans and a hoody. His movements seemed quick and angry. Another figure soon caught up with him: a man in a pair of smart trousers and a shirt. Erik paused the video in order to get a better look. There was no doubt about it, the older man was Markus Johansson. He was standing in front of Joel, his face to the camera. Erik hit play again. There was an exchange lasting a few minutes, and then Markus placed a hand on Joel's shoulder. Joel shook it off and ran away, leaving Markus behind to watch him leave. He was clearly upset.

Petri Forslund had described the exchange as intimate, but Erik didn't agree. On the other hand, maybe Petri had noticed something the camera hadn't managed to capture.

Erik took a step back so he could see everyone in the room.

'I need a deaf person.'

'Why?' asked Daniel.

'So they can lip-read a CCTV film for me.'

'Just because they're deaf doesn't necessarily mean they will be able to read lips,' said Daniel.

'No, I . . .'

'But my mum is deaf, and she can also lip-read.'

Chapter Fifty-Eight

Hanna found her eyes constantly drifting back to the drawer of her desk. Why hadn't she waited to ask for the investigation? She didn't have time to start digging into what her father had done right now. She had a job to do.

She pressed her nails into the palms of her hands in frustration. Did she really think she would be able to prove that Lars was acting on someone else's orders? Or that he was actually innocent? And if she did, what goddamn difference would it make? He was dead.

In reality, it wasn't that simple. Both she and Kristoffer had to live with the consequences of the things Lars had been convicted of. She had to uncover the truth, whatever it was, and she couldn't let anything get in her way.

Hanna needed to break the constant whirlwind of thoughts, so she headed to the nearest bathroom. Behind her, she heard Erik shout for someone deaf, but she simply sped up. Closed the door and slumped down onto the toilet seat. After a few minutes, a message came through from Erik, telling her he had received the CCTV footage from the shopping centre. Hanna got up and flushed, making it sound like she had used the toilet. As she was making her way back to the investigation room, Ove popped his head out of his office.

'Can we have a quick chat?'

It was less a question than an order, and he disappeared back into his office without waiting for her to reply. Hanna had sensed a change in him during their morning meeting, and though she was convinced they should be focusing on Markus Johansson rather than Fanny Broberg, she had barely said a word. She didn't want to be alone with Ove right now. Judging by his tone of voice, he didn't have any new information relating to the case; this was about something else.

Hanna stepped into his office and closed the door behind her. Ove was smiling, but she thought she could see it straining at the corners.

'Take a seat,' he said.

He continued once she had done as he said:

'There's no need to look so terrified. I just wanted to see how you thought your first few days had been.'

'OK.'

She said it in response to his desire to check in, not as an answer to his question, but it felt like Ove had chosen to misunderstand her.

'I think it's probably gone a little better than that.'

'Thanks.' As though that word was any better.

Ove's forced cheeriness made her worry that there was more to come. She wondered whether he had spoken to Erik that morning, and what Erik might have told him. Perhaps that was unfair to Erik. After all, he had voluntarily told Hanna that Ove had asked him to keep an eye on her, and claimed that Ove was acting out of concern.

'You got the investigation?'

Hanna nodded slowly. So, it was her father he wanted to talk about. She should have known.

'Why do you want to stir up all that old business? Wouldn't it be better just to let it go?'

Let it go? How was she ever supposed to be able to do that?

His question took her right back to square one. There was so much that just made no sense.

Hanna looked up at Ove, at his softly hunched body. There was a stain on the sleeve of his blue shirt. Perhaps he had been looking after his granddaughter again. Behind his glasses, his eyes were fixed on her. This wasn't the moment to tell him about the photograph she had seen of Maria and Carina. Nor to ask about the investigation, whether there had been anything that had made him doubt her father's guilt. Or suspect that anyone else had been involved. Few investigations involved a perfectly straight path to the perpetrator.

If someone felt threatened by the simple fact that she was back, she would have to keep her digging as quiet as she could.

'I'm not sure I want to look through it yet,' she said. 'I don't actually know why I asked for it.'

'Good,' said Ove, visibly relaxing. 'Maybe I shouldn't have even given it to you, but I want to help you however I can.'

He sounded genuine, but it was obvious that he wanted to help her in a particular direction: away from her father.

Ove was on the verge of saying something else when his phone rang. He glanced down at the number and answered. Hanna made to leave, but he held up a finger for her to wait. It sounded as though he was talking to Carina.

This time, there was something about his voice that told Hanna there had been another development in the case. He hung up and smiled at her.

'Markus Johansson was on Öland on Wednesday,' he said. 'He bought petrol at the Preem garage by the end of the bridge at seven in the evening.'

In his statement, he had claimed that he hadn't been to Öland in weeks, but Hanna suddenly realised where she had seen his car before.

'I went to Möckelmossen that evening, and I think I parked behind his black Audi. The wing mirror was broken.'

The only problem was that Hanna didn't remember seeing Markus Johansson there.

Chapter Fifty-Nine

The minute the film came to an end, Erik watched it again from the beginning. Daniel's mother was on her way over to the station, and Daniel had gone down to meet her. Erik couldn't glean any more from their expressions alone; he needed to know what they were saying.

His phone buzzed, and he wondered if it was Hanna. She had disappeared fifteen minutes earlier, and he had no idea where she had gone. He sighed as he read the message from Supriya:

Now Mum just called to ask if she can borrow a jacket.

I have to work right now.

Erik regretted the message the minute he hit Send, and Supriya replied exactly as he'd known she would:

Great support you are.

He thought she was overreacting, both in relation to his message and her parents, but he had tried to have that conversation before, and it hadn't helped. He just didn't understand why she found her parents such hard work. They were easygoing and pleasant people to be around, and nothing she had told him about her childhood seemed to explain it. Yadu may

389

have been strict and absent, but Aavika had let Supriya do whatever she wanted, providing she worked hard at school and did her chores at home.

Sorry, Erik replied. *But I really do.*

This time, Supriya didn't reply. He knew he had probably managed to buy himself a few hours of peace, but at what cost?

Hanna came back into the room, and he noticed that her body language seemed different. It was as though she had been to the doctor and found out that the tumour was benign. She came over to him.

'Where've you been?' he asked.

'Ove's office. Markus Johansson was on Öland on Wednesday, and I think I saw his car in Möckelmossen.'

'But not him?'

'No.'

Erik showed her the CCTV footage and explained that Daniel's mother, who knew how to lip-read, was coming in to help them.

'Whatever he's saying there, we need to get him in for an interview,' said Hanna. 'I'll call him.'

'What did Ove want?' asked Erik.

Hanna had been gone slightly too long to have spent the entire time talking to Ove about Markus Johansson, but she simply gave him a quick shake of the head and walked off to her desk.

Just then, Daniel and his mother stepped into the room.

'Erik, this is Gunnel.'

Though they had different hair colours – Daniel's was dark, his mother's blonde – they looked remarkably alike. Both had the same straight nose and the same rounded cheeks, and both were smartly dressed. Daniel was wearing jeans and a shirt,

Gunnel a pair of suit trousers and a pink V-neck top.

Erik held out a hand in greeting, suddenly realising that he didn't know what to do next.

'You can talk to her,' said Daniel. 'Just make sure you look at her while you do it. Like I said, she can lip-read.'

He and his mother smiled. They were probably used to this.

Daniel actually seemed different around her. Softer, somehow. Erik had heard him talk about his mother before, but he'd had no idea she was deaf. Daniel came from Rockneby, just to the north of Kalmar, and his parents still lived there, as did one of his two sisters.

'Thank you for coming in so quickly,' said Erik.

Gunnel signed a reply, and Daniel translated for her: 'Not a problem, I've got plenty of time these days. I'm retired.'

'I've booked an interview room,' said Erik. 'So we won't be disturbed.'

When he'd made the booking, he had forgotten all about her being deaf; she wouldn't be bothered by the clattering of keys or the hum of conversation in the office. Still, he led her to the room and hit Play on the computer. Gunnel focused on the film, her hands still. Only once the clip ended did they begin to move.

'What did she say?'

'That she needs to watch the clip again. It's tricky to see exactly what he's saying because he's so upset. She also wants a pen and paper so she can write it down.'

Erik grabbed a pen and paper for Gunnel, and restarted the clip. Ten minutes later, after showing her the video for a third time, she had managed to jot down the conversation. Markus's part of it anyway. All that was visible of Joel was the back of his head and the side of his face as he ran off.

I just want you to be happy.

Yes, actually. Even though I know it doesn't feel that way now.

You need to tell someone. Start with your mum. Things can't get any worse than they already are.

Why are you saying that? You're being very unfair right now.

Joel, wait . . .

It was as Markus said those last words that he reached out and touched Joel's shoulder. Joel shook him off angrily, and Markus's face contorted in pain.

Erik thanked Gunnel, and she signed to her son, who replied with his hands.

'What did she say?' asked Erik.

'She wanted to know if that's who killed him.'

'And what did you tell her?'

'To stop being so bloody nosy. Also that she could have lunch on the police.'

Chapter Sixty

The sight of Carina's back, the floral blouse a few sizes too large, stopped Hanna in her tracks. She didn't want to talk to her, but she knew she had no choice. Markus Johansson was due at the station in just twenty minutes, and he had forewarned her that he was bringing his lawyer. He hadn't sounded remotely surprised when Hanna called to say that they needed to interview him again.

She walked over to Carina.

'Have you found out anything else about Markus Johansson – other than that he filled his tank at Preem?'

Carina looked up at her, then demonstratively checked the time on her phone. Hanna was well aware that it wasn't long since Carina had spoken to Ove, but she refused to apologise for doing her job. Her colleague sighed.

'I get the sense that he's living a double life.'

'Why?' asked Hanna.

'The arrangement with his wife made me wonder,' said Carina. 'That's why I decided to check his bank statements. There are quite a few trips to the pub, and I don't think his wife was with him.'

'Why not?'

'Because most of the charges are only enough to cover one drink.'

'Thanks, that's great.'

It was more than Hanna had been hoping for, but Carina didn't seem remotely happy with her praise. There wasn't a hint of the joy she had seen in the photograph at Maria's place. Still, Hanna couldn't confront her with that now, not just before an important interview.

'Have you managed to get anywhere with the bloody crane's-bill?' she asked instead. 'Is there anything to suggest it was placed in Joel's hand?'

'No,' said Carina. 'According to forensics, it's more likely he picked it himself, but obviously we can't know for sure.'

'It's just that given what we now know about Markus Johansson, maybe it is something to do with relationships after all.'

For some reason, Carina seemed annoyed.

'When are you interviewing him?' Hanna asked.

'Ten thirty, in interview room fourteen. Let me know if you find anything else.'

Carina nodded and turned back to her screen.

There was still another ten minutes until Markus Johansson was due, so Hanna pulled out all the pictures she had taken at the rest area in Möckelmossen. She sorted them into piles by date, and then flicked through them again. She wanted to find Markus, and on Wednesday in particular. She was sure she had parked right behind his black Audi; the chances of an identical car having the same broken wing mirror seemed far too slight.

Failing to find him, she threw down the pictures in

frustration. Right then, she realised who she was actually looking for, and rummaged through the pile until she found the right picture. Hanna stared down at the image.

It was him.

The receptionist called to let Hanna know that Markus Johansson had arrived, and Hanna shoved the picture into a folder, heading downstairs to meet him. On her way there, she paused by Erik's desk and told him it was time.

It was clear that Markus hadn't slept. He was pale, with dark circles beneath his eyes. His lawyer looked much more alert in her grey suit and black pussy-bow blouse.

Hanna started the tape recorder and reeled off the formalities.

'What is my client suspected of?' asked the lawyer.

'Nothing, yet,' said Hanna. 'This interview is about establishing whether he should be considered a suspect in the murder of Joel Forslund.'

Her eyes didn't leave Markus for a second. Grief was the dominant emotion on his face, but she knew that even people who had killed could be sad. The first time Hanna had visited her father in jail, he had spent almost the entire time crying.

Hanna pulled out the image from the rest area in Möckelmossen and placed it on the table in front of him. She pointed to the blonde woman.

'This is you, isn't it?'

Markus cast a quick glance at the image and then nodded.

'Because you didn't want to be recognised?'

'Because I wanted to come as myself. As Tina.'

'Explain, please.'

'I'm a woman. A trans woman.'

Markus gave them a pleading look, but Hanna asked him

to go on. They needed to understand why he had been at the rest area.

'I've never felt comfortable in my own body, but a few years ago I hit rock bottom and realised I was going to have to do something about it. I told my wife and began looking into the issue. That's why we no longer live together. My son has had a hard time accepting who I am too.'

Markus Johansson's lawyer sat quietly as he talked, but Hanna got the distinct impression that she already knew everything he was saying. In truth, now that Markus had told her, Hanna didn't know how she could have missed it herself: he had the same delicate features. It was just that she really had thought the blonde was a woman. She was wearing jeans and a blouse, with long straight hair and light make-up.

'Why did you lie about having been on Öland?'

'Because I was scared. And because I wanted to protect myself.'

'What was the nature of your relationship with Joel?' asked Hanna.

'We didn't have a romantic relationship. I wasn't lying about that. I was trying to help him.'

'In what way?'

'Joel was confused and unsure of himself. I felt the same way when I was fifteen. Looking back now, I can understand why, but at the time I had no idea. I've been on that forum quite often over the past few years, but it was purely down to chance that I saw Joel's post. I decided to do what I wish someone had done for me at that age.'

'Which was?'

'I started talking to him.'

'Was Joel trans?' asked Erik.

'If you insist on putting a label on him, then yes, I think so. But more than anything, he just felt like something was wrong. At first he thought it was because he was interested in men, and then because he thought he should have been born female. Recently, he'd started to realise that it wasn't that at all, he was actually neither and both.'

Hanna thought it sounded like Markus was talking in riddles.

'Do you have a word for that?' she asked.

'There are plenty. Non-binary, transgender, fluid . . . For Joel, the process wasn't over. He didn't know what to call himself.'

Erik turned the computer towards him and pressed Play.

'What was this about?'

The story Markus Johansson gave them fit with the partial version Gunnel had already provided. Markus, or Tina, had tried to convince Joel to talk to his mother, telling him that the main reason he felt so bad was that the burden was too much for him to bear on his own. Joel had then shouted at Tina to stop sticking her nose in, that everything had been better before they met. That he hated her.

With every word, Hanna became increasingly convinced that this man hadn't killed Joel.

This woman.

'Could you tell me what actually happened to your car?' she asked.

'There are no good places for people like me to go out round here, but once a week I dress up as myself and go for a drink. It was something I started as part of my experimentation, when I realised that I was happier as Tina than I am as Markus, but it's not easy. A few men heard me talking to my wife as I was leaving, and my voice gave me away. They followed me back to the car, and then, well . . . you know the rest.'

For the benefit of the tape, Hanna repeated what Tina had told her earlier: that someone had kicked off the wing mirror and scratched the paintwork. She ended the interview and thanked her for coming in.

'So I'm not a suspect?'

'No, and if you'd told us the truth sooner, we would have realised that much earlier. Didn't you realise this was important information?'

'Joel was struggling even to tell his mother. He really didn't want anyone else to know. I was just trying to respect that.'

Chapter Sixty-One

As Hanna took Markus Johansson and his lawyer down to reception, Erik went over to Ove's office to give him an update. It had been obvious Hanna didn't want to join him, which only made Erik even more intrigued as to what her meeting with Ove had been about. Her father, perhaps, but he didn't want to ask about him again.

Ove looked like he needed a two-week retreat on the French Riviera. He closed the brown paper folder he was reading as Erik came in, but Erik had time to spot the National Board of Forensic Medicine logo on the document inside.

'I hope you're bringing me good news,' said Ove.

'Afraid not.'

Erik told Ove what had come to light during the interrogation, and explained the conclusion both he and Hanna had come to: that the perpetrator was probably someone else.

'Damn it,' said Ove. 'It feels like we're back to Fanny Broberg.'

'I agree.'

Ove took off his glasses and massaged the bridge of his nose before putting them on again.

'Are you really sure it wasn't him?'

'Sure enough. He doesn't have a motive.'

'But he could be lying.'

'True, but there's nothing to suggest he is.'

'What was his alibi again?'

Erik couldn't understand why Ove was still clinging to Markus Johansson. Just that morning, he had wanted to prioritise Fanny Broberg.

'He said he was at home,' said Erik. 'So it's a little tricky to confirm.'

'Try.'

Erik nodded. Ove had sown a seed of doubt in him. Had they been too quick to dismiss Markus Johansson? Though everything he'd said about the meeting in the shopping centre checked out, he could be lying about other things.

'The fact that Joel was . . . trans. Could that be a motive?' asked Ove.

'I don't think so,' Erik replied. 'Virtually no one else knew.'

'Or not that we're aware of anyway,' Ove reminded him.

Erik felt sympathy for the situation Markus was in. For the fact that his wife had found what was happening with him so difficult that she'd moved out. That his son no longer wanted to live in the same town. At the same time, he could also understand them. Processing the realisation that your partner had kept such a big part of themselves from you couldn't be easy. Nor could learning something like that about a parent. And no matter how Erik tried, he struggled to think of Markus as Tina. Perhaps it was simply appearance getting in the way.

After leaving Ove's office, Erik headed straight down to the cafeteria. He needed coffee. More than anything, he wanted

Supriya. Like Ove, he had thought they were nearing some kind of closure in the case, and had been looking forward to spending more time with his family. He sent her a message, hoping she wasn't busy with a patient.

Sorry for being such an idiot earlier.

She replied immediately: *Yeah, you were. But you're my idiot.* Her message was followed by an emoji of a running man in shorts.

It's just really hard-going with the investigation right now.

This time, her reply took a moment to arrive: *You'll manage it. You always do.*

A few seconds later, she added: *I love you.*

I love you, Erik wrote back, taking a sip of the coffee he had just poured.

He thought that he and Supriya were honest with one another, that they could talk about anything, but what did he really know? He headed upstairs and found Hanna sitting in one of the armchairs.

'How did he take it?' she asked.

'So-so. He doesn't want us to drop Markus Johansson.'

'I guess I can understand that, given we don't have anyone else yet.'

'There's Fanny,' said Erik. 'And maybe Lukas and Tilde too. It feels like we're back with them.'

Hanna shook her head. 'I really don't think so. I'm going to call Nadine again. Since she was the person Joel seems to have been closest to, I want to confront her about Joel being trans. I'll take another look at the pictures I took at the rest area afterwards. I can't shake the feeling that there's something I'm not seeing. But first I need to talk to Carina about the latest developments.'

Her voice had lowered to a whisper, and she glanced around the room.

'What's wrong?' asked Erik.

'What do you mean?'

'What's the deal with you and Carina?'

Ever since Hanna had mentioned that Carina didn't seem to like her, Erik had realised she was probably right.

Hanna's cheeks flushed. 'She knows Ester's daughter somehow.'

'How do you know?'

'I saw a photo of them together, at Maria's place.'

'Aha,' said Erik.

'What do you mean, "aha"?'

Erik studied Hanna, unsure how to proceed. He suspected this was the source of her outburst yesterday, but was it really such a big deal if Carina knew Maria? Surely they should still be able to work together.

'Have you asked Carina about it?'

'No,' said Hanna.

'So talk to Ove instead.'

Hanna got up, and Erik sighed. Was what he had said really enough to annoy her again? But when she reached the doorway, Hanna turned around.

'We should talk to Joel's step-father, Petri.'

'For any particular reason?'

'We haven't really done it yet.'

Chapter Sixty-Two

There's something I need to tell you.

The minute Rebecka heard those words – or rather felt the fear that seemed to be clinging to them – it was as though she had shut down completely. As though her mind and body had needed to protect themselves. She had run upstairs to bed and pulled the covers over her head.

Petri had followed her up and sat down on the edge of the bed.

Not saying a word.

Just waiting.

Until he couldn't wait any longer, and pleadingly whispered her name. When that happened, she had pressed her palms to her ears and started to hum. As though she were deranged. That was actually how she felt: like she had lost her footing and been driven over the edge.

A new period of waiting had begun after that.

Eventually, he had given up and left.

I can't take any more. Her entire body was aching with that conviction, but it had gradually loosened its painful grip.

She couldn't stay in bed for ever. Molly would come home

from school at some point, and before that happened, she was going to have to hear Petri out.

Rebecka sat up in bed and the room began to spin. Once the dizziness had passed, she padded over to the door and opened it. She couldn't hear Petri, so she tiptoed over to the bathroom and locked herself inside. Exhausted, she slumped onto the toilet seat. The bottom of the shower curtain was dirty, she noticed. She should take it down and wash it. There were so many things she should do.

What was she afraid of?

That Petri had been unfaithful too? That he had done something else he was ashamed of? That he didn't want to be with her any more?

That was probably what scared her most: the prospect of him leaving her. She would be even more alone than she already was. But she could hardly blame him for that.

She had been such a fucking idiot.

She had managed to destroy their relationship for no reason at all.

In that moment, Rebecka suddenly saw everything that was good about Petri. The way he had always encouraged her to paint. The way he had helped her get started with ceramics when she wanted to try something new. The way he hurried home whenever she needed him – like he had that time a bat got trapped in the house and was flying all over the place. Or the time she was convinced that Axel had slashed the tyres on the Saab.

Rebecka grabbed the shower curtain and pulled it so hard that the entire rail came crashing down. The echo hadn't even died down before she heard Petri running up the stairs. He turned the handle on the locked door.

'Please, Rebecka, let me in.'

She didn't reply. She was staring down at the shower rail, which was sticking up out of the bathtub.

They kept a knife on the chest of drawers in the hallway in case Molly needed help and they had to get into the bathroom quickly; Rebecka was grateful that Petri hadn't used it now.

'I forgive you,' he said. 'Please, just let me in.'

Though she doubted he really meant it, his words made her cry. Perhaps the reason he was so keen to forgive her was because whatever he had done was far worse. She slowly got up and unlocked the door. Let him hug her and lead her downstairs to the sofa.

'I don't care about Gabriel,' he said. 'He's not important. You and me, that's the only thing that matters.'

Rebecka couldn't speak. She was the one waiting now.

'I'm sorry if I scared you before, it's just . . . Damn it . . .' He pressed his fists to his temples. 'I don't know why I find this so hard.'

'Just tell me,' she whispered.

Petri lowered his fists to his lap, and they both stared down at them.

'I've been to prison,' he said. 'I don't know why I've never said anything, but . . . With everything now . . . The police might make a big deal of it, even though it should've been wiped from my record.'

Rebecka's hand had been moving towards his, but she stopped short. How was she supposed to react to this news? All she felt was emptiness, similar to the way she had felt whenever she knew Axel was about to lose his temper. How could he have kept this from her?

'Why were you in prison?' she asked, her voice hesitant.

'Actual bodily harm. I was fifteen, so technically it was a young offenders' institute. And after that . . . well, I turned things around. Sonja had always been so good to me, but when I realised that she wasn't going to abandon me, even after what I'd . . . that's when I really started to trust her. It happened in Nybro, and Sonja pretended I'd gone to stay with a relative for a while.'

His words came out quickly, unsteadily.

'I was so angry back then, and it wasn't the first time I'd hit someone. But the guy had a facial fracture . . . and he reported me . . . he had a whole load of witnesses. I'm not that angry person any more, and I'm so sorry I . . . that I let him out in the past. What if the police think I . . . that I hurt Joel?' Petri sobbed. 'I know I'm bad at showing my feelings, but I really did like Joel, and I miss him. Not as much as you, obviously, but . . .'

It was as though Rebecka was seeing Petri for the first time. His stunted, scared side. She suddenly understood why he was always so cautious, why he wanted to please everyone. The barriers that held him back. Why he didn't dare open up about what he thought or felt. He was just like her: he wanted so many things he was incapable of. The love she felt for him in that moment terrified her, but she refused to let her fears win out.

'We need to get better at talking to one another,' she said.

'I know.'

Petri put an arm around her, and she leaned in to him, resting her head against his chest.

Chapter Sixty-Three

Though Carina wasn't at her computer, Hanna still walked over there. Daniel was also elsewhere, and Hanna quickly scanned Carina's desk. She could see a diary, a notepad, a stress ball and a mug full of pens, but no photographs. The only remotely personal items were the two pot plants; they were both so well tended, and in what looked like hand-painted pots. Maybe it was an interest in gardening that had brought Carina and Maria together, but if so, where? An allotment felt more likely than some online forum – perhaps Ingrid would know whether there was anything like that in the area.

The sound of footsteps made her turn around, but it was only Erik. Hanna regretted having told him about the photograph. *Ask Carina*, that had been his solution. *Or talk to Ove*.

Hanna walked back to her desk. She had no desire to call Carina, and sent her a message about the interview with Markus Johansson instead. She then dialled Nadine's number.

'You'll have to be quick,' said Nadine. 'I've got class.'

'Why didn't you tell us Joel was trans?'

The silence that followed was so compact that, for a moment, Hanna thought Nadine had hung up.

'Hello?'

'Who have you been talking to?'

'Markus Johansson. Or maybe I should say Tina?'

Nadine was silent again.

'What do you know about her?' asked Hanna.

'I've never met her, but Joel said she was helping him.'

'Helping him with what?'

'To feel better.'

'Were they in a relationship?'

'I don't think so. I mean, I thought it was weird they were chatting – I'd never do it – but Joel swore she was cool.'

Hanna didn't speak. Sometimes that was the best way to get someone to talk.

'I couldn't tell you about any of this before,' said Nadine. 'At first, we tried using a bunch of different girl's names, then different pronouns, but not even Joel knew for sure.'

This information could have helped the investigation. If only Nadine had told them right away, they would have reached this point much sooner – not that it really mattered any more. Hanna decided to drop it.

'How would you describe Joel and Petri's relationship?' she asked.

'Nah, screw it.'

'Pardon?'

'That was to a classmate, not you. Screw my class.'

'Sorry, I didn't mean to . . .'

'Meh, I didn't feel like going anyway. Why do you want to know about Petri?'

'Just answer the question.'

'Joel often made fun of him, but I think he liked him. And he was jealous of Molly, of the fact she had a real dad.'

Hanna's attempts to keep the conversation going failed, so she ended the call and dug out Petri's mobile number. The sound of quick footsteps made her look up. Carina was holding her phone out to Hanna.

'What, you couldn't be bothered to call me?'

'I went over to your desk, but you weren't there. I thought maybe you were busy.'

Behind Carina, Hanna could see Erik's watchful eyes.

'Did you have any questions about anything I wrote?' asked Hanna.

'You're not my boss, you know.'

Hanna stared at Carina. She had no idea how to deal with her anger. It all felt so unfair. From the corner of one eye, she saw Erik take a step forward, and felt like hissing at him to stop poking his nose in.

'I don't know how they can just let you waltz in like this,' said Carina, 'and shove the rest of us – who've been here for years – to one side. Especially considering your background.'

Carina turned around, presumably to storm away, and almost walked straight into Erik. Hanna stared down at her desk. She could feel the redness she hated so much spreading across her cheeks again.

She had to fight back.

Hanna refused to let Erik deal with the situation for her. If there was one thing he was right about, it was that she needed to talk to Carina. To make her understand that she couldn't behave like this.

'Carina,' said Erik.

At that moment, Daniel stepped into the room, pausing just inside the doorway. Hanna forced herself to get up and walk over to Carina.

'I'm not my dad,' she said. Her voice was trembling, and she had to swallow before she could go on. 'You know Ester's daughter, Maria, don't you?'

'She's my cousin.'

Carina glared furiously at her for a moment before hurrying out of the room. Daniel watched her leave, then turned to Hanna, as though he needed her approval. She nodded, and he followed Carina out. Hanna walked back to her desk and slumped into her chair.

'You OK?' asked Erik.

'Fine.'

'At least you know now.'

'Yeah.'

Little by little, Hanna managed to compose herself. She was good at her job, and she wasn't going to let Carina take that away from her. If Carina insisted on being hostile, she would just have to talk to her again. And if that didn't work, she would have to speak to Ove.

Hanna dialled Petri's number, and when he failed to pick up, she left a message telling him to call her back as soon as possible. She then took out the photographs from the rest area. She knew she would have to tell Rebecka what she had found out about Joel, that he was trans. Otherwise, there was a risk it would leak to the press.

Her phone rang, and Hanna found herself hoping it was Petri, but it was Joel's friend Linnea.

'There's something I need to tell you.'

Hanna heard her swallow, but the girl didn't go on.

'OK,' she said.

'It was Fanny who sold the hash to Joel.'

'Thank you,' said Hanna. 'But we knew that already.'

Linnea began to cry.

'Do you want to tell me why you're crying?' asked Hanna.

What followed was an incoherent story about Linnea having been given hash by Joel, and going directly to Fanny when she wanted more. Fanny had said it was free, but then she had demanded money for it after all. And if Linnea couldn't pay her back, Joel would have to.

'What if that's why she . . .' Linnea sobbed.

'We don't know who killed Joel yet,' said Hanna. 'Or why. But it's good that you've told us.'

Once she hung up, Hanna turned her attention back to the images. She realised she was going to have to approach them from a new angle, and began by making a list of everyone who had been to the rest area. There were so many people she didn't recognise, and they all looked so ordinary: people from Gårdby and the surrounding villages. Parents, classmates, teachers . . .

She studied their faces, searching for signs of guilt. Hanna spent a long time staring at the image of Tina. There was definitely guilt there, but it seemed to have been almost completely absorbed by grief.

With a sigh, she gathered the images into a pile. That was when she saw him: the man who appeared twice. He was around her age, with blond hair. In one image, his face seemed blank, but in another it was more despairing. Hanna checked through the rest of the photographs again. None of the other faces appeared more than once.

She spotted the man in a third picture – or at least she thought it was him, only just visible at the edge of a group of teenagers. Hanna seemed to have inadvertently photographed him on three separate occasions, which was significant considering she had never stayed at the rest area particularly long. She stared down at the image in which he had a serious look on his face, but couldn't remember having seen him anywhere else.

Hanna added the image to a folder along with a picture of Markus Johansson, and got up to tell Erik what she had found. She immediately changed her mind, and grabbed the other printouts too. They would have to pay Rebecka a visit, and go through the images with her.

Chapter Sixty-Four

The butter on Rebecka's toast glistened, and she lowered it to the plate. It had taken her a while to convince Petri, but he had eventually left for work. She needed to be alone, and in order to make him leave she had promised to eat something. He had asked if she wanted to know more about his assault charge, but she had shaken her head. It could wait. Over twenty years had passed, and he had never raised a hand to her.

He wasn't like Axel.

Rebecka picked up the toast again. This time, she actually took a bite, though she had to wash it down with a gulp of water.

A car pulled up on the driveway. The blinds were obscuring her view, but she knew precisely what kind of car it was. Maybe it was because of the deliberate way the doors opened and closed, the sound of the feet crossing the gravel, but she steeled herself for what was to come: the knock on the door. It was five days since the police had knocked on her door and told her that Joel was dead. Brought everything crashing down.

No, not the police. Hanna.

The situation had been so absurd that Rebecka still had

trouble processing it. She replayed the walk to the door over and over. Everything that had crossed her mind when she had seen who was standing outside, the conclusions she'd immediately come to when she realised Hanna had joined the police. That it must be about Joel, that the worst had happened. The sense of hope she'd clung onto anyway. That it must be about something else. The despair when it wasn't.

This time, when she heard the knock, she was right back there, in the moment when her world had fallen apart. It was Hanna and the other officer again, but she couldn't tell from their faces what they had come to say.

Hanna gave her a hug, and Rebecka reciprocated the gesture, though she still hadn't forgiven Hanna for not telling her that Axel was being held.

'Are you home alone?' asked Hanna.

'Yes. Molly is at school and Petri is at work.'

'Can we come in and sit down?'

Rebecka led them through to the kitchen. She sat down at the table and pushed the plate of toast away from her, taking a sip of water instead.

'Rebecka, there's something I need to tell you. About Joel.'

There's something I need to tell you.

Her body remembered its reaction to Petri's words, but this time Rebecka refused to let it crawl upstairs to bed. Should she tell them that Petri had been to prison? No, she couldn't. That would be a betrayal.

She stared at Hanna. What could she possibly say that would change a thing? What else had she been withholding?

'Joel was trans.'

'What did you say?'

'Joel was trans.'

'What . . . he wanted to be a girl?'

'No. Someone who Joel confided in explained it to us. Apparently this person was trying to help him work out who he was.'

'What do you mean, "who he was"?'

She sounded like a goddamn parrot stuck on repeat.

'He didn't feel comfortable in himself,' said Hanna. 'He didn't feel either male or female, but a bit of both. Non-binary, I believe it's called.'

What did that mean? Rebecka didn't understand a thing, but she held her tongue. Hanna was looking at her like she thought she was about to start screaming, but the male officer's eyes were studying her calmly. What was his name? She had heard it several times, and it bothered her that she couldn't remember it.

Rebecka turned to the window. She had noticed that Joel wasn't doing well, so why hadn't she forced him to talk to her? Coward that she was, she had hoped everything would work out if she just gave him some time, but he had turned to someone else for support instead.

'Did he ever mention the name Tina?' asked Hanna.

'No.'

'What about Markus Johansson?'

'No.'

'Let me show you a picture.'

Hanna pulled a photograph from a folder and placed it on the kitchen table in front of Rebecka. The image showed a man with light brown hair.

'I've never seen him before,' she said. 'What did he do to Joel?'

Hanna didn't reply. Instead, she pulled out another picture.

This one had been taken in the evening. The sun hadn't quite set, but its oblique rays gave the image a strange glow. Rebecka immediately recognised the background: it was Möckelmossen, the rest area where Joel had been found. She could see several people, the police tape. It must have been taken on the first evening, because by the time she went over there, the tape was gone. Hanna pointed to a man in the image.

'Do you know who this is?'

'Yeah, that's Gabriel. My neighbour.'

'Gabriel Andersson? From the blue house?'

'Yes, Linnea's dad. And Elias's. Why are you asking me this?'

Rebecka could see the answer on Hanna's face before she even opened her mouth.

'I'm sorry, but I can't say.'

The glance the two officers exchanged sent a wave of nausea through her. She felt like screaming: *Why are you asking about him?*

Hanna told Rebecka to go through a stack of images from the rest area, but Rebecka couldn't concentrate. All she could see was the picture of Gabriel.

'We have to go,' said Hanna. 'But I promise I'll be in touch again as soon as I can.'

'I want to know now.'

Hanna gave Rebecka another hug. 'I can't. Soon. And please, stay here.'

Rebecka threw off Hanna's arms. How the hell could she do this to her again?

Chapter Sixty-Five

The door to Rebecka's house swung shut behind Hanna. It felt painful to leave Rebecka with so little, but their investigation was still ongoing: they couldn't share their suspicions with her, because it was by no means certain they were correct. There were other possible reasons why Gabriel Andersson might have driven over to the Möckelmossen rest area on multiple occasions since Joel was found dead there. Another kind of guilt. Or his own personal tragedy that he needed to process. Deaths like this stirred up so many emotions.

Erik pulled out his phone and called Ove.

'How's it going?' he asked Hanna once he had hung up.

'It is what it is. What did the boss say?'

He kept his voice quiet so that it wouldn't carry into Rebecka's house.

'He wants us to bring Gabriel Andersson in for an interview.'

That was the obvious next step: to hear what he had to say for himself.

They walked over to Gabriel's house, where a red Nissan was parked on the driveway. Hanna was fairly sure it was

Ulrika's, and she felt the heat of the engine on the bonnet as she passed. There was a light on in the kitchen, and Erik rang the bell. Ulrika answered the door. Since they had met her before, during their interview with Linnea, there was no need to show their ID.

'Are you home alone?' asked Hanna.

'Yes, why?'

'Could we come in?'

Erik took a step forward as he spoke, and Ulrika backed up to let them pass. She was pale and cautious in her movements, and avoided looking either of them in the eye. That didn't necessarily mean a thing in and of itself; some people were simply nervous when the police knocked on their door, because they rarely brought good news. Ulrika had been anxious on their last visit too, but she had directed that nervous energy towards Linnea. It was as though she didn't know what to do with it this time. Hanna wondered whether her daughter had told her about the drugs. She doubted it, but that could wait. When she reached the kitchen, Ulrika paused and glanced around before continuing to unpack her shopping.

'Could we sit down instead?' Hanna asked.

'Hold on, I just need to get the chilled things into the fridge.'

Ulrika carried a carton of yoghurt and a tub of butter over to the fridge. She was moving slowly, as though she needed a little more time to prepare herself.

'Where is Gabriel?' Erik asked once Ulrika had sat down opposite them.

'At work.'

'Where does he work?'

'At the independent school in Färjestaden.'

The minute Erik mentioned Gabriel's name, tears began spilling down Ulrika's cheeks

'Can you tell us why you're crying?' asked Hanna.

'I'm so worried about Gabriel.'

'Why?'

But Ulrika was crying too hard to be able to answer. Hanna tore off a sheet of kitchen roll and passed it to her. Ulrika pressed it to her eyes. A moment or two later, she blew her nose. Hanna repeated her question, but Ulrika simply shook her head.

'What did you do after the barbecue?' asked Erik.

'I tidied up the worst of the mess in the kitchen and then I went to bed.'

'And Gabriel?'

'He did the same.'

'But . . .'

It was clear that something else had happened that evening, and Ulrika was afraid to say what. She closed her eyes. Perhaps she needed to pretend they weren't there in order to answer.

'He got up again. While I was sleeping. I woke up and he was gone.'

'Did you check the time?' asked Hanna.

'Yes. It was twelve thirty. I went to the bathroom, but he wasn't there. He wasn't downstairs either.'

Ulrika had opened her eyes, but she avoided looking at either of them.

'When did he come home?' asked Erik.

'Not until three. I couldn't get back to sleep while he was gone.'

'And what happened once Gabriel got back?'

Ulrika didn't speak. Her face was unmoving. Hanna repeated Erik's question.

'I pretended to be asleep,' Ulrika eventually told them.

'And what did Gabriel do?'

'He put the washing machine on, and then he went for a shower. It must've been at least half an hour before he got into bed. He was so drunk he walked straight into the wall next to the door.'

'Do you know why he was gone?' asked Erik.

Ulrika's face hardened.

'He's been having an affair. Another one. Even though he promised he'd stop. On his own birthday too, after I . . . We had such a nice evening, but then he had to go off and . . .'

'How has Gabriel been over the past few days?'

The hardness was gone. Ulrika slumped forward and buried her face in her hands, her body shaking with tears. They waited for her to finish. Erik tore off another sheet of paper and handed it to her.

'He's been drifting around like a shadow. I've asked him what's wrong, several times, but he just says it's all in my mind, that he's fine. I'm not sure he's actually at work right now. There's no way he can work in the state he's in.'

Another bout of tears filled the kitchen.

'I should have confronted him when he got home, but I was too much of a coward.' Ulrika dried her eyes and blew her nose. 'I *am* too much of a coward. I've tried to talk to Rebecka about my suspicions, but that didn't work either.'

'What suspicions?'

Hanna thought she could probably guess the answer, but she wanted to hear Ulrika say it aloud.

'That Gabriel was involved in Joel's death somehow,' Ulrika

whispered. 'I don't know why or how, but that's the only thing that explains why . . . How he's . . . How do you tell someone something like that?'

She looked up at them as though she thought they might actually be able to answer her. Her eyes locked onto Hanna, pinning her down.

'Did Gabriel kill Joel?' Ulrika asked.

'Right now, all we know is that we need to talk to him. If he isn't at work, where could he be?'

'I have no idea. I don't know anything any more.'

'Please, try to think.'

'He could be at the other woman's place. Whoever she is this time.'

Chapter Sixty-Six

Rebecka slowly opened the blinds. Just a fraction, so that Hanna and Erik wouldn't notice. *Erik*, that was his name. She felt relieved to have remembered it. As though it proved she wasn't entirely worthless.

The two officers were standing by their car, and Erik was talking to someone on the phone. Once he hung up, they began whispering, their expressions closed and serious. They turned towards Gabriel and Ulrika's house, and moved out of view thanks to the stupid bush Petri kept promising to trim.

Rebecka glanced at the clock. Ulrika should be back from her shift at the supermarket by now. She hurried over to the window on the gable end of the house, but the angle wasn't right. All she could see was the front door opening and closing.

The sudden sense of panic Rebecka felt was so powerful she didn't know which way to turn. She wanted to run over to Ulrika's house and storm inside, demanding to know exactly what was going on. Keeping still was impossible, so she paced back and forth between the kitchen and the living room, tearing at her cuticles with her teeth.

Maybe she would be able to see more if she went upstairs?

She raced up to Joel's room, tripping in the doorway and stumbling over to the window. Aside from the yard and the driveway, all she could see from here was Linnea's dark room. But Hanna and Erik were still inside, they had to be. Otherwise she would have heard the car. Joel's room didn't have a window on the front of the house, so she couldn't check whether they had driven off.

Being among Joel's things brought her a sense of calm. Rebecka didn't want to take her eyes off the driveway, but she found herself peering around the room. At his unmade bed. His chair, heaped with clothes that were too dirty for the wardrobe and too clean to be washed. His desk, where his sketchpads usually sat. The little snow globe with a ballerina inside that he'd bought with his pocket money from a flea market when he was six.

Trans? Neither male nor female, but both? Was it really her son they were talking about?

Wonderful, lovely Joel. No, she refused to believe it. It felt as though Hanna had dropped a bomb, seen her lying on the ground with bloody stumps for legs, and then turned and walked away.

Rebecka reached for the hoody draped over the pile of clothes on the chair and pressed it to her nose. It still smelled like him. The scent made her waver, and she braced herself against the window frame with one hand, almost knocking over the small buddha he kept there. The incense was obviously a way to hide his smoking. Had she really been that stupid, or had she simply chosen not to notice?

Joel was gone, and a big part of her still seemed to be fighting that fact. Refusing to accept that this was how things had worked out.

She turned around and stared down at the driveway again. What was taking them so long?

Eventually, she saw Hanna and Erik leave the house and walk down the drive. They were too far away for her to be able to read their expressions, so she rushed downstairs and into the kitchen. Through the blind, she saw them walking towards her. At first, she thought they were about to knock on her door again, but instead they climbed into the car and drove away.

Fucking Hanna.

Fucking everything.

Rebecka didn't even try to hold herself back. She ran straight over to Ulrika's and rang the bell. When Ulrika failed to answer, she began pounding on the door.

'Let me in, Ulrika! I know you're there.'

Her hand was on its way to striking the door again when it swung open. Ulrika's eyes were bloodshot and swollen, and she had her arms wrapped tightly around herself. Wearing that awful bobbly cardigan.

'I'm so sorry.'

'Yeah, so you've said, but what exactly are you sorry for?'

Ulrika said nothing, simply stared down at the floor. Rebecka pushed past her into the hallway and looked all around, though she knew Gabriel wasn't home.

As Ulrika turned to face her, Rebecka began shouting:

'Was it Gabriel who killed Joel? Huh? Did he?'

'I don't know, but I think so.'

'Why the hell didn't you say anything?'

Ulrika slumped to the floor, breaking her fall with her hands. It almost looked like she was praying.

'I tried.'

'You tried?' Rebecka hissed. 'Not very hard.'

She was so angry she felt like lashing out at Ulrika. Kicking her.

'You don't know what it's been like these past few days,' wailed the woman who had once been her friend.

Ulrika managed to get back to her feet and took a step towards Rebecka.

'What about me?' Rebecka shouted. 'How do you think it's been for me? Whatever your sick husband has done, at least he's still alive. Joel is dead!'

Rebecka shoved past Ulrika and stormed outside. With her heart racing in her chest, she ran back towards the house. She needed Petri. She needed him like she had never needed him before, because she had just realised when it had probably happened: as she was hunched over the toilet in the studio, retching and sobbing and convinced that her life was over because Gabriel no longer wanted her. According to the police, Joel had snuck out, but he must have come home and . . .

What had he seen? What was Joel's last vision of her?

The Last Day

Four more steps, then Joel turns around. He doesn't trust the silence behind him. All he can hear is the chirping of the grasshoppers. No engines, no birds. He misses the night singer. Its high, fast song keeping the darkness at bay.

A shadow by the edge of the road makes him jump, sending a wave of pain out from his broken rib.

It's just a bush.

The darkness is full of shapes dancing around him – faster and faster, closer and closer – making it harder to breathe. Could his broken rib have damaged his lung?

Eventually, Joel sees the light. A tiny dot that slowly grows to a square. His head is pounding, nausea washing over him, twitching in the light, but he tries to fix his eyes on it. That is where he needs to go.

His legs give way, and he drops to his knees. Breaks his fall with his hands. The sharp taste of bile fills his mouth. It feels like someone has rammed a fist into his chest and started rummaging around inside.

Staying right there on the ground feels incredibly tempting, but he's so close now.

Joel crawls back onto his feet and staggers forward. He hears something crunch behind him. Footsteps? No, it can't be – just an animal.

He pauses, noticing movement in the light. His eyes take in what he is seeing, but it's like they don't want to pass it on.

Why?

The question tears at him, at the ground beneath him. Everything feels like it is about to collapse.

Joel stares through the window into the studio as though frozen.

Mum.

And Gabriel.

How could she?

Her face is twisted with longing, but Gabriel doesn't want her. She throws herself at him and he pulls away. She falls over, dropping out of sight. But Joel still can't move.

The door flies open and Gabriel comes stumbling out.

'Joel,' he whispers. 'Jesus Christ. What happened to you?'

When he notices the look on Joel's face, he continues, 'It's not what you think!'

Why is he whispering? Shit, he stinks of wine.

Joel tries to move past Gabriel, into the studio. He needs to make sure his mum is OK. Gabriel grips his arm, but Joel tears himself free. Too hard. He falls forward again, and this time he doesn't manage to break his fall.

A searing pain courses through him, shooting upwards from his stomach, and as Joel struggles back onto his feet, he realises that it isn't coming from his broken rib. He shoves a hand into the pocket of his hoody, and when he brings it out, he sees his fingers are slick with blood.

The knife. How deep has it . . .

'I had a . . .' But Joel gets no further before he drops to his knees.

A whimpering sound brings him back. Why is Gabriel just standing there? Why isn't he helping him?

And why the hell is he acting like *he* is the one who is hurt?

'Sorry.'

Joel thinks he must have misheard him, but the word keeps coming, jolting out of him:

'Sorry, sorry, sorry.'

It is getting harder and harder to maintain his grip on reality. Joel feels arms around him, and wants to shout: *No, stop! It hurts too much! Call an ambulance*.

But the arms force him to his feet.

'I'll drive you to hospital,' says Gabriel.

Chapter Sixty-Seven

There was a bus shelter to the right of the road, and Erik realised that it must be where Joel had taken the picture of himself. It was empty, and the afternoon sun was shining so brightly through the windscreen that he could almost imagine it was summer. Erik pictured a bruised, beaten Joel in front of him. Sitting there alone in the middle of the night, taking stock of his wounds. Mustering enough strength to make it home.

Erik eased his foot off the accelerator, passed the bus shelter, and turned off towards Färjestaden. He adjusted the sun visor and glanced over at Hanna, who was staring out of the passenger side window. However much she tried to pretend otherwise, it was obvious that the case was getting to her.

'I'm fine,' she said. Hanna seemed to have a sixth sense for other people's moods.

'Understood,' he replied.

His phone started ringing, and Erik quickly checked the screen. It was Yadu.

'Shit,' he muttered. 'It's my father-in-law; he never normally calls just to chat.'

'Want me to answer?'

Erik shook his head. It was probably nothing. Supriya was most likely in with a patient and couldn't answer their calls. No matter how much she moaned about her parents, she would never ignore them.

'Do you think there's a risk Ulrika will warn Gabriel?' Hanna asked.

'Honestly, I don't.'

'Me neither.'

'But let's call the school and check whether he's there anyway.'

Hanna made the call, giving him a thumbs-up as soon as she had confirmation. Erik could only hear Hanna's side of the conversation, but he managed to glean that Gabriel was currently in a lesson. Without mentioning what they wanted to talk to him about, Hanna told the person on the other end of the line not to interrupt his lesson, but to be waiting outside when they arrived. They were ten minutes away, she said.

'Jesus, she was so stressed,' Hanna said once she had hung up.

'That's not so surprising, is it?'

'No, I know. She asked whether one of his relatives had died.'

'Maybe she's who he was having an affair with.'

Hanna replied with a simple shake of the head.

A tractor pulled out from a track to one side of the road, and Erik braked hard. He swung out into the other lane to overtake it just as a line of cars appeared coming in the opposite direction, and the tractor pottered on like it had all the time in the world.

'Welcome to the countryside,' said Hanna.

'Right,' Erik replied, smiling.

He drummed on the wheel until an opportunity to overtake the tractor appeared. He could have simply used his siren to speed things up, but a minute here or there was hardly going to make much difference. It wasn't like Gabriel Andersson knew they were on their way.

Yadu called again, but Erik ignored him and repressed the flicker of anxiety he felt. Whatever had happened, he couldn't call him back right now. They were almost at the school.

A woman was waiting for them outside the modern glass building. She was in her thirties, wearing a short-sleeved green blouse and a pair of jeans she kept rubbing her palms against. Erik pulled up right beside the main doors.

'Why do you need to talk to Gabriel?' she asked the minute they climbed out of the car.

'We can't say,' said Erik. 'But we need him to come with us, so it would be great if you or another member of staff could take over his class.'

'I can do it. I'm Sandra Dahl, by the way.' She held out a hand to both of them.

It struck Erik that perhaps they should ask Sandra to fetch Gabriel from his class. There was a risk he might panic if he knew they were from the police. But that wasn't a responsibility they could place on her, particularly not considering how nervous she seemed. Gabriel would know something was wrong. Another option was to wait until the lesson was over, but then the corridors would be full of students. Right now, they were almost deserted.

The woman led them over to a classroom, and nodded towards the door, taking a step back.

431

Erik knocked and opened the door.

'Hi, Gabriel. I don't know if you remember me, but my name is Erik Lindgren, from the Kalmar Police. This is my colleague Hanna Duncker. I need you to come with us, please.'

Gabriel looked like a rabbit caught in headlights. He didn't speak, simply stared straight at them. Erik had talked to him during the first day of the investigation, right after they had broken the news to Rebecka. Should he have suspected something then?

There was no point dwelling on questions like that. Nor on the fact that he should have asked to see the images from the rest area, rather than simply accepting what Hanna said about them going over to Rebecka's to show them to her. If he had, he would have been able to identify Gabriel, and they could have avoided going to see Rebecka at all.

'Don't worry about your class,' said Erik. 'Sandra will take over.'

Gabriel seemed to jump at the mention of Sandra's name. He looked, if possible, even more stressed than he had earlier. Perhaps Erik had stumbled upon the truth when he said that she was the one Gabriel was having an affair with.

Though the room was full of teenagers, it was completely silent. Gabriel turned to look at his students, then towards the window. He had a pen in one hand, and the board behind him was covered in equations.

Erik stood perfectly still, watching Gabriel, ready to launch himself at him if necessary. From where he was standing all he could see through the window was the bright blue sky. Gabriel slowly turned back towards his students and closed his eyes. After a few seconds, he opened them, turned towards the door and began walking.

Chapter Sixty-Eight

The corridors were still largely empty, but Hanna and Erik walked on either side of Gabriel, with Hanna keeping a look out to the right. None of the students they passed seemed to pay any attention to them, but an older woman turned and watched them leave. It wasn't the people around them that worried Hanna, it was Gabriel's reaction if any of them said anything. People became unpredictable when they were under stress.

Erik pushed open the main door, and Hanna cast one last glance back inside. Sandra Dahl was still standing in the corridor, watching them leave. Perhaps Erik had been right after all.

When they reached the car, Gabriel hesitated in front of the open door.

'You don't have a choice,' Hanna told him. 'You have to come with us.'

Gabriel studied her for a moment, and his lips moved as though he was about to speak. Right then, the school door opened, and he closed his mouth and climbed into the back seat. Erik excused himself, saying he had to make a quick call.

To his father-in-law, in all likelihood. Hanna was curious, but she climbed into the passenger seat and turned to look back at Gabriel.

'We're taking you to the station in Kalmar for an interview. You're under arrest on suspicion of having killed Joel Forslund, and you have the right to a lawyer during the interview.'

Hanna spoke slowly so that Gabriel would understand what she was saying, but he simply stared at her like he hadn't grasped a single word. As she began to repeat herself, he interrupted her:

'I don't want a lawyer.'

Erik jumped in behind the wheel. Hanna glanced over at him, wordlessly asking if everything was OK.

'My mother-in-law had a heart attack. She's in hospital.' He shook his head. 'Supriya isn't answering her phone – she's probably with a patient.'

'What do you want to do?'

'Nothing right now. I left a message on her answer machine.'

He started the engine and pulled away.

'Is it serious?' asked Hanna.

'Too early to say. Yadu sounded incredibly confused, it was difficult to talk to him.'

Hanna looked back at Gabriel in the rear-view mirror. His eyes were on the door, and he didn't seem to be paying any attention to their conversation. His hands were resting calmly in his lap. He wouldn't be able to get out of the car even if he tried; the rear doors couldn't be opened from inside. Hanna wanted to convince Erik to forget about the interview and head straight to the hospital, but she knew that she would never agree to something like that herself.

As though by reflex, Hanna turned to look out of the

window as Erik drove up onto the Öland Bridge. She felt a sense of calm flooding towards her from the water, but it couldn't quite remove her tension. They were at a crucial juncture in the case. Her gut told her Gabriel Andersson was guilty, but that didn't mean he would confess, nor that they would be able to bring about a prosecution. She studied him again in the mirror. He didn't seem to have moved.

The turn-off to the police station was drawing ever closer.

'Are you sure?' Hanna asked.

That was as far as she intended to push it. Erik responded by turning off.

They led Gabriel up to one of the interrogation rooms.

'Do you want anything to drink?' Hanna asked him.

Gabriel looked up at her like it was the most idiotic question he had ever heard, then shook his head.

Erik started the tape recorder, stating the date, time and who was present, and explaining what Gabriel Andersson was suspected of.

'Could you tell us what happened on the night between the fourteenth and fifteenth of May?' asked Hanna.

Gabriel's eyes darted between her, Erik and the door, but just like in the car, there was no way out. The sigh he let out was little more than a sob.

'It was my fortieth birthday on the Tuesday, and Ulrika threw a party for me. The neighbours came over and we had a barbecue. The whole thing made me realise what an idiot I'd been.'

'Had been?'

'Yes. I'd been having an affair, but I decided to break it off. I was sick of being an arsehole. I love Ulrika. My kids. They're the only ones I want.'

435

It was a good sign that Gabriel was answering their questions. The vast majority of interviews went smoothly, more a conversation than anything else – when the suspect talked, that was. Sometimes they refused to say a word, and they occasionally told stories that were utterly preposterous in an attempt to dodge the blame.

'Did you see the other woman that night?'

'Yes, I went over to her house.'

'So she lives in Gårdby too?' Erik filled in.

'Yes.'

'Who is she?' asked Hanna, fully expecting him to say Sandra Dahl.

'Rebecka. Joel's mum.'

Hanna was so shocked she couldn't hide her reaction. She had heard terrible things during interviews in the past, but she had always managed to mask what she thought. If she didn't, there was a risk the suspect might clam up. But this time, it hit her hard. Why hadn't Rebecka said anything? Had she known who had killed Joel all along?

'Where did you meet that night?' Hanna asked, perfectly aware of how accusatory she sounded.

'In her studio.'

'And how did Rebecka react to you telling her you wanted to end the affair?' Erik asked, drawing the attention to himself.

'Not well at all. We argued.'

'Had you been drinking?'

'Yes, we'd had quite a bit at the barbecue. I also took some wine to the studio, and we shared that. I needed it to give me the courage . . .'

Gabriel paused and stared down at the table.

'What happened in the studio?' Erik asked, his voice calm.

'It was so hard,' said Gabriel. 'She started screaming all kinds of terrible things. Some of it was true, but most of it wasn't. I was just happy that I'd ended things.'

Hanna knew she should keep quiet, but she couldn't.

'How did all of this end in Joel being stabbed?'

All she wanted to know now was the extent to which Rebecka had been involved. Gabriel's eyes were still fixed on the table, and it was clear that he was on the verge of losing control.

'Did you stab Joel?' asked Erik.

Gabriel shook his head.

'If you could just repeat that for the tape.'

'No, I didn't stab him. I told Rebecka I didn't want to listen to her any more, that I was going, and she threw herself at me. I took a step back, and she slumped onto the floor. She was lying there with her arms around my leg, and I told her to pull herself together . . .'

Gabriel's cheeks flushed. Hanna assumed that the words he had used were considerably coarser than that.

'She crawled off to the bathroom, and I could hear her throwing up. When I turned around, I realised there was someone looking in through the window, so I ran outside. At first, I didn't realise it was Joel, because he looked so strange. His face was covered in blood . . .'

Gabriel gazed longingly at the door.

'Keep going,' Hanna told him, only just managing to keep her voice steady.

'I think I grabbed him. I wanted to talk to him, to explain what he'd seen. Tell him he couldn't say anything. But he pulled away from me and fell onto his stomach. When he got back up, he looked even stranger. He shoved his hand into the pocket on the front of his hoody, and when he pulled it out again it was covered in blood . . .'

Gabriel trailed off. It was obvious his thoughts were elsewhere, probably with Joel.

'What did you do then?' asked Hanna.

He didn't reply, but as she repeated her question, he began to tremble, as though he had a fever.

'I panicked. I told him I'd take him to hospital and led him over to the car. That's what I was going to do, but he was bleeding so much. He had a knife in his pocket. Can you believe that? A fucking knife!'

'Yes,' said Hanna, attempting to prevent Gabriel from clamming up.

'He died in my car, and I didn't know what to do. I must have driven round for at least an hour. In the end, I left him over in Möckelmossen.'

'Why didn't you call for Rebecka?' Hanna asked.

Yet again, she managed to keep her emotions out of her voice. She didn't want him to withdraw into himself, leaving her without any answers. But the question made Gabriel fall apart. He slumped forward, onto the table, his body shaking as he sobbed.

'I couldn't face her,' he sniffed. 'And I didn't want her to see. Not in the state she was in.'

'Why didn't you just call for an ambulance?'

Gabriel sat bolt upright.

'I panicked,' he said. 'I thought it would be quicker if I drove Joel to hospital myself. That I'd be able to talk to him on the way. Convince him not to tell Ulrika anything.'

'So what happened?' asked Erik.

'Joel died, and I . . . I wanted to save myself. He was already dead, so it wasn't like I could do anything for him. But my family . . . I had to save it. Ulrika has given me so many chances, and it would have wrecked my marriage if she'd found out I'd been with . . . I love her, Ulrika, I mean. Jesus . . . I don't know how I could have been so fucking stupid.'

Hanna didn't know what he was referring to, and Gabriel seemed to notice, because he looked straight at her.

'I should've called an ambulance,' he said. 'I regret it so much that it's killing me. But it was like my brain short-circuited. I couldn't think straight.'

'How did you leave Joel?' Hanna asked.

'At the rest area in Möckelmossen, where he was found.'

'Yes, but I mean what did he look like when you left?'

'He was dead,' said Gabriel. 'He didn't have a pulse.'

Perhaps he was struggling to understand what she was getting at because he was so upset, or maybe he simply didn't want to talk about it.

'Describe how you left Joel at the rest area,' Hanna persisted. 'And how he looked when you drove away.'

'I pulled him onto the ground,' said Gabriel. 'The knife fell out, and I put it back in the car. I tossed it out the window later.'

'Did you touch it?'

'Through the arm of my jacket.'

'Where?'

'On the blade itself. Next to the handle.'

'And Joel? Describe him.'

'He was lying on his side. He wasn't moving.'

'Did you put anything in his hand?'

'No,' said Gabriel, suddenly sounding uncertain.

'Joel was leaning against the wall when he was found,' said

Hanna. 'And he had a bloody crane's-bill flower in his hand.'

'No,' said Gabriel. 'That can't be right.'

It really did look like he didn't believe her, but that was probably just what he had to tell himself in order to cope. What Hanna needed was air, but she had one last question left to ask before she could end the interview.

'Do you think Rebecka saw anything?'

'No, I'm sure she didn't.'

Hanna switched off the tape recorder.

'What happens to me now?' asked Gabriel.

'We'll need to talk to the prosecutor, but you'll definitely be booked into custody.'

Gabriel clearly hadn't been expecting to leave.

'What are you going to tell Ulrika?' he asked. 'About Rebecka, about what happened?'

'We don't have to say any more than that you're being held in custody. Ulrika already knew you were having an affair, but I don't think she knew who it was with.'

The Last Few Moments

Joel wakes up without any idea where he is. Last thing he knew, he was in a car.

It's so dark here, and the air feels cold on his face. That's probably what woke him. His cheek is resting against something rough. Gravel, maybe.

He lifts his fingers to his stomach, but they quickly become sticky with blood. His body hurts all over, not just there. His head, his ribs, his back . . . But he can still move.

There is a wall nearby, and he shuffles over and leans back against it. Why has Gabriel left him here? Why didn't he take him to hospital? His eyes begin to make out different shapes in the dark, but Joel still can't work out where he is.

He looks up at the sky, at all the stars there.

Mum and Gabriel.

No. He doesn't want to remember what he saw. Mum throwing herself at Gabriel. The ugly look of longing on her face.

Today has been such a shitty day, and it feels like it's never going to end. It just keeps getting worse and worse.

Joel leans to one side. He needs to stand up, to get out of

here, but he doesn't have the strength. His fingers brush something as he braces himself against the ground, and he is surprised to realise that it's a flower. He lifts it to his eyes to get a better look, but it is too dark to see.

He wants to go home. To his bed and to his family. Tina was right: he needs to tell Mum. Something seemed to click when Tina used those words. *Non-binary, they*. It was like everything suddenly fell into place. Maybe that was why he had pushed back against it. Pushed Tina away.

He needs to apologise to her for all the horrible things he said.

Mika.

Joel tests out the name in his mouth.

As soon as he is old enough, he'll change his name to Mika. Unless Mum lets him do it sooner, that is. Maybe it'll be easier to talk to her now that he knows she has a secret too.

Joel leans back against the wall and closes his eyes. His heart is beating like a tiny bird hopping around in his chest. He can hear them again now: the high, quick tones that kept him company as he was walking to the woods.

The night singer.

He smiles. Everything will be OK. If only someone would find him soon.

Chapter Sixty-Nine

Once the prosecutor had sent confirmation that Gabriel Andersson would be remanded in custody, Hanna spoke to Ove. She told him that she wanted to go over to Rebecka's to tell her the news, and he gave her his blessing immediately. Erik had hurried off to the hospital as soon as the interview was over. Supriya was already there, and had sent a message to say that Aavika was through the worst of it.

The charge the prosecutor had recommended was gross negligence manslaughter, which carried a sentence of up to six years in jail. Considering Joel had been alive when Gabriel left him at the rest area, the prosecutor was confident the crime should be considered grossly negligent. It was highly unlikely that anyone else had arrived at the scene and moved his body afterwards.

Hanna didn't feel any sympathy for Gabriel, but her heart ached for his family, and for his children in particular. She knew all too well what they would have to go through now, and Linnea already felt guilty because of the hash. Above all, however, her heart ached for Joel, the fifteen-year-old who would never get to live their life or discover who they really were. And for Rebecka. Hanna hoped it was true and that her friend hadn't seen a thing.

She also felt a deep sense of sorrow for herself. For everything that had happened over the years.

The feeling deepened as she drove into Gårdby. Hanna took in the houses and the trees passing by, and it was as though all the different layers of time seemed to merge together, forming one single, painful present. Would she ever be able to move past it? She knew how hard it was going to be to talk to Rebecka, and she wasn't ready for that yet. Instead, she turned off onto Snegatan. No one had seen Fanny since the search, and neither she nor her mother were answering their phones.

Hanna pulled up in the yard, and the sight of the girl hunched over by her moped sent a jolt of relief through her. She climbed out of the car and walked over to Fanny.

'What do you want?' Fanny asked without looking up.

It was as though she had changed shape yet again. Gone was all the hardness and fear, leaving behind nothing but a troubled child.

'We know you didn't stab Joel.'

'Did you come over here just to tell me that?'

'Yes.'

'Thanks.'

Hanna turned to leave, but Fanny stopped her.

'So who did it, then?'

'I'm sorry, I can't say.'

Hanna climbed back into the car. She could have lectured Fanny about everything she had done – about her beating up Joel, and forcing younger children to give her money, how wrong it all was – but she was fairly sure Fanny already knew.

The question was what the teenager planned to do with that knowledge going forward. It was still too early to say. Hanna would have to talk to her again later, once everything had settled down.

By the time Hanna reached Rebecka's house, both Petri and Molly were home. She decided to talk to the three of them together, for Molly's sake above all else. The girl would be able to sense the tension in the air, and not knowing was far worse than actually being told the truth. Hanna remembered that feeling from her mother's illness. The conversations she had been left out of, but still managed to pick up on. The way everyone had told her and Kristoffer their mother would be fine, even though it was a lie. Hanna also knew that she was in better shape to tell Molly than Rebecka was. She gathered them in the living room.

'We know how Joel died,' she said.

'How?' asked Molly, who was sitting in her mother's lap.

Petri hugged them both to him.

'He fell over and hurt himself on a knife.'

'In Möckelmossen?'

Hanna hesitated to say Gabriel's name, but she knew that Molly would hear it at some point anyway. It was better that she found out now, rather than it being whispered by someone who didn't think she would understand.

'No, right outside here. But Gabriel moved him. He thought Joel was already dead, but he wasn't.'

Hanna studied Rebecka as she mentioned their neighbour, and realised that she already knew. When had she managed to work it out?

'Why did he move him?'

Both Petri and Rebecka were allowing Molly to ask her

questions, and Hanna was answering them as best she could, in a straightforward manner that a six-year-old would understand. To some extent, having Molly present also made things easier for her. She knew it would be much harder once she was alone with Rebecka. But Hanna didn't have a good answer to that particular question.

'I don't actually know,' she said.

'That was silly of him,' said Molly.

'Yes, it was.'

Molly seemed to be thinking, but she didn't have any more questions right now. They would probably come later. It was clear that her parents had plenty. Hanna caught Rebecka's eye.

'Should we go outside?'

Rebecka nodded.

They sat down in the hammock, looking out towards the small wood.

'So Joel saw us?' Rebecka asked, her voice trembling.

'Yes. Gabriel spotted him as he was about to leave, and ran out to talk to him. That was when Joel fell over and injured himself on the knife.'

'Why did he have a knife?'

'He'd snuck out to meet a gang in the woods behind the school. He took it to defend himself, but never actually used it – or not to do anything other than wave it around anyway. He was beaten up in the woods. Since both the teenagers and Gabriel have admitted their parts in what happened, I can answer more of your questions now.'

Rebecka didn't speak.

'You really didn't see anything?' Hanna asked her.

'I was in the toilet in the studio, crying because Gabriel had dumped me. I thought my world was about to end . . .'

'Why didn't you tell us that you and Gabriel were in the studio?'

'You can stop with the accusations,' said Rebecka. 'I can't take it. I'm being hard enough on myself as it is.'

She shuffled away from Hanna.

'I'm not accusing you,' said Hanna. 'I just want to understand.'

Rebecka turned away and wiped her eyes with the sleeve of her sweater.

'It didn't occur to me that it might be important. And . . . because I didn't want anyone to know.'

Now in floods of tears, Rebecka raised her hands to her eyes. Hanna hesitated for a moment, then moved closer and put an arm around her. She wasn't sure Rebecka wanted it there, but Rebecka began whimpering the way she had when she'd first found out that Joel was dead. She continued for a few minutes before lowering her hands and staring at Hanna with a look of such despair that Hanna came close to turning away.

'Is it true that Joel didn't die right away?' she said. 'That I could have saved him?'

'We don't know whether anyone could have saved him, but he was still alive when Gabriel dropped him off at the rest area, yes.'

'Then why did Gabriel think he was dead?'

'I don't know. He was drunk; he probably panicked and couldn't think straight.'

'That bastard!' Rebecka shouted.

'Mmm, that's an understatement.'

Hanna went into more detail about what Gabriel had told her. His excuses for not calling an ambulance or shouting for

447

Rebecka. The kind of thing she hadn't wanted to say in front of Molly.

'If I hadn't been in the studio with Gabriel, then . . .'

Rebecka couldn't manage any more, and Hanna felt an urge to prise the guilt away from her, placing it squarely on Gabriel's shoulders, where it belonged, but Rebecka wasn't susceptible to that kind of comforting.

'Stop it,' she whispered.

They sat quietly for a while instead, staring towards the trees. Hanna decided that she would have to get a hammock for her own little garden, that she would hang it out by the fields.

'Sorry,' said Rebecka. 'Thank you for telling us while Molly was there. I don't think I could have managed it myself.'

'You need to tell Petri too. We probably won't be able to keep all this a secret.'

'He worked it out during the barbecue, that Gabriel and I . . .'

It was plain to see that Rebecka was back there again, thinking it was all her fault. Her face was twisted in self-hatred, but this time Hanna had no intention of comforting her.

After a while, her features seemed to settle down. Hanna knew what it was like, being torn between feelings that didn't fit together.

'What you said about Joel,' said Rebecka. 'About him being trans, or not knowing whether he was a girl or a boy.'

'Mmm.'

'I think that was probably true. It explains so much from when he was younger. One day he would be playing with dolls, and the next he would be kicking a ball around. I know a lot of kids do that, but the switch was always so abrupt with him.

It was like he was searching for something.' Rebecka began to sob. 'Why didn't he just talk to me about it? He must have been so lonely . . . I would have understood. Maybe not right away, but I would've done . . .'

'According to both Tina and Nadine, he wanted to tell you, he just hadn't plucked up the courage yet. It also took him a long time to make sense of it himself. He might not have fully understood it all, and how easy is it to talk about something you don't really understand?'

Rebecka nodded.

'Can I have his sketchbooks?'

'Of course. I'll make sure to get them back to you as soon as possible.'

'I went over to Ulrika's after you left, you know.'

'I thought you might. Your impulse control has never been the greatest.'

Rebecka smiled through her tears.

'I hate her too, because she suspected something but didn't say a word. If she'd just done that, I might have found out sooner. I wasn't so nice to her.'

'Listen, I understand. Let this sink in for a while and then see how you feel. But whatever you do, don't take it out on their kids. On Linnea and Elias.'

Rebecka shook her head.

'Of course not.'

For a few moments, all they could hear was the squeaking of the hammock.

'I don't know what I ever saw in him,' Rebecka eventually spoke up.

'Your taste in men has never been great,' said Hanna.

For a split second, she wondered if she had gone too far, but

Rebecka simply laughed. A moment later, her expression was full of hatred for herself again.

'But Petri seems nice,' said Hanna.

'Yeah, he is,' said Rebecka. 'And he says he's forgiven me for everything with Gabriel, but given it was him who . . . How is Petri supposed to . . . How am I . . .'

Hanna placed a hand on Rebecka's. 'You were the only person who was really there for me while everything was going on with my dad, and I was a total shit who just up and left.'

'You were. But you're here now.'

'I'm here now, and I'll help you move forward however I can.'

They kept swinging. Hanna had deliberately avoided saying she would help Rebecka move *through* this, because she knew her friend would probably never manage that. There was no other side where everything would suddenly be fine.

'Listen, there's something I need to ask you . . .'

'OK.'

Hanna had been thinking that it might help to distract Rebecka if she talked about something else, but she suddenly felt unsure.

'Just say it,' said Rebecka.

'You know what I asked you earlier, whether you had talked about me with Axel? He called you a liar and said that if anyone should know that, I should. He said you'd never liked me.'

Rebecka simply shook her head.

'What did you say to Axel about me?'

'I honestly don't remember. I think I said I was tired of all the drama, but they were just words. I didn't mean . . . You know what Axel is like. He does whatever he can to provoke people.'

'Yeah, I know. It's just . . .'

Hanna trailed off. She didn't know how to explain it. After Fabian broke up with her, it was as though she had been thrown back in time, back to everything that had prevented her from moving on with her life. She had decided to go and talk to her father, but she hadn't made it in time, and that had almost killed her too. She had done everything she could to repress that moment. The way she had lain awake in Bagarmossen, staring up at the ceiling. Her alarm had been about to ring, but she hadn't managed to get a wink of sleep. Right there and then, it hadn't felt like she had anything to live for, and she had gone over to the medicine cabinet in the kitchen and emptied the boxes of paracetamol and ibuprofen. As she'd raised the pills to her mouth, she had caught sight of the tattoo on her arm, reminding her of everything her grandmother had done for her.

She had realised that her life had been good once, and had thrown away the pills, deciding to make some real changes. It was only once she drove over the Öland Bridge that she had really understood what the first step involved: moving back to the island.

She couldn't go back to Stockholm. There was nothing for her there.

'My boss has given me the investigation,' she said. 'Into . . . into my dad and what he did.'

'Why? Don't you already know what happened?'

'I'm not so sure any more.'

In truth, she had never really been sure. Despite his heavy drinking, Lars had never shown any violent tendencies. It made no sense that he would brutally murder a woman like that. Not for the reasons they claimed. The only possible explanation was that someone else had been involved, or that it had nothing to do with the money Ester was said to have stashed away. That it was down to something else entirely.

Though who, and why? That was where she came unstuck.

Get out of here. If you stay, you'll die.

Hanna couldn't leave Öland. If she did, she would still die – in every sense but the literal. The only way for her to move forward was to find out what happened when Ester died, and ideally without anyone else knowing what she was up to. Perhaps she shouldn't even have mentioned it to Rebecka, but Hanna trusted her. She would keep quiet if Hanna asked her to. Besides, Rebecka had her own personal hell to navigate right now.

Hanna would start by reading through the investigation, and then she would ask the questions she had never dared ask before, to everyone who might know anything about how or why Ester had been killed. She would find out who was behind the phone calls. That was the only way forward for her, and it scared the shit out of her.

Afterword

I chose to dedicate this book to Mika, but I could just as easily have written:

To all that never was.

Life sometimes takes turns that none of us were expecting, and this, more than anything else, is what drives my writing. That, and the desire for people to be kinder to one another. It seems obvious that everyone should be of equal worth.

One such turn I have long avoided writing about is the murder of taxi driver Dusanka Petrén in 1991. I was fifteen when three men in their twenties were arrested for their involvement in her death. Almost everyone in my home town, Kalmar, was talking about the case, because they were all local boys, and they had been hired by her ex-husband. Despite that, what I remember most is the silence. In my family, we couldn't talk about it. The man convicted of aiding and abetting – the one known as the 'brains' of the operation by the media – was my sister's boyfriend. We used to spend time with his family. Another of the boys convicted of Dusanka Petrén's murder worked in the same café as me.

I read thrillers long before 1991, but I'm certain that what happened then has helped shape my focus since. What drives a person to kill? How does the murder affect other people – both those around the victim and the perpetrator?

With this book, I have finally drummed up the courage to touch upon the latter, giving my new police officer, Hanna

Duncker, a father who was convicted of murder. I have also returned to the places where it all began for me: Kalmar and Öland.

So many people have helped me in writing this book, and I want to thank them here:

My publisher, Åsa Selling, who managed the feat of making me start to believe I can write. My eagle-eyed editor, Jesper Ims, and the rest of the gang at Romanus & Selling: Lina Rönning, Emelie Hollbox and Susanna Romanus. Everything about working with that particular publisher just feels so right.

Astri von Arbin Ahlander, founder of the Ahlander Agency, which I am so proud to finally belong to, because they really know their texts. My agent, Kaisa Palo, who is working so brilliantly at getting the series translated. To date it has been sold to seventeen countries. I am thrilled that *The Night Singer* will reach English speaking readers through Alice Menzies's fantastic translation. So a deep thanks to Jennifer Doyle and her team at Headline for believing in the story.

Detectives Ulf Einarsson and Ulf Martinsson from the Kalmar Police, who welcomed me so graciously and answered all my questions. I do feel slightly guilty for all the conflict I invented in their station.

My cousin, Jessica Mo, who, unlike me, grew up on Öland.

Elise Karlsson, who knows far more about trans issues than I do.

Björn Ekenberg, Gunnel Mo, Petra Mo, Sara Mo and Martin Falkman, for reading and sharing their thoughts.

My niece Alice too, for schooling me in the ways fifteen-year-olds talk.

The story itself is fiction. Any remaining irregularities are purely down to me.

As I write this now, the world is facing yet another unexpected turn: the coronavirus. We don't yet have the full picture, but I am convinced that many people, like me, will continue to want to read and listen.

Johanna Mo, February 2021

Detective Hanna Duncker's story continues in . . .

THE SHADOW LILY

Discover the second gripping instalment of
Johanna Mo's *The Island Murders* series.

Available to order from

HEADLINE

THRILLINGLY GOOD BOOKS
FROM CRIMINALLY
GOOD WRITERS

CRIME FILES BRINGS YOU THE LATEST RELEASES FROM
TOP CRIME AND THRILLER AUTHORS.

SIGN UP ONLINE FOR OUR MONTHLY NEWSLETTER AND BE THE FIRST
TO KNOW ABOUT OUR COMPETITIONS, NEW BOOKS AND MORE.